THE TREM

Manfred Jurgensen

By the same author

Poetry
signs & voices
a winter's journey
a kind of dying
south africa transit
the skin trade
waiting for cancer
Selected Poems 1971 – 1986 (edited by Dimitris Tsaloumas)
The Partiality of Harbours
My Operas Can't Swim
Shadows of Utopia
midnight sun
carnal knowledge
A Brisbane Kind Of Love

Editor
Penguin's Australian Writing Now (with Robert Adamson)
Cheating and Other Infidelities
A Sporting Declaration

THE TREMBLING BRIDGE

Manfred Jurgensen

Indra Publishing

Indra Publishing
PO Box 7, Briar Hill, Victoria, 3088, Australia.

© Manfred Jurgensen, 2004
Typeset in Palatino by Fire Ink Press.
Made and Printed in Australia by McPherson's Printing Group.

National Library of Australia Cataloguing-in-Publication data:

Jurgensen, Manfred, 1940– .
  The trembling bridge.

  ISBN 1 920787 03 8

  I. Title.

  A823.3

http://members.aol.com/manfredjurgensen

In Memoriam
Hannelore Seidel
and
John Woodward

Manfred Jurgensen is a writer of German-Danish extraction who lives in Brisbane. His previous publications include thirteen collections of poetry, a play, various studies of literary criticism and translations of Australian literature into German.

'He passed from the trembling
bridge on to firm land again.'

James Joyce, *A Portrait of the Artist as a Young Man*

BOOK ONE

THE BEAUTIFUL ENEMY

'To be in any form,
what is that?'

Walt Whitman, *Song of Myself*

I

During autumn the fog hardly ever lifted before early afternoon. St Mary's steeple remained cocooned in a shroud of impenetrable grey. In the harbour the ferries stopped running. Day and night the horns of piloted freighters sounded their ominous warnings. With visibility reduced to a mere couple of metres, navigation in the fjord proved equally dangerous for incoming and departing vessels.

Mark went down to the jetty to fish. But he had no tackle and did not know how to cast a line. Still he joined the old men who were sitting patiently along the pier, legs dangling above the barely visible water, sucking at their cold pipes, in conspiratorial silence. They were not in a hurry for anything.

As he joined the regulars along the breakwater Mark inhaled the pungent smell of the harbour's stale and oily water. He breathed slowly and deeply until his head became dizzy with the stench of paint and fish, refuse and salt. Beyond the call of his mother, he savoured the odour of freedom.

Mark shivered with pleasure. Alone among the anglers, below the bows of rusty cargo boats, he was at home. He would not leave his place next to the old men's worms, their buckets and hooks. It was only when a sudden ray of light cast itself onto the scene that he sensed it was time to go back.

There were days when the sun did not pierce the low-lying clouds and the grey cocoon would continue to envelop him all afternoon. On those days it was difficult to tell when darkness set in. The boats were lit all day. A row of drab warehouses, silos and disused sheds rose like a dark wall around the harbour. Most of the shipping companies had their offices at least one block away from the waterfront. Too many floods had reached all the way to the venerable half-timbered buildings that once had been the pride of ship owners and maritime business firms. As a result, parts of the previously prosperous and picturesque area had quickly turned into the town's shabby, run-down red light district.

Sometimes it rained for days on end. When that happened Mark waited until the water had penetrated his coat, pullover, shirt and singlet, entered his shoes and socks and drenched his skin. 'Rain was good for fishing', the old men had told him. Mark felt it claim his body as if he too had become a vessel, a ferry crossing brackish harbours.

Back in the dry apartment he pretended that his father had returned from the war and together they had claimed the jetty as their own.

But the war continued. Every day was war, Mark knew, even though his home town seemed to take little notice of it. Occasionally air-raid sirens howled through the cobbled streets, as if their wailing could tear the fog and rain apart. If they were a warning, it was of a danger that would pass. Mark listened to the grown-up tales of distant horror, of imprisonment and death, of husbands and fathers who would never return. Yet despite the alarming nature of such reports the war did not seem real. Most townspeople treated it as a rumour, a bad dream from which they would one day wake.

Mark could not tell how many times he had joined his mother and the other tenants of their apartment block in the air-raid shelter. Despite the ever-increasing frequency of alarms everyone still panicked. Only a few small children did not respond to the shrill warning sounds that echoed through the neighbouring streets. They kept playing with their toys until finally their mothers hurriedly bundled them in a quilt and carried them to the cellar. Mark was under strict instruction to leave the flat immediately and wait for the others at the door to the air-raid shelter. His mother stayed only long enough to check the taps and switches, close the balcony doors and open the windows slightly.

At first it had been an exciting game: the urgent herding together of everyone around the house, the handing out of gas-masks, looking funny and scary at the same time, the allocation of bunks in the barely lit cellar. It had all seemed like an adventure, but soon evacuation became something of a well-organised ritual. Even so most tenants remained panic-stricken. The only vaguely reassuring thing was to follow directions, doing what everyone else did.

In the shelter they could hear the planes roar above, like an announcement of evil prophecy. Men and women prayed. Rocking their crying children, mothers sang lullabies to drown the noise outside. Their rhythmic movement seemed to comfort everyone present, all of them held captive by the deadly sound in the sky. They could feel each other's fear. It was so real Mark thought he could touch it. In the semi-darkness his own movement startled those next to him. He was told to sit still, to be quiet, to sleep. How could he sleep at such a time! He listened to their neighbour, Frau Henricksen, sobbing while Herr Weidemann, the toothless old caretaker dressed in a sinister black dustcoat, proclaimed all this was a punishment from God. Mark wondered what he had done to deserve such punishment. He remembered how the old man, looking like death, had informed residents that there were rules for everything, and that children should be seen but not heard. 'Obedience was godly.'

Next time the sirens announced the wrath of God Mark hid in the backyard, inside an open shed housing guinea-pigs, disused furniture, tools and shelves laden with tins and bottles and what Herr Weidemann referred to as 'spare parts'. It was the favourite haunt of the children of the neighbourhood, a chaotic collection of things, complete with a sandbox and the magic of two rusty chains hanging from a leaking roof. They would take turns using an old board to convert the chains into a swing. It seemed the whole shed was moving as they swayed above the ground.

Mark watched the loose chains as they shivered in the wind. Everyone had disappeared. The shelter was locked. He was alone outside where the war was raging. There was an eerie silence. The sirens had stopped. No traffic noises were to be heard. In the stillness of anticipation Mark looked up at the building. Its windows were staring back at him. On a third floor balcony a white shirt was hanging on a line, its arms flapping in the gentle breeze. It looked to Mark as if it were waving at him.

He looked up at the sky. Between the clouds a pale light withdrew. There were no birds, not even gulls or swallows. An empty can fell off the shelves. It startled him, as did the rapid movements of the guinea-pigs. From the corner of the shed came a pungent smell he could not identify. As he walked over he collected an old broom, just in case. Underneath a tarpaulin he discovered a nest of dead rats, many carrying blood-stained bite wounds. In their death struggle they must have ripped into each other.

Bridget's urine stained the sandbox like marks of an animal on the run. Bridget from across the road was already seven, but still could not 'control herself', as her mother kept explaining. It was a delicate condition caused by the war, she informed the caretaker when he complained about Bridget 'soiling the neighbourhood'.

Mark looked up again. He was waiting for war planes to appear. It was strange thinking he had been taught to pray for his soul to rise to heaven. He wanted to confront the angels of death, to watch their flight above his home. They had not come yet.

The backyard was quiet and empty. Mark observed its

bold design as if for the first time, the stark geometry of the iron frame for hanging carpets over for beating, the three steps leading to the stairwell, the communal laundry below street level, the high wooden fence separating their playground from the cooperage next door. On the other side of the wall barrels and tubs were stacked five high, but it was easy to climb over. Mark had been retrieving soccer balls ever since the older boys had allowed him to join their games. The air was filled with the smell of freshly cut timber. Mark liked the fragrance of unvarnished wood.

The five levels of balconies seemed like a staircase to the clouds. In the late morning their railing cast no shadows. Behind the half-open windows of the landlord's ground floor unit curtains moved. The door leading to the yard had been left open. On the pavement Mark could see the chalked lines of a forsaken hopscotch game. Underneath the windowsill of the hairdresser's ground floor salon lay a hastily discarded one-eyed doll. Alone in the abandoned playground, Mark took in its familiar sights, registering details which suddenly seemed to belong to a secret code.

What appeared to be a chance composition of abandonment was to him a careful design welcoming the Enemy. There could be no doubt about the power of the Enemy. The grown-ups talked about nothing else. Even the children invented games in which no one would escape death.

Mark threw a ball from the open shed in the direction of the deserted doll. It echoed in stuttered bounces, missing its target.

Somewhere a tap dripped. He noted the sealed hatches below the ground floor unit and the heavy iron door leading to the shelter. A black skull was painted over each of the bricked-in shafts.

While his mother had locked herself in the basement with the other tenants he had the whole yard to himself. She had disappeared in the dark hole of fear crowded with whispers and prayers. Had he abandoned her or had she left him? Either way, Mark exulted in the sensation of being

15

completely free, of having escaped. A bit like being down at the harbour, only much more exciting.

He was alone, but he was not afraid.

In joyous defiance Mark yelled the first thing that came into his head. 'Vati!' he screamed. 'Hooray! Hooray!'

He rushed out of the shed and ran around the empty yard. Was this what it would be like to win the war? How good it was to be out in the open, to be alone, to be waiting for the heavens to open up! He laughed as he stumbled against the fence, taking in the sweet smell of moist wood. Mark sensed there were promises floating in the air, their camouflage teasing, torturing, tantalising him with every breath. 'Vati!'

His shout rose to the roof of the old tenement house, unable to escape the sound shaft of the yard.

When it was gone the silence returned. Mark felt foolish now, embarrassed by his reckless outburst. Then he listened.

A roar approached from across the harbour. He knew instantly it could only be the calm and confident announcement of The Enemy's arrival. Its droning vibration reminded him of the steady engines of the harbour ferries.

For a brief moment a gust of light poured from behind the low-lying clouds.

Mark saw the grey bodies sleek and silvery as a school of herrings emerge in geometrical formation. As soon as he made out the shape and size of the aircraft they disappeared behind a host of clouds. Counting the planes was quite impossible. But he could see and hear there were enough to cover heaven for a long while and to scare the population of an entire city into hiding.

The noise was awesome now as the bombers seemed to fly even lower. For a moment Mark thought they were circling over the yard. His emotions were the opposite of fear – all excitement and anticipation. There was no need to hide or to defend himself. The Enemy would realise he had come out to welcome them.

Then Mark saw the silver metallic strips on the wings of

the aircraft. Shafts of early autumn sun lit up the lustrous tapes in spectacular explosions of daytime fireworks. It was quite simply the most beautiful spectacle he'd ever seen. He had not anticipated that the Enemy would adorn themselves as they attacked. Perhaps those silver ribbons were the war decorations Herr Weidemann was always talking about. Mark's eyes were beginning to hurt. They had not been exposed to such light refractions before. Could the planes be transmitting in code an urgent message to him? Were they trying to tell him that the war would be over soon and his father would return?

No doubt these flying messengers had come for a special purpose. Had they come for him? Their path had taken them directly above this yard as if they knew only he had stayed outside to await their coming. He got up and waved at the bombers to signal that he understood. 'Vati!' His voice was obliterated by the roar of the planes. He was blinded again by their refracted rays.

Hovering sunbeams and throbbing shadows were piercing the sky. The entire yard now seemed to be trembling. Mark too was shaking. From the corner of his eyes he saw a stray cat climb to the top of the fence, then pause as if afraid to jump. Its black hair stood on end as it hissed in token defiance. When the light hit him Mark could briefly see his own shadow, uncertain of its blurred direction.

Soon the clouds regathered. Only the droning of the aircraft continued uninterrupted. Would it ever end? Mark wondered. It had sounded different in the air-raid shelter, more distant, almost suffocated. But the fear was greater there because you could not see the Enemy.

This time he had stayed outside. He had wanted to face the Enemy alone. Mark never doubted the pilots would be able to see him, but he raised his arms again, just to make certain.

The silver ribbons adorning the planes' wings reminded him of Christmas decorations. His eyes followed their glittering reflections, shivering with joy and gratitude. Hadn't

St Mary's pastor read them some Christmas story of an angel appearing to shepherds in the fields? And hadn't the angel said to them, 'Do not be afraid; behold, I bring you good news of a great rejoicing for the whole people', or something like that? Trouble was, not everybody could actually see or understand angels. They were hard to recognise if you did not believe in them. The pastor had told them they often appeared in some form of disguise. Mark had no doubt the sky above him was crowded with a whole host of angels who had come to deliver a message. 'Do not be afraid ...'. There was no need, then, to hide. Listening to the pastor he had not understood about angels. Now, at last, he had seen them with his own eyes. They had flown over his home, greeted and spared him.

He had to stay outside to meet them as they hovered above dispensing glorious judgment and infinite mercy. Their beauty had startled him. He knew they would help him escape from his mother's imprisonment and lead him to his father. They had come to show him the way. Soon now the war would be over.

The droning sounds were no longer to be heard. The aircraft that had set the sky alight were gone. Mark watched clouds in formation, blockading the rays of the late morning sun. He was alone again.

Like a dream it was difficult to tell how long it had all lasted. In the silence Mark thought of the others in the shelter. He would know that the danger was over when they left the cellar. Perhaps he could pretend he too had been down there with them, that they had simply overlooked him on the way down, that he had been hiding in the darkness by himself. He would have to lie because grown-ups were afraid of the truth. After the all-clear they always cried in relief, kneeling on the coal-dust floor to pray. Mark used to turn away, embarrassed by such emotional and theatrical displays, especially when his own mother took part in them.

The salvation of adults, he found, was based on self-righteousness. Crouching in their cellar, they never doubted that God was on their side. They had to feel safe before they could believe in anything. There was something seriously wrong with their faith, he thought. Mark noticed their gratitude was inseparably linked to indignation. Out in the open, he had witnessed a different spectacle: the beauty and power and freedom of flight. He looked up at what now seemed a deserted sky.

The Enemy had left no trace. His father had not returned. As he began to fight back tears the sound of a nearby explosion filled the air. It was the loudest noise Mark had ever heard. For a brief moment he could feel the ground shaking. He froze. Its unexpectedness tore into his emotions, his memory of the beautiful Enemy. He was shaken by the terrible knowledge. They had bombed his home town!

As the detonation thundered across the roofs it smashed all the windows of the surrounding apartment blocks. The rain of splinters made a high-pitched splitting noise as they spilled into his own yard.

He wondered what part of town had been hit. The noise was much too loud and too explosive to signal the destruction of merely a few houses. Had the Enemy hit the city hall, the dockyard or one of the big freighters in the harbour?

A huge black conical cloud emerged from behind the neighbouring block of apartments. For a moment Mark feared the attacking aircraft might have crashed. Could avenging angels be shot out of the sky? Suddenly he was frightened. There was altogether too much smoke for the bombers to have hit an ordinary target.

By now the wind had carried the dark poisoned cloud in the direction of the yard. Mark picked up a splinter of glass and held it to his eyes. What he saw were divided lines, dissolving colours and fragmented objects. The world had been blown apart. The certainty came to him with a sense of relief. At last he understood the bombers' mission. As the caretaker had warned them all along, this was a punishment from God.

Outside the yard the world was burning. Above the roofs smoke rose in worship of the Enemy. Several smaller explosions, like firecrackers on New Year's Eve, only much louder, followed the initial hit. Lesser clouds offered their fiery celebration. The noise and the smoke would not end. Perhaps there was a bang and a cloud for each plane carrying bombs to liberate the town.

The all-clear sounded. Mark quickly rushed back to the shed, ready to hide himself should his absence have been noticed. From his vantage point he watched a distraught group of survivors emerge from the shelter. Even though the sunlight had faded again, their eyes squinted. A small child fell down the stairs to the yard and screamed. The little girl would not stop crying. The whining, accusing tone of her sobs reminded Mark of the sound of the air-raid siren.

Shortly afterwards a high-pitched scream descended from the second floor. Frau Petersen had just discovered the broken windows of her flat. Peering through what was left of her kitchen window, she yelled out for the caretaker, complaining that she'd only just washed her windows. Mark heard her yell something. Her short curly hair was covered in a bright red headscarf. Two dark red circles of rouge on either cheek and matching claret lipstick made Mark wonder who she might really be under her pantomime mask. All he knew was that Frau Petersen lived with her invalid father. Together they regularly received visitors who looked as though they were impersonating characters in a puppet show. There was something mysterious, even sinister about her crassness, the way she continued to shout from her kitchen. As always, she drew far too much attention to herself.

Mark realised he could not leave the shed while Frau Petersen was remonstrating about her ruined window panes. Nothing escaped her eagle eyes. She would have reported him to Herr Weidemann. Mark was afraid of the caretaker who had threatened him previously with horrific punishment if he did not behave. He looked like death in his black coat uniform. Perhaps he too was part of Frau Petersen's Punch and Judy show.

In vain the other tenants tried to avoid her. She was forever telling horror stories on the stairs or while hanging out her washing. Sometimes Mark thought it possible Frau Petersen's strange behaviour was the disguise of a spy.

Mark raced to the half-landing leading to the stairwell in the hope he would not be observed. Frau Petersen, he was relieved to see, had disappeared inside her kitchen. Someone seemed to be talking to her. Mark could hear the other families returning to their apartments. As they entered their homes there were shouts of anguish, calls of disbelief and outbursts of anger.

Crouching near the back door of the ground floor hall, Mark overheard the word 'gasometer' in the echo of the flights of stairs. As he waited for the right time to make his run to the first floor someone asked, 'How many dead?'

While the tenants speculated about the damage from the air attack he tiptoed up the stairs. The front door to his apartment had been left ajar. He slipped into his home like a thief returning from a burglary. It was difficult for him not to whistle. Quietly he crossed the hallway into the kitchen. From the living room came the sounds of the radio playing patriotic marches. No sign of his mother.

The kitchen table presented a strange but beautiful sight. Sliced rolls, arranged as in a military line-up, were showered with splinters of glass. Mark immediately recognised it as the work of the Enemy. The topping looked like a precious decoration. He checked whether the fragments could be removed, but there were too many quite close to each other, some very small, mere particles of glassy dust. As he touched them, his fingers began to bleed.

A tiny splinter had turned red. Deeply satisfied, he

watched it flow into the pale margarine. His ritual sacrifice of blood had added to the splendour of this extravagant waste.

Hearing his mother approach Mark licked the blood off his fingers. How little it took to cut the skin! It dawned on him that, far from being a protection, his skin was itself in need of being defended. He remembered the changing colours of bruises after soccer games with the older boys. The blows had not opened his skin. It took a special cut to accomplish that.

A gentle breeze through the window cooled his face and arms and calmed his senses. He was still hot from running and the excitement of meeting the Enemy. Mark could tell no one about it. Rehearsing what he hoped would be credible lies, he blushed in anticipation. (Skin could also give you away.) He felt the throbbing of his pulse, the accelerated beating of his heart, not knowing whether it was from triumph or shame.

Inside him the explosion from the gasometer continued to reverberate. The Enemy had spoken at last. They had responded to Mark's calls for his father.

In his excitement Mark began to wonder whether he too had been a target. Could he be invaded and defended? He touched his skin almost in awe. He felt how it marked him, shielded him, separated him. His mother, his friends, people in the street were someone else. Had he ever thought himself the same as them, part of their territory?

Was that why it had felt so right, being out there alone, leaving the others in their emergency shelter, meeting the Enemy on his own?

Instinctively Mark touched himself again, first his face, then his hands and arms, then his uncovered legs. This is me, he marvelled, this is what is meant when someone calls my name. He was overcome by a compassionate tenderness for what he took to be his native parts, his very own land, his personal home. For along with the triumph of discovering himself went the no less intense realisation that he was alone.

No one else could ever take on the task of being him. He would have to defend his vulnerable skin, the fragile border that was like a sky to his body.

Filled with fear and wonder he began to move both his hands to his crotch, registering the warmth emanating from the spot where his legs met his genitals. Slowly he began rubbing, waiting for the explosion.

As he looked up, his mother was standing in front of him.

II

Herr Brodersen is quite old, with hardly any hair on his head. Sometimes his face looks like a soft sagging egg. He's been our form teacher ever since we started school. We all like him because he's kind and never shouts. It's only when it comes to writing that Herr Brodersen is very strict. He orders us to draft a rough copy in pencil before using pen and ink. As if we'd only just learnt how to write!

But I'll do as I'm told. I don't mind using a pencil.

Last week I had to re-do a local history assignment because the ink ran out all over the page! We were asked to list as many street names as we could remember and put them down in our very best handwriting. I had added a carefully drawn sketch of the dock area, showing the precise location of all landing stages, the fishing port and the ship-yard. (Unfortunately I wasn't very good at drawing boats. Somehow they always looked like up-ended beetles.) By the time I was finished my exercise book looked as though it had been hit by an air raid. Actually, I thought the ink blots were no big deal. They made the assignment all the more real. Surely Herr Brodersen would remember the bombs that had just been dropped on our town. 'There's a war on,' he says whenever we complain about the poor quality of paper. As if we need to be reminded.

In the end I had to do my homework all over again.

Well, this isn't an exercise for Herr Brodersen. I'm not writing anything down. I just make up the draft of a fair copy. In my head. That way I don't even have to use a pencil. I want to find out whether I can tell myself things that have happened to me. I know it's a bit strange – like Mutti talking to herself. But it doesn't matter. No one knows I'm doing it.

The idea came to me last week when I found an old notebook in a chest of drawers. Later Mutti explained it was the diary of my dead grandfather. I had never heard of a diary before. Holding the black leather-bound, slightly mouldy calendar in my hands, I turned the stained yellow pages not knowing what to expect.

Mutti told me the book contained 'the innermost thoughts of her dear father'. Calling my grandfather her father made it sound as if she were still a child like me. She gave me permission to read 'her father's' book, but it still felt like something forbidden. It didn't seem right to read 'the innermost thoughts' of a dead person. I wondered what Herr Brodersen would have made of my grandfather's large ornamental writing. The strange-looking figures and unfamiliar dates of the calendar worried me.

The small book felt quite heavy. Flicking through it, I discovered that it didn't just consist of grandfather's notes. Inside I came across several open envelopes, a stack of letters and a set of faded photographs. The pictures showed a group of bearded strangers wearing peculiar clothes, standing next to young skinny women dressed in what looked like short white tablecloths. Some of them wore bell-shaped hats. At the very back of the diary I found a couple of pressed flowers. I think they were snowdrops and crocuses.

If I had a brother or a sister, I probably wouldn't be doing this. Keeping a make-believe diary. More likely, I'd be drawing another map of our rainy city showing them exactly where we lived, how to find the best shortcut to the ferry or the way to St Mary's Woods. Or I'd make up stories about our father. But I'm what they call an 'only child'. Perhaps that's why I'm always secretly talking to myself.

Good thing no one's watching me. Nobody else can read my invisible notebook. So I can say whatever I like. It doesn't matter if it looks like I'm talking to no one. I know that I'm here.

I better stop right now. I need time to think what I want to talk about.

That was easy. Of course I want to 'write' about myself. I don't want to keep a diary like my grandfather. I don't want others to read me when I'm dead. I've been through my grandfather's diary a couple of times, but can't understand it. I want to read what I've written while I'm still alive.

But where to start! Mutti and I live in an apartment building in Toosbüy Street near the harbour. It's not far to school in Castle Road, an ugly cobbled street in the oldest part of town. I hate walking along its run-down half-timbered houses, especially early in the mornings when it is still dark. I'm afraid one day someone will come rushing out of one of them and drag me inside. Don't know what would happen to me then. All the windows are heavily curtained. It's too scary to think about.

Once I'm at school, I feel safe. Our classroom is large and light, with a row of four big double-glazed windows to protect us from the outside. I'm always pleased to see our teacher. Herr Brodersen is an old man, but he is kind and really likes us, almost as if he were our father. He has a thing about apples. During autumn he tests us on the names of the different sorts he places in the windows. And we try to remember: Russets, Coxs, Granny Smiths, Braeburns, Delicious and Gravensteins. Along with the name we have to learn the special feature of each kind. Only when the whole class can identify all apples will we be allowed to eat them. Of course there's always some dummy who cannot recognise what he's seen many times over. I wonder how much longer we will have to wait. In the meantime they're lined up on display inside the double-glazed windows. Inside they're probably beginning to rot.

What makes our classroom really special is a large sandbox at the back. There Herr Brodersen makes us build our town with papier mâché, all the streets and houses, the harbour and surrounding hills, schools and churches, city hall and museum, even the water tower next to the cemetery and the windmill near the border. It's almost finished. We've been working at it for most of the year. Should the Enemy really destroy our home, our model might help rebuild it one day.

It's exciting to construct your own town, even in miniature. 'A world made of paper', Herr Brodersen calls it. Before I started cutting out and gluing together the houses of my street I hardly knew where I lived. It was enough for me to know how to get to my favourite places, how long it took down to the harbour, to school or to Frank Hilmer's place.

Working on our sandbox city has made me see a lot of things I hadn't noticed before. Walking the streets feels different now. Wherever I am, I see myself as part of the model town, checking whether the real buildings are true to our own design. I wonder ...

I just realised that my best friend, Frank Hilmer, and I always knew of course where we were living, but we only thought of our own places – he of the small villa in the suburb of Bellevue and I of our first floor apartment in the middle of town. We didn't include any other houses and only remembered the streets leading to our homes. Funny that. In finding our own places we had left out most of the town. But the town was our home too.

With the sandbox model all that began to change. I suddenly understood what Mutti meant when she said Frank's family lived 'in the good part of town'. But what about us, then? Weren't we right in the middle of it, surrounded by shops and churches, traffic and people?

Our homes were already built when we were born. We just lived there. Wouldn't it be great, if we could choose our own place, build it like we built the papier mâché model of the town and decide what to put right next to it! I wonder what would happen, if Herr Brodersen would allow us to put down our homes wherever we wanted to. I bet our model town would look very different.

Of course we put model ships in the harbour and toy cars in the streets. The footpaths of our sandbox town are crowded with tin people. We even have several dogs and cats straying about. The colour of the harbour is too blue, but it's hard to find just the right shade of green, grey and blue. We have to work with the colours in our paintbox.

These are some of the reasons why I like Herr Brodersen's class.

Do grown-ups prepare rough copies? Does Herr Brodersen teach fair copy local history? Does he carry scraps and notes in his head? (I like the idea of a rough copy in my head!)

Does Mutti rehearse what she's going to say before she opens her mouth? I don't think so. Not to me. She's always telling me the same things: that I should clean my room, finish my homework before going out and that it's not easy being a woman on her own. 'Where are you, Mark?' she calls out, or 'Where are your manners, boy?' or simply 'Where have you been? I've been looking all over for you!' I don't think they're fair copy calls. But then I've noticed she's more and more talking to herself these days.

Or so I thought until I heard her speak to my father. He's away fighting the war. What's the point of talking to someone who isn't there? When she calls out his name – 'Marius!' – it sounds like begging. Often she starts crying when she talks to him. But at other times her voice is normal, the same as when she's speaking to me. On those occasions she seems to treat us both the same, which makes me feel closer to my father. I don't even remember him, while she carries on as though he were living with us. Once she read me a letter in which he asks me to look after her. My father is a ghost.

Mutti's rough copy talk will not let me forget him. I try to ignore her scary conversations with my father, but it's not easy. Especially when she's crying.

Herr Brodersen says we must have faith in our fatherland. In class no one really cares. For most of us the war is a ghost too.

The last period on Friday Herr Brodersen teaches us folksongs, shanties and other little tunes. This is my favourite:

Come, fetch me, ferry,
Take me for a ride!
Come quick and carry
Me to the other side!

It's catchy and clever. I love the words because they know you can talk to ferries.

I wanted to start my 'diary' with something exciting, a real adventure. Perhaps I too can keep a 'personal calendar', as Mutti calls it, just like my dead grandfather. But if it's going to be a calendar, I must learn to be precise.

I'll try to remember what's happening now.

Perhaps I should start by reporting that on my birthday, the 26th March, I woke from a dream thinking I could fly. It must have been very early in the morning. Although my eyes were wide open, I couldn't see a thing. My whole body felt weightless.

Then I noticed I was lying in something wet. Was I still dreaming? Had I fallen from the sky and crashed into the sea? I clawed my fingernails into my skin to make certain I was awake. (I always do that when something terrible happens.) Even then I could hardly feel the pain. There was a lightness in my head that would not go away.

Searching the sheets, I found they were soaked. Calling for Mutti I opened my mouth, but nothing came out. I had lost my voice.

When I came to, the lights of the bedroom blinded me. Now I could only hear. Was it still the same dream, a nightmare in which I was losing all of my senses? At last, in the far distance, I recognised Mutti's voice. She was speaking to Dr Mestring, our family doctor, but I couldn't understand what they were saying.

Later, an ambulance took me to St Francis'. I spent a week in hospital recovering. Mutti's showed me the soaked sheet on my return. It's an eerie sight.

What I was lying on that morning looks like the Danish flag. It's red all over, except for the outlines of my body. When I tell Frank and the others I've got my own badge they're stunned and jealous, I can tell. No one else has a flag made of their own blood.

Of course I was hoping for a different kind of adventure. I shouldn't have boasted. All I got out of it was that even my best friends, Frank Hilmer and Aaron Goldberg, called me names. 'Paleface' and 'Little Bleeder'. Dr Mestring prescribed iron tablets for me. The pills, I told Frank and Aaron, would make me the strongest boy in class. Soon I would be an iron man. That shut them up. I also told them I was a coagulator. They didn't know what that meant, but after the iron pills they didn't dare ask questions.

I don't tell them that once a month I have to go to the Institute of Bacteriology to have my blood tested. It's no big deal. After the nurse pricks my earlobe she spreads a few drops across a small plate of glass. It feels odd seeing my blood displayed like that. After a while it looks as if the glass is bleeding.

I've cut myself on broken glass so often Mutti thinks I might be doing it deliberately. Which is a crazy thing to say, of course. Why would anyone want to hurt himself? Still, she says I've got a thing about blood. Well, after the night of my birthday I guess you could say that.

It's true, I'm both fascinated and disgusted watching it being analysed at the Institute. At first the nurse is merely covering the glass with my blood. Then she mingles it with drops from different bottles until its colour begins to change. The young woman in her white coat explains she is testing 'the sedimentation rate' of my blood. It's like ink running out on my local history assignment. It angers and excites me.

I don't know why, but it makes me feel important that my blood should be measured. With her long black hair, deep brown eyes and the kindest smile I've ever seen, the nurse looks like an angel. I have a personal angel whose job it is to find out about me!

As nobody's going to read my secret diary, I might as well admit that Sister Elke is the real reason I look forward to my regular visits to the Institute. Having my lobe pricked isn't very painful anyway. Not when she's doing it.

Don't know whether I should have talked about that, even if no one can read it. Now it embarrasses me.

Forget about the nurse. It's true, it could've been fun having a sister, even though most girls I know are, well, peculiar. Most of them are so weird I wonder whether they think and feel the way we do. The things they get excited over! I've seen them giggle during the whole break over God-knows-what. Sometimes I would love to throw something at them, just to see them fly in all directions. But that would get me into trouble with Herr Brodersen. Of course, a sister might have been able to explain girls to me.

There's one exception though. Her name's Hanna Lorenz. I mustn't forget another important thing that happened. At the beginning of term Herr Brodersen made us change seats in class. He asked Frank Hilmer to move to the front and Hanna to take his place in the back row, right next to me. Frank, he explained, was forever disrupting class.

Like my mates, I had watched Hanna from a distance. (You mustn't get too close to girls or else you become a sissy.) Her long blonde ponytail bounces every time she moves. As Herr Brodersen keeps reminding us, Hanna is his star pupil. But she's not a swot and no one dislikes her.

Hard to tell whether she's pretty. Guess not. For one thing, she's skinny and a paleface like me. But then she's got the bluest eyes I've ever seen. On top of that, Hanna owns a real grown-up Montblanc fountain pen with very special ink called 'royal blue'. And get this: it matches the colour of her eyes. Going by her clothes, schoolbag and books, Hanna's parents must be loaded.

I'm still not used to sitting next to her, even though it's been a couple of months. I wonder whether she'd allow me to borrow her Montblanc. Haven't had the nerve to ask her yet, but I will, soon. I'm just waiting for the right moment. Pity my own handwriting is nothing like hers, so it probably won't look 'royal' anyway. Still, I'd like to put it to the test.

Not that I need a pen talking to myself!

III

The following winter was the coldest in living memory. The townspeople spoke of a new ice age. Mark could not be sure whether they were boasting or lamenting.

The harbour was frozen, the mole deserted. You could skate across the border. The old men cut holes in the ice to fish. When the fog failed to lift, skaters got lost. A grey infinity of frozen no-man's-land had invaded the safety of the port. No shipping was possible. Freighters were unable to break out of their moorings. Not even the ferries operated. Dark thick ice had turned the harbour into a graveyard.

The older boys tested their courage. They dared each other to cross the harbour in the dark. It was a game they called skating from memory.

At first visibility was still a few metres, but once the shore was left behind the daredevil found himself almost completely enveloped in thick dark-grey matter. In such blindness all he could do was hope the main shipping channel had not re-opened. If the temperature climbed, melting set in imperceptibly. Would the ice hold? If not, the skater would be beyond help. No rescue mission could be alerted. No searchlight, no icebreaker would find him in time. He would drown in an invasion of darkness and unfrozen channels of pack ice.

Mark watched the grammar school boys jump from the

harbour walls onto the ice, cheering loudly as they took off. He could tell they were afraid. Even on these cold, dark days he claimed his regular spot on the frosty pier. In the distance he saw the reckless skaters disappear into the fog. The strange thought came to him: they were fishing for death.

What they were doing was bound to be forbidden. But no one in authority could penetrate the darkness of these winter days, not even the dock police. Mark had seen a couple of officers searching the landing-stages, torchlight beams barely extending beyond their own boots. Enveloped in the same dark grey expanse they were taunted by the sounds of jumping bodies accompanied by triumphant cheers of heedless abandonment.

Even without these cries the frozen harbour had become an eerie place. The fog-horns of captive freighters announced their chilling presence. The imprisoned ships reminded Mark of hooked fish thrashing about on the planks and in the old men's salt buckets. There was no escape.

The war was not over, but he knew it would be lost. Should his father return, it would be to verify defeat.

The winter belonged to the Enemy.

Already refugees had arrived from the East carrying their pitiful belongings on their backs. The town was crowded with cripples, orphans and desperate survivors. For weeks schools had been unable to be heated. All classes were cancelled. At home talk of 'final victory' alternated with outbursts of panic and despair.

Mark escaped to the harbour.

He waited at the quay. There had been war for as long as he could remember. To the grown-ups he was a 'war child.' Yet they assured him the war would not last forever. Spring would have to come eventually. It always did.

Meantime Mark tried to stay away from home.

Now war had broken out between locals and refugees, between those who had little and those who had nothing, between those who kept their homes and those who did not.

In truth, everybody suffered. Some, however, were unwilling to admit it. Even though many townspeople were close to starvation, pride did not allow them to acknowledge their poverty. They had been rich before the war.

Mark did not join the children of their apartment block who, dressed in adult clothing, hands thrown up in horror, paraded up and down Toosbüy Street, remonstrating: 'We've lost everything!' If he was too young and scared to jump with the daredevil skaters into the frozen harbour, he felt too old and embarrassed to take part in imitations of the grown-ups' latest war strategy.

Hunger brought out brutal instincts. People were stealing anything in the hope of exchanging it for food. On a cold and windy January morning Mark watched Mrs Bonishevsky, a refugee who had moved into a single room on the third floor, carry her dead child to a horse-drawn cart in the iced-over street. Her infant son had died of starvation. They had been on the road for over three months. What disturbed Mark most was that the sound of the mother's wailing and whimpering was suffocated by heavily falling snow.

There was so much silence around that winter. Everything familiar had turned into signs, like a frozen language for the deaf and dumb. People mostly talked to themselves, even if they pretended to speak to somebody else. Almost all that was said was choked up by fog and snow. No one listened.

One late, dark and freezing afternoon a farmer unloaded a bag of potatoes in the street. A small crowd gathered around the delivery cart drawn by a pitiful nag to watch the old man's awkward movements trying to lift the sack onto his right shoulder, then disappear slowly through the front door of Mark's apartment building. 'Not many men left to carry such weight,' a woman muffled up in a black scarf scornfully commented. Her voice was bitter with resentment.

Mark was about to turn away when he noticed an increasing restlessness among the group of onlookers. They had turned into hooded creatures shoving and pointing, nudging and urging, communicating in a conspiratorial sign language. It was almost impossible to see their faces while their heads moved in great agitation. Only now did Mark notice they were all carrying scrap paper and shopping bags.

Presently one of them, a man in a camouflage winter coat, abruptly left the formation, walked over to the cart and, without a moment's hesitation, stabbed the hack with a large butcher's knife he produced from inside his coat. The animal reared up in shock. Instantly its blood began to flow onto the icy street. As the others watched, the man quickly glanced around before ramming the blade into the neck of the horse. It writhed in agony. This time its blood gushed out in wild profusion. In vain the creature struggled to break free. Mark saw that the horse was tied to a lamppost. It tried to sever its harness, but the leather straps would not break. The fodder bag the farmer had fastened around its neck was rapidly turning red.

As if a sign had been given, men and women began, in a machine-like movement of precise coordination, to hack into the animal's flank and belly. Intestines burst out of open skin. Piss and droppings mingled with the surrendering of living flesh. With every stab the horse's desperate protest burst into the cold, merciless air. Its neighing was transformed into horrific sounds, a combination of roaring and whining, the carnal outburst of a creature dying in full possession of its senses.

Mark froze. He could not move.

In horror he watched the men and women, people he now thought he could recognise, as they continued to dissect the living cadaver in rhythmic unison. He witnessed their lecherous anxiety, their impatience to claim their piece of flesh.

The horse collapsed with a steamy sound, a final prolonged sigh. The gutter was flooded with entrails.

The killers carried their bloody loot away. The stench of flesh was everywhere. It rose into the winter day like evil, polluting balloons.

The fodder-bagged head lay decapitated on the footpath, one eye staring into the milky winter sky.

The slaughter had been quick and efficient. In despair someone cried out, 'My God!' A few pedestrians briefly turned around, then, shocked by the sight, pretended not to see. Only skin and bones, head and tail, barely more than a skeleton remained, the pitiful remnants of a desperate, brutal murder.

War had come to Toosbüy Street at last.

The ambushed farmer returned to find his cart-horse reduced to less than a cadaver. It looked like a bomb had hit the animal. There were severed legs, guts and parts of a body no longer recognisable. Incredulously he stared at the remains. Puppet-like, hands above his head, the old farmer started to walk around in circles. To anyone not aware of what had happened he might have looked like a comic street entertainer. At last he sat down in the snow, next to what was left of his horse and cart. Stupefied and crazed by his loss, he kept sobbing, 'What am I going to do? They've taken away my livelihood!'

It was Mark who had used the name of God in vain. Paralysed with fright the boy shouted it into the cold February air as if it were a confirmation. He stared at the still steaming rubble of flesh and sobbed helplessly. Overcome with terror he ran away from the street in which he lived.

There was no escape from death. His own hunger had gone. He tried to vomit his horror onto the icy roads leading to the harbour, but his stomach proved too empty. All he spat out was a green-yellowish bile.

Gradually, in the whipping cold air the nausea faded. He was amazed to find he was breathing almost normally again.

The war that had seemed so far away had finally come to claim him. He was sickened by the murderous hunger of people. Catching his breath in the merciless wind Mark was defiantly grateful he hadn't eaten all day. He felt disgusted with his own body because it needed to be fed. He had never thought about the brutality of his needs.

He thought of the old men's catches, fish eyes stunned with pain, graceful bodies stung into a final battle for life. He had watched their slow death, their jolting for air, their trembling before the final surrender. How could he ever eat again?

Grown-up talk about loved ones 'missing in action' whose bodies would never be found took on a sinister new meaning. Mark shivered as he stumbled along the frozen pier. He was afraid of the untraceable dead.

How many times had he been told to wait till he was a 'grown-up'. They had been promises of freedom, of being allowed to be oneself at last. He had been impatient with hope until today.

Now it seemed to him that all adults were murderers. He too would have to become a killer if he wanted to eat. Once he left home, he'd have to provide for his living like any other grown-up. His body's needs were deadly.

Burning tears of shame and impotent anger flowed as he discovered that his daily hunger would implicate him in murder. A flock of seagulls followed him as he crossed the road to a deserted landing stage, their shrieks mocking the helplessness of his humiliation.

As evening fell Mark followed the streetlights to the frost-covered cobblestones of St Nicholas' Square. He used to like coming here on market days, strolling among the stalls displaying rows and rows of dead-eyed fish: cod, mackerel, sprat and perch, slimy live eels looking like monster worms, carp and trout on ice. It was the only food left in ready supply. He had watched uneasily as buyers fingered smoked herrings for roe or spleen. There was something obscene about it. The fishmongers' rubber aprons and gloves could not hide the stains of blood and fat. Their knives cut off heads and slit the skin along the belly to the tail while they casually talked to customers. He noticed how men and women killed with absent-minded precision, scraping off scales with the back of their bloody knives, working from tail to head. The dripping planks of their stalls were covered with intestines.

Women touched and weighed copper-coloured herrings, wrapping them in salt and newspaper. Something in the movements of their hands Mark found disturbing.

When it began to rain he extended his slow walk home by taking a detour via the city centre arcades. He was anxious to allow plenty of time for removal of the remnants of the horse cadaver. Protected against the wet and the cold Mark savoured the shelter of bricks.

As he passed the Roxy his eyes were drawn to a large colourful poster. It showed a bare-chested, muscular man about to kiss a young, half-naked woman. His left hand was carrying a gun, his right embraced her voluptuous body. Although Mark could see the man was about to devour her, she smiled at him seductively. Across their bodies large letters announced: 'THE ADVENTURE OF A LIFETIME.' Just below, a smaller sign in smaller print read: 'Adults Only'. Despite the rain a long queue was waiting outside the cinema's ticket office.

Mark was about to walk across to have a look at the picture display when the rattling noise of an approaching tram shook him out of his thoughts.

His hometown had become a strange place. Like the body, it was in disguise.

When at last he entered his street he wondered whether he was really still living there. But then he saw the treacherous signs of murder, the trail of frozen blood and the tracks of hasty attempts to cover up what had happened.

His mother scolded him for coming home late. ('Where've you been? I've been looking all over for you! The dinner's cold.') He was not hungry, he protested, and went to his room to be alone. She did not call after him.

He wished he could be invisible.

Through the closed door he could hear a woman's voice. Was it the radio news or his mother talking to his absent father again? Lying on his bed he remembered having once asked his mother how and when life began. Her off-hand, belittling reply had infuriated him. He would find out in time. What sort of an answer was that?

With every day the war continued he felt a greater urgency to discover why things were the way they were. Foolishly he had asked Herr Brodersen why their hometown was separated by a border splitting the harbour and was promptly informed it was the outcome of a previous war. He could have guessed as much.

On his tenth birthday Mark had been given his own first adventure book. Its title was *Discoveries of the World*. He loved reading it. Although its explorers and conquerors, savages and pirates belonged to another place, somewhere far away, he knew them as well as the tenants of the apartment building. His heroes lived in the South Seas, Africa or the Andes, yet he was with them all the time. His own room consisted of coral reefs and palm islands, rugged mountains and tropical rainforests, raging rivers and peaceful lagoons. It hid lions and tigers, elephants and leopards, sharks and dolphins. Of course only he could see them.

It struck him that no one seemed to have written about his home. Was it not a remarkable place? Herr Brodersen had told them about the shaping of their native landscape by the ice age's terminal moraines. Didn't the world want to know how his hometown's harbour had come into being? Had his home already been discovered?

Mark began collecting postcards of towns and villages nearby until he decided they did not really show what was special about them. For a while he tried to draw and paint, but found he did not have the grasp of lines and colours to capture an image or a sight. When he showed others his work, they had no idea what it was supposed to be. Apart from his apparent lack of artistic talent, it seemed he always saw something that either was not there or could not be recognised. Disappointed, he came to accept that his native country would not reveal itself to him this way.

Finally he made up his own adventure stories about his

home, the harbour and the older parts of town. He let it be known that somewhere in the backyard, buried deep below the shed and the playground, the dead rats and the children's guinea-pigs, West Indian buccaneers had hidden a fabulous treasure. As proof Mark prepared an authentic map, complete with compass card, directions in secret code and burnt edges on parchment.

Furthermore, he warned, this coming summer a pirate fleet would sail into their divided harbour. Its crew would be savages from the Spice Islands who'd come to pillage the town and set all schools on fire. It would be in revenge for the lies the grown-ups had told. Their leader carried pistols and sabres made of gold. Even the pirates were scared of him. Mark alone knew it was his father.

At first he confided this terrible information only to a few special schoolmates. But later he also told Elsa, who passed it on to the other girls. Although they said they didn't believe it, Mark was pleased to see they were scared. There was little else you could do with girls except to frighten them. They giggled even when they were afraid. None of them knew there was no escaping war, that, like hunger, they would have to live with it all their lives.

But then girls didn't seem to know much about their own lives either. Mark pitied them for not understanding themselves.

Why, then, did he want to frighten them with stories he had made up for himself?

They shrieked with terror-struck excitement when he assured them they would all burn to death. Could it be girls actually liked being scared? It was impossible to shut them up. Well, they certainly became scared of him. He had at least that triumph. (Did that mean they also liked him?)

Mark would not have been able to explain why, playing in the yard, he, in company with the other boys, loved kicking a hard leather ball into a group of rope-skipping girls. It thrilled him to see how they fell over like ninepins. Their howling and wailing gave him deep pleasure. With unrepentant satisfaction he watched how they slowly got up again, sobbing uncontrollably over bruised knees, torn dresses and loosened pigtails.

How little it took for girls to get hurt! In his anger and amazement he felt like running over, demanding they pull themselves together, telling them that the real suffering of their lives was still to come.

But he was most angry with the grown-ups, the murderers and liars who had told him the war was somewhere else. There were times when Mark resented even his mother because he believed she kept his father from him. Had there not been the recent bombing of the gasometer, the stabbing of a live horse outside their house and the ever-increasing flow of refugees, Mark would have thought it possible there was no war at all, that it was all a conspiracy of adult killers playing their own deadly games. But where else could his father be?

Perhaps there were several wars going on at the same time.

On the first day of spring Mark took a rag from his mother's sewing basket, cut it into an armband and, dipping a discarded school pen into a bottle of Indian ink, placed three large black dots on the yellow cloth. Amused by the running ink, he remembered Herr Brodersen's writing class. As soon as the fluid was dry Mark slipped the strip of material over his left arm. To his delight the band proved a perfect fit. Next, he cut off the holed canopy of an old umbrella, turning the handle into a walking stick. For a moment, he was at a loss because he did not know how to paint it white. Then, in a sudden impulse, he rushed to the bathroom. After minutes of intensely nervous rummaging about in the First Aid kit he triumphantly pulled out a gauze bandage. Back in his room he patiently began to wind it around the handle. There was enough material to cover it twice. He congratulated himself on his improvisation skills – the bandage not only provided a perfect grip, it also alluded to unhealed wounds. Finally, he put on the pair of old-fashioned sunglasses he had found in a chest of drawers next to his grandfather's diary. Thus prepared, he defiantly ventured into the centre of town.

Although he forgot to tap with his stick, the crowd soon made way for him. Mark tried to single out elderly men and women, mumbling something incomprehensible under his breath as he charged them off the footpath. They scattered like the backyard girls who believed the war would leave them untouched.

He stumbled awkwardly, ever in danger of running into people. In sweet revenge he jostled unknown grown-ups. 'Pardon me for being born,' he growled and grumbled at unwary pedestrians. Whenever he pushed them, he earned an apology. As his confidence in the ruse increased, he claimed a tram seat reserved for the war-disabled. It proved a risky dare. Passengers soon started to notice his child's clothing and unshaven skin. He could tell they were recognising the home-made quality of his armband. Their increasingly hostile stares convinced Mark to flee the carriage at the next stop before exposure. As he rushed out he left behind the scolding and curses of outraged passengers.

So that's how it was when he took on the role of adults. To the grown-ups his playful acting was no more than a devious cheat. They didn't like to be imitated because they didn't like to recognise themselves.

Yet did they not continue to pretend to him all the time?

Walking down Great Street – a thoroughfare which in fact was neither bigger nor busier than any other road in the centre of town – Mark pocketed his sunglasses. At the box office of the Roxy he ducked his head and, lowering his voice to a husky whisper, ordered a war-disabled ticket to *The Adventure of a Lifetime*. An indifferent woman reading a magazine hardly looked up as she handed him his ticket. The invalid price for adventure, Mark noted, was the same as for the use of municipal lavatories. An old man waving a dim torchlight ushered him into the last row. In his new-found voice Mark acknowledged the service by mumbling a few polite, hoarse, indistinct platitudes like 'God bless' and 'service to the country'. Shortly afterwards the cinema lights dimmed until the theatre was shrouded in almost complete darkness. Reassured and relaxed Mark leaned back in his seat. He watched the national newsreel as if it were directed solely at him. The flickering light of the shadowy screen encouraged him to applaud individual scenes. He felt safe enough now to shout a patriotic 'Bravo!' at the armed forces' resolve to destroy the cruel enemy.

School was no longer a place of comfort and safety. Shortly before Easter Mark had passed the entrance examination to 'Old Grammar', the city's most prestigious high school. There his behaviour soon became characterised as 'rebellious' and 'difficult'. Just before summer vacation one entry in the class-register referred to him as 'obstinate'. His new form teacher, Herr Doktor Schulz, even felt obliged to write a letter inform-ing his mother, with regret, of a 'disturbing volatility in her son's character'. At home Mark tried to explain it all as a mis-understanding. It didn't work. His mother disapproved, shaking her head in long-suffering sadness. Mark understood that he, too, contributed to her grief and pain.

To escape it all some afternoons Mark went back to school to play the piano in the music room. It was an old upright ruined by years of chalk dust and the relentless banging of students who hated the instrument as much as their teach-ers. Despite regular tunings it had acquired a haunting sound of defiance. Harmonious tunes like Für Elise could take on the demonic, sinister tone of a revolutionary song of protest. Once, when Mark was instructed to play it in class, the students bawled with insubordination: 'For a weasel!' In unison with them Mark had howled his own disapproval, even as he was performing the music.

Yet outside school hours everything sounded different. Locked inside the music room by Hennings, Old Grammar's resident porter, Mark was paradoxically overcome by a feeling of freedom and excitement. Placing his hands on the keyboard he became aware of the unlimited range of compositions at his disposal. If he could play.

He was in awe of the instrument's possibilities. Touching the keyboard aroused and frightened him. The piano was a body that could rebel or sing. He would have to learn to play it the way the strong man won over the beautiful woman in *The Adventure of a Lifetime*. 'I want to make love to you,' he had said to her as he threw his rifle away, took her in his arms and carried her to his wagon. (Adults were forever talking about love – love and war.)

Left on his own, he would play for a couple of hours. Not that he could really 'play'. When he had asked his mother for piano lessons, he'd been given the usual answer – there was a war on. So, ill-equipped but with a determined willingness to learn to love the instrument, he began to improvise wilful outbursts of something he had previously kept inside, something which suddenly expressed itself in unsettling chords, sounds of unexpected urgencies like questions he had not dared to ask. They were wild, improvised searches, not unlike his walking the city in disguise, a desperate protest filled with helpless anger and unknowing, unrecognised love.

By the time cranky old Hennings returned to release the voluntary prisoner, Mark often had no idea where or who he was. 'Pretty crazy stuff, that, if you ask me,' the old caretaker wryly commented, closing the door firmly behind them.

Mark left the music room exhausted but strangely satisfied. He had had his say, even if no one had listened. Playing the piano was like 'body talk' – you had to follow it wherever it took you.

In truth Mark knew he had only just begun to discover his body. All it had told him was that he was alone. Both his mother and his father were elsewhere. There was no family, no home.

There was only war.

The world was elsewhere, a place of love and adventure that could be read about in books and watched in movies.

Girls believed in fathers and mothers, in home and family. It was a backyard game they played day in, day out. A single kick of a hard black leather football would suffice to put an end to the doll's houses.

Girls giggled when told about the war.

Mark became impatient with time. He could not wait to get older. Each year was a move closer to the Spice Islands, the South Seas, the pirates and the buried treasure. Sometimes, when his visions made him sweat with excitement, the urgency of being elsewhere expressed itself in a seductive smell. Touching his body, he sensed his future resided in the bulges and crevices of its growth. With every breath he took he inhaled the fragrance of being alive.

Down at the pier, on a day of thick fog, lashed by continuous rain and fierce winds, a few of the old seadogs had told Mark about a beautiful port, far away on the other side of the world, free of ice year-round, where freighters could safely unload their precious cargo. As the harbour town had never been at war, its docks were crowded with merchant ships from many different countries. The old sailors had given the port different names, but when they described it to him it was clear they were all talking about the same place. Still, he had to be on his guard. The cunning fellows had been known to trade in tall tales.

But how could he ever get there? No one seemed to take any notice of Mark's begging question. Had they not heard him? Perhaps the cold and stormy air had blown his words away. Or had he left it all unsaid, confided his impatience only to himself?

Mark felt deserted by the only people he trusted. Could it be that men who had sailed the world shared a secret they wanted to keep for themselves, a knowledge they refused to (or could not) share with a young boy? Would they too tell him to wait till he was grown up? Did the old seafarers not realise that in their age they had returned to a harbour of murder? Was that why they were sitting patiently along the pier, lost in conspiratorial silence?

Mark's burning question had become part of the dark, impenetrable fog.

At last, a croaky, yet quietly triumphant voice filtered through the viscous air, reaching Mark's ears as little more than a monosyllabic clearing of the throat.

'You just get up and go.'

Then, from the thick cloud of semi-darkness the subdued presence of a chorus of other voices emerged. Mark couldn't quite understand what they were saying. Although, up to now, he had only heard the old sailors moan and grunt, it sounded curiously like a giggle.

IV

During the war, when I was still at Castle Road Primary, it was impossible to get wood-free paper. Now the war is over, there doesn't seem to be any paper at all. Perhaps all the mills have been destroyed.

In my first year at Old Grammar we've been ordered to collect scraps of paper, cut them as much as possible to one size and, using a punch, string them together to form a notebook. The occupation forces give priority to printing newspapers and instructions to the civilian population. This is what happens while the enemy occupies our country and we no longer have our own government, the teachers tell us.

We look like postcard sellers or tram conductors when we unpack our homespun pads in class. It's actually fun cutting up unused stationery, wrapping paper or pages out of old books. We're mostly boys now in class and everyone is trying to outdo the other. So far, Theo Kramer who travels to school by train holds the record for the biggest and thickest pad. He comes from Oeversee, a village roughly twenty kilometres away. It's unfair because his family's country pub has been taken over by the occupation forces whose officers let him collect used army envelopes and out-of-date requisition forms. Most sheets of blank paper come in different colours, which makes some of our pads look like lottery tickets.

This time I've actually written something down on paper.

I finished my notebook yesterday, but I'm not going to take it to school. It's made up of shopping bags, old gas and electricity bills and a few blank pages at the back of Mutti's cookbook. I thought I might try again to write something just for myself, now that we've left 'Apples' Brodersen and the war is finally over. I've kept the old exercise book hidden under my bed, inside the *Discoveries of the World*, but I know I didn't do much of a job with my first truly written 'diary'. It's easier writing thoughts in the air. At least with this pad I can tear off a page when things go wrong, like the ink running out or when I don't want to go on writing about something.

Which reminds me, I never did get a chance to borrow Hanna's Montblanc. I guess in the end I was just too embarrassed to ask. Anyway, last Christmas Mutti gave me a fountain pen of my own, a cheaper one, but good enough. It does the job.

Now get this! By a stroke of good luck Hanna's sitting next to me again at Old Grammar. That's more than a coincidence. I might yet get hold of that Montblanc. And, would you believe, Frank Hilmer and Aaron Goldberg have been put together in the front row again, just as before! I bet even teachers from different schools belong to the same spy ring!

But nothing is really 'just as before'. With no schoolbooks available and our self-made writing pads, war and peace are like a paper-chase. Does anyone know where we are going from here?

The days are full of questions. By now, even the adults are beginning to ask each other how all this could have happened to them. There is a missing persons tracing service on the radio. The constant repetition of its questions puts me to sleep. Have you seen? Can you help? Do you know the whereabouts? The program lasts for almost an hour. It's obvious no one knows anything. Mutti listens to it. Does she really believe we will find my father this way?

On our first day at Old Grammar Hanna passed a note to

me. It read: 'So glad. Want to meet me after school?' It's kind of nice getting a short letter like that, written in royal blue, accompanied by a cute drawing that's supposed to be me. But why did she have to write to me? I was sitting right next to her!

Last week I saw an unusual young woman walking in the rain. There was something altogether strange about her. Even though at first I couldn't see her face, I could tell she was very beautiful. She looked like a live painting with running colours. A bright yellow headscarf barely covered her long hair. The only other thing she seemed to wear was a long, heavily soaked, light blue coat, its hem dragging in puddles. I was on my way home from school, carrying Mutti's umbrella. (It's so embarrassing, but she insists I take it along. I hide it in my satchel and only use it when no one can see me. If only its colour weren't bright red!) I don't know what made me offer it to the stranger. She seemed more amused than grateful. (That's the trouble – with women too you have to be grown up before they take you seriously.) For a while we walked together in silence. Although it was my umbrella, she carried it as if it were hers, holding it at different angles, adjusting it to our steps, making sure I was covered. As she was taller, there was little I could do about it. Despite the rain she didn't seem in a hurry. I didn't know what to say. When we crossed the street I told her to be careful. (I was beginning to sound like my mother!)

When we entered Holy Ghost Alley, I thought she took it as a short cut to the main shopping area. But suddenly she stopped, thanked me for 'having been a gentleman' (!), then quickly vanished. I lost sight of her without knowing where she had gone. Left standing under Mutti's red umbrella I realised the only place she could have run to was the small red brick church directly across. I was stunned because it's a Catholic church. In our town almost everyone is Lutheran. She must be a refugee.

Don't know why, but I felt cheated. I wanted to know more about the young woman who had left me in the rain. If only I'd talked to her! Well, it was too late for that now. I'd have to wait till she'd come out again. Slowly I crossed the road to check a noticeboard next to the church's entrance. I was relieved to find there was no service at this time of day. At least she wouldn't stay inside for long. What on earth could she be doing in there?

I waited a very long time, and still she did not return. Finally I overcame my reluctance and stepped inside. The small church was permeated by a sweet burning scent. It reminded me of the perfume I had noticed on Mutti and the body smell of other women when I stood close enough to them. I knew immediately it was something daring, something forbidden. Then I remembered the same scent at St Mary's, especially during Christmas services. What was beginning to make me drowsy was the tangy odour of incense. I looked around. The young woman was nowhere to be seen.

The church was crowded with paintings, crucifixes, sculptures and images. Perhaps that too made me dizzy. Only a few people were crouching in their pews, far apart from each other. It felt strange – all those pictures in an almost empty room. When someone coughed or stood up a stuttering echo rose to the ceiling.

Because it was the beautiful young woman who had led me to this place, I started to think of it as her. (She couldn't have disappeared!) Trembling and giddy, I looked at the altar, the jewel-like rows of candles and the tall whitewashed columns, recognising her in them, a woman dressed for the night. Away from the rain, at last I could see her made-up face, her glorious evening gown, her golden dancing shoes.

As I approached her, the hollow echo of my footsteps embarrassed me. They seemed like sounds of absence, as if I had no right to be here. But right now this was where I wanted to be. I needed to find the young woman in the light blue coat. I wanted to see what she looked like.

I felt the strange urge to light a candle. I had never lit a candle in a church before. Not knowing what to do, I rested on my still dripping umbrella.

To prove my good intentions I tried to remember the only prayer I knew. 'Our father, who art in heaven ...'. That's as far as I got. I couldn't go on. Why do we build churches for a god who is not here with us? It was just like home. Mutti still talks to Vati, even though she's long received a letter telling her that the one she's talking to is 'missing in action'. I've got a good idea what that means. Still she continues to speak to him as if she were praying. Isn't that exactly what people do in churches: pray to an absent father? It wasn't what I had come here for.

By now I really felt very uncomfortable. Hanging from the nearest column was a large wooden crucifix. Its bleeding cuts and wounds made me angry. How did it go? 'For thine is the kingdom, the power and the glory.' Was I looking at them? 'The power and the glory?' Was this my saviour missing in action? Wherever I looked, wherever I went, I was surrounded by death. I was told to believe in it because it was to be my deliverance. Although the war was over, death had remained. Only a few old men down at the harbour were talking about some kind of paradise on the other side of the world. Perhaps they made it up because they did not want to die.

I shouldn't have followed that woman. She's nowhere to be seen. Maybe it's the power of her church's miracles to make people disappear.

It was a relief to see that outside it was still raining. I did not open the umbrella. I wanted the rain to wash the smell of death away. I took my time getting home.

Where had I been? I could see the church had been a woman's place, full of flowers and jewellery. A woman's place that could make women disappear. Strange, that. I thought of witches, but didn't believe in them. Then, suddenly, it came to me. It was Monica Steyer from the top floor of our apartment block who helped me understand.

The church had to be a brothel. Most women call Monica Steyer a slut, a tart or a whore. Some are a little more polite: they call her a 'lady of the night'. I must admit I too watch her when she leaves the house at night, dressed in beautiful clothes that look excitingly forbidden, heavily made-up and perfumed. I can't keep my eyes off her long black hair, falling freely over bare, thin-strapped shoulders. The men in our street call her a 'working girl'. Once I followed her down to the harbour. From the other side of the street I watched her disappear into a bar called The Red Lantern. It was the place everyone in town referred to as a brothel. I've heard many jokes about it, even though I didn't understand most of them. I waited near the door for a glimpse inside. When a couple of noisy sailors staggered outside, The Red Lantern released outbursts of uproarious laughter. I caught a whiff of perfume, smoke and alcohol, a sweet and sour smell like sweat. For a brief moment I could see people at tables and chairs, watching a half-naked woman who appeared to be dancing by herself. It wasn't Monica. Flashes of red light reminded me of our priest's description of Hell, but I wasn't worried. It seemed a warm and friendly place to me.

So I do know something about brothels. Mainly because of Monica I've made it my business to find out. I've listened to talk of older boys, to unwary whisperings of men and women. Most adults think you're stupid because you're young. They believe we don't understand what they're talking about.

What I learnt was no big deal. Brothels are for men looking for women. A bit like the missing persons tracing service on the radio. Or people in churches praying to a father 'who art in Heaven'. Once, in a dream, a terrible thought came to me: what if no one's at home?

I admit I've looked at the drawings in the school toilets.

I've seen pictures of naked men and women. (Some boys are forever carrying them in their pockets.) I find all of them ugly and disgusting. But I would like to know more about real women. It would be good to talk to them, especially the beautiful ones. Not all of them. Just a few, like Monica Steyer or this Catholic woman who vanished.

I better stop. Not that I'm in danger of running out of invisible paper. There's plenty left on the pad. For my written notebook I've used only eight coloured pages – the green ones I tore off from last year's Christmas cards. With my new pen that's no problem because the ink's almost black – dark blue actually.

I feel a bit silly now, because I really wanted to say something about Hanna. Instead, all I've done is talk about Monica Steyer and a woman who was swallowed up by a church. I can still see her walking in the fog and the rain. Maybe she was a ghost. I'm beginning to wonder whether I've made her up. (Mutti's forever complaining that I'm a daydreamer and a liar.) Should've talked to her, asked for her name at least, just so I could be certain she's real. Now it's too late.

I'll go through all this again tomorrow, make sure I don't have to tear off some of these secret pages. Don't want to make a fool of myself.

V

'Name some of the flora and fauna residing in our native forests!' The voice of Mark's Latin and biology teacher marked the beginning of a dreaded oral exam.

It was one of many regular tests conducted whenever the class went on mid-week excursions to St Mary's Wood. Predictably, Herr Dr Schulz was appalled by the abysmal ignorance of his charges. Once a fortnight he would seize the opportunity to coach them on the nature of things. De rerum natura! Ah yes, the divine Lucretius!

Going to St Mary's with Schulz was a school ritual Mark had come to love and loathe.

He looked forward to entering the dark green umbrella of oaks and beeches, alders and ashes, maples and pines with soft filtered light sieving through treetops and the moist ground smelling of bark and moss and fallen leaves. A gentle rustling gave the impression the wood was actually breathing. It was a living place of strangely intimate presence, at once familiar and different; a domain, he sensed, with its own knowledge and its own rules.

He dreaded their teacher's know-all instructions which had in fact done little to explain the special magic of St Mary's. Waving his walking stick like a general's baton the bald patriarch dressed in a green hunter's suit dramatically pointed to his right, then tapped the stick on Mark's shoulder and demanded the correct botanical names of the most common native trees.

In trance-like routine Mark began declaiming the generic names he had learnt off by heart. It sounded like a prayer-wheel, a holy incantation: '*Salix alba, Abies pectinata, Fagus silvatica, Fraximus excelsior, Acer pla-, Quercus pe- ...*' '*... platanoides*', the baton of Lucretius' general came down on him, '*... pedunculata*'. Not only had Mark learnt to remember the words, by now he had actually mastered the art of reciting them as if they were classical verse. Dr Schulz had praised his 'poet's tongue' which knew how to make each syllable sing. With such artistic credentials Botanic Latin had become Mark's password to freedom.

In class they had just begun reading Lucretius' *De Rerum Natura*, a text that surprised Mark with its beauty. ' 'Twas something surely that's Immortal born; /For to a Nothing things cannot return.' He had thought about that a great deal.

'*Ut desint vires, tamen est laudanda voluntas.*' Mark was relieved. Herr Dr Schulz was in a patronising mood. All he had wanted to do was remind his boys that their world consisted of a mixture of parade ground and classroom, no matter where they were.

After an hour's botanical rambling they stopped off at St Mary's Inn near the centre of the wood where their teacher duly rewarded himself with a pint of the local. His students were allowed a couple of hours to explore the woodland on their own. Comfortably settled in the beer garden, Herr Doktor was ready to enjoy what they all knew he had really come here for: his favourite prom orchestra playing popular waltzes, marches and love duets from operettas. Class was indulgently dismissed on condition it 'report back in full force at 1600 hours'. By that time, after the usual encores and throwing of streamers, the uniformed musicians, among them many war-disabled, would pack up their instruments and go home.

St Mary's Wood was located along the northern outskirts

of town, near the edge of the border guarded by military patrols in camouflage. The occupation forces still kept a discreet lookout for diehard soldiers of the defeated army, but in the main they were searching for smugglers. For the townspeople even during the chaotic weeks and months immediately after the war the wood remained the most popular destination for a day's outing, although everyone knew it served as a hiding place for desperate loners who would not accept that the war was lost.

Incongruously in such setting, during sunny afternoons the Philharmonic Players, conducted by a make-believe major-general in white livery, did their best to invoke peacetime idylls. Overcome by memories of 'the good old days', ex-servicemen and civilians alike were driven by the music to learned emotional outbursts, sharing the wisdom of the classics with appreciative patrons at adjoining tables: 'Tempora mutantur, nos et mutamur in illis!' After a moment of respectful silence a chorus of patriarchal voices would venture an appropriate response. Someone like the venerable Oleg Paulsen, director of Holmsen & Paulsen, would bang down his stein and in a croaky voice call out 'Absolutely!' Or ever-elegantly attired Eric 'Beau' Sanders, former insurance director and part-time gambler, now full-time black market entrepreneur, would add the weight of his reflection, drawing attention to himself by grunting loudly before declaring emphatically 'Quite!' It was good to be among one's own, at home, where defeat, humiliation, crime and death could be drowned in Viennese dances.

Next to the beer garden was an enclosure called 'Monkeys' Park' where a handful of down-at-heel chimpanzees earned their keep by allowing humans to imitate and feed them. Once Dr Schulz had taken them to study the exotic creatures. They had witnessed the brutal teasing and mock concern of guests poking sticks into the animals' bodies, the obscene and cruel ridicule of man's closest relatives. How did these creatures ever get here? Mark had choked with anger, vowing never to return to the pitiful compound. But he knew many of his classmates could not wait to come back again.

About a leisurely fifteen-minute walk from St Mary's Inn was a small lake, almost entirely covered with water lilies and seaweed. On a tiny island in the middle of the lake migrating swans had built their nests. Mark loved to watch their elegant gliding between lily pads and buttercups. The presence of the graceful birds turned the stretch of still water into a scene of peaceful beauty.

He had left the others, even Frank Hilmer, to be on his own. The swan lake was on the way to his favourite hiding place. He had to run some distance before he could feel truly alone. As he veered off the main path in the direction of a new plantation the wind still carried bits of music from the Inn. Gradually, however, shreds of chords and human voices were swallowed by the rustle of trees and the intermingling calls of native birds. At last the only sounds were those of the wood. He stopped.

In deep gasps he inhaled the spicy air, nature's own breath of growth and decay. The ground was covered with beech-nuts and acorns. Invisible small animals were scurrying in the undergrowth. He could hear a woodpecker carve his presence into the trunk of an elm. He smiled and abandoned himself to the language of the wood. His senses responded to an exquisitely delicate movement he could hear and see and feel. He became part of a throbbing, a tapping and pounding of bursting pods, fir cones and chestnuts.

As Mark entered the protected plantation area he could hear the voice of Dr Schulz declare that it was strictly illegal for him to be there. Defiantly he kept walking, before choosing a spot and taking off his shirt. The warmth of the sun greeted his skin. He was free at last.

Resting on the moist and fragrant forest soil he was startled by the sound of someone approaching. Before he could move, a herd of red deer appeared almost directly in front of him. It consisted of two stags, bearing their undamaged antlers like crowns, followed by a large group of hinds and their calves. A gentle crosswind kept them unaware of his close proximity. Without hiding Mark watched the slow procession made up of leaders and followers. The animals were both naturally alert and trusting. For a while the herd remained close by, sniffing and grazing, watching and resting, ever vigilant. Then, abruptly, they galloped away.

Lying among pine cones and needles, fallen leaves and moulding bark, Mark let the peaceful setting lull him into a sense of wonder. Arms clasped under his head, staring into the cloudless August sky, he felt at ease, at one with himself. Inhaling deeply, he knew this was where he wanted to be.

Perhaps the war was really over.

Yet soon the quiet moment was interrupted by sounds from inside his head. It was his Latin teacher's voice, instilling in him one more time the categorical rules of civilised life. *'Lex et ratio loquendi …'*. It reminded him that everything governing his life had already been decided. There was nothing left to do, other than to obey the law. For those who wanted to gain knowledge, the world was made up of instructions, regulations and directions.

Mark took a deep breath. It suddenly became very clear to him – he would have to learn to disobey.

Why did adults always talk about 'order'? Because it was theirs? How he hated the way they spoke! The books he had read, especially his favourite adventure stories, seemed to be written in a different language. It made him wonder about words. What about his own stories, things he had made up? And what about the word games the girls played in the yard? He particularly loved their counting rhymes. Pointing fingers at each other they would sing:

> *You're to blame,*
> *And you're to blame,*
> *And you're just the same.*

Some words could surprise, upset and excite him. Others seemed to be saying nothing, as if they were dead.

It wasn't always immediately clear what language was being used. Often Mark had come across expressions that appeared to him strangely 'wrong', made up of words still trying to find their place. On the other hand, he could instantly recognise sayings that appeared 'just right'. The perfect language, he thought, would sound a bit like what he was hearing now – the rustling of the woods, St Mary's 'speaking to itself'. He closed his eyes as he listened to the plantation's gently swaying treetops, the songs and calls of its native creatures and the dry autumn leaves blowing in the breeze.

He had most difficulties with words whose meaning could not change, whose sense had been defined once and for all.

Yet, at the same time Mark felt strangely deceitful when he realised he always saw far more than he could express in words. How little language allowed him to share with others! In words he was taught to understand he often recognised something quite different. Many things spoke to him without the need of intermediary communication. The branches of an ancient oak, for instance, gnarled yet ever bending, still powerfully searching for light, had turned themselves into a large estuary before his very eyes. It was as if the tree had been talking to him, growing its own speech.

There was a crackle in the undergrowth. A busy squirrel raced up the mossy trunk of a copper beech. The air was filled with the chattering of magpies and the busy calls of robins. Across the clearing a hedgehog unwaveringly followed its determined path. In silent precision a buzzard dived for its prey.

By being here Mark had become a part of all this. But his human presence had also brought about a subtle change. Mark did not merely witness, he also imagined what he saw. He could not do one without the other. Looking around him, he marvelled at the woods' continuous transformation.

Fascinated, he witnessed the plantation's thicket become an incoming tide, its crests of hawthorn and elder. With the soothing warmth of the sun on his face, he listened to the sound of gentle breakers and inhaled the sweet and sour smell of sweat on his skin. He was lying on a beach of the outer harbour, away from his friends, sunbathing after a long, solitary, exhausting swim. When he opened his eyes Mark could see a scattered fleet of sailing boats heading towards the horizon. They looked like high drifting clouds in a sunny midsummer sky.

Was he alone forming images, or were all living things capable of transforming themselves? If what he had witnessed was real, what language could ever hope to capture the ever-changing nature of life?

In the distance Mark thought he could hear the giggling babble of a brook. The water's calling mingled with the buzzing of a wasp. For a blurred moment he wondered whether both sounds did not come from inside his head. He barely felt the teasing sting that followed. It was painless, like the pricking of a pine needle. Dreamily he nodded in reply:

> *Call the witches.*
> *Catch the flow.*
> *How it itches!*
> *See it grow!*

The lure of dipping into cool forest water made him rise. Lying in the sun had made him dizzy, as had the smell of pines, moss and bark. Geometric images imposed a wilful pattern on his vision. Black circles interacted with star-shaped objects. Flashing red and yellow dots throbbed into sight.

His head was flooded now with a droning lull, a continuous humming beat. It was a rhythmic pulsation accompanied by a persistent high-pitched tone, itself irregularly complemented by sharp ringing as of thin metal or broken glass.

Unsteady on his feet Mark fell trying to climb over the wire fence of the plantation. Unflustered he continued to walk in the direction of the sound of water.

A swarm of wasps followed his every move. In feverish frustration Mark shook his head as if to relieve it of its content.

When at last he reached the water he felt triumphant. He had tracked the sound down after all. A transparent brook revealed an almost white sandy riverbed. The rapid current carried small broken branches, leaves, pollen and bark. Barely above the surface of the tiny stream swarms of dragonflies hovered. Leaping refractions of the afternoon sun composed their own restless river of light.

Suffused in fleeting patches of gold Mark recognised disrupted images of himself. His straight blond hair looked as if it had become part of the brook's hurried flow. With every deflection of the sun's and the water's movement his face fell apart. Spellbound Mark watched himself drown and resurface, fall apart and reassemble.

His head was still throbbing. He felt hot all over. Staring at the oscillating images directed by light and water he wondered at the composition of this mosaic. It showed many separate parts of him, all of them derived from his presence. So this was what he was made of. Mark followed the changes and distortions of the current's counterparts with alarm and desire. The brook's torn reflections offered an incongruous anatomy – some consisted only of sections of his upper or parts of his lower body. Severed portions linked his mouth and chin to his abdomen. Like a corpse, his dissected torso floated past him.

He quickly undressed. The stream was blissfully cold, although too shallow for swimming. Anxiously Mark threw himself into the water, chasing the current's moving images. He thrust his face under, seeking relief from the droning inside his head. Uncertain how to make himself or the images of his separated body disappear, he tried to shake off his feverish visions. Momentarily he found himself at one with the pure flow of the small river. It seemed to receive him as if he were a natural part of the forest. But when he surfaced he was again confronted with the reflections of his disconnected body, its pale, fluid images, fragile, awkward, distorted and elusive.

Once more he escaped to the bottom of the riverbed. There, holding his breath for as long as he could, he slowly opened his eyes. Above him beams of sunlight pierced the rushing water. Lines, tangents, constellations of a wild geometry lit up in shining clarity of movement. Lying beneath the transparent lustre of its illumination Mark marvelled at the precision of the current's composition. At last he felt safe and sheltered.

Relieved and exhilarated, he had the overpowering urge to call out his name. Rising for air, he tasted cool, clean forest spring water.

Impulsively, he burst out laughing. How good it was to be alive! With gentle deliberation he guided his composite image out of the luminous stream. Along the bank he shook himself like a wet dog, ran around in circles and uttered wild cries, leaving puddles wherever he went. It looked as if he were trying to shed his skin.

Late that afternoon, back in the sunless yard of the forbidding tenement house, Mark for the first time recognised the cracked bricks and stony pavement as unforgiving matter, gritted and cemented, hosed and swept to perpetuate suffocation and fear. Where he was living with his mother no grass or trees were to be found anywhere. Along with the other children he was held captive in a playground built like a fortress from which no one could escape. The desolate walls encircling the courtyard had turned their childhood into a dark place of imprisonment, a theatre of sinister games, a penal cell filled with terror and despair. Even as they were playing together each one of them remained alone. Their games, Mark realised, were diversionary exercises of make-believe, temporary relief from the bleak reality of daily incarceration, clandestine preparations for their eventual release.

Like the grown-ups, Mark could only think of one thing – liberation. Once, when he could be quite certain no one else was around, he had turned to the Enemy for release.

He returned to the familiar enclosure determined not to remain defeated forever. Deep in the shed, half-hidden by a row of upturned crates, he surveyed the yard with the imaginative cunning of a gaolbird. Angry, humiliated and disgusted he inhaled the putrid smell of poverty and fear.

As usual, Elsa was playing on her own with her brightly coloured, gloss-painted balls. Like a mechanical doll the young girl bounced a red and a yellow ball against the stonework. Every now and then she would turn around quickly and clap her hands before the balls returned to her possession. All the while she was nodding or bowing, as if paying her respects. Mark was nauseated by the spectacle, but could not force himself to look away. He noticed Elsa did not need to keep her eyes open when she caught the balls in trance-like reflex action.

He would have liked to have put a stop to her obsessive game. The repellent walls of their apartment building would hardly be appeased by Elsa's mindless ritual. But then Mark remembered learning at school about the Wailing Wall in Jerusalem. They were shown pictures of men dressed in black clothes, wearing long beards and strange-looking hats. Their hair seemed braided and, like Elsa, they were bowing to the Wall. No one in class understood why they were doing it. All their teacher had told them was that they were Jews.

Everyone in class instantly recognised the word. Grown-ups had blamed just about everything, including the war, on 'the Jews'. Who or what was a Jew? Their classmate Aaron Goldberg was a Jew. Mark had no idea why. Could he himself become a Jew? He knew even less about Jews than he did about Catholics. He had nothing against them, but it did seem weird to nod and bow in submission to a wall. What did the pigtailed snotty girl over there know about Jews?

His thoughts were interrupted by a strongly accented voice descending from the tiny top floor balcony into the yard. Its agitated calls dropped and bounced into a captive sound shaft, as if responding to the monotonous bouncing of Elsa's brightly coloured cue balls. Mark was startled to recognise Herr Kirsch, a refugee tenant with thinning grey hair, a quiet man who kept to himself. Was he mimicking a flying trapeze artiste? He looked to Mark like a clownish acrobat, a rooftop contortionist shouting incomprehensible words at his spectators.

What could have happened to the friendly man he had met a few times on the stairs or just outside the building? Like everybody else, Mark knew Herr Kirsch was a popular waiter at The Red Lantern by the harbour. Dressed in a shabby, food-stained tailcoat, he was in the habit of greeting Mark with a conspiratorial smile. Perhaps he didn't want to speak because he knew people had difficulty understanding his foreign accent. To Mark his smile seemed one of knowing resignation, as if to cover a great many things he could not talk about or had chosen to forget.

High on the stark balcony just below the roof, Herr Kirsch, dressed in his professional tails, spread his arms. It looked like the mock blessing of a scarecrow. Was Mark witnessing a clownish conjuring trick? Though still trying to catch Elsa's attention, the resolute voice from above had calmed somewhat. Prompted by curiosity Mark left the shed. Looking up, he tried to signal to the performer that they had trouble understanding him.

Unaware of, or indifferent to, Herr Kirsch's dark appeals, Elsa continued her game, accompanying the throws of shiny balls with a half-sung babble of some kind of nonsense rhyme. Keeping an eye on the man in black Mark focused on the unperturbed childish duet of hopping and clapping. The two performances simultaneously demanding his attention began to establish an incongruous link Mark found increasingly disturbing. In his mind Elsa's self-absorbed chattering and hypnotic movements began to take on a strangely sinister meaning.

Years ago, when the Enemy had smashed all of the windows, a rain of splinters had fallen to the yard. Now Herr Kirsch's words collapsed like broken glass. Even as he turned around to climb the railings of the balcony, sounds of dark and muffled syllables, suffocated or injured words, descended. At this moment the hoarse and urgent voice seemed to speak only to itself. But soon it changed again to sound once more like a desperate pleading. Mark could make out only a few solitary words, among them 'home' and 'children'. Then, all at once, overcome with fear and horror, he understood. The shabbily dressed magician was calling 'Go home, children! Go home!' He was standing outside the railings now, holding on to it with only one hand. With the other he waved anxiously at Mark and Elsa, pleading with them to move away.

In his despair Mark quickly ran over to Elsa and resolutely caught one of her balls. As he expected, she instantly let out a shrewish scream, then began to cry. 'It's mine!' she howled. 'It's mine! I want it back!' Bouncing the ball in front of him Mark pointed to the sky. At last she looked up and saw the man in the tailcoat. They could both hear Herr Kirsch speaking to himself again. He seemed strangely calm now. Three heavy words descended the stony shaft. 'Enough. No more.'

They did not seem to carry any anger. On the contrary, they reminded Mark of Herr Kirsch's friendly greetings on his way to or from work. He continued bouncing Elsa's ball.

When the man in the worn-out tailcoat let go of the railings the girl's mouth dropped open in stupefied awe. Her eyes followed his fall through the air as if it were a circus attraction. The body hit the iron frame on which a carpet was hanging. It crashed into the top of the post supporting the rail. The left side of his head burst open, spilling parts of the brain. Even as the blood dripped down the upright, Elsa continued to stare in hypnotic stupor. Mouth open, spittle running, her hands began to move automatically, as if still trying to clap and catch her balls.

Spread-eagled, half-speared, the corpse lay on the post, arms hanging down, its trunk precariously balanced on the frame. Mark dared not move closer. Herr Kirsch's dead eyes were looking straight at him. Was his disfigured face smiling? Filled with horror Mark was back at St Mary's Inn, with the chimpanzee, Elsa and Herr Kirsch waiting on the table of his biology teacher. A droning pain carried the fleeting image of the cool, clear stream reflecting his own separated parts.

The door to the yard opened. Shadowy people rushed past him. From somewhere he could hear Elsa sobbing. Or was it the pecking of a bird? It sounded strangely comforting. Nearby an angry voice shouted 'For God's sake, someone get him down!' Windows screamed as they were opened and quickly shut again.

Mark saw Herr Kirsch's blood trickle into the drain. Around him people whispered words he did not understand.

Was he lifted or had he grown wings? Would he be flying with the Enemy or fall like Herr Kirsch?

He was briefly aware of lying on the couch in the lounge. Then it got dark.

The plantation took him back. Oaks offered their shelter of roots and branches. Once more Mark was lying on a carpet of moss, attended by squirrels, woodpeckers, forest mice and owls. A row of proud and elegant silver birches kept guard. He took a deep breath, knowing he was safe at last.

A wet cloth was placed on his forehead. Mark heard his mother say, 'He's fainted.' Her words were followed by the sound of beating wings. A blackbird settled over his face. Mark smiled. His lips were forming letters no one could hear or read. Silently they spelled out his name.

In the street whining sirens signalled their shrill alarm.

VI

The paved yard was hosed down, its bricks swept clean of hopscotch squares or oblongs, ball games and nonsense rhymes in danger of turning into nightmares. As if nothing had happened, the shed continued to function as playground for captive children and domestic animals, a Monkey's Park right in the middle of town. Six Toosbüy Street, the grey six-storey *Art Nouveau* tenement building with its dark and forbidding backyard, remained Mark's home.

After Herr Kirsch's 'tragic fall' the landlord added a couple of rabbit hutches to the children's courtyard menagerie. Cats from neighbouring houses climbed the fence to sniff out the albino bunnies nibbling food and air, the sustenance of their imprisoned life. When a cat came too close to the wire enclosure their few constant movements of bodily functions would end abruptly. If there was terror in their red eyes, it was impossible to separate it from their normal stupor.

The guinea-pigs in the back of the shed were busy procreating. It was a race against time. Their survival was increasingly threatened by the children's ever more deadly games. When the caretaker's sons Willy and Johannes came up with the idea of a flying guinea-pig show the situation grew critical. The boys had secured their mother's assistance by appealing to her patriotism. They told her about a project in art class which was to be of national importance. Their task was to create a model re-enactment of the war's decisive battle, which, unfortunately, led to the final defeat of their army. Could she please sew them small parachutes for their miniature soldiers. A few days later they duly took delivery of half a dozen mini-chutes, made to precise measurements taken from the guinea-pigs.

There was great excitement in the yard as Elsa and her friends, the local football playing boys as well as children from across the street and beyond gathered to attend the formal opening of Willy and Johannes' Flying Guinea-Pig Circus. Having taken an oath not to tell any grown-up about it, they all came to witness the promise of truly daring feats. Just as in a real circus they were asked to pay for their seats. It was this touch of grown-up professionalism which helped generate even more anticipation among the local crowd.

The yard had never seen so many boys and girls herded into the shed. Some of the children paid with sweets, others sacrificed their favourite comics. Agnetha, the baker's daughter everyone called 'Aga', got in for two poppy-seed rolls. When Elsa told the directors she could not pay for her ticket, the situation called for an urgent consultation. Willy and Johannes withdrew to deliberate behind the sackcloth curtain. After some tense waiting they reappeared and whispered their decision in Elsa's left ear. In line with the occasion her response proved somewhat theatrical. She blushed, then cried out defiantly, 'No! No! No!' The call was accompanied by an emphatic but graceful stamping of her buckled red patent leather shoes. 'Never!' she declared like an insulted prima donna. Yet, after a brief moment of indecision, she joined the proprietors behind the curtain. There, in angry concentration, she closed her eyes, then, with lightning speed, lifted her skirt and petticoat and pulled down her pants. It was the performance of an experienced illusionist, so skilful and quick the directors hardly got a chance to look. Conscious of the quality of her performance Elsa opened her eyes again, swiftly rearranged her clothes, turned around and in contemptuous triumph took a seat in the front row where she knew she would have an uninterrupted view of the whole sandpit arena. No one dared move her.

'Ladies and gentlemen!' Willy's announcement through a painted cardboard megaphone knowledgeably followed the model of travelling hawkers at the fair. The expectant spectators applauded. 'Observe!'

As the curtain went up, a miniature springboard of approximately five metres height came into view. It was made of plywood and looked a bit like a radio tower. An awestruck hush fell over the assembly. Everyone immediately realised no guinea-pig could possibly survive a fall from such elevation. While pretending to reassure the audience the directors did their best to whip it into a frenzy. By its sheer volume Willy's amplified voice assumed the authority of someone in charge who knew what he was doing.

'Ladies and gentlemen! Thanks to the war it is now possible to teach these hitherto helpless creatures to fly!' The animated crowd responded with anxious whispering, nervous giggling and timid clapping.

'Ladies and gentlemen!' Willy continued. 'The superior knowledge and skill of our military leaders have made the impossible possible!'

Johannes introduced the first two guinea-pig artistes by simultaneously lifting them out of their hutch, an action which drew spontaneous applause. Judiciously balancing them in his two hands he proudly displayed the performance's star attraction to the audience. Conscious of the solemn moment he announced with trembling voice, 'Ladies and Gentlemen – Sir Bobby and Milady Minnie!' To renewed applause he respectfully bowed to both animals.

Accentuating his masculinity with understated elegance, Sir Bobby appeared in natural fur with a black paper top hat proudly bearing his name. Milady Minnie wore a truly stunning gown of frilly pink – 'a lavish dream in organza', Johannes called it – with a cute matching bow carrying her stage name in appropriately ornamental fashion. For the ladies in the audience the tasteful display of haute couture proved an unqualified delight.

Harnessed in their made-to-measure parachutes, accompanied by the rolling of a makeshift tambourine drum, the glamorous artistes were ceremoniously led to the highest level of the springboard. There could be little doubt they knew about the danger of the daring feat they were expected to perform – everyone present could see and hear their chattering of teeth. Their brave climb reached its dramatic climax with Willy's authoritative command 'Observe!' After the pleasures of fashion's momentary diversion the air was suddenly filled again with horrible doubts and fearful expectations. Then, before anyone was ready, all at once, on cue, Sir Bobby and Milady Minnie, with Willy's assistance of a little shove, crashed to their sandy grave. The flying guinea-pigs had failed to open their wings.

Uneasy applause mingled with shouts of disbelief. It was not clear whether the audience realised what had happened. In her bewilderment Aga placed both her hands inside her crotch. Elsa let out one of her inimitable screeches. Only the football boys grinned appreciatively.

To the mournful tune Johannes whistled on a comb Willy approached the crash victims with great delicacy. The star performers did not move. Gently he touched them as they lay in the centre of the arena. When that failed to revive them, he tried pushing, willing them to be alive. In vain. The corpses too had not learnt to fly. Regretfully, Willy announced, the artistes had died from a combination of over-excitement and unspecified complications of free fall.

Despite this tragic mishap, the directors were determined that the show must go on. Both Willy and Johannes proved to be in possession of a truly professional sense of timing. Johannes quickly put away his comb and reverted to the makeshift tambourine.

'And now, ladies and gentlemen!' In a quick follow-up

attraction Willy introduced Prince Lionheart and his damsel, Lady Guinevere. To provide the Prince with a truly leonine appearance the brothers had glued on his neck a mane of wood shavings gathered from the cooperage adjacent to the shed. The Lady's elegant white fur was complemented by jewellery made up of small adhesive golden stars one of Elsa's girlfriends had offered as the price of her ticket. Sadly, they too died a tragic death. Lady Guinevere's chute did not open, while Prince Lionheart missed the sandpit altogether, his chivalrous body splashing over cement. This time all of the children were stunned. No amount of haunting comb-whistling by Johannes could disguise the enormity of what had happened. The drum-rolls were sombre now, sad and inconsolable. A tragedy had occurred. A few girls were crying, and some of the boys from across the road started throwing stones.

'Ladies and gentlemen!' Willy began again, but the audience had turned ugly. 'These beautiful creatures,' he shouted, 'have made their ultimate sacrifice for the sake of the fatherland!' But it was too late. The spectators booed. 'You have been privileged to witness today ...' As he implored his audience to remember that the deaths of these creatures were truly patriotic, fateful and noble, patrons were leaving the shed, threatening to reveal all.

They had been promised guinea-pigs could fly. There was no reason now not to tell the world they couldn't.

Mark too had watched, but from a distance. Unwilling to leave his vantage point on top of the carpet-hanging frame, he remained there even after the end of the show. What he had witnessed was for him something like a double spectacle. A part of him began to realise he had been watching himself not so long ago. He knew everyone present, the touch and smell of the shed, the mixture of sawdust and sand, white mice, guinea-pigs and rabbits, rotting wood, urine and paint. Much of his life had been made up of these ingredients. But now he felt he no longer belonged here, that the time had come for him to leave the shed behind.

Following the performance, he had grown restless, even angry. The yard with its walled and fenced-in space of playing games and daily chores, friendships and brutality, nursery rhymes and hopscotch, dirty laundry and whitewashed linen had held him captive. It was here that he had called out for the Enemy to take him to his father. It was here, underneath the dark grills of cell-like balconies and the bleak towering walls suffocating everything around it, that he had begun to imagine himself elsewhere. Remembering his favourite stories and pictures from *Discoveries of the World*, he wondered why the world was so far away.

Mark wished he was not imprisoned in a place of death.

He watched the agitated and distraught children as they left the yard, in small groups or by themselves. After they had gone Mark could hear quiet sobbing, fearful whispers, nightmarish screams. He looked around, but there was no one there.

What was he doing here, sitting on top of the carpet-hanging frame like a monkey? The show was over. He had seen Willy and Johannes, anxious to destroy the evidence, leave in a hurry, carrying the dead animals away in a chocolate box. Only the frayed sackcloth that had served as curtain and two rows of pillowed crates now turned upside down gave a hint that the Flying Guinea-Pig Circus had made a brief appearance.

How easy it was to hide death!

Not only his mother had called him a war child. He did not like it, but more and more he himself felt that it was an accurate description. He had been a child during the war, and now he found that his childhood was just like the war. Although it lay in the past, he was unable to leave it behind. It remained present even after it was gone. He would have to live with it for the rest of his life. There was no escape from it.

By late May that year spring had reached even the northernmost parts of the country. Parks and gardens were staging their revival of nature as if to encourage man to do the same. Catkin flowered on willows, daffodils and lilies spread their festive colours.

On his thirteenth birthday Mark's mother gave him a globe, a chemistry set and a camera. With it came a present he had not dared hope for, a cruise on the recently refurbished Alexandra to the outer harbour 'and beyond'. It was the 'beyond' on the ticket that excited him the most.

He had to be patient. It took another two months before the Alexandra was ready to sail. The vessel had been used as a human cargo ship transporting refugees from the East. Now that she had at last returned to her native harbour, all temporary superstructures were being dismantled again. No effort was to be spared to restore the Alex to her former glory. She had been part of the harbour city for generations. Built around the turn of the century she was a grand steamer, with luxurious staterooms and an elegant semi-enclosed upper deck where the town's polite society spent balmy summer nights cruising along the southern parts of the inlet.

The local shipping company boasted five sleek, modern motorboats, but the Alex remained the favourite among young and old. Her very presence was reassuring proof the war had really changed nothing.

Squatting at his usual place along the pier Mark had watched the crew cover the rusty hull with paint, scrub planks and walls and install new seats. At bow and stern her name was being lovingly restored.

At last she was docked at the landing stage, flags atop and festively decorated with garlands of coloured lights.

She looked a new ship when Mark finally boarded her on an overcast July morning. Blowing dark smoke through her huge funnel, the Alex sounded her hooter. From his seat next to the bridge Mark waved his mother goodbye. Her moving hands seemed an apparition. Could she really see him, or was he just imagining it? On the pier a brass band was farewelling the first boat since the war to cross the border with traditional shanties. Determined not to offend the former enemy, the local officials had decided to celebrate the return to normality with strictly non-patriotic marches.

On board, Mark's eyes wandered across the jetty to where the old men were fishing. Would they miss him, wonder why he had not joined them this morning? They looked up wearily as the Alex pulled back and slowly turned into the main shipping lane. Of course, to the old seadogs she was little more than a coastal steamer, not to be compared with the 40,000 plus tonners that had taken them to the other side of the world.

Mark had crossed the inner harbour on motor boats many times, and once, a long time ago, someone had taken him to one of the islands close to the border. Not that he could remember anything. He only knew about it because of a photograph which showed him sitting on the lap of a stranger in uniform. He had to be reminded by his mother of who the man in the picture was.

This was Mark's first cruise on a steamer, and the first time he would cross the border. He took a seat next to the pilot-house so he could watch the skipper's manoeuvring between rudder and engine room. Like the Alex, Captain Morsen had become something of an institution with his regular passengers. He was considered a fine figure of a man, even though, as with his ship, his time of youth and splendour lay well and truly in the past. But what a past it had been! The townspeople fondly remembered extravagant weddings, midsummer night dances, weekend excursions to the outer harbour, resort voyages, day trips to the beaches. How many of them had first fallen in love on the Alex!

The most prominent equipment of the pilot-house was a beautifully polished copper instrument displaying, in old-fashioned Gothic letters, the signs FULL STEAM AHEAD, HALF, QUARTER, STOP and REVERSE. To its left, next to the rudder, was a shiny mouthpiece which looked like a record player from the twenties. Mark watched closely when Captain Morsen used it to speak to the engine room, and he followed every move when the skipper pulled the levers. He couldn't help wondering what would happen, if the skipper gave his orders verbally, then pushed the handle for a different instruction.

Gracefully the Alex passed the inner harbour resorts of Hawk's Nest, Forest Lake and Solitude. Although the war was over and the weather summery, the beaches were deserted, the seaside cafés closed and the promenades empty. The beautiful shoreline had taken on a ghostly appearance. It was difficult to imagine that once yachts had crowded the firth and other pleasure steamers had entered and left the harbour at regular intervals. Now the entire inlet looked abandoned. Despite the sunshine the hilly landscape projected an atmosphere of doom. Some of its lush gently sloping meadows remained covered in mist. Although seemingly within reach, they appeared inaccessibly withdrawn. Few cattle were grazing. Farmhouses disappeared behind overgrown hedgerows. The entire land had gone into hiding.

As they sailed past Mark watched the scene in disbelief. Was all this his home?

In local history lessons they had been taught about wars between north and south, of the fierce competition between two national economies almost entirely reliant on farming and fishing. Mark saw a fertile countryside where no one seemed to be living. The fields lay bare, their rich soil wasted, and the paddocks were empty of animals. The other side of the harbour looked just the same.

Soon the Alex was leaving the protection of the southern peninsula, venturing out into the open sea. A stiff breeze had sprung up. Many of the passengers were beginning to leave the upper deck. The air tasted salty and the shrieks of gulls astern seemed wilder now, more demanding like arrogant birds of prey. The waves alongside the bow were spraying white foam. Further out whitecaps were punctuating the sea.

Captain Morsen passed the rudder to his First Mate before stepping outside the pilot-house. Jovially he walked up to Mark and handed the young boy his binoculars. It took him a while to bring them into focus, but then Mark saw the far-away lightship as if it were right in front. It was painted red, with the white-lettered name of the port prominently displayed across its hull. From both masts powerful beacon lights spread their signals across the entrance of the outer harbour. Even on a sunny day their flashes could not be missed. It looked to Mark as if they were warning ships not to enter. Wasn't the lightship supposed to guide them into safety? And what about the lightship itself? Mark liked the idea that it bore the name of his hometown. He imagined being part of its crew, having to live on the anchored vessel rocking helplessly in the heavy swell.

'Is it safe?' Mark asked the captain. He was assured lightships could not sink.

Why was light always associated with safety? Mark thought unsinkable ships somewhat of a cheat. If he himself could not drown, what would be the point of learning to swim? In Latin and Greek they had been taught what it meant to be immortal. The gods of antiquity, they were told, lived forever. Heroes too. You could actually become a god if you were heroic enough. Or, if you were a strong ruler, you could declare yourself a god. In his collection of adventure stories the heroes were really only brave because they were not afraid to die. And in his favourite book, *The Corsair*, even the largest galleons sank, and heroes and villains alike drowned in the ocean where they were eaten by sharks. If all that were not true, they would have been only fake adventures. Nothing to get excited over. Immortality would make life a trick, a forgery, an adventure story of make-believe.

'Water is an unstable element,' Herr Brodersen had told them at primary school, 'it has no planks.' But men had always taken their vessels to sea, venturing away from the safety of firm land. The only ways of conquering the sea were sailing and swimming. What a curious expression, then, 'to be all at sea'. Where he came from, it was the only way to be. Sailors talked differently; that's why their stories were always daring. They were spinning yarns to stay above water. For those who remained on land there were only dreams and adventure stories.

Mark would have liked the Alex to take them to the lightship, but he noticed the First Mate had steered her port-side. Through the open window of the pilot-house he was communicating with Captain Morsen. The skipper quietly nodded to the helmsman. Their faces were serious, almost grave, then exploded in short bursts of reckless laughter. Linking thumb and index finger both raised their right hands and pierced the air like he had seen the make-believe Major-General conduct the Philharmonic Players in the beer garden of St Mary's Inn. Then they quickly returned their attention to the sea.

Retrieving his binoculars, Captain Morsen pointed to several large buoys just ahead of them, each carrying a red lantern. As they came closer Mark could hear a high-pitched signal emanating from them. Next to him came the defiant voice of the captain: 'The border, my boy, we're about to cross the border.'

There was laughter of passengers below. Sounds of drinking rose from the stateroom. Were the travellers toasting the moment or oblivious to it? The Alex had entered foreign waters. On the upper deck, not far from them, a small group of older men and women, obviously refugees from the East, was standing at the rail. Every now and then they pointed to the shoreline. The wind carried shreds of their conversation. '... Just like home ...'. Arms around each other, they continued to look at the passing landscape, the geometrical marking of its hedgerows, a distant wind-mill, wild fields of flax and rye.

With the crossing of the border Mark had claimed his

birthday present. In future he could say he had been north, in the country of the Enemy. How close it was to home! He did not doubt the importance of the event. Yet despite its significance Mark had to admit to himself there was little that had been truly special about the trip. Captain Morsen had spoken to him, he had kindly lent him his binoculars, and he was allowed to watch the pilot-house. But that was all.

Crossing the border had not turned out the spectacular event Mark had assumed it to be. Perhaps it had something to do with being 'all at sea'. He had not learned to speak the old sea dogs' sailor's yarn. There were demarcation buoys, but the water looked just the same on either side. Now, after the event, he wasn't so much disappointed as embarrassed, even slightly amused, by his own foolish expectations. How could water suddenly look different?

What was the big deal about crossing a border? When he had stopped playing in the yard, withdrawn from the children and become a spectator, when he had felt the need to keep a distance between himself as he had been and as he was now – had he not also crossed some kind of a border then?

Back in his room he had been looking at himself in the mirror more closely than before. In fact, he had to admit he was in the habit now of doing it much more often than before. He needed to look at himself. But for all his scrutiny he could not detect anything about himself that looked radically different. There were no obvious marks on him. Unless you included the fact that he continued to grow and gain weight. He missed such signs during his daily checks because they were normal and hardly noticeable.

Sailing on the Alex through a beautiful but deserted landscape had proved something of a ghost-ride. The other passengers, mostly middle-aged women and old men, had taken little notice of him, and he preferred to be on his own. Many of the women had hard and bitter faces. Mark could tell they were war widows, trying to forget their husbands by eating and drinking. They drank in a hurry, as if to make up for lost time, and got drunk very quickly. Mark was afraid of their laughter. Some had linked arms and swayed from side to side. Others let themselves be kissed by whoever happened to be sitting next to them. Their presence added to the unreality of the voyage. Watching them through doors and windows, Mark thought they looked like conspiratorial deaf-mutes.

He wondered what Captain Morsen might think of his passengers. After steering hundreds of refugees through mine-infested waters, with little or no food on board, babies being born and many of the injured dying, how could he return to coastal cruising, weddings and dances aboard the Alex as if nothing had happened?

The outer harbour was covered in bright sunshine. It was suddenly a glorious summer's day. The breeze had died down and visibility was excellent. Yet the Alex remained a ghost ship. No other vessels were to be seen. The local fleet of trawlers had not yet returned from their fishing grounds further out in the open sea.

'Here, get that into you.' A seaman offered Mark a glass of hot tea mixed with Jamaican rum. From the first mouthful the drink felt like a cleansing of his body. With each sip the alcohol made him gasp.

'There's a tombola in the lower stateroom, with lots of prizes,' the sailor announced.

Mark was non-committal. 'I'll see.'

The cheerful deck-hand urged him on. 'Music, drinks and ladies. Think about it!'

Displaying an infectious smile, the seaman stayed around, as if on unfinished business. 'You're old enough,' he tried again. Mark thanked him, handing back the empty glass. He did not like his chances competing against the surviving deaf-mutes' anger and defeat. They scared him. He preferred to stay up in the fresh air, with the wind in his hair and the taste of salt on his lips. The sailor left him, staying put next to the pilot-house.

The sun on his skin and the effect of the alcohol combined to make Mark pleasantly tired. Half closing his eyes he could hear the Alex gently slicing the fairway, as if cutting or tearing the sea open. They were gliding through the inlet, stealing back into the harbour. Mark took stock of the familiar sights, the abandoned landscape of his home. Neither town nor country had been burnt to the ground as in the south. Inaccurate bombs had destroyed only a few official buildings, damaged parts of the shipyard and one or two other port installations. Yet they were passing an inland scenery of defeat, a deserted countryside of waste, the outskirts of a town populated more and more by native refugees. When would the farmers start tilling the soil again?

His head dropped; his breathing, pulse and heartbeat slowed. In his sleep Mark skippered his body into forbidden territory. Captain Morsen reminded him they were not on a lightship. Mingled with his laughter were the urgings of the deck-hand to go below. He kept telling him that he was not too young. Too young for what? His mother informed him the empty countryside belonged to his father, an absentee landlord who would not allow his fields to be tilled. Like everyone else, he too had gone into hiding.

Mark awoke from the ringing of the ship's bell. Located between funnel and pilot-house, it rang out loudly. He saw the Alex had switched on her garlands of multicoloured lights in bright sunshine. She was sailing home proudly dressed in dozens of flags. In the late afternoon they made a noisy entrance into the harbour. Air-raid sirens were howling. Freighters and factories blew their approval. It was a triumphant welcome, in strong contrast to the refugees' arrival one foggy winter morning three years ago when there had only been stunned silence. This time Captain Morsen stood at the bridge, a forbearing smile on his face, one arm around the boy who would not leave the pilot-house. Mark knew from countless adventure tales this was how victorious battleships returned to their native ports, how pirate ships defiantly delivered their splendour of exotic spoils.

But all they had done was sail his home until they reached the border. And the border was water. He had seen the lightship, the anchored beacon that could not sink, but only through binoculars.

As arranged, his mother collected him at the jetty. Mark tried to tell her about the trip. But she was not listening to him. He could tell, she had heard voices again.

VII

Dr Mestring has had a word with me about Mutti's condition. She's not well, he says, but I mustn't worry. I should try to think that sometimes she's not really here. Is he kidding?

Despite his advice he's asking me to let him know any changes in her behaviour. I should take notes. What does he think I am – a spy, a traitor, an informer? She's my mother!

Admittedly, sometimes I think she's just another child playing in the sunless backyard of our home.

Mutti, who gave me such wonderful birthday presents! A trip on the Alex, a chemistry set, a camera and a large globe that lights up at night! I have no idea how she can afford to be so generous.

The globe stands close to my bed. I love looking at it, gently rotating it, imagining the countries my fingers travel. Thanks to my mother the whole world has come to my room.

When I light the globe at night it reminds me that the world never sleeps. I know the sun is shining on one half of the earth while the other is shrouded in darkness. Whatever the time, there are always people awake. That's a scary thought. I would prefer it, if for a while at least everyone were at rest.

I've learnt a new word: Antipodes. It means the opposite side of the world. Our new Classics teacher, Dr Gerson, explained to us that the word is Greek and really means 'having the feet opposite'. That's funny. Sometimes I dream of people walking below each other, touching the soles of their feet. When I can't fall asleep I think there's always someone walking below or above me. Like reflections on water. It's a crazy idea. That's what can happen when I keep the globe light on all night.

I've tried to talk to Mutti about this, but all she does is nod or say 'Really?' She constantly mumbles to herself, just like an old woman. I suspect she's not only forgotten me but also herself. When I speak to her she hardly ever listens. She's busy with something else, but I have no idea what that might be. Sorry, Dr Mestring.

Mutti talks gibberish. It's pointless listening to her. She lives in a globeless world. Her days and nights are filled with darkness. She's long forgotten to keep time. But she never misses the tracing service for missing persons. Even though she has no watch, she turns on the radio on the dot of two o'clock. 'Do you know the whereabouts ...?'

Watching my mother, it is difficult to believe in 'standard time'.

When I went shopping with her, assistants wished her a speedy recovery. From what?

Now I do all of our shopping on my own.

VIII

For Mark, the town was like his body, intimately familiar, yet strangely apart. He loved walking the streets, past shops and houses he knew, filled with strange expectation. It was good to live in the centre.

Overlooking all was the imposing steeple of St Mary's. Sometimes he thought of it as a guard, a kind of angelic recorder of their daily lives. At other times he felt they were prisoners being watched from an observation tower. 'God sees everything!' his mother had warned him.

Mark didn't know about God, but he himself had begun seeing things that he had missed before. Now that he no longer spent most of his afternoons in the backyard, he often strolled around the town on his own. When dusk set in, he was drawn to the lights of neon signs and window displays. He let himself be guided by the vision of a seductive geometry. Eyes wide open, he saw letters change contour, lines mingle to create strange formations, bright dots turn into squares, triangles, circles or stars. Precisely formed shapes changed their size or altered their appearance until, in the end, he found himself surrounded by a silent fireworks of images.

Although Mark lived in the heart of town, his daily life's radius was small, comprising little more than a couple of intersecting streets. With the deterioration of his mother's illness he began to take care of all of their shopping. It was not something he thought of as a chore. For him the shops of his neighbourhood had always held a special attraction. Each one announced a trade with its very own, specific odour – the smell of flour and yeast when entering Weidemann's bakery, the spicy scent of Schwab's delicatessen, the intriguingly mingled, intoxicating fragrances of St Mary's apothecary, even the pungent smell of fish entering the footpath from Butendyke's seafood or the stench of rotten eggs coming from Salon Ingwersen. There were so many different traders on which their life depended. Doing the shopping was a daily reminder of how much they were an essential part of them. Life consisted of buying what was available. It was a lesson the war had taught them. Mark could only bring home what the shops were selling. In the immediate postwar economy he soon discovered what was essential and what was not. He was quick to learn the price of food.

Almost everything he and his mother needed could be found in the shops. They were the real providers of life. There was something mysterious and splendid in visiting them, cautiously checking out their latest offerings. It seemed suspicious how there could be such abundance of merchandise so shortly after the war. Some shops gave Mark the feeling supply was inexhaustible. If money were no problem, he could have bought just about anything.

It was this wealth of goods, with its potential fulfilment of almost any dream, which made up part of Mark's attraction to shops. But it was also their diversity, his sudden realisation how many things were needed in life, that customers had different needs and were therefore forever buying different things.

Not all of what was bought and sold was food.

It did not surprise Mark that, being in charge of dispensing the seemingly limitless provisions of life, many of the local shopkeepers tended to behave like rulers. The way they spoke and behaved seemed somewhat exaggerated, like the actors he had seen in a pantomime. Owning a business meant to take part in a drama the outcome of which had to remain uncertain. Would the supply never stop? Would they be able to continue distributing life's goods, feed the hungry, heal the sick, even entertain the bored?

Mark suspected there had to be a trick somewhere. He understood why anyone in business had to be a bit strange.

Next to the Roxy two elegant non-smokers ran the small tobacconist's Overbeck. The seemingly ageless men had a constant superior smile on their face. Did they know something the rest of the world was unaware of? Of unnervingly similar appearance, exceptionally tall and handsome, they were in fact father and son. They might just as easily have been twins. Both regularly waved at Mark whenever he walked past. Sometimes they would step out from behind the counter to greet him in the street. Their conversation was always the same. They would urge him either to go and see a particular film or not to bother. Once or twice they actually gave him money for the ticket. Standing in the doorway of their shop Mark came to think of them as sentinels guarding the Roxy, their palace of pictures. Could it be they were tobacconists like film detectives, leading a double life, pretending to be shopkeepers to avoid drawing attention to themselves?

Collecting his mother's prescription medicine from St Mary's Apothecary proved one of Mark's shopping highlights. He was fascinated by the array of strange medical apparatuses, sinister-looking appliances, some of them featuring rubber hoses and pipes. Despite their crude and clumsy design he could not tell what they were to be used for. Their unknown functionality tortured his imagination with suggestions he did not wish to envisage. But the best thing about the apothecary was its combination of so many different scents. Together, they amounted to an intoxicating perfume of its own, made up not only of the spicy odour of various pharmacological preparations, together with the sweet, enticing promise of recovery and health, scents you could trust. Mingling with them were other, more disturbing odours emanating from the dispensary – the ingredients of ominous ointments and emulsions, the names of which appeared on barely readable prescriptions marked 'Confidential', dispensed to awkward customers with an understanding nod and a professional smile, along with evil-looking tinctures and concoctions in small brown bottles carrying red warning labels 'Danger. Poison!'

Surely this was a place both of life and death!

Mark liked the paradox that not all scents derived from benevolent, harmless substances. Poison too could be beautiful. It often carried a strikingly unusual, seductive colour. He remembered the polluted sections of the inner harbour, the rainbow effect of oil on water. So what if poison was dangerous? Did that not make the bright blue or deep yellow liquid even more attractive? Weren't almost all the beautiful and spectacular mushrooms poisonous? You could not drink perfume either.

St Mary's Apothecary was like an aquarium of exotic fish, some harmless and some deadly, all of them beautiful.

For much of their daily food Mark went to Schwabe's delicatessen, an apothecary of unusual meats and cheeses crowded with seductively exquisite spices from all over the world, olives, sausages and a seemingly infinite variety of salads. The smell was so stimulating it made everyone instantly hungry, even after one had just eaten. Though most of what Mark saw proved too expensive, he loved going there, if only to inhale the exotic odour of smoked fish and roasted or seasoned meat, cheeses and chocolate, together with the warm, inviting smell of freshly roasted coffee.

The most extraordinary thing about the delicatessen was that it offered its customers tastings, so they would know what they were buying. Sometimes Mark pretended to be interested in a particularly exotic cheese or pâté, just to taste a sample. It was difficult to leave the shop looking disappointed after he had just delighted in the most exquisite delicacy. 'It's not quite what I had in mind,' he'd explain with regret, adopting the excuse as his line in the uncompleted drama of buying and selling. The salesperson understood perfectly.

Frau Schwabe and her assistants were immaculately dressed in white coats, rather like doctors or chemists. Mark considered it to be the uniform of life-dispensers.

Right next to Schwabe's was Schmidt's greengrocery. Its potatoes, cabbages and carrots belonged to the earth. Mark recognised the familiar scent of the countryside. Inside the shop it smelled of St Mary's Wood and the soil of pot plants when they were being watered. Here everything was regional produce – whatever Mark bought, his mother would turn into a local dish. They were both eating part of the landscape of their home – a basic, unfulfilling dish, the best his mother could do with what had been on offer.

In the centre of town buyers and sellers were trading in life and death.

Mark's home territory ended opposite St Mary's, near Neptune Square, where one of his classmates, Peter Moritz, lived alone with his father in the shadow of the tall steeple. Herr Moritz was a coffin maker. Appropriately the front of his shop was almost bare; it consisted of a small selection of open caskets, black curtains and an array of artificial plants. Mark was reluctant to visit his friend at home because he and his father lived upstairs from the shop. It was difficult to say where the shop ended and the home began. A sad and eerie place, he first had to walk past a long line of coffins until he reached the 'reception area'. From there Herr Moritz directed him through his office to a couple of stairs at the back leading to Peter's room. Sometimes Herr Moritz would join them upstairs, checking on their homework or just talking to them. He always greeted Mark warmly and was kind and generous to his son. Mark was relieved to find that when no customers were around Peter's father was a joyous man who laughed a great deal. It looked improper somehow, Herr Moritz laughing over his own jokes, dressed in his professional black suit and tie. But his jokes were really funny.

It was this incongruity which encouraged Mark to look for humour in the place of death. He found it hard to pretend that what he saw was funny before he noticed a sign promising the customer some kind of guarantee. How could that be? Would mourners come back after the funeral to check on the state of the coffin? Hanging from the walls were quotations from the Bible and a reminder that 'death was forever'. Mark interpreted that as an attempt to influence customers to spend as much as they possibly could afford because there would be no second chances. Looking at the inside of coffins he wondered why they were luxuriously lined with white silk and other precious cloth. Surely the dead could neither feel nor see it. At last Mark understood that most of what he saw was in fact designed for the benefit of the bereaved buyers. Death, it dawned on him, must be a very peculiar business because Herr Moritz was really selling illusions. Mark noticed that, as in life, there were deaths not everyone could afford.

Life and death were most closely linked at Butendyke's fish shop where customers chose live fish from huge aquariums, then watched as rubber-aproned and rubber-gloved assistants removed the fish before cutting off its head and tail with another routine movement, slicing the belly wide open. In the course of these ritualistic actions the conversation between buyer and seller continued unabated. For Mark, the fish shop was a confronting place where people habitually carried knives. Often, he noticed, the sold fish weren't quite dead yet. The thought that he and his mother had to eat something dead in order to stay alive unsettled him deeply. Despite this apprehension he continued to buy smoked eel, mackerel and salt herrings. Both he and his sick mother loved fish. Everything else they could eat had also been killed. What were they to do? Living off the dead presented no problem to people who had survived the war. But secretly Mark remained horrified that all life seemed to feed on death, in war or peace. He did not want to be a killer so he could live.

Not all shops were selling food. In the thick early winter fog the lights of Paulsen's Electrical shone like a mirage. It was October. It was dark. And there was light.

Mark remained in the wet and cold mist outside the store for a long time, marvelling at the blurred, beautiful apparition. Paulsen's lights looked as if they were forever celebrating a moveable feast the rest of the town had forgotten.

Inside the warm display area he closely inspected the many designs of classical 'royal' chandeliers, colourful hat-like lampshades, modern cone-shaped standard lamps as well as office and desk lights. Each fitting distributed a specific kind of light, which in turn created a particular quality of sight or a special kind of mood. It was true: light could really determine thoughts and feelings. Mark wondered how different the town would look if it weren't covered in clouds of darkness, fog and rain. Would it turn into a more cheerful place? Perhaps its inhabitants would even learn to forget the bitterness of war!

He thought of his own globe lighting up at night and smiled. In the early dark of autumn and winter afternoons the lights of Paulsen's Electrical were a beacon of hope. Mark never actually bought a lamp, but kept returning to the store which, not unlike the movies at the Roxy (ah, the excitement and anticipation when the cinema lights were dimmed and the curtain drawn!), could project so many images, moods and places. In his own thoughts and dreams light was a constant creator of films about himself. Mark found it impossible to tell whether he was their director or simply an actor playing his part.

What an exciting thing that was: to trade in light, to direct where it may shine, to determine the mood it should convey! He delighted whenever they burnt a fuse or blew a bulb because it gave him a legitimate reason to visit Paulsen's, to inspect the latest lamps and light fittings while waiting to be served. 'Take your time,' he obligingly reassured the sales assistant. 'I'm in no hurry.'

Dropping in at Herr Henrick's cycle shop proved a similarly rewarding if somewhat unsettling experience. Mark liked listening to the old man while he was repairing axles and tyres.

Herr Henrick was a great storyteller who told his tale working on upturned bicycles. He habitually spoke from behind a bike. Sometimes he would interrupt himself spinning a wheel to test the rims or the calliper brake. To Mark it looked like a wheel of fortune or a Ferris wheel. Whenever he asked Herr Henrick 'Is that really true?' the repairing storyteller would turn both wheels in emphatic affirmation before replying, 'You better believe it, son!'

The pungent smell of rubber in the workshop unnerved Mark. It seemed a curiously shameful odour, especially unsettling when mixed with the smell of soldering. Repairing a puncture did not seem so very different from putting a bandaid on human skin. He found it most difficult to watch Herr Henrick glue tiny plasters on inner tubes. It was never a clean fit, with leaking thick yellowish glue dripping down the rubber like pus from an infected tissue. The sticky liquid seemed to run way past the point of incision, an embarrassing give-away of imprecision and imperfection. Mark tried to avoid looking at the pink rubbery 'nudity' of the tube.

But then there was the dynamo on the right-hand front wheel. Once Mark understood how it worked, he thought it a most ingenious invention – to convert mechanical into electrical energy by simply pedalling! To turn on the light all one had to do was ride a bike! In a way, then, Mark himself could be trading in light; he himself had the power to create electricity, to direct light, to shine! The simplicity of the device delighted him, as did the fact that he could do two things at the same time – enjoy himself riding his bike and produce the shining glow that was the energy of light.

He thought about that a great deal and began to wonder whether there were other things he might be capable of doing that he knew nothing about. One night, his sleep interrupted by the howling of foghorns in the harbour, a curious idea came to him. If his dreams were like films, could it not be, then, that his body – or a part of it – was a projector? Where else could the dream images come from? Who lit the many stories he was told in his sleep night after night? What if he had taken the place of Herr Henrick, telling tales from behind upturned wheels?

In the light of morning Mark was not so sure any more. Reluctantly he admitted to himself that such thoughts may have been rather fanciful. But in future, every time he visited the cycle shop it reminded him of the possibility that he himself might be a carrier of light. For he knew now that there was a vital connection between the Roxy, Paulsen's electrical and Henrick's cycle shop. None of them may have sold food, but clearly they all were distributors of something important in his life.

The smelliest places in his neighbourhood were the pub 'Burghers Brew' and the hairdressing salon Ingwersen. Mark had never been inside the pub, but passing it he inhaled its stench of sour beer, burnt potatoes, fatty food, stale perspiration and cigarette smoke. It was a foul, obnoxious smell, as if a drunk had burped or vomited in the street. From the inside he could hear the sounds of coin machines ringing and dance music blurring from defective loudspeakers. They'd put an iron gate in front of the pub's large front window because too many drunks had smashed into it. Those who frequented the bar were mostly crippled or demoralised war veterans and what Mark's mother called 'loose women'.

Mark became particularly interested in women he had been told to keep away from. He watched with fascination as they opened their handbags, took out a lipstick, casually redrew the lines of their already overly made-up lips, then tested them by letting their tongue slide over the glossy red wound like cats licking their prey. He couldn't help staring as one of the veterans lit them a cigarette and they, with a dismissive nod of acknowledgment, blew smoke into the air like a magician. It was easy to see that they were casting a spell over the bitter, defeated men sitting at the bar waiting to get drunk.

But the most disgusting place in his hometown was without a doubt 'Salon Ingwersen'. The pungent stench escaping from its front door and windows was more than Mark could bear. His mother had explained to him that what he described as the smell of rotten eggs was in fact the ammonia of women's perms. Mark took a look at the women who had had the treatment and described their hairstyle as a 'fart eruption'. Busybody Frau Petersen from the second floor was in the habit of wearing her curlers all day, as if they were a crown of thorns. Why would anybody pretend to have curls when they had none? It was a stinking deception, that's all. The hairdresser's smell was particularly unpleasant because it entered the stairwell, the backyard and the lower floors of the apartment building where it would linger throughout the week. Only on Sundays and holidays the air seemed almost back to normal.

By contrast, Helma's stationery shop across the street carried a fragrance of cleanliness, accountability, decency and hard work. It was mainly the pure smell of paper. While at Castle Road Primary Mark had bought his very first copybooks at Helma's. Now at Old Grammar, he was still getting his exercise books from the same place. But under the pretext of looking for a present he had also started to ask for expensive diaries and other notebooks bound in leather. There was nothing quite like an unwritten book, an as yet unkept diary, clean white, virgin paper. Such pages contained the promise of everything imaginable. Unused pocket or desk calendars, reams of foolscap, sheets of white paper – they all had one thing in common: they were like a landscape of snow, still unmarked, untouched, signalling a new beginning. It almost seemed a pity to interfere with the purity and beauty of the empty page. Like a dog Mark would sniff the paper, momentarily closing his eyes as he did so. Yes, it was the same smell as in new books.

There could be no cheating with paper. Any impurity would show, any interference could be clearly seen. Blotting paper was something entirely different. It was there to soak up mistakes. Pure white paper, on the other hand, was reserved for what was right, what had been written correctly, beautifully, truthfully. (But it was good to have blotting paper as well.)

At Helma's Mark looked longingly at rows and rows of fountain pens displayed in a glass cage. One day he, too, would write in royal blue. For the time being he had resigned himself to buying pencil sharpeners, rubbers and rulers. Yet as he left the shop his knowing eyes quickly took stock of other stationery, more exciting writing material on offer, such as special gift wrapping paper, business ledgers, guest books, calendars and postcards from faraway places.

The very first shop he was ever sent to he still visited every day. His one task before school was to go across to Weidemann's bakery in the early morning and buy fresh rolls. There Mark inhaled the smell of yeast and flour while he was being served by one of two young women dressed in bibbed starched aprons. They both reminded him of nurses. He loved watching them as they reached behind to pull out different breads from the shelves or used tongs to select a variety of rolls from a huge wicker basket on the counter. Sometimes the baker's apprentice would enter the shop to unload fresh new rolls. The basket would overflow with warm poppy seed and raisin rolls, croissants and caraway seed bagels. Quite a few missed the basket, ending up on the counter and the tiled floor. The way the young women and the apprentice laughed as they recovered the rolls made Mark think something else was going on.

He was strangely aroused by the blonde and busty pinafored shop assistants. Mark could tell their bodies would smell of yeast and freshly baked rolls. The way they moved behind the counter, dressed in starched aprons, they seemed like graceful nurses dispensing sweet, tasty medicine. Back home he couldn't help thinking of them as he bit into his croissants.

One of the baker's five sons regularly came over to play football with them in the backyard. Rudi boasted to Mark how the shop-girls were fooling around in the bakery when his father was away.

'What do you mean, fooling around?' Mark was keen to learn what it was they had been doing, but equally anxious not to show his ignorance when it came to young women.

Determined to enjoy the moment, Rudi decided to keep his listener on tenterhooks. In a calculated tease he dismissed Mark's curiosity with the condescending observation, 'Why do you want to know? You wouldn't understand anyhow. I'll only tell the older boys. You're still a kid.'

Mark quickly replied, 'If you knew some of the things the old guys have told me down at the pier!' An appreciative smile came over his face. As part of his own challenge he pretended to have lost interest. He made a move to leave. 'I've got to go anyway.'

It was enough to make Rudi change his mind. Suddenly he seemed very keen to share his secret.

'I was hiding behind a stack of flour sacks and saw them do it. Hella, the pretty one, and Ferdie. She squeaked like a piglet, and he was grunting like a wild boar. Should've seen them at it; two grown-ups behaving like pigs!'

Rudi had got excited over his own description. His freckled face was covered in sweat, and his nose was running. Mark too felt his blood rush to his face. He tried his utmost to hide it. There was no way he could allow Rudi the satisfaction of seeing him aroused.

'Did they?'

He left his playmate standing on his own. It was not the reward he had expected for his revelation. Disappointed and angry, Rudi came rushing after him.

'You don't know anything!' he yelled at Mark. 'I'm never going to tell you anything again!'

With provocative slowness Mark finally turned around. 'You've got snot running out of your nose,' he replied coolly. 'Blow your nose, you creep. It's disgusting!'

Back home it felt different biting into his croissant. He thought of the yeasty, milky shop assistants in their stiff aprons and found it difficult to hide his excitement. He looked at his mother across the table. She was sitting there as always, absent-minded, seemingly unaware of what he was doing, seeing things instead that weren't there. When at last she noticed that he was looking at her, she smiled. Anxious and awkward, Mark reassured her by smiling back.

He had discovered that eating the croissant was like eating the young woman who had served him. What did snotty Rudi say her name was? Hella. 'Hella, the pretty one.' Lost in thought he started to slowly tear his croissant apart. Once more he took in the sweet yeasty smell and tasted the sticky strawberry marmalade on his tongue, wondering what it would be like to do with Hella whatever it was Ferdie had done with her. He still didn't really know what that was, but he was beginning to get a pretty good idea. He was certain it would taste something like this.

Mark checked the time and found that he was late for school. Confident in the knowledge that he would continue to buy rolls, he rose and gave his mother a hurried kiss. He'd be back at Weidemann's bakery. First thing tomorrow morning.

IX

I suppose nobody can pry into a pretend diary. Isn't there a song called *Thoughts Are Free*? Still, I'm nervous. There are supposed to be people who can read other people's thoughts. I can only hope no one I know can do that. What a disaster that'd be! I'd be caught red-handed! My hands, my arms, my fingers spell out the same desperate warning DO NOT READ!

Thing is, I have to let out what's been happening. But there's no one to talk to. It's hardly the kind of thing you can discuss with your mother, even if she were, well, all right. I'm no longer showing up in the backyard, but even if I did, there'd be nobody I could confide in. And the old men down at the harbour wouldn't be interested. They'd just smile and say 'It'll be all right'. Or tell me that in another part of the world all this would be very different and, of course, much nicer. They've got their own things to worry about.

So I can't tell anyone that there's something scary going on with me. Looks like I have to keep it to myself. What is it? Hard to describe. It's like war has broken out in my body. There's no escape. Nothing I can do about it. My body's on fire.

Perhaps it's still the Enemy. At last he's entered my body and won't let me be. First he makes me do stupid things, then he makes me feel excited over what I've done. He controls my dreams. Day and night I'm hunted by a strange, impatient feeling. I don't know what it is, but I know this is why people go to war. It interferes with everything I'm doing. In the middle of *Treasure Island*, *Sinbad the Sailor*, *Leatherstocking*, or *The Last of the Mohicans*, I have to put the book down because the pirates are ambushing their own ship or the bravest redskins are betraying their own tribe.

I'm back at Castle Road Primary, clumsily drawing the beautiful Enemy, then watching the ink run out in my copybook. Do I have to start all over again?

I'm afraid I might have seriously fallen ill. I suffer from a hunger which cannot be satisfied by food. Truth is I'm hungry only for myself, for the taste of my own body. They might as well close down all the food stores in town! How can a body feed on itself! Am I going crazy like poor Mutti?

Don't know whether she's noticed. Probably not. She doesn't live in the real world, as Dr Mestring says. Sometimes, when I gulp down my dinner, she sends me a benevolent smile across the table and says, 'I can see you've got a lot of growing up to do, Mark'. Wonder whether she ever felt what I do when she was young. Can't believe that.

Do young women get ambushed too?

Whenever 'it' happens there's a triumphant tingle in my blood. I have to control myself not to cheer because I have the crazy feeling that there's nothing I cannot do. It's difficult to suppress such certainty when it is part of my body. Don't want others to see me tremble with confidence. They might misunderstand.

Mind you, it's almost the opposite, afterwards. Then, all of a sudden, I feel extremely tired and dejected. Although the sticky fluid running out of me smells of nothing, I can't stop testing its texture and sniffing at it. It's both light and thick, quite different from my bleedings, although both make me feel exhausted. In the morning stiffness I feel myself.

Have I become a toilet drawing?

Here's a crazy idea – what if one could write with it!

Wouldn't that be something! It'd be like Hanna letting me use her Montblanc, the colourless secretion our personal ink for communicating an invisible code. Hanna and I would be spies, the only ones who could decipher our messages.

Mostly it calls me when I'm in bed, but sometimes I'm ambushed in difficult places. It's a nightmare when that happens. What am I supposed to do when I go all stiff in a crowded tram, or in class, just when Dr Svensen asks me to come to the front? For such emergencies I've worked out a special technique. It's quite a sad trick really, designed to outwit my body. What I do is think of Mr Kirsch's broken body. It's a brutal exercise conjuring up the image of him lying on the stony ground of the backyard, blood all around him. But it's the only thing that works. I really need to concentrate hard. It upsets me terribly. I don't care if people notice a strange expression on my face, so long as they can't tell the reason.

Saw Hanna in town on her own the other day. She pretended not to notice me. Well, perhaps she really didn't. I followed her as she strolled along Great Street in the direction of Neptune Square. Every now and then she stopped in front of window displays.

You'd think I know what Hanna looks like, seeing that I sit next to her every day. But that day I noticed something different about her. Hanna already looks a real woman. I watched her upright walk, the way she carried her handbag and her long hair blowing in the wind as though I'd never seen her before. At first I tried to catch up with her. I even called after her a few times. But then I decided to follow her secretly, like a spy on a mission. I suddenly realised I didn't want to speak to her at all. I much preferred just watching her, spying or no spying.

You could say Hanna is probably the only girl I've ever been interested in. Everyone in class knows I've always liked being with her. There's something special about her. We know and understand each other. It's almost as if she were my sister. But recently that's changed. Don't know exactly how to put it. Hanna's become a bit of a stranger, but I still like to be with her. I recognise a movement in her walk I didn't see before, the gesture of placing combs in her hair. Watching her I'm joined by the beautiful Enemy. Once more I feel that familiar prickling, stinging, throbbing tremble in my blood. It only started now she's become somewhat strange. Do I want Hanna to be different? Is that why I suddenly find it more exciting to spy after, rather than to be with her?

So we actually never met that day. At home, when I'm by myself, I imagine wild things about Hanna, like pirate stories set in a foreign land. They're all about my having to liberate her from slavery. But there are plenty of other adventures, some of which I can't talk about, not even here. As I fantasise about Hanna and me, the sticky fluid pops out of me like seeds from an overripe gooseberry. It spreads a drowsy feeling all through my body.

Whenever it happens I think of the beautiful Enemy. By now I know that I'm carrying the Enemy inside. Together we are flying dangerous sorties. Despite the risks it feels right. It's what we have to do, those of us whose fathers have not returned from the war. I could never tell Hanna about all the things we have already experienced together. But perhaps she already knows.

A couple of department stores send Mutti mail order catalogues twice a year. She likes shopping that way, relieved not to have to leave the house. When she's finished with them she wants me to look for shirts and socks I like, so she can order them for me. I never like any of them. I prefer buying things in real shops, especially things to wear. Browsing through the catalogues makes me feel like I'm doing something forbidden. It's as if I'm looking in other people's bedrooms. Everything is shown, all the clothes and models are on display, and there's always a price and an order number underneath the picture. When I look at women in underwear I shudder. Is that what Hanna looks like, half-naked? Why on earth do women have to wear such weird and complicated outfits? It's a prison uniform! But then I dream of liberating Hanna from her enslavement, and suddenly all the models look strangely appealing.

Even if she shares her humiliation of imprisonment with mail order models, Hanna's not the least like them. Anyone can see that. She's wearing her captivity like an abducted princess knowing she's about to be released. With that I'm back to my favourite fantasy.

Later, tired from the insistent throbbing and heavy sweetness, I mark a couple of 'practical checked summer shirts for boys in three popular colours, Catalogue Number 260340', so Mutti has something to order.

The trick is to know when to expect the onslaught. I have to be careful watching women in the street, try to ignore certain types of cinema posters and avoid women's underwear pages in mail order catalogues. Unless, of course, I want it to happen. But that's something I can't write about.

It's such a dicey business. Sometimes 'it' occurs in strange places and for very odd reasons, announcing itself while I'm racing Frank on the bike, during class tests or when playing truant. When Mutti behaves strangely, Dr Mestring says it's her nerves. Perhaps that's all it is with me too. But here goes! I have the nagging suspicion this fizzy, tingling, swelling, seething something-or-other may be what grown-ups call 'love'. The word on every toilet wall. With or without a drawing.

How can it mean the same as it does in novels and films, or when Mutti says she loves me? I know I love Mutti, even though she's not quite with it. I also love poor dead Vati whom I can't remember. Both of them are a part of me. But then this other thing must really be just a 'nervous condition', as Dr Mestring keeps decribing Mutti's illness to me. In that case it's something I've got to learn to control. I can hardly ask Frank or any of my other friends for advice because I've always pretended to know all about 'love'. Serves me right for being such a show-off!

Do I 'love' Hanna, then? I'd love to see her naked, but not in a catalogue. Don't want anyone else to see all the things that make her a desirable woman, her breasts, her long hair, her whatever-you-call-it. With me, it's all imagined. I'd love to see my own imagination come true. Is that what happens when men fall in love with a woman?

I see so little of Hanna these days. But, for me, even missing her may be a kind of love. Last time I rang, her mother answered the phone. Hanna wasn't feeling well, she informed me. When I asked her whether I could visit Hanna, she didn't say no. She said it was 'too early'. I don't like the sound of that. Already she's missed school for over a week.

Feels strange thinking like this about Hanna, 'love' and all that stuff.

The good thing about not keeping a proper diary is that you don't have to follow dates. You simply remember what's important. Seems my body's a notebook with its own sense of time.

During PE, three days ago, I fell off the horizontal bar. Bit of an accident. Could've happened to anyone. Except I'm now the only one in class attempting the giant circle. All the others have given up. For me, it's become an obsession.

Entering the gym, taking in its familiar smell of floor polish, stale sweat and fear, I felt fine. It was an odour hovering above the shiny parquet of a slippery human circus, a bit like Dr Svensen's description of those Roman theatres in which Christians were put to death. For us, in our fourth year at Old Grammar, it is the place of trials in athleticism, muscle control and physical discipline. It's also the classical arena where boys unable to complete ten pull-ups on the horizontal bar, followed by the same number of push-ups on the floor, are routinely mocked and humiliated.

I loathe the brutality of the ritual. Class is divided into four squads of six. In small groups we're turned simultaneously into terrified performers and sneering spectators. We all know there are only two ways of surviving: either you receive Emperor Engholm's thumbs-up, or, if you are really lucky, you escape the notice of our classically trained PE disciplinarian ('*mens sana in corpore sano*'). Emperor Engholm stylishly sports a short-cropped fringe and knee-length white toga-like shorts. With Caesar keeping a constant eye on us, it's not easy to discover for myself what my body can and cannot do. But that is precisely what I'm determined to find out. Looked at from the outside, it may seem Engholm and I are after the same thing. Nothing could be further from the truth.

Actually, the brutality of the gym provides an almost perfect cover for something I want to do by myself. It's not easy to explain.

Often I feel so completely separated from my body I can't be sure it actually belongs to me. There are times when I don't want it to be a part of me. Since I've discovered the beautiful Enemy within me I'm even more confused. When Mutti's out, I stand in front of the full-length bathroom mirror staring myself to death. I find something distorted about my body. How can the mirror produce an inaccurate or incomplete reflection of me? I barely recognise myself, and I don't like what I see.

I've tried combing my hair back, but it makes no difference. In the end all I can do is pull a face in disgust. One thing's for certain: I'd have made myself look more convincing. Still, I've got a fairly strong body, despite my blood problems and that other thing. It works like a machine. Living with it, owning it, is a bit how I imagine it must be riding a high-powered motorbike. You've got to learn to handle, balance, steer and control it.

Trying to own my body is what the horizontal bar is all about. At least for me. Testing my physical powers I'm bound to discover how much of myself is under my control. If there's more to me than my body, only the body will tell me. I want to know what I can do with myself.

Standing in front of the horizontal bar an insistent throbbing tells me my blood wants out.

At that moment nothing else exists but my body and the bar. I stare at the metal rod the way I stare at myself in the bathroom mirror. I don't see myself, I see lines and circles, movements waiting to be materialised. With those movements, with this geometry I'm going to write myself in the air. Strange that: just before I need the body the most it hardly seems to exist. I'm about to turn it into a geometrical design.

According to Engholm, completing the giant circle on the horizontal bar holds about the same degree of difficulty as a double somersault on the mat. Both, of course, can be done. All the athlete has to do is turn himself into a projectile, or 'catapult himself into a weight-defying composition', as The Emperor puts it. He's forever talking about 'live construction of images', or he carries on about 'scientific precision linked to artistic beauty'. You'd think he's our art or science teacher. Meanwhile I'm concentrating all my energies on the exercise. I don't need his kind of talk trying to explain why both freedom and concentration require energy. I know at the horizontal bar freedom and discipline are one and the same.

Transforming myself into movement is something I have to want to do. I do it because the giant circle belongs to me. It's part of my body. It's got nothing to do with anyone else, least of all with Emperor Engholm and his squads of jeering spectators.

This is how it happened.

Starting the pull-up, I raise myself slowly, deliberately, holding my breath and closing my eyes, as always. Engholm and his cohorts have taken up position below. Hands covered in chalk, I finger the high bar like a blind man, checking my grip, measuring the distance between my wrists, testing my muscles. I don't have to look down to know Frank and Aaron have stationed themselves on the other side in backup position, just in front of the two large mats almost three metres away. We've tried the exercise many times before.

As my body begins to swing below the bar its pendulous movements produce a high-pitched squealing sound. Rapidly criss-crossing, as if endeavouring to catch each other, my clasping hands beat a rhythm of swift rotation. Switching my bandaged wrists the radius of turns extends progressively. I can feel my body propel itself into ever-widening circles. The rapid alternation between hold and release dictates its increasing urgency. My body rotates around its own axis. Eyes wide open, I draw giant circles. I've become my own composition.

The moment has arrived. My limbs swish through the air like mill blades. The self-generated circles grow wider and wider. I'm a skipping stone ricocheting on air. Finally I let go. I've taken off, hands and forearms measuring the distance of flight.

Released from the pressure of my wrists, I hurl myself across. At the instant of discharge I smile triumphantly. It's possible! I've released my body from itself.

They tell me I landed face down, just outside the mats. At the moment of impact I must have bitten my tongue. According to Frank, a grim-faced Engholm was first on the scene, placing the top of his tracksuit underneath my head. I remember Engholm wiping away the blood while instructing someone to ring the school doctor. Shouts of 'split eyebrows' and 'forehead cut open'. Class was dismissed with a curt 'Showers and dressing-room!' I was bleeding from nose and mouth.

And I recall Engholm's unfamiliar calming monosyllabic words, strangely in tune with my own heavy but regular heartbeat.

'Lie still, boy. Don't move.'

His new voice is like a hypnotic drone which makes me want to sleep.

'Breathe slowly.'

In my numbness Engholm's barely audible, quietly intense words are the only sounds that reach me. They seem to be coming from far away.

'You did the giant circle, my boy!'

Was there pride in his voice? I make an attempt to smile or nod. But the pain holds me back. All I can do is moan in tired recognition.

Engholm must have thought all I did was complete his prescribed exercise. He didn't get it. He had no idea what it was really about. And I was in no position to tell him.

For him, the giant circle consists of five 'run-ups' or 'altitudes'. They're like a kind of musical notation, what Engholm calls a 'weight-defying composition'.

One of Mutti's unused diaries has just the right kind of manuscript paper. Let's see now. The exercise looks something like this:

I'm not very good at drawing and, as old Hennings says, I'm a bit young to be a composer. If the staves are like contours on a map, the five stages or 'altitudes' are musical notes. I can even think of words to go with them: Dr Svensen's infamous 'nos et mutamur'.

Don't know what Hanna would make of this record of my accident. She did ask me next day at school whether I was all right.

I think the giant circle has become an important part of my life right now. Maybe it's foolish to write about something that went wrong, unless it's done as a kind of rough copy. But Dr Svensen had a saying: 'Accident accounts for much in life.' I record mine in one of Mutti's old unused family diaries.

Today is 3 July 1939. The date carries a reminder in old-fashioned handwriting: 'Birthday'. It doesn't say whose, but I know it's my father's.

X

It is the week before Christmas. Mark lies in his room listening to the radio. Late at night the music turns mellow. The time for big orchestras has past. He is alone with a few instruments and an occasional single voice. And with the yellowed photographs of an album he has found among old newspapers, letters and magazines.

Its pages show people he does not know. Most of them are no longer alive. He ponders how he might look one day, putting an arm around his wife (he would have a wife, wouldn't he?), smiling possessively to the camera while holding the hand of his beautiful daughter (he would have at least one child, wouldn't he?).

He can feel the fog outside closing in, suffocating the forbidding apartment building that is his home. His favourite picture is of his father, elegantly dressed in a grey Italian suit, boldly wearing a dashing off-white panama hat. Someone must have released the shutter twice: the snapshot of his father is superimposed on a photograph of the harbour. The distinguished-looking gentleman appears to be nonchalantly walking on water. Or else he has drowned without losing his composure. Either version would explain the mischievous expression on his father's face. He is a magician specialising in disappearance acts. The similarity of features between the bronze statue and the man in this photograph remind Mark of the Neptune Fountain in the old town square. His father is a triumphant Neptune stirring the waters, assuring his son that life is the art of trickery. Mark is convinced there is nothing accidental about the composition. He notices the conjuror's clowning wit: under his right arm his father carries a fashionable umbrella, as if to protect himself against drowning.

From now on Mark imagines his dead father this way; his immortality of double exposure, protected forever against decay by a photograph coincidentally capturing the trickery of history.

Studying his family's photographs Mark encounters a history of himself without him. Why would his father return to them?

Mark's bed is warm, even though the room is not heated. The curtains are not drawn. There is no need. It will not get light in the morning, not before midday. The night sky is overcast. There are no stars shining through the window. He has placed the pillows in such a way that he can look out without moving his head. But there is nothing to see. The only light is the reflections of the radio dial.

The house is quiet. He can hear his own breathing and the beating of his heart. Someone returns home late; echoes of footsteps carry from across the stairwell. Mark falls asleep with gentle music and images shaped by his body's chemistry. They are dreams of no beginning, no middle and no end. He recognises the pattern from which he cannot escape. It is the persistence of their return which makes them real. There is something urgent about their design, but he is much too tired to respond. For he is floating, hovering, sailing. On a sea of ever-changing forms and colours he swims into the night.

In the early hours of the morning Mark's mother finds him lying in his own blood. Her screams are not enough for him to wake up. In vain she searches his body for a wound. Her hands are covered in blood. His face is smeared, mouth and nose covered in scab formations. On closer inspection she notices a persistent trickle coming from both sides of his nose. For a moment she is relieved: it is a nosebleed after all. Then she notices the thin red line flowing from his mouth and panics again. Sobbing and shaking she calls his name the way she used to call Mark's father. This time it is her son who does not answer.

When the doctor speaks of a 'massive haemorrhage' and gently tells her to be 'prepared for the worst', she is frantic, beyond reassurance.

Mark lies there quietly, submitting to the sea within. He hovers between fainting and consciousness. When he awakes, it is for short periods during which he vomits bile and whispers words they cannot understand. A fever makes him shiver and causes his teeth to chatter.

Sailing in his own blood, Mark survives, but only just. They rush him to hospital where he is given regular blood transfusions. The patient is too weak to receive visitors. His arms are tied to tubes, his face is as pale as the sheets.

New Year's Eve he is back home. He has lost weight and looks like a little boy again. The doctor comes twice a day. The only nourishment his patient manages to keep down is water and rusks. Mark lies in his bed seemingly listless and self-abandoned. His mother and a nurse take turns keeping watch over him. Dr Mestring explains the need to combat further complications of anaemia. Should his condition improve, Mark will have to be sent away, as soon as possible, to take 'a cure by the sea'. Not along the mild and gentle shores of the Baltic, but somewhere around the north-western archipelago, exposed to the fresh, wild, iodic air of the North Sea.

Mark continues to just lie there, wrapped in sheets, looking more dead than alive. Cold sweat on his forehead, he breathes very slowly. Peace has broken out in his body. He is on the Alex sailing home. The Handsome Enemy has boarded him and offered his blood. His father is at the bottom of the sea.

As soon as he can walk Mark has to go to the Institute of

Bacteriology. Dr Mestring puts him on cod-liver oil, iron tablets and glucose. He falls asleep at school and is excused from PE. No more giant circles for this boy. Emperor Engholm calls it 'a tragic loss'. At times Mark has trouble just keeping upright. Back home he ventures from chair to chair, collapses on the sofa or spread-eagles on the carpet in dog-like fashion.

In early summer Mark's mother receives a letter from the Red Cross. She goes over it carefully several times, word for word, as if she'd just learnt how to read or were trying to learn the text off by heart, then she bursts into tears. The letter informs her that her son, diagnosed as 'suffering from acute anaemia, haemophilia and chronic malnutrition' has been granted a six-week recuperation in a sanatorium on the North Frisian island of Amrum. All expenses are to be borne by the International Red Cross. The congratulations that follow read like a mockery. She keeps reading, searching the two typewritten pages for information about her husband. Wasn't the Red Cross responsible for the missing persons tracing service? Where is he? When is her husband coming home? Doesn't he know he's needed here? His son's in danger of dying.

On arrival at the transfer station Mark wound down the window of the compartment, eagerly awaiting a first glimpse of the sea. People were rushing across the platform to catch their connections. Others jostled to the exit of the small station.

He got out and walked the hundred metres or so to an even smaller wing station from where a narrow-gauge railway was to take him to the boat. Still no evidence of the proximity of water.

The red and black steam engine carrying ten green cars looked like a toy train. A whistle reminded passengers of the urgency of their transfer. Carrying his mother's old-fashioned suitcase across the platform Mark rushed to board one of the small carriages. Their polished wooden benches and inside walls decorated with paintings of mythological animals in an exotic landscape reminded him of the fair rides back home.

Mark had never been to the western side of the peninsula. Here, he was told, the sea whipped up a real surf, some waves as high as twelve metres. Along the Baltic coast the water was always calm, with hardly any tidal rise or fall. The countryside around his hometown was hilly, but the sea coast remained flat.

Where he was going it was the opposite: the lowland was regularly flooded by king tides. Dykes criss-crossing the countryside in an effort to contain the sea obscured it from view.

As the small local train began to move and climb above the first embankment a vista opened up which overpowered Mark. Behind lush marshland dotted with countless sheep, Frisian cows and long-maned grey horses, the silver-blue tongue of the sea reached to the very base of the dyke. Heavy clouds hung low as a stiff north-westerly combed through unruly blades of grass, churning up the fleece of the sheep. In the distance a couple of white windmills were grinding the sky. The landscape looked like a painting.

Mark opened the window and took in a deep breath. The tingling air, chilly even in summer, was exhilarating. Dr Mestring had instructed him to spend most of his time in the open, as iodine was considered a vital benefit of the islands' bracing climate. He had been sent to the West Coast to recuperate. From what, exactly? He had read the letter's official medical diagnosis, but his sudden illness had never been clearly defined. Perhaps it was no more than 'a natural part of growing up', as his mother used to dismiss most of his concerns in the past.

A small tug-like boat carried him to the Red Cross sanatorium on the main island. There was no surf this side of the mud-flats. Mark would have to wait till they reached the ocean side. In all, eleven islands made up the North Frisian archipelago, many of them little more than tiny islets. Only the largest was big enough to boast a small town. It was here that the sanatorium was located.

Sailing through channels separating the islands Mark saw that some consisted of no more than single elevated farmhouses. He had read stories of how during winter most of the tiny islets 'went under'. Families had to move to the roof, taking their cattle and most other belongings with them. The constant threat of such emergency called for a special architectural design. Viewed from the outside, the island farmhouses seemed to be split in half. The need for upstairs and downstairs living quarters included provisions for a roof stable.

Mark wondered what it would be like to live on one of these lonely islands, in a 'double house' which would allow him to rise above storm tides while the other half of his home went under. Surviving the flood, living on both land and sea, Mark imagined, would have to be a bit like the immortality of a Greek hero.

He was expected. At the mole a lanky fellow sporting a sailor's beard and a cold pipe in his mouth had come to collect him. Mark found it impossible to guess his age. He looked somewhere above twenty and below fifty. 'Call me Ben,' he introduced himself in a grumpy voice which didn't match his cheerful, almost laughing eyes. With ridiculous ease he lifted Mark's suitcase onto a dray. A silent nod signalled the visitor to join him on the coach-box.

At the crack of the whip the shaggy carthorse turned around and without further directions began to trot along a clearly familiar path. It must have picked up so many patients in its time there was no need to pull the reins. At leisurely pace they passed picture-postcard houses with colourful front gardens in full bloom, a couple of corner shops, a tiny school, a telephone booth, a post office and a red brick church surrounded by tombstones that looked like whitecaps in a sea of windswept marram grass. Where the bitumen ended, the buggy came to a halt.

They were confronted by a vast whitewashed building in the local style, with thatched roof, blue and white doors, bulls' eye panes and a gravel path leading to the main entrance. A matronly figure dressed in pinafore and cap came rushing towards them with open arms to welcome the new arrival.

The air was salty. Even Sister Anna's sturdy hug tasted of the sea. As she guided Mark to his room she kept assuring him, 'You'll like it here. Trust me. Everything will be all right.' Throughout her chatter she kept one arm around him, as if to make sure he would not run away. Mark was uncertain how to respond. At home his mother rarely touched him. Sister Anna's hands on his shoulder or around his waist seemed to lay some kind of a claim on him, which made him feel uncomfortable.

His room, its large window framed by wild roses, was on the ocean side of the island. The high white walls inside were covered with prints. Some of the paintings of sunflowers and landscapes he recognised.

At last, Sister Anna left. Tentatively Mark sat down on the bed, got up again and began to touch the furniture, then looked out of the window. It was too early to settle in, to become part of the unfamiliar environment. He would unpack later.

How much light there was in the room! It pierced through the blue-and-white check curtains as if to prove that nothing could stand in its way. Mark pulled them aside, impatient to feel the sun on his skin. He stood there for a very long while, staring into the far distance. When he undid the catch a stiff westerly carried sounds of screaming and laughing children from the foam-swept beach. High tide's majestic breakers seemed to beckon him. He acknowledged their call with an unwitting smile of recognition. The cool, prickly sea breeze had entered his room, and the midday sun was now shining directly on his face. Spellbound, he did not move. Suddenly he had no doubt he had come to the right place. He could not tear himself away from the view, the light, the surf, the distant horizon. Inhaling deeply he tasted the tingling air and felt the restlessness of his blood.

Unpacked, his meagre belongings consisted of little more than clothes and what his mother considered 'essential toiletries'. But from the bottom of the suitcase, cushioned by what he considered to be a superfluous amount of underwear, Mark carefully recovered two books printed in old-fashioned Gothic letters. One was an anthology of Greek and Germanic sagas, the other a novella set in the North Frisian countryside, Theodor Storm's *The Ghost Rider*.

Mark quickly settled into the daily routine of the sanatorium. Part of the ritual of new arrivals was to be weighed and measured. Mark noticed how doctor and nurse double-checked his weight, mumbling something about malnutrition. He could not tell whether he felt more ashamed of his body's nudity or its loss of weight. The indignant nurse kept looking at him in undisguised pity. She had no doubt about the nature of her calling. Patients were sent here to be restored to health and normality. The staff would see to it they were nursed and fed properly before they would be allowed to return home for a new life.

Many convalescents were adult ex-POWs who had barely survived the war. They congregated in small groups, looking like an assembly of ghosts. Mealtimes were the worst. Mark tried not to look at their haunted faces whenever he sat near them. They frightened him more than any missing limbs or unhealed wounds. He dreaded in particular having to watch them try to eat soup or dissect fish. Some could barely hold fork or spoon. Mark felt guilty about his disgust. He knew they couldn't help it. They may have survived, but their bodies were as good as destroyed.

There was one young fellow in the dining room who had no such compunction. He scathingly referred to the emaciated former soldiers as 'our stumbling heroes' or 'the unholy ghosts'. Mark met Sannes over dinner the very first evening. The older, handsome fifteen-year-old with long dark hair and olive skin told him nonchalantly he had been living in convalescent homes for as long as he could remember. It wasn't clear to Mark whether his parents were unable or unwilling to look after him. Sannes too was suffering from a mysterious incurable illness.

Despite his unidentified chronic disease, Sannes had an almost athletic build. His brown, oriental-looking eyes, radiating a nervous, feverish energy, lent him a fanatical appearance. Everything about his body appeared tense, barely held together by an overwhelming effort of restraint. Paradoxically, in the opinion of his doctors it was the undiagnosed illness which kept him alive. What would happen to this young man, Mark wondered, if his body were given free rein?

As their rooms were on the same floor, it was natural for them to visit each other. Soon they went to the beach together, taking long afternoon walks and collecting bilberries in the dunes.

In the sanatorium everybody thought Sannes was special, not only because rumour had it he came from a famous and wealthy family. There were a great many rumours about this young patient, which by itself was sufficient to perpetuate his special status. (His father was in fact a well-known industrialist, 'something in rubber', Sannes ironically explained. He was the only child.) Sannes was a celebrity among the sick and the dying because he had survived his illness for so long. Those who considered themselves healthy admired what they took to be his tenacity. At the same time, however, they were unsettled by his acid tongue and stubborn wilfulness.

On his arrival Sannes had caused a minor sensation. He had brought a motor scooter to the island, an Italian-designed bright red Vespa. Mock-apologetically, he presented Sister Anna with a special permit issued 'on medical grounds'. Sergeant Walter Olsen, the islands' only police officer, had never seen such a document in his thirty-five years with the force. He intended to check up on its authenticity. As far as he was concerned, the shred of paper was a forgery until proven otherwise. In the meantime, however, the young man with his defiantly long black curls was given permission to ride his shiny red scooter along the island's few graded and bitumenised streets, 'so long as he behaved himself'.

As if to demonstrate their independence and new friendship, Sannes took Mark on his Vespa all over the island. Together, hair blowing in the wind, they were an incongruous sight. From a distance they seemed wild, like members of a bikie gang. But close up they looked more like children joyriding at a fair. Pretending the scooter had a powerful engine, they tried to frighten the locals by noisily revving the motor. They weren't fooling anybody. Sister Anna scathingly informed them they were carrying on like circus monkeys on a mini bike.

It made no difference to the boys. Defiantly they parked the shiny Vespa right in front of the small town's police station, along the row of tourist shops at the promenade or outside the local hotel. Soon the locals referred to them with mock horror. 'The Reds are coming!' Mark and Sannes were calling themselves 'Ghost Riders', a name more in tune, they thought, with what had brought them to this island. Knowing they were to be returned home 'healthy, normal and obedient', they regarded their scooter escapades as rehearsals of escape. But they knew on a tiny island like this there was nowhere for them to go. It only seemed to exist so they could be sent to a sanatorium where their adolescent mystery illness was to be cured. (What diseases were the other islands of the archipelago catering for?)

Yet in their shared confinement Mark and Sannes were no longer alone. They had met someone of a similar disease. What a relief it was not to have to explain oneself! Soon they became inseparable. Listening to Sannes, Mark discovered, was almost like thinking aloud. Exploring the beaches, roaming the dunes or riding the coastline, they were really searching, discovering and claiming each other. Together they recognised places neither of them had ever been to.

On their first weekend together Sannes dared Mark to join him in crossing the mud-flats at low tide. If they kept time, he assured him, they could easily walk to the adjoining island. They had both heard of tourists caught by the incoming tide who had to be rescued by the coastguard. Only a few months ago a foreign visitor had drowned. The tideways had risen very quickly until suddenly it was no longer possible to cross them. The current of the incoming flood proved too strong even for experienced swimmers. Surrounded by rising channels the unwary found themselves trapped on patches of dry mud.

Sannes scorned such warnings. He ignored the advice of the locals not to attempt the crossing without a qualified guide.

'We can make it,' he appealed to Mark. 'We've got plenty of time.' Dismounting the Vespa on the beachfront promenade, they surveyed the vast sandy seascape of low tide. In the near distance, flying low, gulls, albatross and herons were scanning the narrow channels. Further out, on the horizon, they noticed what appeared to be tiny moving dots – guided groups of tourists on their way to the other islands.

'So long as we don't join the shell collectors.' Mark was thinking aloud. 'We're not after plaice or flounder, are we?'

'If we're lucky we might find some amber.' Sannes' reply was more of a challenge. Quietly they continued to stare at the mud flats as if searching for something. They were still busy exploring each other. For a long time they stood next to each other in complete silence. The only sound was the whimpering breeze.

'Let's do it,' said Mark.

They grinned conspiratorially, then embraced to seal the pact. 'No plaice, no flounder, no amber.'

'Tomorrow we shall walk on water.'

In a final validation of the dare, they shook hands.

'Your health, my brother!'

Sannes switched on the engine, the start of the motor drowning in their laughter.

On their exploratory rides across the island neither of them spoke about why they had come here. It was enough to know that there was something wrong with both of them. Why go into details about an illness the doctors could not cure? They had other things to talk about. Like what they would do if one day, against all odds, cured or not cured, they should be released.

Mark and Sannes agreed they would do a lot of travelling. More than anything, they wanted to get away, as far away as possible. There was no need to explain from what.

It was early afternoon the following day when they made good their promise. Defiantly they entered the mud-flats, tentatively navigating their feet around gravel, broken shells and cutting sea grass. Before long they reached sandy patches criss-crossed by low-level tideways, then passed warm, sunlit sandbars where fish were left stranded and could be caught with bare hands.

As agreed, they ignored them, intent on keeping their sight on the neighbouring island in the distance. A lighthouse on the horizon and the angle of the sun, now reaching just behind their shoulders, was to guide them in the right direction. Jumping across a flood channel they could see their shadows follow below. These dark figures were part of their bodies. They would not be left behind.

Sannes stooped, picked up a shell and wrote something on the wet sand. When he got up again he asked Mark, 'Do you believe in God?' He did not wait for an answer. Triumphantly he pointed to the word in the sand and declared, 'When the tide comes in, God will drown.'

'Who's the flood?' Mark wanted to know.

Sannes remained defiant. Stepping on small heaps of sandworms he declared, 'The flood's the flood. The word's a word.'

Mark thought of telling Sannes how, as a child, he had welcomed the Enemy because he had hoped the Enemy would deliver his father. But his father had not returned, and now the war was over. What if 'father' too was just a word.

'How long till we get there?'

Sannes put his arm around Mark. Jovially patting him on his back he shrugged off his friend's concern. 'Who knows.' His indifference seemed both beautiful and reckless.

On reaching the neighbouring island they headed straight for the small tourist pub. In a boisterous mood Sannes ordered aquavit and beer. Although Mark, afraid of his friend's defiant mockery, ordered the same for himself, Sannes must have read his thoughts.

'The doctors know nothing.' Then, after a moment's silence during which they avoided each other's eyes, he added, 'Anyway, no one else's responsible for me.'

In an attempt to soften Sannes' apparent bitterness Mark quickly replied, 'Well, I'm glad you're here.'

It sounded awkward, but he was relieved to have said it. Best not to think too much about what it meant. Neither of them believed their being here was part of a health cure. But it felt good to go island-hopping with somebody like Sannes.

Mark watched his friend's long dark mane blowing in the wind like a revolutionary banner demanding freedom through anarchy. It was the most beautiful hair Mark had ever seen. With its colour almost completely black, Sannes looked like Tyrone Power or Robert Taylor. The way he sat there he could have been the leading man on any Roxy poster, a dashing hero promising romance and adventure. There was a studied elegance in his drinking, a rehearsed casualness, which made Mark look positively clumsy.

Without envy he admired Sannes's self-assurance and sophistication. But Mark did not want to be like his friend. Inseparably linked to his urbane charm there was something unsettling, mysterious, perhaps even slightly devious about him, something disturbingly secretive and elusive. Mark had to remind himself that he and Sannes were the same age, no more than boys whose childhood had coincided with a world war. The worldliness of Sannes was so different from the world they had grown up in. Where had he gained such knowledge from? What had turned him into a film star while his body was dying?

In Mark's home town embittered adults had begun to rebuke their children by reciting nursery rhymes of hate and resentment.

> So young and ill-behaved,
> So young, yet so depraved.

Was Sannes one of these depraved children? Were they both?

How could he admire someone about whom he knew so little? Sannes' mere presence was enough to release him from his own doubts and insecurities. His new friend's reckless ideas and exuberant defiance disturbed and excited him. In his company thoughts came to Mark he would never have dared to consider before.

Pointing to the incoming tide, Sannes raised his glass and proclaimed in a solemn voice, 'Behold, my beloved brethren, God's just died!' He threw his head back and grimaced as he downed another aquavit.

The sun's reflection caught in the raised glass made it look as if Sannes were drinking pure light. He threw the glass in the air with an exuberant cackle. As he tried to stretch out his arms, the extravagance of the sudden movement made him lose his balance. He fell off the chair with the graceful gestures of a magician. Sannes could make even accidents look like clever disappearance tricks.

Unimpressed, the publican came over to tell them they had had enough.

Outside, the strong wind made it difficult for them to walk upright and straight. Like mime artistes they copied each other's half-drunk attempts to keep balance. Struggling to regain control over his body, Mark knew they were in no condition to attempt the return trip across the mud-flats.

The stiff northerly was a welcome relief from their rapid intoxication. Hot from the alcohol and unsteady on their feet, using the wind as an alibi for their ungainly staggering, they sauntered in the direction of the light-house. From there a ferry would take them back to town.

In his drunkenness Sannes kept talking to his preceding shadow. 'Don't you worry,' he assured the dark figure, 'I'll get us back in time.'

He did. They reached the lighthouse, waited for high tide and took the ferry. Mounting the Vespa the ghost riders decided to withdraw to their rooms quietly and reappear only for dinner. There was no need for anyone at the sanatorium to be informed of their unauthorised excursion.

T he following Saturday they became more daring. Shortly after breakfast they informed the nursing staff they were planning to take the inter-island ferry to one of the land-marks of the archipelago, an outer reef featuring a small grove and a few fishing huts. This time they planned to reverse the crossing, walking the mud-flats home. It was a far greater distance, but Sannes assured Mark there would be no danger.

In the preceding days, whether by design or chance, they had gone their separate ways. Mark found the air, the pre-scribed walks and exercises quickly made him tired. Resting in his room or lying on the beach, he read Storm's *Ghost Rider* or just dozed. At night, he lay in his bed looking out over the moonlit sea. What a different view it was from his room back home! He thought of his mother. She had not replied to the picture postcard he had sent her upon his arrival. They had never written to each other because he had never been away. Perhaps he should not have sent the card. It might have confused her. He should have checked with Dr Mestring first. She may not know how to respond. Mark had never seen his mother write, not after the letters to her husband were returned unopened. It was painful and confusing to have a mother who was physically present while her mind was somewhere else. His father's absence was more brutal and final. He was definitely not there. No point in writing him a card or letter.

Mark had been deserted by both his parents.

Yet, while reading or looking out of the window, sooner or later his thoughts would return to Sannes, his rebel friend, the Vespa boy from the south, the terminal patient who did not care about his health, the handsome stranger to whom he felt so curiously, so irresistibly drawn. Their communication did not require anything more than each other's presence.

When the launch berthed on the fishing reef they were the only ones to get off. Heading for a half-timbered cottage in the near distance they crossed patches of pristine white sand and small tideways. As if anxious to leave their mark they threw themselves onto the windswept sand. Had it not been for the dilapidated shacks and beached trawlers they could have easily imagined themselves to be the very first to walk the ridge.

Outside the tiny group of huts a fisherman sat repairing nets. Mark thought he looked like the model of a tourist poster, the very image of a life in natural harmony with the sun and the sea. It was rare to come across such a healthy young man, even in these parts. He exuded self-reliance, masculinity and strength. No more than in his early twenties, he must have just managed to escape conscription. How else could he have survived the war in such physical condition?

But when Mark made reference to his good fortune, the sun and the sea, the tanned islander gave a forbearing chuckle. 'Hardly an easy life,' he corrected them, shaking his head in quiet amusement. Still, he didn't look unhappy, they decided, with what he was doing.

'What's that next to your house?' Mark demanded to know.

'The smoking chamber. We smoke our own. Salmon, cod, mackerels, herrings.'

'I love the smell,' Sannes said. 'May we have a look?'

'Go for your life. But be careful! There are herrings dripping from the roof joist. If you like, you can sit inside, there's a table and a couple of chairs, but don't touch anything.'

'Do you remain on the island the entire year?' Mark asked before they left for the smokehouse.

'No one stays the winter out here,' the fisherman replied. 'Trick is to know when to leave.'

'How do you know?'

'You know. Time teaches you.'

They could see his trawler near the mooring, left stranded by the low tide. On the mud-flats it looked big and sturdy, but Mark imagined out on the open choppy sea it would be little more than a nutshell.

'How far out do you go?' he shouted into the wind.

'As far as the fish!' the skipper called back with a boyish grin. He put his hand to his cap and returned to his nets.

Sannes opened the door to the smoking chamber. Immediately they entered they were enveloped by a tangy, sooty, salty fragrance. The smell of wood intermingled with that of smoked fish. Above them, high in the ceiling, rows of herrings turned into silver and gold. Glistening flesh shone upon them. The image of the Enemy returned to Mark, their flights spitting fire from above, their shining planes reflected in bright sunshine. Acrid spice began to settle on their skin and lips, flavouring every word they spoke.

Taking a deep breath, Sannes solemnly proclaimed, 'Verily I say unto thee: this is the spice of life!'

Mark took the bait. Sniffing the aromatic air, inhaling it with unabated relish, he confirmed his friend's finding. 'May it remain with us for a long time!'

Intoxicated with their own inflated rhetoric they began to compete for other formulations of worldly wisdom. 'We smoke our own!' Mark echoed the quotation of the fisherman. Amidst their laughter Sannes crowed, 'Trick is to know when to leave!'

For the moment they were one, two boys who had come together and recognised what united them, their friendship a chance encounter brought about by the illness they shared. Then Sannes turned into a stranger again. In a curiously monotonous voice he started to chant a number of exotic words. Priest-like, with outstretched hands, he sang, 'Morotai, Buri, Halmahera, Batjan, Ternate, Obi, Sula, Ceram, Ambon.' The seductive vowels seemed to melt in his mouth.

For once there did not appear to be a hint of irony in what he was saying. He quickly responded to Mark's quizzical look.

'There's a place called the Spice Islands. At least that's what they used to be called. On the other side of the world. Somewhere in the Dutch East Indies. They were conquered and turned into colonies by the Portuguese, the Dutch and the British. All that's left of them are their spicy names.' And, as in a prayer-wheel, he began again: 'Morotai, Buri, Halmahera, Batjan ...'.

'How come you know so much about them?' asked Mark. He remembered having read about the Islands in his *Discoveries of the World*.

Smirking appreciatively, Sannes adopted the pose of a man of the world. 'Let's just say I've always cultivated an interest in everything spicy.' Mark had never heard anyone their age use that kind of language. The way Sannes pronounced the word 'spicy' made it sound like the hissing of a snake or a flick knife flying through the air. It made Mark shiver. They left the smoke house, taking its sweet fleshy fragrance with them.

When Sannes put his arm around him, he recognised the gesture from the pirate film *Under all Flags*. He instantly understood they were blood brother privateers, the only survivors on a spice island where infidels were sacrificed to a cruel, greedy god.

Sannes led the way to a small wood at the northern end

of the island, no doubt to protect their loot. They needed to go into hiding and wait until the tide would be favourable for their daring escape.

To reach the trees they had to cross a small channel. They quickly undressed and dived into the cool, clear water. The current was weak. Effortlessly they swam to an unspoilt beach reflecting the warm afternoon sun. Still naked, Sannes triumphantly rolled his body across the unmarked white powdery sand. His wet face and limbs covered in mud, fiery eyes glowing, he took on the wild appearance of some kind of feral animal. 'I'm the tidal monster!' he screamed at Mark. 'I've come to get you!'

In sudden movement, yet with calculated aim, as though he had waited for the right moment, he threw himself at Mark and quickly pulled him down. Playfully they wrestled in the midday light, the salty breeze entering every crevice of their bodies. Resting on each other's skin they detected on them the tangy smell of the smokehouse. With each sharp pungent touch they confirmed their desire to escape. Buri, Sula, Obi, Halmahera.

Lying on top of each other, they resumed their wrestling. Mark's face too had turned into a muddy mask. He tried desperately to keep his mouth shut tight, but Sannes' unerring hands proved stronger, force-feeding him warm grains of crystal white sand. As he did so, holding Mark by the throat, he began to shout. 'A spicy word, Saint Mark! A word, me lad, a spicy word, my boy!' Doggedly they continued. Yet, had they been fighting upright, their contest might have almost looked like a dance. Rolling together on the ground, feeding each other with warm white sand and the scent of their skin, their movements became indistinguishable from an embrace.

At last, biting and spewing, Mark's lips exploded. 'CUNT!'

Sannes let go of him. Silently they got up, entered the water to remove the sand from their skin, then peaceably moved on to the nearby grove. They were both relaxed now, as though there had been no fight between them. They were brothers again.

But as they walked together Mark's body reverberated with the delicious brutality of their contest. It had not been a fight either one of them was meant to win or lose. They had celebrated the joy of a strength within them, triumphing over their illness, playfully asserting itself in conquest, taking delight in the power of its force. They had not been adversaries but fellow pirates sharing their loot of the Spice Islands.

'Have you ever seen one?' Sannes asked as they reached the edge of the wood.

'What?'

'A cunt, you cunt!' Sannes threw the word at him in boisterous triumph.

Mark shook his head.

In front of him Sannes' naked body blocked his way. 'A cunt's an oyster,' he explained, reverting to his role of the rake instructor. 'Or a smoked herring.' As he spoke, his penis began to grow and stiffen. Noticing Mark's quizzical look, he cryptically added, 'It depends.'

Why was everything about Sannes, every word he used, so intensely physical? Wasn't he supposed to be a convalescing war child? From where did he derive his energy and strength? Could his athletic looks be like his intimidating language, claiming a perfection too carefully designed and beautiful to be real?

In vain Mark tried to dodge his friend's body. It kept blocking his way. Whatever move Mark made, Sannes' muscled frame parried like a fleshy shadow. They were ducking and weaving in perfect rhythmic concord.

'And smells like it.'

Sannes would not let go. Mark lowered his head, then rammed it like a steer into the abdomen of his torturer. As they touched he felt the stiff but silky penis dancing on his face. He heard a voice come from above, 'Sex smells like death. Did you know that?'

Half-heartedly Mark kept pushing against his captivity of smooth and fragrant skin. Everything he touched demanded a response in kind. With every breath he inhaled the sweet smell of Sannes' moist genitals. Once more he could hear the triumphant voice of his captor coming from somewhere high above him. 'It smells like under your fingernails. Or like the sweaty skin between your thighs.'

Mark wondered whether he should make a run for it. But he knew he had left it too late. Sannes had found him out. There was no escape now, no hiding.

'That's why people fuck,' the voice from above continued. 'They're randy for death.' Despite their violence the words sounded seductive, as if they had been sung. When Sannes' scrotum splayed against Mark's face, voice and body had become one. 'We're fucking death, you fucking cunt!' they were ringing.

Then, abruptly, it all stopped. The sudden release left Mark breathless and dizzy. He had barely got up when Sannes hurled himself at Mark's shoulders. Once more they were linked together. This time neither of them was trying to break free.

They collapsed on the edge of the mud-flats. As he pressed himself against Mark, Sannes' voice continued with its intoxicating singsong. But now it merely consisted of deliciously incomprehensible words, made up of crazy syllables invented by his stirred tongue. Triumphantly he held Mark down. His hands clawed into the wet sand, Mark turned his face away. Above him, Sannes' erect penis descended.

At last Sannes let go of him. Hurriedly he swam back to where they had left their clothes, waving for Mark to follow. Silently they dressed, carrying their gym shoes for the crossing.

Sannes' mood had changed completely. Cleaned by the short swim, his face was handsome and calm again. A couple of big wet curls had fallen across his forehead. Mark had to fight the instinct to push them back.

Instead, he pointed to the outgoing tide and asked in a matter-of-fact tone, 'Isn't it time we crossed?' Sannes' reply seemed blithe, but Mark noticed an underlying urgency in his voice. 'If not now, when?'

They entered the wet soft soil back to their island as if nothing had happened. Immersed in the late afternoon light they led their shadows into a stiff breeze. Silently they plodded under low clouds, accompanied by the formation of a spectacular sunset. Some of the larger flood channels were already beginning to rise, but there was plenty of time yet.

Marching briskly now, they passed a couple of tardy mudflat wanderers collecting worms and dying fish. Mark and Sannes kept their eyes on the island's coastline directly ahead of them. The familiar seashore gave them both incentive and direction. When they stopped to catch their breath they thought they recognised the sanatorium, the village and the seashore road. But they could not be sure. While they were plodding ahead, the horizon appeared to recede. Out in the mud-flats it was difficult to measure distance. Even the low-lying clouds seemed within reach. It was like walking into a landscape painting without dimensions – wherever they were, whichever direction they took, however far they proceeded, they remained in the foreground.

The wind was getting colder; they were thankful now for their woollen polo-neck sweaters.

With the passing of time their steps began to assume greater urgency. They no longer took a breather or bothered to look back. Slowly but unstoppably, the mud-flats were being reclaimed by the incoming tide. Already they were walking in low water, with a powerful current running through their toes. Mark could feel its whirl underneath his feet. His legs were beginning to grow stiff, but he was sure they were making good progress. They would be safe so long as they followed the right direction.

Almost imperceptibly the tide continued to rise. The water rose to a level where it became necessary to carry their shoes around their shoulders before relinquishing them to the incoming flood. Shortly afterwards Sannes defiantly surrendered his shirt, socks and pants to the tidal channels. Relieved of their load, he let go a jubilant shout, then ordered Mark to toss away most of his clothing. There was no sign of anxiety on Sannes' face. On the contrary. He had rid himself of a burden. His precaution had been an act of cheerful abandonment. He revelled in his loss.

If they did not reach shallow waters soon, they would have to swim.

The colours of the landscape changed. Daylight's dying rays had become smudged. Sunset melted into wild formations of pale, oppressive, suffocating clouds. In the distance they noticed first reflections of electric light. It could only come from the small town on their island. Long beams flashed from the lighthouse across the dark sea. Dusk was closing in.

By the time they were close enough to make out the sanatorium, the shops along the promenade, and even the yellow telephone booth outside the post office, the water had risen to just below their chests. They were entering the home stretch reassured by the sight of familiar images. In semi-darkness their field of vision had at last taken on dimensions allowing them to measure the distance to safety.

In preparation for one final effort Sannes called out to Mark. His words were swallowed by the wind.

High tide had overtaken them.

They knew they were swimming for their lives. A strong undertow kept holding them back. Mark now felt the suction between his legs, an unnerving sensation reminding him of being held down by Sannes. He had begun to swallow water. As darkness fell, he wondered for the first time whether, despite the close proximity of the island, he would last the distance.

Both were good swimmers. Both drew on the energy they had put to the test on the reef, a strength which would not allow them to be defeated. Their strokes growing steadily weaker, they continued to press ahead. They knew they were on their own, but hadn't they always been? There was no need to panic then. As they swam towards the safety of the shore, they listened to their breath, the gurgling ripples, the howling of the breeze and the splashing sound of their arms parting the waves.

In their rhythmic unison Mark and Sannes were one again. Mark recognised the Beautiful Enemy daring him to accept his body, rely on its senses, trust its knowledge and its needs. The tide was the Emperor urging him on, challenging him to do the giant circle.

Like a buoy pitched and tossed in heavy seas, Sannes' head was hovering in front of Mark. In the distance, to their left, they could see the lights of the tiny landing stage. If they kept their direction, they would step ashore outside the embankment near the general store.

Yet the island that seemed so close refused to come any nearer. Despite his determination Mark found it more and more difficult to move his legs. Then, abruptly, he suffered a cramp. Mercilessly the pain cut into him, making it impossible to uphold his previous rhythm. When he let go, it was a desperate relief. In sweet surrender his body gave itself to the sea.

Mark made no attempt to float. He had forgotten about his arms. From somewhere came a familiar, confident, commanding voice. 'Keep your head above water!' But he had no more strength to do so. His breathing had become as uncoordinated as his muscles. He wilted into the illness of defeat. Giving himself up, he surrendered to the tide. As his body went under, a painful smile appeared on his face. 'I'm going to visit my father', he thought, 'the man with the umbrella at the bottom of the sea.' Someone would take a picture of his drowning and add it to the family album. He would have to learn to live under water.

He was still breathing when Sannes pulled him onto the beach. Unable to move or open his eyes, his pale blue, almost naked body was lying on the cold sand. He looked like a drowned corpse.

Numb and wet, Sannes stumbled to the telephone booth, imploring an old woman for help in 'an emergency', 'a matter of life and death'. A native islander, she immediately grasped what must have happened. Calmly she rang the sanatorium and raised the alarm.

It was completely dark now. Out of the night Sister Anna's white uniform emerged. Like a hawk she descended upon her charge, rubbing Mark dry, wrapping him in a towel like a child, all the while groaning 'What's to become of you! I don't know. I really don't!'

It didn't take long before Ben and his shaggy carthorse arrived on the scene. Somewhat ignominiously, Mark and Sannes returned to the sanatorium much the same way they had arrived. Covered in Red Cross blankets, both were handed mugs of Frisian tea into which Ben had slipped a generous dash of rum.

It was difficult to guess what Ben, the coachman, was making of all this. During the short ride he did not speak a word to either of the boys. After her initial outbursts Sister Anna, too, had stopped scolding and wailing. For those who knew Ben, his silence certainly did not signal that he had lost his composure. Mark and Sannes, on the other hand, had no way of knowing what mood he was in. For one thing, sitting on the box, Ben faced the other way. In any case, it would have been much too dark to read his face. Only for a fleeting moment, while the dray was passing an occasional street light, might they have recognised the ruefully tender expression of a man deep in thought. But the castaways, Ben's medicinal mugs of tea firmly glued to their lips, were in no condition to read anybody's mind. Right now, all they wanted was to hide inside the cover of their blankets.

Catching the defiance in Mark's farewell wave to Sannes, Sister Anna warned them their unauthorised adventure would have serious consequences. For the moment she sternly ordered them to take a hot bath and go to bed immediately.

That night Mark relived the strangely pleasing sensation of letting go as well as the deliverance of his final rescue from drowning. Even now, in the safety of his bed, the two remained inseparably linked. Could Sannes have planned their test of courage for this very reason?

Through the open window the high tide's crushing surf delivered his rescuer's mocking voice. 'Give me a spicy word, Saint Mark!' As if in answer he walked over to the sill and looked at the clear night sky sprinkled with stars and a bloated moon. The heavy low clouds of their afternoon crossing had disappeared. Never before had Mark seen a moon so big, so close, so glorious, a big fat yellow blot in the salty darkness, barely hanging above the dunes. It looked like a child's drawing. Only the gently smiling face was missing.

Then Mark remembered it was this moon that was causing the turn of tides. He could hear the words of their science teacher trying to explain to them the magnetism of the planets. In the language of physics it was 'the alternate rising and falling of the surface of the ocean and of water bodies that occurs twice a day, caused by the gravitational attraction of the sun and moon occurring unequally on different parts of the earth'. Something like that. No doubt that was the reason for high tides and low tides, but in his teacher's scientific description Mark thought he recognised something else. Wasn't that a bit like what was happening to his own body? Could what he was feeling for Hanna and Sannes be like the magnetism of the planets?

Had he, unwittingly, come across the explanation of love? Was the big, fat moon out there a sign of passion? A distortion caused by attraction, an aberration ruling the planet, a gravitational love?

Ah, how exciting, then, was the science of love! It would not let him sleep. This afternoon Sannes and he had taken part in the movement of the planet. Mark was jubilant. The universe did care.

'A spicy word!' A four-letter word. Why not 'life'? Sannes would mock it, of course, but tonight, in this bright darkness, it was the right word. He may have been a war child, but Mark never doubted that he would survive. Surrounded by death, he had taken his own life for granted. All his plans were based on the assumption that he would live. But now he had been rescued, saved by someone who was both his brother and his enemy. He looked up at the moon in a mixture of gratitude, pleasure and disbelief. Perhaps life and love, the world and the universe were made of opposites. He had been rescued from drowning by an unlikely ally. His captor was also his saviour. Despite his bath he could still smell the spice of Sannes' skin.

The voice of Sannes, his Spicy Island words came back to him. Mark was all at sea again. No longer ignorant of the nature of its desire, he watched his penis grow. He had lost all anger over its self-righteous demands. He held on to the window-ledge as the rolling thunder of the crushing surf came bursting upon him. In helpless jubilation he celebrated the night flooding into his open hands, life's silent explosion of nothingness, timed breakers of triumph and surrender. He sobbed into the tide calling Sannes' name.

Slowly he raised his sticky fingers to his face. The Beautiful Enemy had taken him across the mud-flats. He had joined the inspector of tides and tasted the moon.

Back on his bed, Mark strained to listen to the raging sea, the restless reverberations of the night. Through the window he could see the tireless warning flashes of the lighthouse.

He had been rescued.

The splendour of the spices would not be denied. Islands went under, but stayed alive. There was a light that shone in darkness. It gave birth to the tides. Like Sannes, Mark would do anything to stay alive.

XI

The unwritten diaries in my possession belong to the dead. Anything I write is on the empty pages of their lives.

There are still a few more unused notebooks, but I think I'll let them be. I'm not the diary-keeping type. Guess I started the pretence because I felt more and more responsible for the old unused books I found. Seemed such a waste to throw them away. But writing something about each day is too much like homework. I've got better things to do with my time.

However, this one's special. I came across it trying to find some letters Mutti claimed had disappeared. It's bound in bright red leather and bears the inscription 'Our Honeymoon'. Like the others, it's all empty inside. I think it must have been an extra copy, a duplicate wedding present of my parents. Its deckle-edged paper is handmade and looks very precious. I didn't dare write in it till now.

Actually, so far all I've done is draw lines, geometrical shapes, parallels, triangles, tangents and circles, wilful patterns such as I scribble in my exercise books. Only I know what they're supposed to be.

With Mutti, things have taken a turn for the worse. More than once she was found walking aimlessly in remote parts of town, not knowing how she got there or what she was doing. Each time the police brought her home, telling me she was lost. 'Lucky we found her,' they said in an accusing voice. She could not even remember her name. It was only because she carried a handful of letters addressed to herself they were able to return her home.

I feel sick whenever that happens because it means I haven't looked after her properly. She's as lonely as ever and still talks to people who aren't there. Sometimes she even offers them tea! 'Wait,' she says, 'I'll get you your favourite!' And smiles to someone only she can see. All Dr Mestring says is to keep an eye on her. How can I when I'm at school or doing the shopping!

From her first war pension cheque Mutti bought me a junior school microscope. She must have found out it was something I wanted very badly. How could she know that and not know where she was in her own hometown! Why can't she see Vati won't return! She's not only talking to ghosts, she's also talking to the dead. But I can't tell her that.

For a long time I was crazy about a globe, but since then I've moved on. I've tried to trade just about everything – books, knives, model planes, stamps and bird eggs – for a magnifying instrument. But no one's interested. Well, now, thanks to Mutti, who Dr Mestring tells me no longer lives in the real world, I've got my own.

It all started in biology class when we were shown how aquatic amoebae changed their shape by splitting cells. We could actually watch a one-cell being grow into a larger form of life. I was hooked. It wasn't just that I'd witnessed life reproducing life. There was something especially beautiful, I thought, about the different shapes and patterns that emerged. Maybe I'm not that different from Mutti – I want to see things invisible to the naked eye.

Poor Mutti! She really must be worried about me. She's trying so hard to make sure I don't miss out on anything. How often has she told me I have to become 'an educated gentleman'! The day after she gave me the Zeiss microscope she announced it was time for me to learn 'how to behave in the company of young ladies'. She would make arrangements for me to 'attend dancing school with other educated young men from good homes'. 'Good homes'?! Is she kidding? Thanks to the war, there's hardly a normal family left in town. Locals and refugees are still fighting over whose homes were destroyed. Truth is there are no more homes, least of all for the many latchkey children whose fathers have been replaced by ominous so-called 'uncles'.

Don't know about dancing lessons. As Mutti says, it's really all about 'behaving yourself', wearing a suit, carrying on, 'courting' a girl and learning 'the latest steps'. A real drag. On the other hand, it might mean getting real close to the action. You could hold a girl, touch her skin, inhale her perfume, feel her petticoats and who knows what else. Not bad! Perhaps I'll agree to becoming 'an educated gentleman', just to please Mutti.

Otherwise not much's been happening lately. Oh, that guy from the island, Sannes, sent me a couple of postcards. All from different places. It's been two years now since we crossed the mud-flats. Wonder how he feels. He's always writing from spas, so I guess he's still doing the rounds, as he used to call it. Still trying to convince the whole country that he's not really sick. Or the whole country is trying to find out what's really wrong with him.

'Course I haven't forgotten him. How could I? If I haven't replied to any of his cards, that's because it still upsets me when I get too close to him, even if only in my thoughts. But the cards keep coming.

Most of my spare time I spend hunched over the Zeiss, staring at all sorts of things. Under its magnifying lens even an ordinary piece of cloth becomes exciting. I love examining minute parts of any matter, the interaction of colour and texture. It's a bit like watching a painter. As a special treat I put shreds of my own skin under the lenses, so I can see what I consist of. The microscope turns even parts of me into a composition.

I also look at my blood. It's easy. All I have to do is what Sister Elke's doing at the Institute of Bacteriology. Prick a finger with a pin, put a couple of drops on a piece of glass and smear the blood all over. The sight under the microscope's amazing. Thought of putting my semen under it, but must admit haven't had the courage to do so as yet. (God knows what 'nothing' will look like close up.) 'Course I haven't told anybody that I'm experimenting with myself. Mutti would have a fit. If I'm asked what I'm doing, I'll say I'm doing research for a school project. That should satisfy them.

When I'm not goggling into the Zeiss, I play Vati's piano. I've never taken lessons, but it doesn't matter. Once I've found the left hand's harmonic chords I start 'improvising'. It's a word I've heard used a great deal on late night radio jazz programmes, but with me it doesn't mean variations on a theme or anything like that. I play whatever comes into my head.

Still, when Frank came to visit – we're doing Latin and Maths homework together – he seemed genuinely impressed. 'I had no idea you could play,' he said. So far it's the only confirmation I have from anyone that I 'can play'. When asked what I'm playing I invent 'little-known Baroque' or 'minor nineteenth century' composers. It always prompts the same response: 'Sounds surprisingly modern.' I'm quick to agree. 'Doesn't it.' And I tell them that's precisely why I'm playing their sadly neglected or underrated work.

It's all a game, of course. But there's something about music, especially piano music. Apart from listening to late night jazz programmes on the radio I play records of Bach's Goldberg Variations with Schnabel and Schubert's piano sonatas performed by Elly Ney. While the music's playing, I see patterns and geometrical forms moving like molecules. It's not how one is supposed to listen to music, I've been told. But I don't think anyone could tell me how to listen 'correctly'. What I see is no illusion. I'm convinced music doesn't 'mean' anything. It's about movement, design, logic of form, order, arrangement of parts. All I can do is recognise the pattern. In that way music's like the microscope. It lets me have a closer look at life.

Is that why I'd only scribbled lines and circles in my parents' formal Honeymoon book? Here's something funny. Last weekend Herr Mommsen, our slimy dance instructor, complimented me on my 'natural sense of rhythm'. I showed promise of becoming a good dancer! Frank nearly spewed! The girls sitting on the other side of the room giggled. My God, they're dumb! Don't they know anything? All I'm doing is miming the movement of musical molecules.

These are pretty uncoordinated thoughts. I'm jotting down whatever comes to my head, just scribble really, filling the pages of my parents' empty honeymoon record. I wonder whether they did keep another diary of their first holiday as a newly married couple. Or was their honeymoon not worth remembering? Where did they travel? Mutti never told me. They must have been happy once, before the war. It's difficult imagining your parents as lovers.

Which makes me realise how much I relate to other lives about which I know very little, even in my own family. Strictly speaking, I've always been a part of someone else, never fully myself. My beginning is with others who do not reveal themselves to me. How much do I need to know about them, I wonder.

Families are a bit like occupation forces. The enemy soldiers who marched into our city left years ago, but we think they're still here. We haven't noticed yet that we are free. Actually, I think life got much more difficult after the foreign army withdrew. It's the chronic housing shortage which has led to more and more violent clashes between locals and refugees. There've been demonstrations in the city for months. After the withdrawal of the occupation forces food became prohibitively expensive. The authorities seem unable to resolve the conflict. I think everybody would love to be ruled again by martial law. I've heard some people refer to 'the good old times during the war'.

It's different for me. My father did not return. He's remained on his deadly honeymoon trip, leaving me a spare diary of precious blank pages.

Wish I knew the corresponding words of lines and patterns, triangles, parallels, tangents, circles. There. I've drawn a few more across these precious pages. Let them be my sign language. Unlike Mutti, I can't talk to people who aren't there.

The story of *The Ghost Rider* describes how in the past babies and animals were buried in newly erected dykes. The Frisians were convinced life could only be protected by the sacrifice of life. I remember my horror and disgust the night on the island when I first read it. How could our ancestors be so cruel? But now I realise that what they were doing was not so different from what I've seen under the microscope. And isn't that also what Pastor Handmann is preaching at St Mary's, that the Son of God had to die so we may live? Perhaps that really is the logic of life.

At the Institute for Bacteriology they keep talking about antibodies. Surely that must be the wrong word. One of the doctors there explained it to me. It's meant to refer to 'blood proteins produced by the body in response to foreign bodies trying to poison it'. It was the first time I've heard the expression 'foreign body'. Does that mean the body turns against itself? Is the poison – 'antigens' the doctor called it – not part of it? Is it possible to separate and divide the body from itself? How many bodies are there? If I am all of them, how can I be 'anti' myself? How can the body be against itself? If *The Ghost Rider* is right (I thought it was just a story) and the body's a dyke, I want to know even more about the living thing inside.

It's thoughts like these that lead me back to the microscope. I need to look more closely at living things. Never know what people mean when they're talking about 'life' in general. The only life I know is the one made possible by my body. Before I had a body I did not exist. All this talk about 'the meaning of life' makes me suspicious. I think the meaning of life is life. Even Pastor Handmann agrees. If you've lived 'a good life', he says, you'll be rewarded with 'eternal life'. Like music, I don't believe there's anything above or beyond life. But I've seen there's a lot inside life itself. That's what I want to know more about.

I have to keep quiet about it. Pastor Handmann already calls me a heathen. Don't know whether he's serious about that. At school I pretend to go along with what we're being taught. But a lot of it I don't believe. Why do they teach us that parallels meet in infinity? I'm no mathematician, but it's obvious no one's ever witnessed the great event. Isn't it much more likely parallels don't 'meet' but – what's the word – regenerate? Like life they just go on and on. Wasn't that supposed to be the meaning of infinity?

Two years ago, at the end of confirmation class at St Mary's, we were all invited to select a text from the Bible that should help guide our future life. When Pastor Handmann saw what I had chosen, he hesitated. 'Wouldn't you rather choose one of St John's more poetic sayings?' he falsely enquired. I could tell he disliked my choice intensely. I've kept my confirmation certificate. It's on the very top of my shelves next to my science textbooks, and it reads: 'Your motto: It is your own selves you should be testing; it is your own selves you must put to the proof. Corinthians II, 13, 5-6.' Funny thing is the words actually moved me very deeply. Why didn't the church approve? After all, the text came from the Bible! But the pastor's right about one thing. They're hardly reassuring words. I may have chosen them, but most of the time I put them out of my mind.

What is it about my generation of war children that so many of us seem to be suffering from blood-related illnesses? Are we in some way contaminated? Many soldiers have lost 'life or limb', as they say. All around me I come across war cripples demonstratively displaying their loss or injury. Most of them accusingly, some almost in triumph. There seems to be a kind of affected behaviour unique to our war cripples – demanding, self-righteous, even arrogant. Many of us, on the other hand, are carrying our illnesses inside. It's as if we're hiding death. All you can see of Hanna's leukaemia is her pale skin. That's why her sudden faints are so scary. Of course, when it comes to covering a life-threatening illness, Sannes remains the absolute master of disguises.

Hanna's hidden illness is one of the reasons why I'm looking at blood particles under the microscope. Pity my lenses are not more powerful. Haven't yet been able to get a single drop of Hanna's blood. Imagine what'd happen, if I asked her for some! She'd probably think I'm some kind of Dracula and demand to be seated elsewhere. She's still top of the class, but I can tell it takes all of her strength. Made one of my stupid mistakes the other day when I asked her whether we could go to dancing school together, 'to trip the light fantastic'. Should've seen her sad smile! 'Thanks for asking,' was her polite answer. Could've howled.

Saying things about Hanna isn't easy, even though it helps clear my mind. Truth is she's confused me from the very start. Our friendship's like her illness. Outwardly we're just sharing desks. Didn't take long before I'd become dependent on her sitting next to me. We didn't 'carry on'. I tried not to distract her. It was enough that she was near.

Hanna's not beautiful. Not in the usual sense of having a pretty face, a good figure and clothes to go with it. She's skinny, gawky and pale-faced – in fact pale all over. Her long blonde hair reaching below her shoulders makes her look even taller than she really is. Most of her dresses are pretty ordinary. I suspect her mother makes them. Her arms are too long and her legs too thin. The boys in class refer to them as 'match-sticks'. Cruel, but pretty close. She walks awkwardly and carries her satchel as if she's walking the dog.

Hardly the stuff beauty queens are made of. Yet Hanna's not only the best student in class, she's also by far the best liked. Though she keeps pretty much to herself, we're all convinced we're her friends. Don't know why that is. Not everyone's as wrapped in her blue eyes as I am, but even the other girls in class think she's 'special'. Sitting next to her I've become familiar with her habits. The movements of her hands, the way she holds her head or pen when she's writing. Can't imagine Hanna without her Montblanc. Hers is the most beautiful writing I've ever seen. It'd take a microscope to do justice to the steady lines, the elegant angle, the steadfastness (can I say that?) of her letters. Looks like she's turned the alphabet into a work of art. Boy, would I love to get a royal blue letter from Hanna! But I have to be content with borrowing one of her exercise books pretending I need to copy something.

All the ungainliness of Hanna's body seems unimportant. For me the colour of her skin's not pale but ivory, her walk's restrained, cautious and vulnerable. Sometimes, on the way home after school, when I see her cross the street, I've got this crazy idea that she's really testing the ground, checking whether it is safe to walk the earth. Safe for what? I have no idea, but that's what it looks like. Hanna's not elegant. She's got something else instead. A grace only those possess who know about the fragility of their body. Who know they're carrying a fatal illness inside.

This thing about the body still has me worried. Keep thinking about 'the ghost rider' or the 'dyke reeve', as he's called in the novel, a warden responsible for safety and maintenance of the embankment. Dr Schulz, our old form teacher, assured us that the book is historically correct. To let the death of a child safeguard the life of the father is not the idea of some morbid writer after all. Why do we have to build dykes in the first place? Why not let the floods come and cover the land? As far as I know, there've never been many settlers in the west, just a few farmers and plenty of hardy Frisian sheep and cattle. A fertile, rough and windswept country which at storm tide would go under like the islets off the coast. So what? There'd be plenty of time to move.

Why can't we let ourselves be flooded? Why do we think our bodies are dykes? Hanna walks as if trying to discover whether the ground will carry her. I remember her horror during last year's school excursion when we visited the site of an ancient Viking settlement. We were shown well-preserved bog corpses a couple of thousand years old. Among them were the skulls of two women whose necks clearly displayed remnants of a rope. Hanna asked the guide whether they were wearing a chain or string of beads. She was told they had been executed for adultery. Hanna clutched me, took a deep breath and fainted. When she came round I was asked to take her outside the excavation area. After a glass of water she slowly regained control over her body.

It was a grisly sight. But I kept thinking how the soil, even the moors, had managed to preserve so much of the dead women's bodies. Was Hanna afraid of her body being preserved in death? Is that why she moves so tentatively, as if she doesn't trust the very ground she's walking on?

Hanna's fainting's been getting worse lately. Whenever she feels dizzy I'm authorised to leave the classroom with her, get some water, make sure she takes her medicine, ring her mother if it's serious, go to the principal's office and ask his secretary to ring for an ambulance in an emergency. Despite the initial upheaval her breakdowns are a strangely quiet event, almost peaceful. Once we're out of class Hanna seems to let go. She just stands or sits or lies there, eyes shut, breathing quietly, saying it'll be all right. As if I needed to be reassured! Never heard her complain, never seen her cry. It's terrible what I'm saying, but I find these moments with Hanna very beautiful. She lets me wipe her fringe off her forehead and pretends not to notice when I'm gently stroking her cheek. We don't talk. I feel Hanna's cold hands in mine, her pulse barely noticeable, and in the midst of my concern I'm strangely happy. Perhaps happy's not the right word. What I mean is Hanna and I are at peace together.

It's difficult to say why Hanna means so much to me. She's not like other girls. I mean, I don't imagine her naked. I don't even go out with her. Perhaps she's like a sister. I don't know. Can't pretend I understand these things. Isn't that what calendars and notebooks are for – to ask questions that can't be answered? There are still so many empty pages in my parents' honeymoon diary! Wonder whether Hanna'll ever get married.

One day I'll find out about bodies and antibodies. Right now I can't do it on my own. It's no use talking to teachers about it. All they do is quote textbook laws of biochemistry and the physiology of the blood. I've noticed that with teachers. They always substitute language for the thing because they don't know the thing's the language.

Just had a crazy idea. What if one could put words under the microscope, watch them split and grow, form and reform, shape and design ever-new patterns!

I better stop. These entries in my parent's honeymoon record are not much different from their empty pages. I'll never know anything about their honeymoon. They'll never read what I've written. It's only the book that links us. We're separated by death. Because of my father my mother pretends there's no death. I know father and absence are the same.

Death's all around us. Even so, I want to live unprotected by dykes, go under with the flood and start anew. It may take a while, but I'm determined to discover what it is we carry within our own bodies.

Think I'll go to the lounge now and listen some more to the Goldberg Variations. Later I might tickle the ivories myself, invent another little-known, underrated composer of a previous century. Frank and I've decided we're going to form a combo for our school formal. We've already got a name for it: The Dykebusters.

Mutti's gone. She's sneaked out again, pretending to do the washing. Don't know where she might be. Probably at the markets asking people whether the war's over yet.

XII

Among his schoolmates Gunnar Nielsen, a stockily-built eighteen-year-old with short cropped curly blond hair, held the part enviable, part dubious reputation of being 'experienced'. Everybody at Old Grammar knew what that meant. Some of the girls bluntly called him an oversexed tomcat. By contrast, Gunnar was fond of using what he himself described a more refined, codified speech. Occasionally everything he said seemed to consist of peculiar euphemisms.

During morning recess he took Mark aside.

'Wanna do a bit of conducting?'

'What d'you mean?'

'Get a fish on the line.'

'Haven't got a clue what you're talking about.'

Gunnar acknowledged the recognition of his linguistic sophistication with a condescending smile.

'An allegretto with the fair and foul maidens of Newtown, Maestro. Soubrettes anxious to perform. Auditioning for parts.' He winked conspiratorially. 'Live from the fish factory "La Scala", next to the gasometer. Whenever they feel the urge. No need for fine tuning.'

Mark's classmate was in fine form. They were standing in the smokers' corner of the schoolyard. Gunnar lit a cigarette as if he were firing a grenade, then took a deep, relishing breath and began conducting tiny smoke-clouds in the air. He oozed confidence and aggression.

'One thing though. Seems no amount of perfume covers the stench of fish. Would that put Herr Kapellmeister off?'

Mark shrugged his shoulders. 'Not necessarily.' He was anxious not to appear timid. The truth was he didn't know how to respond to Gunnar's blunt invitation. No amount of language could hide what he was suggesting. But Gunnar's crazy words seemed just right for the crazy thing they would be doing. Mark could feel the familiar response of his body. It would not be denied.

'All right, then, Mark. Let's go fishing. Say Neptune's Fountain around eight?'

'*Con amore.*'

'*Con brio.*'

Newtown, the industrial quarter, was in the northern part of town. The ruins of a rusty gasometer towered over factories, an electric power station, the municipal abattoir, run-down warehouses and various dilapidated shipyard repair sheds. The air was heavy with chemical pollutants and the sickening stench of carcasses. Overcast skies were unable to absorb the exhaust fumes from industrial plants working round the clock. The entire suburb was in danger of suffocation. Its residential streets were stripped of trees or gardens. At Newtown only the hardiest weed survived. It was almost touching how, against all odds, a few tiny wild plants managed to push their prickly stems and dusty leaves through misshaped cobbles of wretched, dirty and deserted streets. Here life and death were equally brutal and unforgiving.

They arrived outside the gasometer shortly after dark. The group of young women standing around a small kiosk seemed to be waiting for a bus. Day shift had just been relieved. Mark and Gunnar saw a few women outside the factory unlock their bikes and ride into the dark.

The boys tried to look casual as they approached the kiosk. As if to legitimise their being here Gunnar went to the booth and bought a pack of Prince. Lighting their cigarettes as they had seen it done in the movies, they discussed where they were planning to spend their holidays. Not Italy again! Had Mark ever been to Spain?

For the five women nearby it seemed to be feeding time. They took turns telling each other stories that were drowned in screams and laughter. Their screeching voices cut the air.

'The birds are singing,' Gunnar observed.

'The fish are biting,' Mark replied, much to his own surprise.

Every now and then one of the women would open her handbag, pull out a pocket mirror, readjust her hair and check her make-up. Despite their pretence of having ignored the young men's arrival their every move was being monitored. A furtive side glance and a quick check whether the bus was coming were sufficient to evaluate the visitors.

To their relief Gunnar and Mark could not detect the smell of fish, at least not from this distance. But the odour of strong sweet perfume was overpowering.

After a while the women began to whisper, then burst out laughing again. It was an explosive sound challenging the young suitors.

Gunnar and Mark went into a huddle to exchange preferences. Gunnar would take the dark-haired one now looking straight at him, then, having been discovered, quickly turning away; Mark, the one next to her with a long blonde ponytail. They grinned at each other. As far as they were concerned, the matter was settled.

Defiantly the women continued with their show of indifference. Chewing gum, their tongues recovered the sticky sweet dribble and saliva. It reminded Mark of an animal eating its afterbirth. He shivered in fascination and disgust.

'Over sixteen then?' the dark-haired one finally opened negotiations.

'You talkin' to me?' Gunnar pointed to his heart in a condescending gesture. In unison the group replied with a giggle. A chain of smoke rings rose in the cold night air like halos.

'And your side-kick, what's 'is name?'

Mark took the bait. 'It's our athletic figure. Keeps us young and pretty.'

'Yeah? Well, what'ya doin' to keep fit, like?'

'Oh, you know, bit of this, bit of that. The usual.'

It wasn't clear whether the fish women were impressed or amused. Their laughter began to sound nervous. Some of the others turned away, indicating their loss of interest.

'Boxing, wrestling, sailing, diving. That kind of thing.'

Gunnar's nudge warned Mark not to exaggerate. The ponytail opened her red patent leather bag, pulled out a tiny mirror and slowly painted over her lips, pressing them firmly against each other. Her overuse of mascara made the eyes look like smoked mackerels. Mark recognised the invitation and shuddered with anticipation.

'How 'bout it then?' Gunnar suggested in his most worldly manner.

' 'Bout what?' the dark-haired demanded.

'You an' me, babe.' Gunnar relished using the words of a pop song, rather pleased with his no-nonsense approach which he considered had just enough of the common touch.

'What 'bout your athletic mate, then?'

'Name's Mark. He's a saint. He'll come too.' The lads bowed theatrically, prompting a further outburst of cackles from the women.

'Charming, I'm sure,' the ponytail mackerel offered in reply. 'I'm Rosy,' she volunteered, then added, 'In name and in nature.' Gallantly the boys grinned their appreciation. ' 'Course you are.'

Gunnar pushed Mark in her direction. They shook hands as if at a formal dinner dance. It was pure theatre, the acting out of a comedy of manners, a collusive imitation of polite society. They were rehearsing scenes from another life, beyond the reach of canners, slicers and boners of the local fish factory, outside the realm of local grammar school boys. There was something grotesquely serious about their behaviour. Mark remembered Errol Flynn – or was it Tyrone Power? – claiming every lady needed to be treated like a whore and every whore like a lady. But were these fish women really whores?

'I'm Barb. Come on then, you two.' Her head pointed in the direction of the abattoir. 'We've got a caravan. Quite comfy really. You sure you know what yer doin'?'

Barb, the dark flounder, led the way. Nonchalantly she threw her handbag over her shoulder and walked off as if to work. Gunnar caught up with her, possessively putting his arm around her. After they had walked a while Rosy and Barb looked back at the others still congregating around the kiosk. The women were waving exuberantly. Laughter and shouts – 'Be careful if ya can't be good!' – followed the two couples until they disappeared in the dark. It looked as if the gasometer had swallowed them.

They entered an industrial wasteland where some factories were operating on nightshift. Others, closed since the end of the war, remained vacant and abandoned. The wind howled through broken glass and empty windows. Across the sparsely lit street rhythmic thumps echoed from the abattoir. The air was filled with the smell of gas, fish, urine and blood.

From unfenced vacant land copulating feral cats screamed their high-pitched angry pleasure. There must have been dozens prowling around the deserted sites and warehouses. It disturbed Mark that sometimes they sounded like crying babies, sometimes like frenzied killers. He felt an urgent need to talk to the woman who had agreed to come with him. What was her name again?

Conscious of the brutality of their near-anonymous encounter, Mark wished he could be as casual about it as Gunnar and his woman who, walking ahead, were whispering and laughing, stopping regularly to embrace and kiss each other.

'This ya first time, then?' The voice startled him. Rosy, of course! For too long they had walked next to each other without saying a word.

Mark had to say something. The cats' piercing predatory cries got to him. Rosy's high heels provided the beat to some very disturbing sounds. They seemed to answer the pounding noise from the abattoir. Out of the corner of his eye he watched her ponytail bounce. Even her breasts bobbed up and down in the same relentless rhythm.

Walking arm in arm in front of them he saw Gunnar try to lift Barb's skirt. She always pushed him back, disengaging herself from his embrace with teasing rebukes. 'Not so quick!' she laughed in a way that made it clear she did not really wish to discourage him.

They were approaching a large vacant lot along the waterfront. A solitary street lamp swaying in the night breeze flickered over what appeared to be a haphazard assembly of industrial wreckage. Strange shapes of machinery cast twisted shadows across the street. As Mark came closer he could see the block also served as a car dump, a rubbish tip and a drainage ditch for the abattoir. A tiny creek leading straight into the harbour carried the stench of blood and intestines.

In the distance the outline of a dilapidated circus caravan came into view. Occasional gusts cast light across lions, tigers and monkeys painted in garish colours on the outside of the old-fashioned trailer. Trunks of elephants were peeling off, as did the stripes of zebras and the red saddles of white horses. Large indecipherable letters emerged from the dark, then quickly disappeared again.

Mark grew increasingly ashamed of their dishonourable intentions. The unexpected starkness of the surroundings disturbed him. He had never been here before. Yet at the same time he felt an exciting anger. His body seemed to be saying, 'You try and stop me now!' How grotesque it all was, how unworthy! A tinselled clown and mermaid were about to enter the shabby arena of a long dissolved circus to face the king of beasts. To the sounds of an off-tune fanfare man and creature would wrestle in the sawdust until it was soaked with blood. In the end the wit and strength of man would prove superior. Triumphantly the clown and the maid would rise above the defeated beast of prey to acknowledge the applause.

Mercifully she did the talking for him. She looked around.

'Some glamorous setting, eh?'

'Yeah.'

'What d'you wanna be? Later, I mean.'

'Dunno.'

Her heavy sigh was without a hint of protest. 'At least you won't have to work in a factory. That's for sure.' It was a statement of fact, free of envy or malice.

Mark did not know what to say.

'Are your parents rich?'

The question embarrassed him. 'Not really,' he stuttered.

They left the road to turn into the lot. Resolutely she took his hand and led him to the caravan. Her touch released the smell of fish mingled with that overpowering sweet perfume.

'D'you like me, a bit?' The question was hardly seductive, more a kind of naive begging, a desperate appeal pleading for reassurance.

'I picked you, didn't I?'

For the moment it seemed enough to satisfy her self-esteem. As he spoke, Mark could hear his own voice as if it were someone else's. He sensed their exchange was part of a ritual which had to be adhered to, even in this raw corner of the night. Was what they were about to do really what people referred to as 'making love'?

'S'pose you did. Gimme a kiss, then.'

She stopped walking to offer her lips like a girl expecting to be kissed at a family gathering. Her sudden confidence derived from the simple knowledge of how it was done. In the passing light Mark saw the moisture of her heavily coloured lips. He was overcome by disgust and desire, unable to keep them apart. The moment he touched her he was greeted by Rosy's tongue, searching, pushing, feeding its own impetuosity. Like dancers they began rubbing their bodies against each other. When she felt his hardness she urged him on to the caravan.

Gunnar and Barb were already lying on a mattress, half undressed, drinking rum out of the bottle and listening to a portable radio. It was warm inside, the air filled with cigarette smoke, alcohol, the smell of bodies, fish and perfume. There was something exhilarating about the brutality of their desire, the location and the undisguised nature of what they were doing. Humiliation seemed to have its own triumph, pity its own despair. Mark found there could be something merciless in human instincts.

He and Rosy joined the others on the bed, taking gulps from the unlabelled bottle, smoking, talking, laughing, teasing, still showing off. Whenever the pounding of the abattoir threatened to drown their talk they quickly turned up the radio. Although the women were less nervous, Mark noticed they too were waiting for the cue when at last their bodies would take over.

XIII

Final year at school meant ever-increasing frustration as well as the promise of relief. Mark was impatient to be released. He had grown tired of the knowledge he had acquired at school, a truth to be learnt off by heart and repeated as if it were one's own! Wasn't book learning really copying, a kind of cheating?

Schools taught the discipline of copying. All their knowledge was history. Why should their students want to perpetuate that history? If they did, they would remain schoolboys forever. Had they not witnessed the most brutal and shameful of exposures – so-called timeless truths being revealed as lies? Had the generation of Mark's teachers not been responsible for the war? Trying to force their truths on the world, the world had hit back and defeated them. Mark believed in the world, the Beautiful Enemy. School had taught him what it did not want him to know – that thoughts and beliefs could be misrepresented and abused. For all its reputation, Old Grammar too perpetuated a conspiratorial history of learning.

It was a bit like his hometown's reaction to the news that peace had been declared. At first, the entire population was relieved. Soon after, everyone pretended either they had won the war, or it had never happened.

It was possible to couch such lies in deceptively reassuring language. The national army had never been defeated on the battlefield. Yesterday's enemy was today's ally. The occupation forces were welcomed as liberators. Words revealed themselves as a collusive code. Mark wondered whether it was just his native tongue that made it so easy to mislead, distort or hide the truth.

He had discovered how, in language, nothing was ever the same. Words meant many different things, not only to different people. The word summer could invoke the two months he and Sannes had been ghost riders on a Frisian island, the times he'd been sailing on the outer harbour with Frank Hilmer, the dismal, rainy weeks he'd stayed home looking after his mother or his plans for the coming holiday. His mind, mood and memory chose what he wanted it to mean.

General words such as knife or door were really abstractions. In his mind Mark invariably envisaged a particular knife and a specific door. The real language was all that existed. The world defined itself. Words were always lagging behind. They were shadows of what was real.

It was even worse with abstractions. When Mark had to learn a famous Goethe poem off by heart, its opening line 'Let Man be noble, helpful and good ...' left him confused. How was he supposed to respond to the poet's rhetoric? What was 'noble, helpful and good'? Wasn't each person likely to define those words differently? What did the line mean to Goethe's contemporaries? Surely not the same as it did today! What, then, was the reality, the truth of language? Reading was a dancing with shadows. Anyone could read into words what they felt like. Wasn't it dangerous to build a world on such understanding?

The word was not, and never would be, the thing. Yet school was all about words. Despite his scepticism Mark decided not to rebel openly. In a kind of self-discipline he confined himself to expressing doubts. He wanted his teachers to acknowledge the ambiguity of language. Once, in a philosophy class, they had come close to it.

'So you see, according to Plato', Herr Doktor Gerson,

their white-haired classics master, explained, 'the world is an imitation'. As always, he was dressed in a badly stained white coat, with its bone buttons done up unevenly. What made their philosophy teacher feel the need to don a uniform more appropriate to the teaching of natural sciences? Perhaps it was meant as a sign, professing to a scientific claim of the humanities. More likely, he wore it in pretence to a clinical objectivity of his discipline. He was a doctor of knowledge, the bearer of culture, a man with a calling, an intellectual detached from the trivialities of everyday reality, a classical pedagogue with a spiritual commitment to higher things. It was understandable, then, that from time to time he may have also needed the white coat to protect himself from the messier parts of his profession. Sadly, teaching was not always what Plato had promised it to be.

'Which is another way of saying the world's not real,' Gerson continued. He was hovering like a vulture over rows of seemingly dead prey. It was the last period of the afternoon. The man in white knew his only chance was to stir the corpses with unsettling thoughts.

Friday afternoon periods were traditionally the realm of what the curriculum euphemistically referred to as one of the 'less demanding' subjects from the humanities. For good reason. With barely half an hour to the end of classes the challenge of keeping students' interest alive proved too much for all but the most inventive or insensitive of Old Grammar's teaching staff. During early autumn the mild midday sun was enough to put the entire senior class in a hallucinatory trance.

Gerson spoke with a deceptively soft, melodious voice which fooled no one. All his students knew inside the right pocket of his white coat he was carrying several pieces of chalk, ever ready to use them like a foreign legionnaire deploying bundled sticks of dynamite.

'Why then do we believe we have a soul?' the bird of prey kept stimulating the corpses.

When no one answered he stopped dead in his tracks, turned around and dispatched a chalk missile in the direction of the second-last row. The projectile hit a student whose lanky body had only just collapsed on his desk. Holding the back of his head, he shot up and looked around.

'Henning!' Gerson's quiet voice almost sounded like pleading. 'Do you have a soul, I wonder?'

'I don't know, sir.'

The accosted stammered not because he was embarrassed or dim-witted, but because the unexpected ambush had rudely interrupted his pre-lunch navigational charting of the weekend. Henning would defy anyone to remain philosophically alert while planning a cruise to the outer. Especially for this coming weekend, likely to be one of the last when it would still be safe to venture out to the Baltic. Any day now the weather would take a turn for the worse.

As if sensing what his student had been thinking, Gerson countered with a relatively gentle rebuke. 'That's right, Henning, you're all wind.' It was enough to send him back to his nautical dreams. Momentarily awoken by the missile, the rest of the class burst into nervous cackles.

Following his own kind of navigation, sharpshooting Gerson seized the moment. 'Well then, what about the rest of you?'

But already the class had withdrawn to its earlier state of suspended animation. White-coated Gerson had turned into a ghost again, stalking rows of unattended graves in a cemetery for the sublimely ignorant. What had ever made him think he could offer the ungrateful dead the consolations of classical philosophy! Clearly, there was nothing left they cared about. The war – what did these untrained youngsters know about war! – had given birth to a generation of hard-nosed survivors.

'How do we know there is a soul, sir?'

Mark realised his teacher's nod was no more than a thinly disguised gesture of disgust. Still, he tried hard not to make his challenge sound aggressive or flippant.

'I mean, who thought up the idea, the idea of a soul? It must have been someone's mind. If so, doesn't it remain simply a product of that mind, another Platonic idea? There's no evidence the soul exists outside the human mind, is there? The world and our mind are not the same.' He took a deep breath. 'The soul, sir, the soul is just a thought.'

From the back row came half-suppressed, uncertain laughter. Encouraged by the spasmodic giggle, Harald Sörens, the class clown, called out, 'Yeah, as I recall, life was one hell of a bore before I invented myself.'

The chalk projectile landed just in front of him. As well as a warning to Harald Sörens, the timely shot served as a wake-up call for everyone else. Suddenly there was uproar in the classroom.

Hanna was alienated by the underlying tension of what was meant to be a philosophical discussion. Male belligerence had turned even the search for the human soul into a war. Would it never end? With all that aggression she preferred to remain silent.

But another girl, two rows behind, raised her arm. Nibbling the frame of her glasses as she spoke gave Angela Carstens a devious, furtive look.

'I believe the time will come,' she suggested, 'when all thinking will be done by a machine. Maybe that'll be the end of all ideas, as well as the end of the human soul.'

Gerson confiscated an ink-stained ruler from Theo Kramer who, swinging on his chair, had been conducting an invisible orchestra. With one casual push he forced him back to the upright position. The interaction between teacher and student had all the precision of a circus stunt. Gerson's face lit up as he slowly proceeded to perch himself across Angela Carstens' desk.

'I see,' he said in an insidious voice, beaming with delight and sarcasm. Without glasses, Angela's eyes, barely centimetres away, looked dead. Staring at them, Gerson continued with his falsely jovial tone. 'You would like that, wouldn't you, young lady? And how, may one ask, is that likely to come about?'

Unperturbed, Angela Carstens returned to nibbling the frame of her horn-rimmed spectacles. 'Well, sir,' she replied, 'it's like this. I'm sure you agree there's already far too much for any one person to know and to remember. In future all knowledge will be stored, you see. The machine will do it for us, sir.' She sounded like a professor patiently explaining what to her was patently obvious. It wasn't just her teacher she had to persuade. Her classmates, too, were uncertain of what she was proposing. It sounded quite audacious. Was she making it up as she went along? Did she intend to mock or challenge Dr Gerson? Or did she actually mean what she was saying?

Sensing an implied challenge, several of her classmates were anxious to come to her assistance. Hands went up demandingly, hands Gerson chose to ignore. The man in white decided to adopt a new role, that of impartial referee. 'Settle down,' he announced with uncharacteristic calmness. A high-pitched voice soared above subdued moans of disappointment. Its crowing pitch sounded positively defiant. Overruling the arbitrator of fair play, Theo Kramer did not wait for permission to speak.

'I don't believe we'll be all that important, sir. Not any more. Looks like we won't be needed much longer.'

Slowly Gerson slid off Angela Carsten's desk, discreetly checking his remaining supply of ammunition. Realising he had nearly run out of stock, he decided on a tactical withdrawal to the front of the class. In a moment of truce both sides reflected on the state of the battle. Mark's questioning of the soul, Angela's conjecture about the future of thinking and Theo Kramer's almost total dismissal of the usefulness of man – all barely ten minutes before the end of class – had brought an abrupt end to their pre-lunch philosophy warfare about the meaning of life.

In the middle of the armistice something startled Henning,

about to doze off again, into a reflex defence. 'Who? What? Why?' he screamed, suddenly nervously alert, eyes wide open. The unprompted outburst proved unsettling. His questions sounded like a cry of guilt. This time no one laughed.

Mark remained disturbed by what had been said. More and more his mother's illness had become a challenge to his own concept of reality.

'But if the machine can only think us,' he concluded Angela's argument, 'and Plato is right in saying we're not real, its intelligence would be merely imitating the imitation of an imitation.'

In frustration Angela Carstens threw her glasses on the desk. This was not what she had meant. Mark was taking her reasoning too far.

'The body, the idea and the soul are all concepts of human thought, sir. Outside it, there are no ideas and no imitations. Plato was wrong. There's only one reality.' His voice was trembling with passion.

As if alarmed by the intensity of Mark's reasoning, Gerson raised his hands to pacify the class. It looked like a sign of surrender. No one could tell whether he too was agitated or rather pleased. Against all odds he had led his class to more questions than he could have hoped for. Grateful and relieved, he adopted the role of forbearing conciliator. Indulgently he summarised: 'That, my friends, was quite a discussion. As we have seen, philosophy does affect all of us.'

'Well, almost all of us,' he corrected himself, casting an eye across to Henning slumped in his chair, hovering somewhere between blissful oblivion and startled exhortation. To everyone's amazement, Gerson resisted the temptation to dispatch further guided missiles in his direction. He would not tempt the gods to grant one final last-minute metaphysical awakening.

That very moment the bell rang. Class broke up with the usual pushing and shoving. Despite the heated discussion no one had any trouble leaving the human mind, the soul of man, the world and its possible meaning behind and get the hell out of there. Mark couldn't wait to get home for lunch. He hadn't been as hungry for a long time.

Whatever his contribution to Old Grammar's final year philosophy classes, Mark did not see how thoughts or words should attempt to separate what he had found to be one. Weren't mind, body and soul one reality? How, then, could any part be different? He could not separate his own body, or any parts of it, from the life of the world. All of his senses made him feel whole. It was his body that would let him grow into the world. It spoke the only language that mattered. Everything else was school talk.

Nonetheless, it was good to have discussions about these things. To Mark's surprise the debate continued the following week.

On that occasion it seemed lab-coated Gerson tried on the role of the mad scientist. Triumphantly he proclaimed, 'The world's made of fire!' True to the principles of didactic warfare, he hurled this piece of retrospective prophecy at them with the speed and precision of one of his dreaded chalk missiles. The camouflaged use of literary and scientific cross-references was his favourite strategy of philosophical warfare. In a devious double disguise he was quoting Goethe's *Faust* citing Anaxagoras.

'What say you to that, Master Olevsen?'

Mads, sitting near the window, would not be rushed. His long wavy blond hair covered his forehead like a heavy curtain. Slowly, deliberately, he brushed it aside, signalling he was open for business. Calmly leaning back in his chair, he ventured, 'That would explain volcanos and geysers, sir. Deep inside the earth is a ball of fire. That's probably how people got the idea of hell.'

It was pouring outside. Although only just past midday, it was getting so dark the classroom lights had to be switched on. Wind and rain created wilful patterns on the windows. It was no longer possible to look out. As heavy drops whipped against the glass they momentarily formed starlike shapes, replaced almost immediately by a downpour of seemingly endless watery constellations. The window-panes turned into screens displaying a rainy avalanche of shooting stars.

Mark was captivated by the spectacle, the rapid movement of its continuous creation and destruction. He wondered whether what he was watching could also be a kind of knowledge. Would he ever be able to read its watery message?

'I see.' Gerson remained uncommitted, leaving Mads Olevsen's answer up in the air. 'Anyone else opting for fire and brimstone?'

Gunnar Nielsen was getting restless. He had a reputation to defend, having come top in geography for two years in a row. They were talking about his favourite subject, the world.

Once Mark had visited Gunnar's home. They'd spent most of their time in his father's study. Gunnar was keen to show Mark an enormous antique globe, prominently displayed in front of rows and rows of heavy oak bookshelves. Mark had never seen one this size, so carefully detailed, so beautifully crafted, so extravagantly large. Turned into a luxurious piece of ornamental furniture, the world looked comfortable and orderly, precious and finite. Mark could see that for the rich it was much more open, larger and friendlier. But it also seemed to have lost some of its mystery. Nonchalantly Gunnar gave the globe a push as if it were a billiard ball. 'My dear Mark,' he boasted, 'as you can see, we're men of the world.'

Mark took a step back. 'Not quite. From where I'm standing, we're looking at it from outer space,' he replied. 'Or from another planet.'

Gunnar remained unperturbed. 'Well, actually, we're looking at it in my father's library.' They laughed. They had both won.

Mark secretly compared the tiny globe in his room with

the huge piece of furniture in front of him. Where in their small apartment could he and his mother have put anything this size?

Prompting disparaging hissing from the back of the class, Gunnar Nielsen volunteered a high-handed token support to Dr Gerson. 'It's true that volcanic eruptions have shaped the surface of the earth.' What had come over him? Gunnar was famous for trying to contradict just about anything their teachers put to them. But he quickly redeemed himself. There was an audible sigh of relief as he continued. 'However, as you know, sir, actually most the world consists of water.'

Surprisingly, Gerson showed no signs of irritation. No missiles were launched from his pockets, no sarcasm parted his thin, seemingly bloodless lips. Uncharacteristically at ease, he was content to look around, waiting patiently for someone to put up a hand.

Mark could not take his eyes off the windows. The rain's rhythm continued to draw short-lived, strange but beautiful formations, geometrical compositions made up of lines and circles, visual movements of coagulation and dissolution. Barely established patterns interrelated, then quickly disappeared. If they were signs, what did they mean? Mark preferred to think of the spectacle as a kind of music. From far away he could hear the voice of Henning. 'I've read about Pacific Islanders who walk across fire.'

Gunnar nodded wisely. 'As do some holy men in India.'

Elke Fischer's comment that not so long ago wise women were burnt at the stake drew a hostile response from the boys.

'What does that have to do with anything?' Mads Olevsen demanded to know.

Instead of reprimanding, a curiously tolerant Gerson simply ignored him and proceeded with his next announcement.

'In fact, life does originate from water,' he now declared with absolute certainty. It was another double-quotation – this time Goethe citing Thales.

From the back of the dusky room came a moaning sound. 'It's getting dark in here. Could we please have more light!' It was Henning innocently quoting Eckermann misquoting Goethe.

Outside, the rain continued to bear down.

As if Gunnar Nielsen had guessed Mark's thoughts he wondered aloud, 'What if it never stops? The rain, I mean. What if one day it's the biblical flood all over again?'

'In that case we'll build another ark, stupid.' Harald Sörens' laughter was followed by a hearty yawn. Still Gerson did not lose his composure.

As in a dream, a wide-awake Mark experienced strange visitations of light and fluid reflections. They were visions he had never seen before, forming continuous beginnings and endings, an apparition of an interdependent organism, designed by interlinking images. Like a volcanic eruption it blew itself up, spraying red-hot sparks of minute particles. Substance, form and matter drowned in each other. Mark could not tear himself away from the spectacle. Did no one else see it? Was he the only one captivated, the only one to witness its mutations and transformation?

But then, what exactly had he seen? Mark could not be sure. In vain he tried to capture the logic of the vision. Was it a portent of his own body growing and disintegrating? Was it a pattern of the whole world drowning?

He was sweating. The rain's endless formations had sent him into a state of hallucination. Drops of water changed into sparks, rain into fire. Flames set alight tiny globes, worlds exploded. The tide of history was coming in, carrying all before it. Mark heard babies cry inside dykes. Images he could not escape pierced his consciousness. Dripping down the window-panes the rain had turned into pools of blood. He and Sannes were swimming home. Flying through the air like a rag doll was the body of Herr Kirsch. Explosions and broken glass announced the arrival of the Beautiful Enemy.

'The world's made of both fire and water.'

Mark heard his voice, but did not recognise it. Washed ashore in his classroom he listened to himself, unable to intervene.

The bell rang. Slowly he rose, embarrassed yet oddly defiant. He felt the burning growth in his crotch. Conscious for the first time of the absurd simplicity and grandeur of the observation, he wanted to call out, 'I'm here!' But he seemed to have lost the power of speech.

In the gloomy afternoon the heavy staccato rain continued. Leaving behind the drumming beat on the windows, the insistent designs of something he could not fully grasp, Mark was the last to leave the classroom. Yet for once he felt he was not alone.

On his way home it seemed to him the density of the rain was pouring out a brightness that shone its own light. Mark felt he was walking through liquid fire. Drenched to the bone, his body was burning. He was down at the harbour again, sitting next to the old men, soaking wet, the delicious texture of liquid fire next to his skin.

Autumn was drawing to a close. Streets filled with brittle leaves, red and yellow or rusty-coloured in the final beauty of their splendid decay. Days remained cold and rainy. Already the fog was beginning to strangle the city.

Cocooned in his room Mark listened to the world on his father's old radio. Night after night he lay in the dark, watching the dial light up the names of foreign stations, listening to unfamiliar sounds from far-away places. Exotic cities he only knew from his school atlas addressed him in their native languages. Alone in his bed, he was enveloped by the sounds of the world.

Mark's place of belonging was marked by absence. His father was gone for good; the daily worsening illness of his mother had long crossed the boundaries of mere absent-mindedness. Truth was she wasn't there, even when she stood right in front of him. Helplessly Mark watched his mother lose herself. In his suffering he too was in danger of losing his grip on reality. Being who he was, he considered himself an impostor. He painfully discovered there was no certainty in knowledge. Angrily he wrote in one of his notebooks 'Nothing's certain – not even that.' Like his mother, he had lost his way.

Together with Hanna, he had come top of class in maths, yet he did not believe in some of the subject's fundamental assumptions. Why was it possible to work with unverifiable symbols of infinity and arrive at verifiable finite results? They had been taught that phi was an essential value in the construction of bridges. It made crossing rivers, ravines or roads with the aid of an imagined eternity more than just an engineering feat. There had to be a trick, as impossible to prove as the assertion that parallels met in infinity. Sometimes Mark thought mathematicians were like his mother pretending that his father was not dead. Yet bridges were built without collapsing. People crossed them every day. They had become part of the traffic of reality. There was even a bridge in Cambridge built entirely without the use of a single nail!

Alone in his room, Mark tried to force his own mind to become part of a reality he did not believe in, but could not deny. Infinity was a construction without nails. Carelessly people crossed it, without any knowledge or concern about how it was built. Bridges were unrecognised everyday miracles. What if infinity and immortality were the same? Was his mother busy bridging death, her illness the construction of a miracle? If absence was a vital factor in building bridges, why did Mark remain unable to determine what was real?

As always in moments of conflict, Mark turned to music. It alone could help resolve his confusion. Music, he knew, didn't ask questions. It didn't say anything, it just was. Its very existence was enough to comfort and reassure him. A foreign orchestra was playing Mozart. He turned up the radio. The familiar sounds of the piano concerto put his mind at ease. The music was accompanied by steady rain tapping against the window. Mark drew the curtains, turned off the lights and listened.

Soon it became difficult to tell whether it was day or night. Images of crossing the mud-flats with that strange, beautiful boy appeared. Was it already so many years ago? He had not forgotten the spicy words they had exchanged. Nor had he forgotten Sannes. How could he? Sannes was a creature of the fog, a tidal ghost beckoning him even now. Why had he never replied to his postcards? Was he still afraid of their love? When Sannes eventually stopped sending him cards, Mark was triumphant. Now they would be forced to remember each other as forever alive.

Mark made it his habit to walk once a week to the Church of the Holy Ghost, an ugly red brick building in the centre of town. Was that the best they could do building a house of God? He thought of the elegant, exclusive villas on the outskirts of town, the homes of Gunnar Nielsen's and Frank Hilmer's parents near St Mary's Woods, small palaces built in worship of postwar affluence.

Outside the sacristy of the Holy Ghost a glass-fronted noticeboard bore the inscription CATHOLIC FILM SERVICE. It informed the faithful of movies currently shown in local cinemas. Overwhelmingly its advice consisted of warnings of moral dangers or un-Christian ethics, giving particular attention to films considered to be 'sexually explicit' or of 'gratuitous violence'. In its endeavour to protect the town against moral decay the service adopted a hierarchy of codified classifications, reaching from warm recommendations such as 'wholesome and uplifting for the whole family' to outright condemnation, expressed in uncompromising enumerations such as 'evil, sinful and abominable'. Each category carried its own code of abbreviation.

One of the most common acronyms was 'BYP', which

meant 'banned for young people'. Mark, who made a point of seeing as many 'BYPs' as possible, thought it might as well have meant 'ban young people'. Invariably the censured films were accused of containing too much sex or glorifying the criminal mind. It meant they showed brutality, unfaithfulness and prostitution, behaviour at odds with principles of civilised society. Where had the Church been during and after the war?! Did it really believe the young people of today could be protected from what, thanks to their parents' generation, they had already witnessed outside the cinema in the past?

Once, as a child, immediately after the war, Mark had pretended to be blind. It had been an angry gesture of rebellion. Now the time of disguises was over. On wet and foggy nights he went to the local cinema to watch the truth. 'Stalls' became the magical password for celluloid bodies violating each other, men fighting women, women fighting men, men fighting men, and women fighting women. Somehow, out of all this, someone emerged the winner, a hero who'd get his woman or a heroine who'd get her man, and all others getting their just deserts. It was the typical 'BYP' plot, a war epic, a postwar love story, a Sannes film, salacious variations of moral corruption, the violence of love, the love of violence, the infinite pattern of a bridge without nails, Mark's favourite of B-Grade sexually explicit gratuitous violence, *White Slaves for Tangiers*.

Films became another kind of school. While at Old Grammar he was taught the rules of abstractions, the cinema showed Mark life as it was imagined and desired by ordinary people. He knew perfectly well that most of what he saw was a different kind of make-believe, projecting fantasies of those sitting in the dark next to him. Films, he quickly discovered, were real because they showed the true desire of the people. They came to watch their real fantasies. For that reason it was a deeply satisfying ritual, allowing spectators to identify with their favourite actors. Films created reality from plots of make-believe. Its glamorous stars played an important part in people's everyday lives.

Mark fell under the spell of motion pictures because their shadowy images told important stories of the human body, forever staging variations of its demands and desirability. The logic of film was the logic of the body: the fantasy and desire of its celluloid projections were the anatomy of love and war, triumph and humiliation, crime and punishment. Bodies were both targets and perpetrators of violence. They were dangerous because they themselves were in constant danger. It was important, therefore, to know the story of the body.

How to become a competent actor of one's own body! Mark had begun rehearsing a whole range of important gestures in front of the mirror. He needed to learn how to look aggressively confident or callously indifferent, how to express sorrow or seduce with a disarming smile. (The latter proved particularly difficult; so far he only managed to produce a lewd, suggestive grin that would have frightened any woman away.) Most of all, he wanted to know how to act like a man.

Once he took Hanna to a Lemmy Caution film. He loved the charm and cynicism of the popular French-American actor Eddie Constantine, the self-mocking, ballet-like ritualised violence of the plot and, in the middle of fistfights and murders, the star's slightly snotty voice singing audacious chansons about love and life. Already Lemmy Caution films had become cult movies. To Mark's relief and amazement Hanna seemed to enjoy the satirical acting almost as much as he did, even though almost all the women in the film were whores. The rough treatment handed out to beautiful women did not seem to shock or surprise her. In the semi-darkness she startled him as she shook her long hair not in horror but in recognition. How could Hanna know about these things, or had he misread the gesture? Hadn't her illness confined her to a sheltered home life with her mother? Fortunately the sex scenes turned out not to be nearly as explicit as the Catholic Film Service had promised. (There was no relying on the Holy Ghost after all.) Still, Mark considered them daring enough to make a young woman uncomfortable. Yet Hanna continued to sit next to him – at times it felt like she had sat next to him all his life – without looking away once or withdrawing her hand from his.

After the late show he walked her home in the steady rain. Although neither of them carried an umbrella, Hanna refused to take the tram. Silently they followed the narrow cobbled alleys of the old part of town. Passing street lanterns they could see the heavy rain pouring down. It looked as if it were combing the light. Still there was no urgency in their steps.

Soaking wet and cold they reached Hanna's new housing estate. The entrance to her apartment building was brightly lit. As they approached the door Hanna gently dragged him into the darkness of the front garden. There, slowly, deliberately, eyes wide open, she kissed Mark's wet face. Cautiously their lips touched, then parted. With the rain quietly falling on their faces, they shared breath and tongue. Mark held Hanna in an embrace not to possess but to shield her. For a very long while they both stood still, abandoned in a kiss neither wanted to end, floating on a searching touch of surrender.

Mark dared not seek her breasts. With one hand he caressed Hanna's heavy drenched hair, with the other he drew her ever closer until he could feel her heart pounding. When at last their lips parted, he could hear himself beseeching her not to go, not yet. Holding her face now in both hands he kissed her eyes reverently, then gently rubbed his cheeks against hers. Hanna anticipated and responded to his every touch. Was it really the very first time they had held each other? In sudden familiarity they recognised their bodies. It was a joy not without apprehension. How cautious, how gentle, how considerate they both were! Mark felt the same serene intimacy as during one of Hanna's fainting fits. Then as now their bodies shared a fragile intimacy permeated by the fear of loss.

Slowly Hanna opened her eyes and smiled. 'You,' she

whispered in frightened recognition. 'You!' Once more she kissed his cheeks. Through her open coat Mark could feel the warmth of her fragile body. Apprehensively he waited for its response. Again he drew her to himself, impatient to inhale her presence. For a brief moment he thought she might faint in his arms.

He wanted to tell Hanna that he loved her, but that was movie talk, and after Eddie Constantine he wasn't sure how she would take it. While he was searching for the right words, she suddenly freed herself, ran away, turned the key and rushed through the door. It happened so quickly Mark could not be sure he had ever held her. Had they actually kissed, had they literally shared the same breath a brief moment ago?

If only school were over! It was still six more months to final exams. The coming winter threatened to be particularly severe. For weeks the cold weather had taken hold of the city, and it was only the beginning of November.

Lights were left on for most of the day. In the thick fog and heavy rain Old Grammar took on the appearance of an impenetrable fortress. Inside that stronghold of learning Mark and his classmates remained captives of a knowledge passed on to them from previous generations. Their teachers kept reminding them how privileged they were to attend such a prestigious school. At graduation they would leave well prepared for the world. The way they said it, there was little doubt they considered 'the world' they were referring to a rather inferior proposition, an institution not unlike the army, necessary but uninspiring, undeserving of the qualifications of higher learning. The only conclusion students could draw from such talk was that they were prisoners about to be released into an unworthy freedom.

They would take their chances being free.

In anticipation of their liberation Mark and his classmates studied with dogged determination. Like his confirmation three years earlier, Mark would graduate around Easter, the time of his birthday. He shuddered when he added up how much of his life had been taken up by school. For what? A freedom his teachers did not believe in? If their generation had been responsible for the war, why should he want to be released into a world still ruled by their kind of knowledge? How preposterous of teachers to assume they were acting in their students' best interests! As far as he was concerned, they had disqualified themselves for life.

Over the last two years Mark became convinced that some of his teachers did not believe in what they were teaching either. Anxious to cling to employment, they were just going through the motions. To Mark, that seemed the greatest hypocrisy of all.

Everyone in class was desperate now to leave the cloisters of venerable Old Grammar behind. During recess Gunnar Nielsen informed anyone who cared to listen that his brain had reached the limits of its tolerance. Even model student Hanna seemed to have lost faith in a knowledge confined to the classroom. When she asked Frank Hilmer what he looked forward to most after leaving school, he responded with an outburst of lyrical passion. 'Ah,' he enthused, 'the beauty and joy of making mistakes!' Hanna smiled in silent approval.

Nonetheless, for the time being they continued to study as if it mattered. For Mark, pretending to believe, or suspending disbelief, was something like parallels meeting in infinity. Endorsing assumptions of learning was not the same as discovering the truth. Assumptions were like bridges. Crossing chasms, they lead back to safe ground. But they had no purpose or meaning of their own.

When Hanna did not turn up for classes after New Year, Mark was concerned, but not alarmed. She had probably caught a cold and would join them in a couple of days. To put his mind at ease he tried to ring her one afternoon. No one answered. The following day Dr. Gerson announced to the class that Hanna's mother had informed the school her daughter would not be returning for the final exams. She was 'currently receiving urgent medical attention' in a special hospital down south. It was a tragedy, Gerson proclaimed, that something like this should happen to the school's most outstanding student so shortly before the final exams.

Mark's classmates shared his anxiety, and there was much speculation about the nature and state of Hanna's illness. Deeply worried he went back to the new housing estate where Hanna lived. Standing outside the familiar entrance to her apartment, he rang the bell. As with the phone the day before, no one answered. Of course, Mark foolishly realised only now, her mother would have gone with Hanna, wherever she might be. He stood outside the entrance, unable to tear himself away. At this very spot they had held each other not so long ago. When they kissed that night, did he have a premonition of what was going to happen? Was that why he had pleaded with her not to go? To go where? Now she had gone, without letting him know where she was.

The only way Mark could handle the void Hanna's absence left was by concentrating even more on his studies. He prepared himself for the finals as if his life depended on it. Never before had he swotted as hard as this. His anger over what he had to learn became inseparable from the frustration over his inability to find out what had happened to Hanna. He felt as if he had to learn her absence off by heart. Late at night, in deep exhaustion, he began to think of his studies as the gawky, awkward, ever-pale body of Hanna. He found it unbearable to look at the empty chair next to him. He had no sensual fantasies about her, least of all now. Hanna's body remained an assumption impossible to verify. If he loved her, it was not a love of her body.

In early February, Hanna's mother wrote another letter to Old Grammar, thanking class and teachers for their kind thoughts. She wanted everyone to know that Hanna had been very happy at school. She hoped Hanna's classmates would understand her decision to have a private funeral only. The letter was signed 'Respectfully yours'. Mark was struck by that old-fashioned term. It sounded polite, but it also seemed to express a need or desire to keep distance.

Mark was the only one who had actually met Hanna's mother. He remembered the afternoon in their small newly built flat, the kindness she had shown him, how pleased she was he and Hanna had become friends. When Mark rang Hanna's mother she asked him to come to a funeral parlour on the outskirts of town.

Snow fell as he walked the three blocks from the terminus of the tramline to a building that from the outside looked like a garden centre. As soon as Mark had entered, a large door closed soundlessly behind him. He was greeted by a cold, distinguished-looking man dressed in an elegant, dark-striped suit. A mane of silver-grey hair, immaculately manicured hands and incongruously tanned skin gave the mortician the appearance of a waxworks film star. Foolishly Mark wished the funeral director could have been Moritz's father. No one else was present. He must have come too soon. Not even Hanna's mother had as yet arrived. But the undertaker informed him that no one else was expected. He led Mark into an adjoining chapel, in the centre of which stood an open casket surrounded by orchids and roses. They looked unreal. On top of the coffin lay a large crucifix.

'You'll want to be alone.'

The refined dummy withdrew, bowing mechanically as a token of professional respect. Slowly Mark approached the casket, until he could see Hanna's body lying in state. Bride-like she was dressed and covered in white. Her hands lay on a sheet of lace. There was a pink tinge on her pale face. Was she embarrassed by her death, or had she at last regained her strength? As he got closer he noticed it was make-up. Hanna's hair was much shorter. It must have been cut by the mortician. Why? Mark had no idea under-takers interfered with the body. Wasn't there a law against that? With her different hairstyle and fake rosy cheeks Hanna looked a different person. Even in death she seemed ill at ease. What else had they done to her? Only her long eyelashes signalled rest and acquiescence.

Finding it hard to keep his eyes open, he forced himself to see what he did not want to see. Not a sound penetrated from the outside. Why was swallowing so difficult! Cautiously Mark approached the body. As he did so, he unwittingly adopted Hanna's tentative, testing walk. Unnerved by the continued total silence around him made him want to speak. But he remained silent.

He hesitated, wondering whether he would be allowed to touch Hanna's hands. Were there laws or rules of behaviour on how to deal with the dead? Was there an undertakers' school of etiquette? Did funeral directors have to sit for a final examination on death? Mark thought of the waxworks film star as a butler serving corpses.

When their hands met, he quickly withdrew. Their once caressing touch had turned icy cold. No medicine, no rub-bing would make them warm again.

Overcome with impatience and anger, Mark felt the urge to turn back the lacy sheet and strip Hanna naked. He needed to see the fragile body that had carried her through life. What part of herself had she hidden from him?

At last he spoke to her. 'You didn't try hard enough', he rebuked her in a voice choked with tears. 'War children don't die over a bit of blood! Do you have to be the first in every-thing? Couldn't you just go on fainting? Have you forgotten how good it was when you recovered while I was holding you? Did you know the others were teasing us? Whenever I had to take you to the doctor, they said it was one of our dates. "Lucky Mark," they'd say, "she's swooning again!" '

He walked around her coffin. Filled with bitter despair he tried to mock her. 'Best in class and couldn't finish school!

Now I suppose you want to meet me in infinity? I don't give a phi!' He thought of saying things he believed would have shocked her. 'Did you know sex smells like death, Hanna? That's what someone once told me, someone who refused to die. Well, I guess you've found that out for yourself.' He offered a mock apology. 'Sorry, I forgot you weren't interested in sex.'

He needed to be still more brutal to make certain she knew about his loss. Sobbing uncontrollably he hurled his pain at her. 'Good thing is, Hanna, I can spread out, now you're no longer sitting next to me. Looks like I'm going to do all right in Maths and Latin, too,' he boasted, 'even without you. Wanna know why? I copied all of your books. We were going to do the finals together, remember? Aren't you going to wish me luck? Don't bother. I begged you not to go, didn't I? But still you left.'

At last he fell silent, exhausted from grief and self-pity. It wasn't easy talking to the dead. Perhaps there was a need for a school of death after all. The soundproofed, windowless mortuary seemed like a bunker. He was a child again, locked inside the air raid shelter. The war was a killer stalking the dark. One more time he needed to find an escape, to face the Enemy out in the open. Where had he taken Hanna?

Despite his school friends he had always been on his own. Standing at Hanna's open casket Mark felt the full weight of his loneliness. There was no one he could turn to, no one to whom he could talk about Hanna.

In his distress he thought of his mother. It seemed she knew how to talk to the dead. Perhaps she wasn't lost at all. Perhaps it took an illness like hers to understand life. Perhaps, in the end, she was the only one who could teach and comfort him.

The thick carpet and drawn curtains swallowed every sound as he was leaving. Mark scarcely noticed the dark-suited figure of the undertaker approaching him. He was handed an envelope. Walking past a display of open coffins, he nodded an absent-minded acknowledgment, anxious to escape the silent shelter of the dead.

Outside it was still snowing. In no time his bare head and clothes were covered in thick flakes. The world was silently suffocating. A car drove soundlessly past. Mark turned up the collar of his coat. The large ancient pines along the road to the terminal looked like unforgiving sentinels of death. He looked around and found his tracks already obliterated. His body had become a ghost.

The day was as cold and white as Hanna's corpse.

Six weeks after Hanna's cremation Mark graduated top of the class from Old Grammar. He joined his friends Frank Hilmer, Gunnar Nielsen and Mads Olevsen in a wild night of drinking and dancing at the Hansa, an old harbour pub. They were celebrating their freedom. How good it was to be released!

'The war's over!' Mads shouted, prompting a verbal relay.

'At last!' Gunnar triumphed.

'We've survived!' Mark rejoiced.

'We've won!' Frank declared.

They raised their glasses. Intoxicated with themselves and the special moment in their lives, they ordered another round. Some nearby guests wondered about the young men's belated celebration of peace. A grumpy war-disabled drinking rum by himself shook his head, 'Would you believe it, they've noticed at last!' The boys in their exuberance took no notice of him. This was their day, and they were going to make certain it would be a memorable one.

With that in mind Mads went over to the bar to invite a couple of good-looking women to their table. While Frank kept feeding the jukebox, they danced with groping hands, inhaling the young women's sensuous perfume, enjoying the delicious confidence of their own male bodies. Now they had graduated, no one could doubt they were at last fully grown men.

It is true, later that night they got into a fight with a couple of foreign sailors who wanted to dance with their girls. It was an uneven match. They had neither the physical strength nor the alcoholic stamina of the seamen. One by one they were punched to the floor. After helping them up, cleaning their clothes and attending to their cuts and bruises, the women waved goodbye and left with the enemy.

The incident did little to dampen their spirits. They pretended nothing had happened and ordered more drinks. No one would be allowed to spoil the grand occasion. So what if they were defeated by some foreigners? They still considered themselves winners, free men now, ready to enter their future professions and lead the country in a new direction.

By the time Mark got home morning had broken. He was unsure whether the thick fog was outside or inside his head. In a drunken stupor he managed to open the lock to the apartment. He fell in the hallway without waking his mother, staggered on to his room and collapsed in drowsy, restless surrender.

When Mark awoke it was late afternoon. The fog had not lifted, either inside or outside his head. He got up in semi-darkness to discover he was still dressed in last night's clothes. Stale sweat intermingled with the stench of cigarettes and alcohol. Was that the sweet scent of victory?

Stripped naked, Mark noticed the smell of sex. How could that be? He thought of one of his mother's severest reprimands – 'Have you taken leave of your senses?' Apparently he had. (Or had he been with a woman after all?)

In the kitchen he found a note from her, letting him know she had 'gone shopping'. Mark knew what that meant. Fortunately most shopkeepers were aware of her condition. They promised anything she bought would be charged and delivered. Like the letters to her husband, her orders never arrived.

But in recent times her absences had taken a new, worrying turn. More than once his mother had been seen around the harbour, trying to hire a sailing boat big enough to take her to Norway. She had told the boat hirer she was on her honeymoon.

Mark returned to his room. Getting dressed, he stared at the fog-covered window. The small, unlit globe on his desk looked forlorn, as if in the wrong place. Despite last night's celebration of freedom, he had remained a prisoner in his own home. He was comforted by his prized possession, the young student's Zeiss microscope. Placed on a special bench, it was twice as big as the globe and dominated the room. His head was still spinning from last night. The room was moving, as if he were riding on a merry-go-round, his books threatening to fall out of their shelves, the radio and record player ready to get up and walk away. Like poles of an electromagnetic field, only the globe and the microscope remained steady. In his dizziness they formed a place of rest.

He was both proud and ashamed of his mother's generosity. Whatever the nature of her illness, she had given him the best presents of his life.

From the harbour came the regular muffled calls of the foghorn. Why did he always think it was directed at him? His eyes returned to the blind window. In the deafening silence he could hear the ticking of the alarm clock. It entered his head as a relentless throbbing noise. Or was it his own pulse, each beat marking time with an accusing urgency? Unnerved and disenchanted, Mark threw the alarm clock to the floor. His time of celebration had been short-lived.

He continued to look around his room, as if searching for something. At last he started shifting papers across his desk, in the process knocking over a stack of his parents' old notebooks, some of which he had used as diaries.

Startled and suddenly sober, he picked up the heavy fountain pen next to the thick white envelope bearing his name in Hanna's writing, filled the pen from an inkpot bearing the label Montblanc Royal Blue, opened the calendar closest to him and pensively began covering its pages with lines and circles, parallels and tangents, squares and triangles, eyes fixed on the figures as they assumed patterns of a bold and intricate design. He would have preferred writing on glass, covering the fogbound windows of his home, copying a language unspoken and unrecognised.

Soon it was too dark to continue. Rubbing his eyes, he switched on the miniature globe.

Inside his blood the alcohol was still singing, spreading its illusions of promise and despair. Like his blood, Mark remained a captive of his body. In echoes of drunken confidence he was designing blind visions of his life. All his plans had one thing in common. He would have to leave home to find what he was looking for. He would leave the deadly shelter and face The Beautiful Enemy. He would dare his body to discover itself, its mind and soul, its knowledge and idea. He would find the place where absence and death were no longer the only guardians of his life.

He was jolted out of his intoxication by a ring at the front door. Mark knew it would be the police returning his mother to him.

BOOK TWO

THE CALL

'Where, then, are we going? –
Always home.'

Novalis, *Heinrich von Ofterdingen*

I

Whenever Mark's friend Frank Hilmer got into trouble at home, he used to say, more in mock despair than truly disparagingly, 'You can't choose your parents.' It wasn't meant to be hurtful; on the contrary, it was an attempt to make light of recurring problems he had with his family's expectations. As far as they were concerned, his entire future was already fully laid out. All he had to do was follow their advice and instructions. If he did, his life would surely prove a spectacular success.

Mark just wanted his parents to be around. What troubled him was a much more radical thought. He would have rephrased his friend's frustration, saying something like 'You can't choose your country.' Even though he hadn't said it to anyone, he was alarmed by the apparent callousness of what he was thinking. It amounted, at the very least, to disloyalty, a lack of love for his native land, a denigration of his family, home and country. In times of war it would be downright treason. To prove the value of patriotism people were shot. Could there be anything worse than being a traitor to the Fatherland?

Yet the truth was Mark felt he had been held captive by his home town, its never-ending days of grey, of rain and fog, of wind and snow. The town in which he was born had proved a place of death. Oh, there had been nights when he felt almost safe in a cocoon of books and music, imagining a life elsewhere. His room had been an intimate shelter, inviting the world in through distant radio stations, exotic pirate stories and dreams directed by passionate senses. He had kept his little globe lit all through the night. And there were days at St Mary's Wood that had lifted him high above the medieval walls of the city, even though he was lying on the ground of a protected plantation area or at the bottom of a crystal clear brook casting fluid reflections on a current of light. But these moments were rare, and despite their beauty and inspiration they were not strong enough to protect him against the drabness and brutality of the town. All they did was intensify his desire to free himself from the impositions of a coincidental birth.

In the end, the town, like his parents, had died on him. There was nothing left of his home, just familiar streets and buildings and the memory of too many dead. He was angry and ashamed of the generation of his parents and teachers. They had fought, and lost, a war that was not his, even if they kept repeating their lies that they had done it all for their children.

Mark did not believe he was a traitor. But he did believe that he could leave a country, if it had deserted him first. It was a conviction he knew would not be shared by many.

Secretly, he had made plans to extend the freedom he and his friends had celebrated at the Hansa. He had made plans to join the Beautiful Enemy, wherever he might be. The day his mother died, Mark knew that it was time to leave.

He had never flown before. Looking out at the tarmac from the airport's departure lounge he surveyed with suspicion the Super Constellation's bulky silver body, its bold jet propellers and the letters BOAC proudly displayed across its superstructure. Anxious not to reveal any public signs of unease, Mark wondered how a machine that size could actually take off into the sky and stay up there for hours and hours. Even days perhaps. It was Friday afternoon, and he'd been told they wouldn't reach Melbourne till early the next week. Once more his eyes glanced at the potbellied plane that to him began to look more and more like a portly whale. Hardly the kind of getaway vehicle he was familiar with from the gangster movies! This giant was to take him across two continents to the other side of the world! It seemed an outrageous proposition, a wild boast, a self-evident absurdity.

'Super Constellation'. The name at least carried some glamour, but it was a title this graceless monster did not deserve. During the war the enemy had flown elegant fighter planes across Mark's hometown sky, bombing targets at will. The leviathan standing on the tarmac like a well-trained circus performer seemed clumsy and awkward by comparison. 'Super Constellation'! Moby Dick, more likely! Mark forced himself to believe that despite its appearance the strength of the huge metal creature would indeed raise him to the sky and carry him away. There was no choice in his belief. Any moment now he would have to board it as an act of faith. There could be no flight without it.

It had come from enemy territory, he discovered, or rather, the land of the former enemy, arriving in his country as a mere break in the journey to collect displaced persons and refugees. On its global flight his place of birth was listed as no more than a temporary stop. The Super Constellation had only landed for a couple of hours. It was in a hurry to move on.

Mark was not surprised so many refugees had no wish to stay. Now they were all reclassified as emigrants. He had watched them surrender their luggage at the check-in counter, then present their documents to customs officials. What was left of their meagre belongings they carried on their backs like gipsies.

Until their arrival in Australia they would officially remain in transit. Being in flight lent the emigrants yet another, if temporary, identity. When Mark thought of it, their additional classification made sense. While they were flying, they were 'up in the air', in no-man's-land, following a passage without having reached its destination. Still, it was an unfamiliar thought, to cross the world in transit. It added to the exotic nature of flying. In newsreels Mark had seen famous film stars arrive at international airports, looking glamorous, stepping out of planes as if they had come from a different planet. It was most unusual for ordinary people to travel by air. Yet, apart from a handful of paying passengers this flight was carrying poor and desperate survivors of a terrible war, emigrants looking for a new life in another country, and the odd young man searching for his own kind of freedom. Whoever they were, for the duration of their journey they would all be equal.

A loudspeaker announcement urged passengers to proceed to the departure gate immediately. Ground personnel and aircrew, customs officials and security staff grew anxious for them to leave. 'Time to go!' they urged the hesitant emigrants, directing them into a queue. 'Get a move on!' There were tears, but no goodbyes. None of the passengers turned around.

The engine droned and shuddered as Mark tentatively stepped up the ladder to the open cabin doors. He took a quick glance at the silver hull's rivet joints, to make sure they wouldn't fall apart. Inside the cabin everything seemed to be trembling. Above the roaring engines he heard the propellers start to turn, ever increasing the speed and intensity of their rotation. The overhead lockers were rattling, and there was a hissing noise coming from the oxygen supply. The flying whale was shaking and breathing, uncertain whether to surface or not.

There was no turning back now. The glamour of flying quickly made way for more ambivalent feelings. From his allocated window seat Mark kept an eye on the fiercely turning jet propellers. It still seemed to him an audacious assumption that it was safe to fly. His body vibrated with the aircraft's thrust. Racing down the runway, he was willing the take-off, exhilarated by the elation of being in the air at last. In triumphant release Mark hardly registered his own erection. He had abandoned himself to the flight. His body was singing a delirious relief of being airborne.

The old man sitting next to him signalled benevolence in a smile. He had lost almost all of his hair. A few white strands fell to his forehead as he put his arm around the young woman next to him. He turned to Mark. 'This is Esther.' The woman greeted Mark by leaning forward without leaving the old man's embrace. There was something painfully fragile and beautiful about her wide open look, her shiny almond eyes and her long, nearly pitch black hair. Although her face was that of an adult, she had retained the body of a child.

Mark didn't understand the old man's name – was it Shmuel or Samuel? He quickly introduced himself, in his embarrassment adding nervously he hoped they'd have a pleasant flight. Smiling at each other, they settled back in silence. They'd been polite, shown their good manners, made a move. There wasn't much else to say or do. They were complete strangers who happened to share a row of seats on their flight into a new life. Should they crash, they'd be forever united in death. If they made it safely to their destination, they'd never think of each other again. That was all.

But then the old man said, 'I lost everything in the war.' He said it calmly in the manner of a statement. There was no accusation or self-pity in his voice. It wasn't even clear to whom it was addressed.

Without thinking, Mark replied, 'Me too.'

The man sat up and looked at him. Their introductions had been little more than customary social courtesy. Only now was he taking real notice of Mark. He eyed him quizzically.

'But you are – ,' he began.

'– an orphan,' Mark quickly completed. He knew his

words could be misconstrued, but he also believed it to be the truth.

The man whose name was Shmuel or Samuel raised his head and sighed. Holding the hand of Esther, he said, as if to explain something to himself, 'It is evil.' Then, as if presenting his passport, he rolled up the sleeve of his left arm and showed Mark the number on his skin. It was a high figure.

Mark had heard about concentration camps, but never met a survivor. What must this man think of him, his parents, his teachers, his people! How could anyone ever repay his suffering!

'Esther's all I've got left,' he whispered in a hoarse voice. 'All the others died in the camp.' There were no tears in his eyes. He must have said these words too many times before, mostly to himself.

Foolishly, Mark enquired, 'Your wife?'

The old man nodded. 'Three children,' he added. 'My sister. One grandchild.' He patted Mark's arm, as if to comfort him. Then he turned away, not in anger but exhaustion, hugging Esther once more before closing his eyes and waving his hand in a final gesture to let it be. The woman of indeterminable age too had closed her eyes.

Mark was left alone with the window.

The Super Constellation flew in the direction of the late afternoon sun, as if the light were its target. Mark watched its silver metallic wings penetrate hosts of clouds, taking them higher and higher, until at last they reached an altitude of pure, uninterrupted vision. Reflections of bright sunshine seemed to set them on fire. Mark knew, at last he had entered the territory of The Beautiful Enemy.

It took time to get used to cruising on a clear blue ocean of light high above the clouds. He had become part now of the continuous droning of the engines. When the sun set, the snow-covered Alps below shone like fiery, champagne-coloured diamonds. He watched the splendid reflections until at last the spectacle faded into darkness.

Flying through the night was both scary and oddly familiar. How many times had he imagined travelling the world, trying to fall asleep with the lit globe by his bed!

Mark marvelled at being separated from the sky only by glass and welded, riveted sheets of metal. It frightened him when he thought of what little separated him from crashing back to earth. He was sitting on a height of almost thirty thousand feet! Better not look under his seat!

Thousands of lights greeted Mark and his fellow passengers as they descended into Beirut. It looked as though the constellation of stars above were reflected and multiplied on the ground below. Beirut lit up the night, as the lights of all the great cities of the world had done on his small globe. Joining the other passengers for a three-hour wait in the airport's transit lounge, he became frustrated. How often had he sought out Beirut with his fingers on the globe! Now he had actually landed here, entry was denied. The flight hadn't really taken him any closer. How could he get so near, yet still miss out on where he wanted to be! How could he truthfully say he 'had been to Beirut', when he hadn't set foot in the city! In the language of the airline staff he remained a transit passenger, Beirut no more than a 'refuelling stop'.

Waiting for their take-off, Mark's disappointment and frustration gradually melted into exhaustion. When they were finally allowed to board again he was relieved to return to his seat, anxious to fall asleep as soon as possible. He would let himself be cradled by the Super Constellation as it crossed the night sky. But the other passengers took some time to settle down – families with crying children kept changing seats, the man sitting next to him began removing his luggage from the overhead compartment, and in the row behind someone started to sob inconsolably. An old woman's wailing voice kept repeating, 'I'll never see them again!' Mark had forgotten about the noise of the engine, the vibrations in the cabin and the litany of loudspeaker announcements. By the time they were heading down the runway he found himself wide awake again. Already flying had proved not quite as glamorous as he had imagined. At the same time the potbellied plane he had mistrusted began to invoke in him a new sense of loyalty. So what if it didn't look particularly stylish? He was going to barrack for this noisy, inelegant, boisterous upstart called Super Constellation. It's not the handsome team that wins the game.

Esther had taken the old man's seat next to him.

To pass the time Mark imagined himself inside a whale. He pretended they'd all been taken by a monster that would carry them across the sky. From time to time it'd spit them out, only to swallow them whole again.

He surveyed his fellow passengers at rest in their seats like terminal patients, eyes closed, prepared for, ready to submit to, anything. Their very existence was part-rescue, part-torture. Where were they all going, he wondered? Incongruously, the migrants were dressed either in their Sunday best or in clothes that gave away their desperate poverty. Some women wearing village scarves, peasant skirts and sturdy boots clutched their possessions even while they were sleeping. A few paying passengers, sporting casual outfits, displayed their flight experience by the condescending way they ordered drinks from the hostesses and ignored everybody else. Part of their pleasure was to show others that, for them, flying was no big deal.

Even with these privileged travellers on board they had become something of a group, an involuntary family almost, at least for the duration of the journey. They were united by the prevailing mystique, the exotic triumph, the barely sublimated dangers of flying. The whale had swallowed them altogether.

Looking out of the window, as they finally took off into the night, Mark said a silent goodbye to the lights of the big city. Flying in the dark proved even eerier. No longer could he check the state of at least one of the wings, making sure the rivet joints had not dissolved. Nor could he see the approaching clouds that suddenly blotted out the lights below. All at once they were travelling in complete darkness.

After their food-trays had been collected the cabin lights were dimmed. Once more Mark felt like being back home in his room at night, lying on his bed, listening to the radio. He tried to sleep, but found it difficult. As he thought about what he had left behind, every fibre of his being trembled in unison with the vibrating plane. Eyes closed, he conjured up scenes from his dark and rainy home town, its streets he knew so well, the harbour, St Mary's Wood, his old school.

In an unguarded instant he was confronted with the image of his mother. He felt guilty because, no matter how hard he tried, her face remained out of focus. All the apparition retained was the sad beauty of her absent-minded smile. In death, as in life, his mother appeared too preoccupied to commit herself to a full presence in the world. Her knowing eyes seemed to convey she had always been aware life was an impossibility.

What Mark found most upsetting was that, despite strenuous efforts, he was unable to reassemble the fragments of their final moments together.

His mind had blocked out all details of the coroner's report. The horrific nature of her death and the gruesome photographs in the newspaper had obliterated her image from his mind. How helpless he had always been in the love he felt for his mother!

Attempting to reconstruct the terrible event, he kept rehearsing unlikely scenarios for her rescue. But, confronted with the finality of her life and death, he eventually found he had to let her be.

He knew that with her death his own life had changed irrevocably. From now on he would be truly alone. As he tried to fall asleep crossing the night sky, somewhere above the Gulf of Akabar according to his estimates, Mark reflected on his new identity. 'I am an orphan', he repeated what he had said to the old man, then, in a bitter outburst of self-mockery, added, 'an orphan nearly coming of age.' It was a realisation ruling out any self-pity. He wasn't so much an orphan as a young man responsible for himself.

His head was crowded with uncoordinated images. As so often, his thoughts turned into vision. Although his mother's image remained blurred, he tried once more to talk to her. Invaded by signs and reflections, he began to speak with the dead. His brain discovered a code in which his mother came alive. As if she were sitting next to him, he passed on to her the announcement that their next stop was to be Karachi. Perhaps that city would reveal itself as more than just another set of lights nestled in the dark.

Esther awoke from their loss of altitude. Stretching herself, her arm touched his. When she saw her companion still asleep, she turned to Mark. 'Where are we?' she demanded to know.

For him, intermingling with the approaching signs of life thousands of feet below were memories of The Beautiful Enemy bombing his place of birth. Were they diving for a target, aiming for light? As the Super Constellation sliced through the night he saw himself walking again the wet cobbled streets of his home town. In their descent he was entering a hovering darkness uniting past and present in a no-man's-land, the most dangerous and heavily guarded section of any border.

To distract from the impending landing manoeuvre he asked Esther, 'Where's your home?' She seemed surprised by his question. Stopping abruptly her attempts to rearrange her hair, she looked at him in puzzled amazement. 'Why, Israel, of course.' It was the voice of a child, but the reply carried the tone of a particularly patient teacher.

Mark quickly echoed her response. 'Of course.' He wondered whether she was referring to the new state of Israel.

'But where do you come from?' he tried again. Esther had stuck a couple of hairpins in her mouth. As she took them out, the old man raised himself in his seat and answered,

'We're originally from Krakow in Poland.' He helped Esther fasten her seatbelt.

'So Jews always have at least two homelands', Mark thought. If they were going to settle in Australia, they'd have a chance to make it their third home. Mark felt a pang of envy. How comforting it must be, to know that wherever you were going, you would be going home!

They taxied the tarmac of Karachi Airport, back in the lit-up world. The transit lounge exuded an exotic sweet smell. Mark again despaired over the restrictions of his movements. Had he been allowed to walk through the customs door, he would have truly been in Karachi. As it was, he had to be content with inhaling the spicy scent of an exotic place remaining beyond his reach. Why wasn't Sannes with him now! Once more the exhausted and disappointed travellers were kept in anonymous transit lounges, watched over by security guards dressed in bizarre uniforms, some carrying old-fashioned rifles. What were they defending? Mark recognised a tall Sikh sporting a twirled moustache and dark red turban as the proud-looking stranger in an illustration from *Tales of India*, a travel and adventure book of his childhood.

The wait proved much longer at this airport. Large ceiling fans sliced the humid air, unable to cool it down. The sweet smell began to nauseate him. Finding it difficult to breathe, he wondered what it would be like outside, in the overcrowded city of millions they had heard so much about in geography lessons at Old Grammar. Would the air be even heavier? Discreetly he observed the locals, marvelling at their tanned skin, their brown eyes, the rapidity of their speech. They seemed an excitable lot, strangely tense, keen to use their body to express emotions. Everyone appeared determined to persuade everybody else. Of what?

He followed the graceful movements of barefoot, braided women sweeping the floor as if paying homage to a fastidious but benevolent god. How beautiful they were! Mark tried to imagine their homes. Would they really be as pitiful as they had seemed in his geography textbook? How could they be, with hard-working women like these?

Home! The long flight continually forced him to think about the meaning of home. How far removed he was from his place of birth after just twenty-four hours! He had a rough idea of the distance, if it could be measured by geography alone. He had left behind all and nothing. The harbour, the town, St Mary's Wood – his mother, Hanna ... They had all been a part of him. He had left behind the people he loved because they had left him. Death had claimed his home. Waiting for his father, separated from his mother, had his early years not also been a kind of transit? Home, too, had been a flight destination. He had got close to it, but in the end it had remained outside his reach.

As he watched the graceful movements of the airport sweepers, the words of the state radio's missing persons tracing service returned to Mark, the repetitive, monotonous announcements: 'Missing; served in; last seen; present whereabouts; any information.' Like heartbeats these unanswered appeals would stay with him forever. For he had done something like his father – he had left home, never to return. But unlike his father, he knew there was no one waiting for him.

Back in the confined spaces inside the Super Constellation, Mark tried replacing the whale image with that of a giant womb delivering him to a distant birth, but found the analogy too disturbing. It reminded him that he had once lived inside his mother. How could any young man put himself back in that position? It was, well, unnatural. Too daringly intimate, like thinking about his mother as a woman being made love to by his father.

Racing down the runway Mark was again possessed by a sense of simultaneous abandonment and total commitment, an erotic arousal of life and death. Even before take-off there could be no return. Conscious of his own passivity, he had to restrain himself from calling out: 'Yes, yes, yes!' They were leaving at last. They were flying again. He was no longer in earthbound transit.

After they had risen above the clouds the reassuringly calm voice of the captain seemed something of an anti-climax. Mark listened to the dispassionate litany of twenty thousand feet, outer temperature, air turbulence, weather forecast and approximate landing time in Singapore. Everything about their flight was pre-programmed. Nothing unusual was expected. How could this be? Mark burst out laughing at the false sense of security conveyed by the announcement. Nothing untoward would happen, unless it happened.

Through the open door of the cockpit he had caught sight of a multitude of lights and switches, buttons and levers, as well as a screen displaying bold interconnected lines of a navigational chart. Despite the dashboard's complex coordination of instruments and controls it seemed a curiously familiar sight.

Esther and Shmuel – he had overheard the ageless woman call the old man by his name – quietly submitted to the rituals of flight. Every now and then they whispered or mumbled to each other words he could not understand. Mark surmised from their apathy they were used to being shoved around. He did not want to intrude on their privacy, their experiences, their grief. Mourning seemed to have become their normal response to life. It held no more surprises for them. In their defeat they had developed new, impenetrable defences. Their unconditional dependence on each other built its own emotional shelter. He left them alone.

'I'm an orphan,' Mark thought again, then quietly corrected himself, 'I'm on my own.' The stewardess came to check whether he was a passenger sponsored by the Department of Immigration. When he confirmed his status she made him sign a form before announcing, 'You'll be getting out in Melbourne, then.' As if to explain her encouraging smile, she added, 'I'm from Melbourne.'

Mark knew all along where he was going to 'get out'. What he really would have liked to know was what was going to happen to him then. But, of course, that was not something an airline stewardess would be able to tell him, even if she was from Melbourne. Still, he was strangely reassured by her comment. At the very least it confirmed Melbourne did indeed exist, and this plane was definitely going there. Any certainties were welcome!

Sometimes Mark thought of himself as an impostor on the run. Where he came from, fleeing one's home, 'emigrating' was perceived as something frivolous or shameful, if not downright dishonourable. Was it possible to escape his origin, or was he born to remain forever who he was? Would moving to the other side of the world turn him into a different person? Could he ever become somebody else? He could hear the voice of his German teacher quoting a line from a Hölderlin poem: '*Das meiste nämlich vermag die Geburt.*' 'For birth determines most in life.' Most, he thought, but not everything.

Imagining a kind of rebirth inside the uterine hull of a Super Constellation was the kind of crazy thing an intercontinental flight could do to you. He would never get used to flying, not long distance, with days and nights in the air. What could be more frustrating than refuelling stops at some of the world's most famous cities where all he could see were their lights as they landed! As the airports' transit lounges were clearly designed to invoke languor and stupor, Mark decided to rename them 'trance lounges'.

Inside the cabin the smell of food, clothing, sweat and human flesh continued to accumulate. Rows and rows of crumpled up seats took on the look of a dormitory of unmade beds. More and more, passengers became victims of a forced intimacy. It was as though they had grown into one body. After a couple of hours the stench from the tiny toilets permeated the air. Day and night the cabin was filled with sounds of moaning, crying and snoring.

Mark listened to the collective body sharing its hunger

and digestion, revealing its exhaustion and mortality. He had never been in a camp, but he was beginning to understand how the total lack of privacy could become an early stage of terror. Being a passenger had made him an inmate of a body camp in the sky. He shuddered. But then he thought of Esther and Shmuel, and he felt ashamed.

He had joined a body of refugees, displaced persons and asylum seekers on a collective flight. It was time to acknowledge he belonged with them. Once more Mark rehearsed his new identity. 'I'm an assisted migrant'. It sounded wrong. The bureaucratic classification failed to identify him. There were many reasons why people left their home. He knew his were different from those with whom he shared the flight, haunted by the knowledge that almost all had suffered at the hands of his own people. How, then, could he possibly claim their kinship! He was an impostor. Whole families were clinging to pieces of pitiful belongings, whispering subserviently, eyes begging for encouragement or approval, exhausted children in their Sunday best, crying or reciting nursery rhymes in their native language. Mark knew only too well who they were. He recognised them as refugees, just like those who had come to his home town immediately after the war.

'I am a refugee', he tried again. Wasn't he too fleeing his home? Or was he trying to escape himself? Was that why he felt guilty in the company of those who wanted to remain themselves, but had been forced out of their own country, separated from their families and friends, precisely because of who they were and who they wanted to remain? What was the official category for an only child, a young man who had lost his parents and a girl he loved, whose home had condemned him to living with the dead? Where did he fit in? Was there a provision for someone like him in the classifications of Australia's Department of Immigration? Was there any group he could become part of without feeling dishonest, fraudulent and deceptive? Would there be no end to his isolation? His despair left him exhausted.

By the time the plane touched down in Singapore he had given up finding the right word to describe who he was, or might become. Despite his shame, perhaps he did belong to a family of displaced persons after all. Did one have to be like others in order to belong?

While they were cruising on the runway Esther and Shmuel sat like dummies in their seat, seemingly oblivious to what was going on. Their apathy began to irritate Mark. Wasn't there anything they could get excited over? They had just landed in Singapore! The old man had his eyes closed, while Esther pretended to read a magazine. Mark could tell by the way she turned the pages that she was not really interested.

'Well, here we are,' he tried drawing her back to the real world. 'Or rather, we're nearly there.' It was a feeble attempt at being witty. Esther looked at him politely and smiled. How gloriously beautiful her eyes were! After all they must have witnessed Mark thought of them as a defiant beauty. He, too, had seen death while he was young, but nothing like what he had read about the sufferings of Jews.

Why had Shmuel shown him the tattooed number on his arm? Mark wondered. Had he done it to accuse him? Shmuel must have recognised where he had come from. Mark remembered something about the sins of the fathers descending on following generations. But perhaps Shmuel had shown him the concentration camp number because it was his only means of identification. Long ago he had watched Elsa in their backyard clap her hands and bow to the wall. What was a Jew, he had wondered. As always, his teachers had not been able to give him an answer.

Mark looked like a monk absorbed in meditation as he entered the Singapore 'Trance Lounge', joining the ritual procession through bargain temples. Outside, the world was reciting its prayer-wheel of efficiency, technology and commerce. Life at the airport was a precision exercise of starts and landings, arrivals and departures, crowded with luggage trolleys, catering and refuelling vehicles.

His view was partly obstructed by a row of tall palms outside the terminal, their fan-shaped leaves gently swaying at the top. Set against the horizon of the late afternoon sun they looked part-temple guards, part-sacred dancers. He watched the graceful movement of their long, fan-shaped, pinnate leaves with awe and fascination. Unfortunately he could not see whether the trees were bearing coconuts. Their stem seemed to consist of scale-like bark. Where he came from, palms were symbols of paradise. Would there be palm trees where he was getting off?

Mark used his transit pass as a fan to ward off the stifling heat. The overcrowded lounge quickly resembled their flight cabin – an untidy mess of jam-packed humanity. Exhausted parents, many still dressed in winter clothes, attended to crying, tired and thirsty children. He watched a group of emigrants writing glossy postcards to people they'd left behind. Even refugees and displaced persons knew someone who had stayed at home. Were their greetings from 'The Jewel of the East' meant as a 'sign of life', a pretence indication they had been there? Mark noticed the popular choice of cards – exotic landscapes featuring palms at sunset.

They flew through another night before reaching the coastline of Australia. Just before sunrise they touched down for a refuelling stop at Darwin. This time Mark and his fellow-passengers were not confined to the transit lounge. What a relief! Walking behind a high wire fence, unsure on their feet, they eagerly took in the fresh early morning air. They may have looked like prisoners in an exercise yard, but in fact they felt mostly relieved. It was good to breathe freely again. A strong wind was blowing. All they could see were barracks and what appeared to be military installations. Although Mark had identified a few houses as they came in to land, no city was evident. Covered in dry overgrown grass, the landscape looked unfamiliar, desolate and inhospitable. Gathered around a few leafless, ghostly looking trees were strange, crippled shrubs that appeared lifeless. 'Better not look too closely', Mark decided, as he read the disappointment and concern on his co-passengers' faces. This had to be some sort of outpost, not the real Australia. In the brochures of the Immigration Department the photographs of Sydney and Melbourne looked much like European cities, except they had not been destroyed by war.

Worse was to come. On the last stretch of their flight all they could see from their windows were vast uninhabited areas of red rock and soil, occasionally crossed by serpentine rivers. Mark couldn't help thinking of Gerson's philosophy classes back at Old Grammar. A rueful smile came over him. 'The world is made of fire and water.' Down there it must have been more fire than water. They appeared to be flying above a desert of death.

While the Super Constellation was taking them across the wild and barren Australian outback, the blurred image of his mother reappeared in the strange formations of the country below, hovering like a mirage, staying with him even as he closed his eyes. 'Mutti!' His lips formed the familiar word without making a sound. He had taken her death with him. He would not be able to ignore her presence. Already she had become part of the Australian landscape.

Back home, the papers had called it a disaster, a tragic accident that should never have happened. His mother was not a water person; she could barely swim. Not that it would have made any difference, the way things turned out.

In his dazed exhaustion the droning of the engines became one with images of the country below. Shapes and patterns he had first encountered under the microscope, russet-coloured vessels on a sky-blue current, swamped his mind to the monotonous sounds from a drone-pipe. A vast landscape of death claimed and entered him. He was invaded by its inescapable, all-consuming presence. Once more it felt as if his body were flying. How much longer to its destination? Was there no end to this flight? The territory below bore no signs of life. He became alarmed. Had he escaped from one place of death, only to arrive at another?

The week before graduation he had attended a public lecture on Existentialism. The speaker had made light of death, insisting it was not a philosophical problem. When asked how he personally felt about dying, he brushed the question aside, claiming it was unworthy of humans to be concerned with their mortality. Mark's immediate response had been the man could have never loved. For it was love that had taught him to think beyond himself. From Hanna, the girl whose blood disease he shared, he had learnt that caring was just that – a thinking beyond oneself. People who didn't care were people who didn't think. What had offended him at school was that his teachers didn't care about the quality and motivation of thought. Those he had loved and lost remained alive in his thinking. (Was that what mathematicians meant when they insisted parallels met in infinity?) He continued to care about Hanna, his father and his mother. Thinking of them meant thinking with them. In their death they remained part of his thoughts and feelings. It had offended him deeply hearing the philosopher dismiss death as of no consequence.

According to the captain, they had passed Sydney to the East almost an hour ago. Mark was disappointed. He would have liked to have looked out and seen the biggest city of Australia, if only to reassure himself that people actually lived on this seemingly empty and desolate island continent. Instead, all he could make out were endless patterns of soil and rock, colour and light, mountains and rivers. Mark sensed it would be a country strong, cruel and demanding enough to absorb or suppress his native landscape, the sights and sounds, the people and buildings, the foggy days and rainy streets he had called home.

The announcement that they were about to start their descent into Melbourne took Mark by surprise. So there was to be an end to the flight after all! He looked at Shmuel, the old

Jew, and his ageless, beautiful but elusive companion. They did not seem at all disturbed by their imminent arrival. Now, so close to his destination, Mark himself wasn't sure whether he was anxious or relieved. Could he assume that soon he would simply leave the plane, take a bus to the city, find work and a place to live? Would an 'Immigration Department passenger' be allowed that kind of freedom? Truth was he had no idea what was going to happen next.

Mark remembered the jubilant shouts of triumph he had shared with Frank Hilmer, Gunnar Nielsen and Mads Olevsen while celebrating their freedom at the Hansa. How foolishly confident they'd been!

Below, the patterned red and brown landscape had dramatically turned to green. Suddenly the country looked 'civilised' and orderly. Mark could make out individual farms and a few roads linking them, which, from the plane, looked like pale blue veins. At last they had left the landscape of the dead behind. Then, just as abruptly, the outskirts of the city emerged. That large, flat expanse consisting of symmetrical squares put together like a jigsaw puzzle had to be Melbourne. On the far horizon Mark could see water.

During their descent they barely flew above rows and rows of single, almost identical houses. It was a sobering sight for Mark who had imagined a more exciting destination. From what he could make out, the settlement below could hardly be compared to a European city. It looked improvised, incomplete, temporary. He had to remind himself they were still only crossing the outer suburbs. Even so, he worried. Would he have to fit his new life into the rigid pattern underneath? Would he end up living in one of those drab, identical bungalows? Nervously Mark was on the look-out for the city centre, the spires of churches, the town hall, museums, galleries, government buildings, railway stations, traffic, busy intersections, parks and squares. All he could see were endless rows of similar houses built along symmetrical streets.

The plane's shadow was superimposed on the miniature

puzzle below. Anxiously he followed its path above the roofs of the sprawling city. It was a curious way of watching himself. For a brief moment he thought he was being shadowed by Shmuel and Esther.

As they got closer and closer to the ground, the engines started their familiar rattle, then the whole plane began to shake. The wheels were noisily dislodged from the under-carriage. Mark looked around. In the faces of the arriving immigrants he could read how they responded to the rattling engines with their own tremble of relief and apprehension.

Just when it looked as though they were going to slice the roof off a house Mark saw the runway. The plane no longer cast a shadow. They were on the ground at last.

Impatient passengers rose to check their hand luggage and personal belongings. They had been advised not to leave anything behind. Esther looked enquiringly at her guardian. Shmuel gently shook his head.

'I wish you a happy new life.' The old man took his leave with patriarchal European formality. They bowed and shook hands. When Shmuel prompted Esther to say her own good-bye, she seemed confused. Staring at Mark, she slowly rose from her seat. In her bewilderment she whispered, 'You too!' He looked into the deep almond eyes of her beautiful face, unable to laugh at the apparent misunderstanding. He would have liked to hold her damaged body, to embrace all of her, but she quickly turned away.

One by one they were directed to a low yellow brick ter-minal. Above its windows a sign read ESSENDON AIRPORT. Mark and his fellow-passengers were herded into a customs and immigration reception hall. Soon overflowing queues reached back to the outside. The long flight and mercilessly hot afternoon sun first caused a pregnant woman, then an old man to faint. Hungry and exhausted children cried in their own languages, 'I want to go home!' Through the windows Mark watched young luggage handlers carelessly unloading the meagre belongings of the new arrivals.

Even from inside the hall he became aware of a dazzling, glaring light, so different from the European sun. The sharp contours it projected gave an impression of looking through binoculars. How could he be bleary-eyed with such overly precise vision? What he saw seemed to be transparent, as if carrying an X-ray of itself. In such light it would be difficult to hide. Or was all this an optical illusion, the result of being tired and over-sensitive? Whatever the reason, right now his sight had acquired a different perception. Like a microscope, it no longer took in an object as a whole, but dissected it into many parts. Leaving the terminal after customs clearance Mark saw not the building, but the pattern of its composition of bricks.

He looked back, searching for Shmuel and Esther, but could not find them. In the vastness of the continent it was unlikely he would ever see them again. For nearly two days they'd been captives of the confined spaces of the Super Constellation, eating and sleeping next to each other, sharing their fateful escape from what had been their home, only to be separated again as if they had nothing in common.

Two hours later the migrants and their luggage were put on a bus that was to take them to a place called Bonegilla. They were not told how long their journey would take. They would be more comfortable travelling through the night, officials reassured them. January's heat might cause severe discomfort to those not used to it. Everything was taken care of.

Mark noticed they were driving north, back in the direction of the land of the dead. Disembodied spirits outside the windows accompanied them. He was the only one who remained awake. The rest of the passengers seemed to have lost all consciousness. What was he doing on this ghost-ride? When he moved to the front, near the driver's seat, he could see it was a cloudless starry night. There was a full moon, as incongruously bright as the light's precision in the late afternoon. The movement of the bus had a lulling effect, but his nerves remained on edge. From underneath the driver's door an invisible creature blew its hot breath. The road was beckoning him with dark reflections. Alarming images, patterns and designs emerged from the night, pretending to be animals, trees or passing cars. A branch was tapping at the window.

Mark knew he was not alone. As he looked out he saw his mother looking in. Her image was stark now, overly focussed, shining on him like a transparent dark sun.

II

In the beginning was the camp.

Mark had read and heard about field camps, school camps, scout camps, holiday camps, military camps, prisoner camps, training camps, refugee camps and concentration camps. Sometimes, during summer vacations, he and his school friends had gone camping along the shores of the outer harbour. *Campus*, he recalled from Latin class, meant 'open country, field or battlefield', leading to German *Kampf*, 'struggle, combat, battle'. The camp was in the early stages of transformation from rural peace to military conflict.

Although he had never been inside a place where troops had been lodged, Mark instantly recognised at Bonegilla signs of their prior occupation. During the war, would his father have been kept in such confinement? Was that where the Enemy had hidden their prisoners, some never to be released?

Mark had himself become a refugee, a displaced person, a prisoner even. How could that be? The war was long over. He had come to this country to leave the rule of death behind. Yet on his arrival he was put in a military camp, thinly disguised as a migrant reception centre. Did freedom always begin with imprisonment? What a role reversal from having been a native resident all his life! He would never be a native again. From now on his closest relatives would be refugees like Herr Kirsch and that strange young woman he had accompanied to the Church of the Holy Ghost.

He remembered the resentment and suspicion with which the locals had reacted to the arrival of refugees from the East. It seemed he was now put in the very same position.

An official in army-like uniform directed him past a manned barrier to long rows of crude wooden barracks looking like oversized chicken pens. Following a zigzag of dusty tracks they stopped in front of an unpainted hut marked '17'. Mark entered it by way of a couple of half-broken wooden steps. The heat inside was so intense he instantly felt nauseous. Exhausted and close to fainting, he dropped the two suitcases, his only luggage. An instant cloud of dust was raised. Squatting on the floor crowded with empty beer bottles and self-rolled cigarette butts, an unshaven, uncombed stupefied threesome, dressed in what appeared to be identical shorts and singlets, eyed him coolly.

Yawning, then smacking his lips with relish, one finally grunted, 'Don't worry, you'll get used to it. The door doesn't shut. We leave it open day and night.' Mark recognised the voice of a fellow-prisoner.

'Ja,' another added in a thick accent as he threw a bottle top past Mark. 'Australia's committed to an open door policy.' The drunk, down-at-heel residents cackled and howled, intoxicated as much by the oppressive heat as by alcohol.

'There's nothing here. Make yourself at home!' Another slurred voice came from the corner of the room. It wasn't clear whether it was mocking him or bidding him a sardonic welcome.

How did he end up here? At school he had read some works by the French Existentialists. Camus' *L'Étranger*, for example. 'There's nothing here.' How incongruous! That scathing piece of sarcasm mumbled by a drunk inmate could have come from the novel his teachers had praised for its 'insight into the human condition'. Even Gerson had praised the Existentialists in his philosophy class. Had he been allocated the role of the imprisoned stranger? Was this 'nothing' going to be his new home?

Anxious to escape the heat inside, he stood near the door as they exchanged their names like passwords into indifference. Mark was deeply disturbed by his room-mates' morale. They were burnt-out people in a burnt-out landscape, defeated by the rigours and boredom of the camp. He turned down their offer of cigarettes and left the shack. 'You can't escape!' they called after him in bitter despair.

He retraced his path from 'Hut 17' to the entrance of the camp, alarmed by the realisation that he, too, was trapped. The huts he passed were overflowing with people. Children played in the dust. Women had hung out their washing to dry. There was no shade anywhere. The camp had been bared of all trees.

As he approached the manned barrier he took a closer look at the dead landscape. Behind the barbed wire fence the grass had turned yellow-brown. On arrival only a few hours earlier, they'd been told it had not rained in Bonegilla for over a year and that during the months of January and February temperatures regularly reached 'one hundred'. According to Mark's arithmetic that equalled about 38 degrees Celsius. Back home it rarely rose above the mid-twenties. (Why was he still using that expression – 'back home'?) Although it was only early morning, the heat had already become unbearable. In the distance Mark could see what looked like a lagoon surrounded by a couple of dead trees. A flock of large white birds had settled on their bare branches. Their animated screeches sounded like that of parrots. Despite the heat he did not move. His first confrontation with the open Australian landscape fascinated and horrified him. It seemed appropriate that he was looking at it through a fence. What he saw was not 'nothing', but he had no words to describe it. It was a *L'Étranger* scenery, a composition of death, a painting of absence, a vision of hell. The sight of forlorn nature matched Mark's despair perfectly.

Next to the camp's entrance was a general store. Mark sauntered over to it, attracted more by the promise of shade than the desire to buy anything. Above its entrance hung a sign 'Welcome to Australia!' Inside, the first thing he recognised were endless rows of the brand of cigarettes his room-mates had offered him. Capstan. In this hot, humid, dry inland the brand name seemed like a mirage. The only possible mooring would have been in the small lagoon outside the camp local staff referred to as a 'billabong'. None of the inmates knew what it meant.

Most of the migrant customers bought washing powder, toiletries, soft drinks, ice-cream, fly-spray and tobacco products. The camp appeared not to provide any but the most basic of its residents' personal needs. Mark wondered how much money they were given.

The answer came to him the following morning when he witnessed dozens of men stripped to the waist climb into open trucks. He was told they were being driven to farms to work as day labourers. Others were transported to distant orchards to pick fruit. They returned to the camp in the late afternoon, anxious to buy enough cigarettes and beer to see them through the night. The tired men were welcomed back by groups of women who made sure that at least some of the daily earnings would be left for family expenses. Many of these men had been working on the land, Mark learned, for more than six months.

As he slowly returned to 'Hut 17' the subdued activities in the camp were interrupted by a loudspeaker announcement. Incredibly, it was in the language most residents would have come to know in previous European internment and POW camps as the enemy's tongue. There was going to be a film night under stars, a crackling disembodied voice declared, and everyone was welcome. Parents were encouraged to bring their children. After some high-pitched sounds the message was repeated in English. Listening to the announcement Mark was reminded of the precarious nature of his position – to many of his fellow-inmates he was a representative of the hated enemy whose deadliness they had come to escape, while he had been sent to this camp because he wanted to live with the Beautiful Enemy. Would he ever be able to speak to the others?

Different noises were coming from the hot and dusty rows of huts. Women were busy hanging out their washing, attending to their children or engaging in animated exchanges with their temporary neighbours. As he walked past, Mark could tell some were Poles, others Czechs, while the houses closest to the fence appeared to be occupied by people from Yugoslavia. Single men were kept separate from families, irrespective of their nationality.

To get into his own hut he had to climb over the German Wolfgang, who occupied the top step. His other room-mates were still lounging on the floor. Their greetings seemed surly, their stares blind, their bodies unfamiliar with the upright position. Dushan, a wiry dark-haired unshaven man in his early twenties, had stored the newcomer's belongings next to an unoccupied bunk. Mark took it as a sign of acceptance. On his arrival Tadeusz, the stocky Pole whose age Mark found impossible to guess, raised his left hand to acknowledge his room-mate's return. He looked like he was taking an oath of allegiance. Tadeusz inhaled the smoke of his Capstan as if it were a religious exercise.

'What happens now?' Mark asked no one in particular.

After a prolonged silence the sharp, abrupt syllable of a single German word filled the air: 'Nix!' Wolfgang's language could make 'nothing' sound like a sharp axe or a precise explosion. Mark could understand why so many people found German an ugly language.

Resigned, Mark took his seat on the flight of steps next to Wolfgang. Already he had become one of them. The day grew long.

Did it make sense to speak of a beautiful and an ugly language? He had made up the term 'Beautiful Enemy' to escape the squalor of his home, the endless darkness of hunger, fear and lies. If Australia was part of the Beautiful

212

Enemy, it had not welcomed him with open arms – or the others who had suffered under his people's aggression. What had made him think he could join the 'enemy' without becoming someone new? Changing from an 'ugly' to a 'beautiful' language would be part of a much more devastating transformation. The new country would demand he become another person.

A howling wind rose, blowing clouds of sand, paper, cans and cigarette boxes through the narrow, dusty tracks. The four residents of 'Hut 17' watched the sand and refuse as if it were a passing parade. From next door they could hear the blaring sounds of a radio. Its programs seemed to consist mostly of advertisements they failed to understand. All they could hear was a range of enticingly silky or brutal voices urging them to buy. Perhaps the sounds reflected the promise of the new land, its gentle lure of harsh demands.

Mark had been told to listen to the loudspeaker. When the time was right it would call him. His immediate future would depend on this call. It would almost certainly come from the camp's employment office. He might be lucky. Who knows, perhaps they'd find a job for him in Melbourne. Getting to Melbourne was considered the first prize. Almost everyone in the camp dreamt of going to Melbourne. Once more Mark found himself listening to a tracing service, except this time he was waiting for his own name. He realised it would be the only way to escape from Bonegilla.

In the meantime he would be waiting. They were all waiting to be called.

Some of the inmates busied themselves learning the new language. Mark had been told about classes he could attend. During lunch at the camp's mess he could hear a smattering of English in the midst of a host of other tongues. Usually they were expressions relating to food and work, plus a couple of swearwords they had picked up. The mixture of native and foreign, old and new sounded disturbing, like a third language of brutal syntax and tortured pronunciation.

Those who spoke it seemed somehow injured, as if their bodies were marked by wounds that would not heal.

Although Mark had studied English at school, he knew he, too, was carrying an accent that would identify him as a foreigner. Like most inmates he was unlikely to lose it. He would speak the language of the Beautiful Enemy without it being his beautiful language. Bonegilla was a Babylon of accents, a camp of the unclean. Whenever its occupants spoke they were bleeding. There was nothing to be done about it.

Mark continued to walk the grim and barren precinct. By now temperatures had risen well above thirty-five. Apart from the pitiful huts there was no shade. Dead grass and weeds marked territories of abandonment on both sides of the fence. One glowing cigarette butt would have been enough to set them alight. In a strange way the dry landscape complemented the dullness of the camp's military discipline.

That night they all decided to watch the movie in the open air cinema. Wolfgang had persuaded someone working in the camp's kitchen to provide them with two crates of beer. By the time they settled in their deckchairs they were already heavily drunk. The place was crowded with well-behaved, well-dressed captives determined to enjoy a night out as they had done back home. Like young lovers they were looking forward to an evening of unspecified promise and excitement.

Mark thought it was more of a conjuring trick. He had hardly taken his seat when he was startled by an outburst of stuttered laughter. Introduced by a cackling kookaburra and a grazing kangaroo, the screening had opened with an officious newsreel bearing a close resemblance to propaganda movies he had seen shortly after the war, the 'Cinesound News'. Soon the animals made way for an authoritative male voice confidently reciting the glory of Australia, its droughts and floods, sheep and cattle, mining and shipping. What a challenge and what a privilege it truly was to belong to 'Her Majesty's Jewel of the South'! The voice cracked with emotion. 'There she goes, our beautiful young Queen! Long may she reign over her loyal subjects here in the young and privileged Commonwealth of Australia! God speed, your Majesty, god speed!' The man seemed close to tears. The film showed Queen Elizabeth and Prince Philip boarding the royal yacht. Bonegilla's captive audience remained noncommittal. Mark wondered what the Catholic Film Service would have made of this. 'Wholesome entertainment for the entire family' or 'BYP', banned for young people?

During and after the newsreel the spectators were busy exchanging information and gossip. Tomorrow the store would have a special on washing powder, and it was rumoured next week a busload of Greek migrants were expected. All agreed their arrival would put an even greater strain on the already overcrowded camp.

The wind and the heat had at least died down. Up in the sky a multitude of stars shone brightly. They seemed so close, almost within reach. Mark sank back into the canvas of the deckchair. At regular intervals Tadeusz passed him another bottle of lukewarm beer.

When the large screen turned into a pale flicker the spectators grew restless. Although no one knew its title, they were impatiently waiting for the main feature. In the ensuing tension a woman a few rows ahead suddenly started screaming and shouting in a language Mark did not understand. Sobbing incomprehensible accusations she began hitting the man sitting next to her. Attempts were made to calm her while she continued to remonstrate with him. As she ran past his row Mark saw she was young and beautiful. Shortly afterwards the man she had attacked followed her.

The others hardly raised an eyebrow. What they had witnessed was a familiar scene. Nervous breakdowns were a daily occurrence, part of life at Bonegilla, its air of unreality, the tensions and incongruities of inhabiting an overcrowded void in the middle of nowhere. Determined to ignore the dried and burnt-out surroundings, desperate men and women, survivors of a war that didn't seem to go away, endeavoured to prepare themselves for the promise of a new life. It was a make-believe projection requiring nerves of steel.

The main feature turned out to be a Doris Day movie. Halfway through the show a black cockatoo, attracted by the light, flew into the giant screen, screeching its violent protest and casting live shadows across the actors' images. The intrepid spectators treated the incident as part of the performance. It took more than an intervention of reality to unsettle those who had learned to live double lives.

Later that night, in 'Hut 17', Mark and his room-mates were kept awake by the sounds of urgent love-making mingled with cries of despair. It was impossible, Mark found, to separate them.

When the heat woke him in the morning the camp was in uproar. Tadeusz, Dushan and Wolfgang were nowhere to be seen. The narrow lane outside was choked with an agitated crowd.

Leaning half-naked against the doorframe Mark pieced together from the welter of languages that a young Yugoslav woman had drowned herself during the night. She'd been found in the 'billabong' just outside the camp.

In response to the general upheaval loudspeaker announcements urged inmates to remain calm and vigilant. The authorities would be carrying out a thorough investigation of how the victim had managed to 'escape'. To that effect the commandant would address all residents after a general roll-call in the assembly hall at nine o'clock sharp.

So Bonegilla was a place where people committed suicide in small lakes called billabongs. Gillabone – billabong. What sort of deadly words were they? Was that what happened where he was now living? Or had the words come to him in a dream? Had Sannes come back to haunt him? Could the woman have been the one who had rushed past him as she ran out of the cinema? What had she been fighting over with the man? Why had she drowned herself in the clean, shining dark of an Australian night?

Pensively Mark went inside, grabbed a towel and walked across to the communal washrooms. He was wide awake now, but the memory of the distraught woman would not leave him. Perhaps a cold shower would wash it away.

The toilet facilities lay deserted. Entering the men's washroom he was overcome with revulsion. It smelt of urine, sweat and soap. Cracked tiles were covered with blood spatters from squashed dead mosquitoes. The cement floor's drain was blocked by thick, yellow-green slime. In an open cubicle tepid water came pouring down on Mark with an irregular burst. As it exploded on the floor, it sounded like remonstrating captive voices. He listened intently with his eyes closed.

It was pouring unclean, muddy memories, all the oily, brackish water of his native harbour. He stood there perfectly still, surrendering himself to the brown-coloured, luke-warm sludge. His face drowned in corpses floating in slow motion. Mark found it impossible to haul his mother to the surface. Whenever he held on to her they both immediately sank to the bottom of the harbour. Where was Sannes? Surely he would still be alive.

'You finished?' somebody asked.

Mark did not move or open his eyes. The polluted, smelly water continued to gush down, a maelstrom enveloping his naked body.

Somewhere in the stuttering bursts of swill Mark thought he recognised the pathetic figure of 'The Emperor', his gym teacher from Old Grammar, floating as if someone was holding him in a swimming harness. He was busy saving his own life. Mutti should've learnt to swim.

Mark saw the school of herring cadavers. Nothing to be afraid of. They're poisoning them across the border, Frank Hilmer's convinced. He'd seen shoals of silver herrings in the sky, a shiny squadron of the Beautiful Enemy. He'd seen them because he wasn't hiding underground with all the others.

Now he was drowning, just like his mother, only on dry land. In a place called Bonebillagong. A nothing-sort-of-place, with just enough what-d'you-call-it to kill yourself.

It felt like someone was pissing on him. In his disgust Mark tried to leave the shower, but found himself pinioned by memories. His mother had been afraid of water the way most people were afraid of fire. Had no one ever told Mutti that water meant life? How could anyone be frightened of being alive? His mother had never been an outdoor person. Shelter was what she'd sought.

The warmth of the muddy water was revolting. How could he wash himself in dirt! He was bitten by mosquitoes buzzing inside the filthy discharge. Mark, too dazed to defend himself, felt their sting. With every bite images of his mother's death invaded him. Or was it the young Yugoslav woman who'd killed herself? Mark's fevered mind could not keep the two women apart.

The water was tepid, stale and oily, yet in the heat of the morning it seemed to hold the only promise of relief. Soiled and defiled, Mark submitted to its deception. The ghost of his mother would not let him go.

A voice called out again, 'You finished?'

He opened his eyes, but the washroom was empty. When he closed them again, he saw a pastor praying over a wrapped body. 'In my end is my beginning.' Someone put an arm around his shoulder. 'Remember her the way she was. This is not your mother any more.' The harbour's alive with salvage vessels, police boats and small craft. Across the docks the shipyard's siren howls aimlessly. 'It's stuck,' one of the onlookers explains.

Mark had fallen to the ground. Above him the vile water kept running. When he opened his eyes he found he was alone. The communal showers lay deserted. He made no immediate attempt to get up. From the distance he could hear the ringing of a solitary bell drowned out by the loudspeaker announcement. A powerful voice summoned the inmates of

Bonegilla to a memorial service. The dead Yugoslav woman was to be honoured as if she belonged to the country in which she decided to kill herself.

Crouched naked on the slimy cracked cement Mark quietly began to cry, his sobs drowning in the broken jet of water and the calls from the camp mess.

Pouring with sweat and bitten all over, Mark returned to 'Hut 17'. In his last clean shirt he walked over to the communal hall with Tadeusz and Dushan. In line with the camp's exotic dress code, there was nothing in their appearance to suggest they were going to attend a speedily arranged funeral service. Dushan wore sandals, white socks, tight black gym shorts and a colourful, sleeveless shirt featuring a pattern of sinister-looking parrots. Tadeusz had donned a navy blue track suit with nothing underneath. He remained barefoot. Dressed in proper shoes, pants and a white shirt, Mark looked curiously formal. In the unbearable heat it didn't matter what they were wearing. The mere fact they bothered to get dressed at all amounted to a gesture of respect.

Inside the mess sweating men, women and children huddled together under a row of barely moving ceiling fans. They had come to confront death, the demon of their flight from home. Mark could read his own fear in their faces.

After solemnly announcing the tragic suicide of 'a valued member of the Yugoslav community' the camp commandant offered his condolences to 'relatives and friends'. A young Serbian beating his breast rose to bid the departed a tearful farewell. The same man, Mark surmised, with whom the dead woman had fought the night before. To the sounds of 'God save our gracious Queen' the Union Jack was solemnly lowered to half-mast. (Unfortunately the camp could not provide the national flag of Yugoslavia.) Uniformed attendants signalled all those present to stand while officers gave a rendition of 'Abide with me', then shook hands with a couple of inmates sitting in the front. Only staff members actually knew the words of the hymn, but everyone present pretended to sing along. It was strange and frightening, listening to make-believe words from speakers of half a dozen or so languages. Their singing, punctuated by persistent children's crying, was more a kind of howling which in its inarticulate helplessness rendered poignant expression to the agony of shared loss and powerless mourning. It greatly contributed to what the commandant, in his closing remarks, declared a most satisfying and moving ceremony. Out of respect for the dead there would be no farm duties today, he announced. They were dismissed.

While almost everyone in the camp was attending the memorial service Wolfgang had seized the opportunity to break into the kitchen store and steal a crate of beer. When Mark returned to the hut he found the German surrounded by bottles, trying to open a carton of Capstan. It was only mid-morning and already he was well and truly into the routine of his day. Momentarily snapping out of his stupor, Wolfgang assumed the voice of experience, 'Bet she was knocked up. Women go fuckin' stupid when they've got a bun in the oven.' He brought world weariness to his opinion. 'I've seen it happen, believe me. Sooner or later all chicks turn into mother hens. Why do you think I'm here?' He flicked the ash off his Capstan with pimpish grace.

Mark did not respond. Stripped to the waist again, he settled down on the steps, hoping his name would be included in the loudspeaker announcements. 'No farm duties' did not mean the end of the daily camp routine. 'What's the hurry?' Dushan counselled him. 'You've just arrived!' It was only a matter of time, Mark knew, before he too would be sent to the fields. At least he would escape the monotony and boredom of the camp.

In a brochure issued to all inmates the Department of Immigration offered a brief introduction to Australian history. Two hundred years ago a penal settlement was established near Sydney. In the beginning was the camp. How could the officers guarding the convicts be considered free, Mark wondered, sharing the hardships of a primitive environment on

220

the other side of the world. Were they not banished too? The real prison must have been the vastness of the unknown, hostile land. Escapees from the convict settlement would surely be defeated by the immense country.

It was a new idea for Mark – that too much of something could be destructive. Was that why they were sent to Bonegilla, to become Australians by being imprisoned in endless space? But why the fences? To protect them against suicide? He wondered who, apart from the army, had lived in this area before their arrival.

Mark's name was not called. Skipping lunch he wandered around aimlessly, following the shade cast by the larger staff barracks. On what appeared to be a former drill-ground he saw a couple of men lift a steel coffin into an unmarked hearse. They seemed in a hurry. An officer kept looking around, urging them 'to get on with it'.

On the perimeter fence Mark discovered the hole through which the woman must have found her way to the billabong. The lighter non-corroded wire gave it away. Just repaired.

Over the next few days Mark bought the daily paper from the general store. He wanted to know how Australians would be reporting the death of a Yugoslav woman. The front pages featured articles about Australia's commitment to immigration, with government and opposition alike strongly supporting a 'White Australia policy'. The future of the country was safely in bi-partisan hands. The favourite slogan among public figures appeared to be 'Populate or Perish!' Elsewhere the paper was mourning a 'tragic loss' suffered by the national cricket team. Mark's ignorance of the game meant that he failed to grasp the full impact of the tragedy – apparently a vital player on his way to making a substantial contribution had been 'left stranded'. As a result, the Test was lost. Pages were devoted to court proceedings, murders, break-ins, fires and accidents, but no reports of suicide.

One clear and calm night, with the darkness splendidly lit by an abundance of stars that as usual appeared almost within reach, Mark walked round the outer boundary of the camp. Drawn to the pattern of luminous points, his eyes were fixed to the night sky. How different from the darkness back home! Even at night, rain, clouds or fog covered the skies like a thick curtain. At home, the darkness truly proved a cover. Only rarely, in the clear air of frosty winter nights, had he been able to discover the elusive lights of constellations.

To his delight he thought that for the first time he could make out the Southern Cross. He still could not get used to the transparency of the dark. Not only during the day was the light different in this country, more dazzling or glaring.

As he approached the camp kitchen the night wanderer suddenly found himself surrounded by a group of men. Shouting something he did not understand, they punched and kicked him until he fell to the ground. In the clear dark Mark could only glimpse their faces, without recognising them. He tried to get up, but was pushed back. Next, his attackers started throwing empty bottles at him. Soon his head and arms were bleeding profusely. Crouched between garbage cans, crates and containers, he suffered the anger of strangely accented voices cursing and taunting him.

Words of hate rained down on him like bullets. They did not seem to belong to any particular language. Nor did they appear to carry any specific meaning. They were grenades thrown to destroy, hissing and spitting sounds of death, overpowering explosions frightening Mark by their very senselessness. He remained lying on the ground, wrapped in a mantle of pain.

Then, as suddenly as they had emerged, his ghostly attackers disappeared. One moment they were tormenting him, the next they vanished. In the ensuing silence Mark tried to collect his thoughts. Unable to make use of his arms and hands, he felt the blood trickle and mingle with the cold sweat of his forehead. His face was cut by glass and covered in kitchen refuse. His own breathing was the only sound he could hear. Above him the stars shone as radiantly as before, sublimely indifferent to the troubles of the world below. Whenever he opened his eyes, he was confronted by their distant light.

Mark was found by Wolfgang and his room-mates at first light. Far from being alarmed, they treated him like a hero. None of them wanted to know what exactly had happened. Like a rite of passage his fight in the dark had made him one of them.

Dushan dryly asked, for all of them, 'How many?' Mark's response raised him even higher in their esteem. His initiation as resident of Bonegilla was now complete. Together they carried him over to the camp hospital as if he were a trophy.

The grumpy nurse who attended his wounds pointed to a bed and in a firm voice ordered Mark to rest. It was much cooler in the ward than in 'Hut 17'. There was a large ceiling fan of the kind Mark had first seen at Karachi airport. An 'angel of air'. He reassured his room-mates that he would be back soon.

In the light of day the unprovoked night-time attack seemed even more ghostly and horrific. What made it so frightening was that it appeared devoid of any motive. Its violence was like a form of spontaneous self-combustion. Mark recognised the war, the onslaught of an uncontrollable force. Why had he become its target?

Although he had clearly seen the thugs' faces, Mark knew he would not be able to identify them. Their transparent darkness was the exotic revelation of an Australian night, precise but without recognition. Where were they now? Outside, the usual merciless sun was shining. Scraps of voices in different languages sieved through the window, interrupted by official announcements and the usual litany of names over the loudspeaker.

The staff officer who came to interview Mark promised to 'get to the bottom of the matter'. But there was no bottom to what had occurred.

He had lost himself.

For a while the 'angel of air' helped keep him awake. The

surly nurse came to check his temperature and give him a needle. The injection made him dizzy, sleepy and thirsty. In his exhaustion he soon lost all sensation of pain. Along with it he lost all sense of time. He was back at the harbour, collecting fragments of his mother.

He awoke late afternoon the following day. As he glanced around, he noticed his luggage neatly stacked in the far corner of the room. Closing his eyes again he took in the noise from outside. It reminded him of his old schoolyard. There was even a bell ringing. It must be time for dinner.

The nurse who came to check on him was not the one he remembered. She was much younger and, Mark thought, prettier. With an infectious laugh she called out to him, 'Welcome to the world! Are you hungry?'

He was. In no time the young nurse delivered a tray of food. She watched him eat, then washed him like a new-born, made the bed and did her best to cheer him up. 'You'll be getting a visitor tomorrow', she confided. 'I don't believe you'll be staying with us very much longer.'

Mark felt uneasy to be mothered by someone not much older than himself. Whenever she came to his assistance – helping him sit up in bed, adjusting the pillows, passing him a glass of water – he kept protesting, 'I can do that myself!'

The young nurse would not hear of it. 'Better keep your strength for later,' she replied light-heartedly. 'You might need it.'

Mark watched the unselfconsciousness of her graceful movements. She was the first Australian woman he had encountered. Why would someone as beautiful as her be working in a camp?

'What's your name?' he asked her as casually as he could. She was quick to reply, as if to make up for an embarrassing oversight, 'Cathy'.

'Mine's Mark.'

'Yes, I know. I know all about you.' She was laughing again which made her words sound like a conspiratorial promise.

'The doctor will see you in the morning to check the wounds. If he gives you the all-clear, someone from the employment office will come and hand you a train ticket to Melbourne. You'll be free at last.' Mark couldn't decide if she only meant to encourage him or whether she also wished to convey a tinge of irony in that last statement.

Left alone again, he drifted asleep with Cathy's cheerful voice ringing in his ears. It was good to surrender to her all-knowing, no-nonsense good spirits. In his dream he imagined being released to life outside. Hadn't she promised as much? Relieved and determined, he smiled at her wholesome image. She saw to it the night would not call on him to dive for his mother's body or search the sky for war planes delivering his father.

He had moved on, even in the dark.

Instead of his dead parents he was invaded by the wastelands of red and brown, deserts and death valleys, unnavigable meandering rivers and ancient rock formations. What he had seen from the sky had turned itself into images and patterns of something he had not yet learned to read. In his sleep Mark could feel the throbbing pain of his wounds, but it was not enough to lend the camp a reality of its own. Bonegilla was a non-place, a make-believe settlement, a purgatory without expiation where lovers committed suicide and enemies spoke in deadly tongues. It buried hope in barracks of indifference. It killed passion in the heat of fatigue. It punished prisoners with promises of freedom.

In the morning he was called into the head office of the camp, as predicted. He was given back his passport, a one-way train ticket to Melbourne, a document confirming an interview with the recruitment officer of a large trucking company and 'ten quid'. Soon after, he was driven in a staff car to Albury station where he was to wait for the train to Melbourne.

'Hut 17' was empty when he returned to say goodbye to his room-mates. Inside, the floor was covered with bottles and butts, traces of the residents' addiction to stupor and defeat. It looked as if Mark had never been there.

Was he, as Cathy had promised, 'free at last'? Would he allow the vastness of his future to imprison him again? If he was still a refugee, he was no longer taking refuge from his old home but from the camp. He would not be like the war refugees who had come to his town lamenting their loss, searching for what could not be recovered. He was impatient to get to Melbourne, carrying his wounds and his past in silence, ready to go wherever the city would take him.

On the platform of Albury Station, Mark found himself on his own for the first time in this country. The realisation left him both apprehensive and elated. Discreetly he looked around. Scores of passengers were boarding the train. Some travelled alone, others in the company of friends or family. They were, Mark noticed with relief, ordinary people going about their ordinary business. Some may have looked at him quizzically, but that, he reassured himself, would've been prompted by the cuts and bruises on his face. All he needed to do was smile back apologetically, implying he'd been in an accident. None of them seemed to associate him with Bonegilla.

He lifted his two suitcases as joyfully as if embarking on a holiday. The dark red wooden, old-fashioned train inspired confidence. It looked as though it had done its job for a long time. As he took his seat in the second-class compartment he was reminded of the narrow-gauge railway that had taken him to the North Sea all those years ago. Suddenly he was overcome by travel nerves, just as he had been then, an undernourished boy on his way to the sanatorium. When at last the engine driver blew the whistle and the train began moving slowly out of the station, Mark was as excited as on his first trip to the islands. Would the past be always travelling with him? Even if it could, even if he was becoming a child again, one thing was for certain: he would not be the same as he had been.

Leaning back in his seat he looked around, listened to shreds of conversation and politely nodded to passengers who appeared to look in his direction. 'I just have to pretend I'm an Australian,' Mark thought to himself. 'I simply have to act as if I'm one of them, that I belong here.' The daring idea reverberated within him. He could hear Cathy's voice promising 'You'll be free at last', adding with ironic laughter 'I know all about you'. Was he an impostor because he wanted to belong to ordinary people?

'Going all the way, son?' an elderly gentleman sitting next to the window asked in a friendly tone.

Mark found it safest to nod enthusiastically, assuming 'all the way' could only mean Melbourne.

The man seemed deeply satisfied. 'Great city, isn't it?'

Again, Mark nodded before replying with increasing confidence, 'Sure is.' He was relieved the old man hadn't noticed his accent.

'First time for you?' he persisted.

Mark had to think about that. After a short while he answered, 'Yes. But I always knew I'd go there.'

The man who called him 'son' seemed to have lost interest. 'Quite,' he mumbled as he began unwrapping sandwiches, then triumphantly held them out to him. 'Like one? Go on! Help yourself!' he offered.

Mark shook his head politely. 'No thanks. I'm fine.'

The man persisted. It would be 'a long journey', he reminded the young traveller. 'All through the night.'

'I know,' Mark replied conspiratorially.

III

For most of the long train ride Mark slept. He was not ready for another encounter with the Australian dark. For the second time in a few weeks he believed he'd escaped. But he was more sceptical now, anxious not to be disappointed again. The rattling of the carriage reminded him he was still fleeing. His sleeping body translated the bustling sound into a trembling of its own, a resonant quivering as if in conversation with itself, a probing of his true intentions. Sometimes he felt a jolt; momentarily the train's engine appeared to hesitate about whether to continue its fast forward motion. His sensation that the train occasionally stopped or changed into reverse was an illusion. In his sleep it established a rhythm rather like breathing. Mark's body took it all in, sensing there would be no return. No dreams, no visitations conspired to hold him back.

It was on a grey morning that Mark got off the train, looking like any other traveller as he carried his two suitcases, and followed the general surge of passengers to the exit of Flinders Street Station. The size of the railway station, with its huge boards listing dozens of arrivals and departures, reassured him. He was closer to the world again. A large city held promise of easier moves; its very essence was traffic. Waves of people entered and left the station.

He deposited his suitcases at the cloakroom. Out in the

street he bought himself a paper, then ordered breakfast in a small café. It amused him to come across a newspaper called the *Age*. The age of what? The age of now! he thought. When, if not now? Perhaps he should make that his slogan. The paper was heavy, with many different sections. Judging by its size, a lot of things must be happening in Melbourne. It took him a while to find the column 'Rooms to let'. He wrote down a number of addresses. Through the open door came the noise of passing trams, honking cars and the rush of pedestrians. Already he began feeling at home in a city he didn't know.

Within two hours he'd rented a room at the top end of Swanston Street in Carlton. His new home was an old terrace with a white lace iron balcony and a tall palm tree in its front garden. The fact that his room was towards the back of the house and its only window was broken, revealing a cracked view over dilapidated backyards, did not diminish his joy. Collecting his luggage from the station, Mark triumphed in the knowledge that on his first day in the city he had found a place of his own. He took it as an omen of even better things to come.

Tomorrow he would ring the trucking company and ask for an interview. But at night in his bed, the breeze from the broken window providing relief from the hot summer air, he changed his mind. A daring idea came to him. Back home he would've attended university by now, studying medicine, specialising in haematology. As his mother said, he had a thing about blood.

What if he tried to do the same thing here? He realised he would first need to find a job to pay for his studies, but he would be earning a living to do what he really wanted. It was an audacious thought – to have left death behind; to have left his home, all he loved; to have taken flight to a dot his tiny globe had lit up in the night; to have been imprisoned in the name of freedom – all to study life here in the place in which he found himself released.

The next day he boldly went to the enrolment section of

the university and put his name down for 'First Year Science'. The man behind the counter informed him all overseas qualifications would have to be checked, but in his case he did not foresee any difficulties. They would confirm his enrolment by mail. Mark gloated as he wrote his new 'home address'. After signing still more forms he was directed to the Student Counsellor's Office.

It wasn't easy for Mark to explain how he'd arrived there, but the intrigued counsellor showed more concern over Mark being on his own and his apparent 'lack of funds'. Indeed, in Mr Priestley's professional judgment the situation amounted to an emergency, calling for immediate action. After a number of intensive phone calls, in the course of which he discreetly scrutinised the unusual visitor, he handed Mark a map of the university, circled the Old Law Building and told him to go to the first floor and 'report to Mr Johnston's office at two o'clock'. Mark looked at his watch. It was approaching midday. He would still have time for lunch. Mr Johnston, the student counsellor explained, was 'the Head of Public Exams'. As Mark rose, the counsellor asked again, 'Where did you say you came from?'

He was nearly hit by a dart as he entered the Clyde. The air tasted of cigarettes, beer and piss, and from the back, behind a door marked LADIES LOUNGE, came the smell of cooking. An ecstatic voice yelling from the radio sounded as if it were trying to overtake itself. Men in various stages of dress and undress, some wearing blue singlets and strangely shaped hats, congregated around the horseshoe-shaped bar. Running along its foot was a kind of channel or gutter which to Mark looked like a urinal. But its main use appeared to be for spitting and dropping butts. In places the drinking crowd was three rows deep. It took a while before he could place his order. In response to his shout of 'steak and kidney pie' a matronly full-bossomed barmaid handed him a knife and fork wrapped in a napkin, and poured him a beer he hadn't ordered. He took the glass, handed her five shillings ('five bob', he'd have to remember that), took the docket and allowed himself to be pushed from the counter.

Mark watched the men throwing darts at a green round board. Some aimed with such intensity and deliberation it was hard to believe they were playing a game. By contrast, others merely pushed back their hats without letting go of their glasses before nonchalantly piercing the air with their missiles. Mark noticed a few uncollected plates on a small ledge against the wall. It took him a while to realise the occasional calling of numbers was not part of the races broadcast but order numbers for counter lunches. He checked the docket and waited for his turn.

Mark ate his counter lunch standing up against the wall, surrounded by boisterous grabbing, shouting, laughing, sweating drinkers. Every now and then someone beamed at him, took hold of his shoulders and like a password called out 'Howyermate'. Mark grinned and nodded in acknowledgment, anxious not to drop his plate. He checked his watch – habitually noting that 'at home' it was still night – knowing he would need time to find the office of 'the Head of Public Exams'. He wondered about the name. Who was examining whom – or what?

A friendly looking bloke with what he judged to be an Irish accent tapped him on his back. 'Raffle for Sain' Vinnies!' While collecting coins and dispensing tickets with his right hand, he balanced a meat tray above his head. Again, buyers received a number and had to wait to hear whether they'd been lucky. Mark didn't understand much of what was going on around him, but for a stranger on only his second day in the city he felt oddly at ease among this noisy, hectic crowd. What a mixed lot they were too!

Looking around he noticed three businessmen formally dressed in suit and tie raise their glasses to a couple of construction workers. Together they nodded and cheered. Mark heard them call out 'Big Nick' to each other. Then one of them threw another name in the air – 'Serge!' then 'Loftie' – and once again the whole group started to toast each other.

Reluctantly, apologetically, Mark made his way to the door through this strange brotherhood of drinkers. He could get used to their company, he thought. It made him feel confident that for a while he had been part of this noisy pocket of men drinking and feeding off each other.

When Mark entered the main office of 'Public Exams', an old lady with a huge pencil in her white hair (so smooth he thought for a moment she might be wearing a hat) informed him that 'Mr Johnston had not yet returned from lunch'. Subdued giggling came from various desks. Would he like to take a seat? she politely enquired. 'Mind you,' the old lady sighed in sudden afterthought, 'it might be a while.' Mark could not be certain the comment was still directed at him. It was possible she had simply thought aloud. Again her remark prompted suppressed laughter. Perhaps in the mean-time he would like to have a look around? As she spoke she shifted a black leather volume of enormous proportions from one desk to another. No one came to her assistance. Mark was stunned the fragile woman could carry its obviously heavy weight. By her action she'd signalled that, as far as she was concerned, the interview was over.

He was about to leave when a young man who appeared to have been engaged in knitting left his desk in the depths of the room and offered to show him the place. Speaking with a heavy lisp and an American accent (which in fact proved to be Canadian), he introduced himself as David. He told Mark he was a professional skater who'd been left stranded with 'Holiday on Ice', found a job at Public Exams and 'never looked back'.

'You've come for a job, I can tell. Don't worry. If you can read and write, he'll take you. Just make sure your figures are right.'

Mark had no idea what the ice-skater was talking about.

David dragged him along the corridor. As they were passing a large intimidating door to their right, he explained, 'That's Mr Hooper's office. Hoopy's second-in-charge. He checks all the results.' Mark found it simplest just to nod.

They were approaching another, slightly smaller room. 'That's Wal's and Ted's. They're mates from way back. War buddies, if you know what I mean. I'd be careful if I were you. Where are you from, anyhow?'

When Mark told him, David repeated his warning. 'Be very careful, then. Wally lost his balls in Malaya. Literally. Would you believe it! Shot to pieces! Poor bastard! Better watch it!'

They continued moving down the passage. To their left they passed a number of strongrooms which David described as the 'Holy of Holies'. 'That's where all the records are stored, man!' he exclaimed in mock awe. 'It's like the FBI. You need clearance to get into there!' Mark tried to look impressed. The stranded ice-skater seemed satisfied with his response.

He pointed at two young women typing away furiously in another office. 'The left's Lorraine, the right's Sue,' he informed Mark, as if they were pieces of furniture. 'They're typing the certificates that go to Hoopy. After they've been checked and double-checked he presents them to Mr Johnston who then signs them.' One of the typists was Chinese. Mark had never seen such a huge woman. 'Sue's an ABC – an Australian-born Chinese,' David clarified. He sounded like a circus director proudly displaying one of his more exotic animals.

They had reached the end of the first floor corridor. 'That, ladies and gentlemen, concludes this afternoon's inspection tour,' David announced. Mark did not know much more about 'Public Exams' than before, except that it involved keeping records and attracted a wide range of somewhat peculiar people. He wondered whether that was why the student counsellor had sent him there.

'Where our offices end, Law begins.' David explained the layout of the building, unaware of any philosophical implications. Slowly they started walking back to the main office. 'Mr Johnston,' he warned Mark, 'may be a bit under the weather. Some of his lunches tend to have a lasting effect on him.' The more Mark learnt about the place, the more confused he became.

He had to wait another twenty minutes or so before a tall, sunburnt man in his fifties, elegantly dressed in a three-piece suit, finally staggered into his office. He displayed all the signs and routines of a confirmed alcoholic trying to keep up appearances. His red face bore a frozen smile, his watery green eyes stared at nothing in particular, and his slightly slurred speech was slow and deliberate.

'Welcome to our team,' Mr Johnston began, anticipating the outcome of what was supposed to be an interview designed to test Mark's suitability as an employee of his department. 'Let me have a look at your handwriting, lad.' Jovially Mr Johnston passed him a sheet of foolscap paper. 'And while you're at it, could you write down the numbers from one to ten. There's a good chap.' He gave a hearty yawn.

Mark did as he was told. While he was writing, Mr Johnston appeared in danger of falling asleep. It required repeated polite coughing for him to notice that the intellectual side of the test had been completed. Rubbing his red eyes, he gave the paper a stern look, then sadly shook his head. 'That won't do, my boy. For starters, you don't put a line through the seven. Where'd'ya learn that!' He seemed genuinely disappointed. 'And another thing,' he remarked, 'I don't care for the look of your one!'

The brief interview had reached a stalemate. Neither the head of 'Public Exams' nor Mark knew what to do next. Mr Johnston pretended to give the matter some thought, a lengthy and complicated process occasionally interrupted by loud snoring noises. It did not take long before, as in a gesture of surrender, the upper part of Mr Johnston's body finally collapsed on the desk. Mark looked around the office, wondering whether it was time for him to go. Behind the glass door of the office he could see David pulling faces at him.

Then, all of a sudden, Mr Johnston's trunk rose again, life returned to his bloodshot eyes and his arms took up their former position, clinging to the back of the chair. 'D'you think you can do that, then?' he asked. Mark was quick to respond. 'Certainly, Mr Johnston!' This time he'd found the right answer. As if to prove he was fully alert again, the tall man in front of him left his chair and with surprising agility grabbed a form from a filing cabinet near the window. He indicated a line, passed the paper to Mark and said, 'Sign here, lad!' He watched the foreign recruit's awkward signature, shook Mark's hand and rang a small copper bell on his desk. 'Young David will show you the ropes. That'll be all.' As they left his office Mr Johnston called after him. 'Good man!' Mark didn't know how to respond to that. David pushed him outside. But then, his left hand on the door, the newly appointed clerk of 'Public Exams' turned around and, adopting Mr Johnston's military jargon, said, 'Thank you, sir.' Just before he shut it he heard his boss mumble to himself, 'Dismissed.'

Back in the main office the time had come for Mark to meet the other clerks. Three older women introduced themselves as 'Noreen', 'Mrs Adams' and, the lady with a pencil in her white hair, 'Mrs Osborne'. The job of 'Noreen' and 'Mrs Adams' was to check and double-check exam results before they could be entered in the Big Black Book. Mrs Osborne was the senior clerk in charge of recording grades and authorising the issuing of certificates. Mark noticed that despite her age she had a remarkably delicate rosy skin, not unlike that of a very young woman. She was, according to David, 'quite potty' and not a little cranky, obsessive, self-righteous and absent-minded; yet, for all that, capable of disciplined, prolonged concentration and in full possession of a considerable brain.

Noreen was an 'honest working class soul', an indefatigable chain-smoker displaying a home-made perm that had gone seriously wrong somewhere. Her desk was shrouded in clouds of Capstan smoke. Only at close range was it possible to make out her small, ashen face with large glasses almost totally hidden behind piles of examiners' booklets, school sheets and student lists. Noreen gave Mark a comradely grin of encouragement. 'You'll be right,' her nervous but kind smile assured him.

She was aspiring to a friendship with her colleague 'Mrs Adams of Kew', who, David informed Mark somewhat tautologously, was a true lady 'of good stock'. Noreen understood it was only because of an undisclosed shattering tragedy befalling her husband that Mrs Adams had ended up at 'Public Exams'. That a lady like her friend should have to leave home and go to work seemed nothing short of an outrage. During morning and afternoon tea Noreen loved to listen to Mrs Adams' accounts of garden parties and recollections of her friend entertaining Melbourne's rich and famous. Occasionally Mrs Adams would actually join Noreen in a smoke, even though she was partial to her own brand, Revelation, 'in a flip-top box'. She just couldn't warm to the pungent tobacco and loose tips of Noreen's Capstan. 'How do you do?' she politely enquired when David presented Mark to her. His equally polite formal response was met with only partial approval by the lady from Kew. 'That accent,' Mrs Adams turned up her nose. 'You're not Welsh, by any chance?'

Mark had begun to like the ambiguity of the name 'Public Exams'. When it was finally explained to him that they were administering the state's public examinations from Intermediate and Leaving to Matriculation level, he was disappointed. His own conjectures of the place had been much more romantic. He had imagined them performing tasks similar to medieval monks preparing and preserving precious manuscripts. But the large heavy leather-bound folio books stored in the strongrooms, he was told, contained no more than the school results of the

State of Victoria's past and present students, reaching all the way back to 1920. Well, it was a bit of history.

Apparently people were actually afraid of 'Public Exams'.

David led Mark to a desk close to Mr Johnston's office. His first task consisted of adding rows and rows of figures. He worked especially hard at standardising his European ones and sevens. Once he'd settled behind his desk, the main office quickly grew quiet again. Only the ticking sound of an antique wall clock bearing Roman numerals filled the semi-dark, smoke-filled room.

During afternoon tea break Ted and Wal joined them, as did the typists Lorraine and Sue. A stocky, bespectacled Mr Hooper formally shook hands with Mark, uttered something like 'Good to have you on board', then quickly disappeared for an executive cuppa in Mr Johnston's office. While Noreen asked him how he liked his tea and David passed around a plate of biscuits, Mark realised he'd become part of a group. It'd all happened so quickly. He couldn't believe how easy it all was. A deep sense of gratitude came over him. Everyone had been so kind, so helpful, so anxious to make him feel welcome.

'We fought you lot,' Wal pointed out as he introduced himself. 'You and the Japs.' Mark nodded into his tea. 'Anyhow,' Wal said. He had a habit of saying that whenever he wasn't sure what to do next.

'You've just started, then,' Ted prompted.

'Yes,' Mark replied, 'I've just started.'

IV

At ten in the morning and at two in the afternoon Mark carried the departmental mailbag down to the postal counter on the ground floor. The first time he delivered it the lethargic young woman behind the counter didn't even look up. She was pretending to sort the morning's mail. In fact, she was reading the paper and listening to the radio. When he reappeared in the afternoon she seemed a different person: friendly, energetic and curious. Dressed in a short black skirt and velour pullover, her dark hair and heavy eye make-up gave her a theatrical appearance – like a deceptively beautiful vampire in a horror movie.

'Who are you, then?' she asked him with a cryptic smile. As she parted her lips, her eyes were simultaneously reduced to tiny slits. It unnerved Mark because he did not know whether it was an expression of critical assessment or a pacifying gesture of acceptance.

'I'm Mark, from upstairs,' he replied in what he hoped was an acceptably jovial tone.

'Are you now? You must be new. They're always hiring and firing up there. You're a part-timer?' Again she smiled at him, and again her eyes nearly closed. Mark thought her automatic movements were those of a doll. Didn't Elsa, one of the girls back home, have one that looked just like her?

'I'm Maree, from downstairs,' she joked.

'I'm full-time,' he explained. 'But they give me time off for lectures.'

Maree took her time licking an internal mail envelope that didn't need to be closed. He waited for her slit-eyed smile. When it came he grinned back at her and said, 'I'm off.'

'Yeah, Mark, see ya round.' She removed the mailbag from the counter, holding it like a lover. As he left the office Mark heard it crash to the ground.

'That's spider woman,' David told him with a knowing smirk. 'She's a student at the conservatorium. God knows what instrument she plays.'

'All right you two, get on with it!' Hoopy called them back to work. They were adding numbers for the '58 Intermediate and Leaving. Mark was still restricted to the use of pencils. Only the senior staff had the authority to enter double- and cross-checked figures in ink.

The hours passed slowly. In the semi-darkness of the large office it was hard to tell whether the sun was shining outside. The light of the departmental lamps was designed not to extend beyond the clerks' desks. It shone on a confined world of names and figures.

After a few weeks Mark realised he could learn off by heart biochemical formulae and data while filling out rough copy examinations sheets. In one of his drawers he kept his most recent lecture notes. He would open it after the completion of a column and consult what he'd written. Working for 'Public Exams' proved a surprisingly effective way of studying.

Most of his lunch hours he spent with David at a Parkville café opposite the Conservatorium, just across Royal Parade. David, who was in the habit of taking along his knitting, kept feeding the jukebox. Whenever he played his favourite, an instrumental called *The Lonely Bull*, he would get up and dance around the room, raising his banderilla needles ready to thrust them into the neck or shoulders of the invisible bull. While admitting the grace of his movements, Mark was embarrassed by his friend's self-conscious pose. He kept eating his sandwiches and drinking coffee as if nothing had happened.

And nothing had happened, of course. Dancing in public was the kind of thing out-of-work professional ice-skaters were likely to do, he reminded himself. But when David used his knitting to dance to a pop song called *Silver Threads and Golden Needles* Mark decided he'd had enough.

Out in the tree-lined street the sight of green and yellow trams passing by gave Melbourne the appearance of a European city. The familiar scene reassured Mark. It was a reminder of images he had not left behind, memories of his childhood that would stay with him, wherever he went. But what imbued him with greater confidence was the realisation that in the short time since his arrival in this country, he had become a part of it. Already Mark felt he belonged. He had become part of Carlton like the Greek family with their delicatessen in Drummond Street, the Italian coffee merchant torrefazzione in Lygon Street or the Maltese fruiterer in Elgin Street, whose unmistakable accents revealed they, too, were recent arrivals. To speak the same language in a variety of different sounds made it appear generous and rich. From the beginning it gave Mark the feeling he was one of them.

In Melbourne he'd never felt like an outsider or a mere spectator. Like a non-swimmer at the municipal baths of his home town, he'd been thrown into the deep end, and managed to stay above water. He hadn't drowned in the city's pronouncements.

Mark thought of where he was living now. Although it was getting cold at night, the broken window in the tiny back room he rented had still not been fixed. There was only a bed, a wardrobe and a chair. He had turned a rough pine crate into a kind of table and covered it with a tea towel. Inside it he kept the little food he bought – fresh white Italian bread, butter, sugar and a bottle of Rio Vista sherry.

Because there were no cooking facilities he continued to rely on counter lunches at the Clyde. Within days he was recognised as a regular and offered a table in the Ladies' Lounge where he could take his time over a steak and salad, a shepherd's pie or meatballs, sausages and eggs. When the proprietress learnt he was living by himself, her maternal instincts were aroused. She decided to take the young man under her wing. Mark found his plates over-loaded, bursting with special treats he hadn't ordered and didn't have to pay for.

People were good to him. From the start he'd been quite certain that Melbourne would be the right place for him. The city 'felt' right. Suddenly everything had fallen into place. He'd rented a room, found a job almost immediately, even become a university student during the first week of his stay. In the country of his birth these things would just not have been possible. Why, then, could it happen here?

Was it just in contrast to life in the camp, or had he really found freedom in the city? Mark had read about the colonial history of Australia, the country's European beginning as a penal settlement. In a small way, could it not be said that he, too, had come here as a prisoner? Perhaps conscious freedom may only be gained from previous imprisonment. Mark found it incredible that he could rent a room without having to register with the police. There didn't appear to be a municipal residents' registration office. It made him wonder why a person's home needed to be registered. Here, it seemed, people could come and go, live where and how they pleased – an unheard-of sloppiness no 'civilised' European city would tolerate. Mark began to question many customs and rules he'd taken for granted.

It made him think, not for the first time, about that other kind of imprisonment – the inescapability of origin, of birth and identity. Many people in this city, ordinary men and women he encountered in his daily dealings, carried accents from different parts of the world. They were living proof of the freedom to change, to become a different person, to discover a home they didn't know they could claim. Even those who'd been forced to leave their native countries seemed to harbour no intention to return.

Mark's thoughts were interrupted when he caught sight of a familiar figure across the road. It was Maree leaving the Conservatorium, carrying a large folio of music under her arm. A young man walked closely behind her. As Maree turned in the direction of the Old Law School the two waved at each other. Mark looked at his watch. It was almost two o'clock. Time to get back to the office.

He must've asked too many questions about 'spider woman' because at afternoon tea David and the girls started to sing in mocking chorus 'And Maree's the name of his latest flame'. It was no more than a good-natured tease, but it embarrassed him because in truth he was beginning to find the postal clerk from downstairs very, well, intriguing. Wal and Ted simply dismissed her as a slut who shouldn't be allowed to work at a university. Noreen and Mrs Adams turned up their noses at the whole unworthy, unladylike subject. Mr Johnston and his deputy Mr Hooper seemed to be blissfully unaware of the existence of 'spider woman'. Only Mark, it seemed, had fallen under her spell.

Despite Wal's barely controlled hostility towards him, Mark could not help feeling sorry for the old soldier. Surrounded at his workplace, as he was, by the combined hostile forces of a gay skater, a promiscuous young woman and an enemy lecher, his reactions to all of them had the effect of turning the tragedy of his war wound more and more into involuntary cruel comedy. When Lorraine told him Mark was 'fascinated by the postal clerk downstairs' Wal exploded. 'That foreign lout'll fuck anything that moves!' he foamed in angry disgust. In vain Sue tried to calm him down. 'But he's not doing anything, Wal. I'm just saying he finds her interesting, that's all.' In the hope of closing the subject Ted offered his mate another cup of tea. 'Disgusting, that's what it is,' Wal continued to growl his disapproval. 'Makes you wonder what the world's coming to.'

Next time he collected the mail Mark was more daring. 'Are you in mourning?' he asked Maree. His remark prompted her eyes to turn into a slit, without the usual accompanying smile.

'You talkin' to me?' she dared him to repeat the question.

'I notice you're always wearing black.'

'You're some joker.' Maree seemed genuinely disappointed.

'I saw you at the Con a few days ago,' Mark tried again. 'You really a music student, then?'

'You really a nosy office boy from Public Exams?'

Mark refused to be put off by her continued mockery. 'You know I'm studying science, part-time.' As an afterthought, he added, 'It's just that I like music.'

'You're also an office boy at Public Exams,' she retorted.

'Don't call me that. I'm just trying to be nice.' He thought of what else he could say to pacify her. 'I'm interested in you. What's wrong with that?'

Maree shuffled the mail, pretending to be busy. 'I haven't got time to talk to the likes of you. We're actually working down here, you know.'

'We?' Mark quoted. 'I don't see anyone else.'

'Oh, go away, Mark,' she dismissed him, but then, in what he took to be a conciliatory gesture, added, 'If you really want to hear me play, you can join me for lunch tomorrow. Now go. I've got work to do.'

In his office, going over his lecture notes while completing the State's overall Leaving results for the previous year, he found himself whistling. 'And Maree's the name of his latest flame ...'.

The next day he followed her to a brightly lit room on the first floor of the Conservatorium. She took out a key and opened the door to Practice Room 4. Inside was a Steinway, surrounded by a couple of folding chairs. Maree sat down at the grand piano. As she did so Mark noticed a couple of large holes in her black stockings. Her short skirt now looked more like a pair of shorts. He followed her movements with curious fascination, entranced by the way she placed the sheet music on the instrument's stand, then, almost without transition, bowed her head and began to play.

Mark was disappointed it was not Bach, but what was instantly clear to him was that Maree could really play. He recognised a nocturne by Chopin – the right music for her to play, he acknowledged. The music possessed the same kind of nervous tension linked to a demonically flirtatious beauty he thought he'd discovered in Maree. He closed his eyes, intoxicated by the romantic composition and its empathetic playing. The notes came gushing down like windswept rain. Mark thought he could feel them on his skin.

His emotions were as seductively volatile as the music of Chopin. Hands folded over a chair he'd turned back to front, Mark pretended to remain calm as he listened intensely. But with his nails he was feverishly pricking the skin of his thumb and index fingers. Sitting barely two metres away from her, he continued to pierce himself until he could at last feel the moisture of small drops of blood. The chair served as a seemingly casual shield covering his desperate arousal. Maree's performance registered as an outrage, an invasion of his senses.

The music stopped as abruptly as it had begun. Slowly, reluctantly, indignant at the sudden ending, he opened his eyes. Maree had swung around on the stool, leaning back onto the instrument, legs apart, the black tights lifted to the waist. She wore no panties, openly displaying her shaven genitals. Her slanted eyes were accompanied by a blind smile. Again, Mark found it impossible not to think of a mechanical doll.

She excited even as she offended him. To his amazement, he felt himself assaulted once more, beaten and thrown among Bonegilla's kitchen garbage. 'In the beginning was the camp'. The sentence entered his head like the damning opening pronouncement of his personal Book of Genesis. In the city of the free he was a condemned prisoner staring at the spectacle of Maree's blind compulsion. Her eyes were shut as she summonsed him, 'Come over here, office boy!' They were both caught in an irresistible urge, a desire of self-fulfilling passion. The music had become flesh, demanding to be played.

The rattling of a passing tram outside startled Mark from the trance. With slow deliberation he rose from his chair, walked over to the Steinway, kissed Maree on the forehead and left the room.

Once, when Mark was careless enough to say how beautifully Maree played the piano, David commented wryly, 'You too! I hear she's quite an instrumentalist!' Mark resented his scathing derision and tried his best to change the subject. In vain. 'She's a real nympho, that one. Everybody knows about her lunch hour performances.' Mark felt an overpowering urge to defend Maree, to take her side, to tell David – and anyone else who wanted to know – that she truly was a very gifted player. But anything he said merely prompted renewed ridicule and sarcasm. He could tell the 'gay skater's' comments did not really address themselves to Maree. They merely reflected the age-old envy of one body, one desire over another.

The truth was that Mark did not care what his co-worker thought of his relationship with 'spider woman'. Because he was much more concerned about Maree's reaction he asked to be relieved of his postal duties for the coming week. He wanted time before facing her again.

After the drudgery of the day Mark looked forward to his evening lectures. At last he was learning things he really wanted to know! He felt most comfortable in the lab where he could put biochemical processes of living organisms to the test. Scientifically at least life clearly made sense! What a long way he'd come from his boyhood chemistry set!

With his first two pays he bought himself a number of

textbooks and put a deposit on a portable typewriter. In future he would submit his assignments neatly typed, giving them a more professional, 'scientific' appearance. He loved preparing analytical reports of practical experiments. They proved the supremacy and certainty of facts, exposing all errors of speculation, prejudice and false judgment. In accordance with the accuracy of the scientific investigation itself, it was appropriate for such demonstrations of facts to be presented as tidily and methodically.

One Saturday, on his way back from the Clyde, a young woman dropped her shopping bag almost exactly in front of the terrace where he lived. He quickly went to her assistance. 'Did she have far to go?' he enquired.

She shook her head in relief. 'No, thank goodness, I live just two houses further down.' Mark could not resist telling her where he lived. 'Well, then,' the grateful young woman said, 'we're practically neighbours.'

Politely she asked whether he was a student. Not without a certain amount of pride Mark replied, 'Yes, I'm a science student, but in due course I'll be switching to medicine.' Too late, he realised the phrase 'in due course' was a bit pompous. He was embarrassed. His short answer sounded altogether too much like a carefully thought out programme. In his mind, at least, it was.

'You seem to know exactly where you want to go with your life.' There wasn't a hint of irony in her comment. Indeed, she meant it as a compliment, even though she couldn't resist adding, 'Wish I felt as confident.'

It was a remarkably personal exchange for two strangers meeting casually in the street. Most likely she was a student too, Mark realised. Her age, casual appearance and friendly, relaxed conversation appeared to suggest that. She must've noticed his accent, but didn't ask him where he came from.

Days later, when they ran into each other again, they both seemed genuinely pleased. Over a cappuccino at the students' café, Genevieve's, she told him her name was Sonja, that she was a second year arts student majoring in English and Indian Studies. Sonja explained she was sharing a terrace with three student friends, Julia, Belinda and Mignon. After she found out that Mark was living by himself, she spontaneously invited him for tea at their place. 'It must be terrible being on your own in a tiny back room,' she commiserated. 'And you can't just live on counter lunches. Sooner or later you'll have to find a place where you can cook.' It was important for him to eat sensibly. Was he eating plenty of fruit? Didn't he know the pub vegetables were all overcooked? He needed to make sure he got enough vitamins. Sonja may have been a young student, but she displayed all the manners and concerns of a mother or a nurse.

He would not have called her beautiful. She was a slightly overweight blonde, with huge green eyes and an infectious smile. Around twenty, Mark guessed. Her femininity projected warmth and kindness, protectiveness and a willingness to please. Her enthusiasm was easily quickened. As their friendship blossomed Mark noticed how her keenness to admire others stood in marked contrast to her habit of belittling herself. She took great delight in the promise of those benefiting from her support. Mark soon felt his friend was the kind of person who needed to be protected from herself. Her very presence offered shelter, shielding him by laying herself bare.

Although comprising only a ground floor, the rooms in Sonja's terrace were considerably larger than those in Mark's house. To the right of an extended hallway were four spacious bedrooms, each occupied by one of the students. Located behind was a lounge or dining room, next to an old-fashioned kitchen. At the rear of the house was a tiled courtyard with a small garden.

Sonja's room was an expression of homely femininity: cushions everywhere – on a large bed, over a couple of armchairs, spread out on a couch and on the floor. Its feminine intimacy was accentuated by the decoration of the high ceiling with what appeared to be extravagant layers of silk petticoats, but in fact proved to be an open parachute. The lamps were covered with coloured scarfs, the bookshelves and a couple of small coffee tables decorated with exotic paper flowers. The wall next to the bed bore a poster of Indian dancers.

Despite the casualness of her invitation Sonja proved an energetic hostess. Mark had never seen anyone take such delight in preparing a meal. Her 'guests' included her co-tenants Belinda, Julia and Mignon. Sonja's colourful stories about 'the young guy next door' had aroused their curiosity. To her delight they were not disappointed. Finding him 'intriguing' and anxious to know 'everything about him', they asked him questions Sonja had not. Where was his home? What made him come here? What were his plans after university?

Mark tried to explain himself as best he could, but it became clear he was unable to do so, at least not to the satisfaction of all his listeners. Belinda, Julia and Mignon failed to be convinced. In his embarrassment he avoided giving straight answers; instead, he tried to be flirtatiously evasive. But such manner did not come to him naturally. Belinda in particular, a strikingly beautiful law student with curly black hair and hazel eyes, sensed he was keeping something from them. She unnerved him with her persistent follow-up questions. Mark could tell she would become a feared, relentless, ruthless cross-examiner in court. With fake naivety she demanded ever more detailed explanations. Talking to her, Mark found himself an untrustworthy suspect with no alibi.

Julia, by contrast, found everything he said 'interesting' or 'fascinating'. A tall woman with enormous wide and thick lips accentuated by an overuse of dark red lipstick, she kept interrupting the conversation with outbursts like 'Oh, it must be wonderful to travel!' Mark was grateful for her misunderstandings.

While Sonja tried her best to mediate, her impish friend Mignon, impatiently shaking a wealth of straight shoulder-long blonde hair, chastised Belinda for being 'a bully'. Picking at her food she demanded, 'Give the guy a chance!' Every now and then she would raise her fork as a sign of indignation and declare, 'For god's sake let him finish, Linda!' In the course of her pleadings she helped herself to another glass of plonk.

Mark's reactions continued to be elusive. He was grateful to have been invited – once more, it seemed, he had been made welcome by a group – but he was unprepared for the young women's social inquisition. When it came to relating to others he clearly still had a lot to learn. Hospitality, he discovered, had to be reciprocated by being amusing. Part of that entertainment appeared to be the obligation to reveal or to explain oneself.

It surprised Mark that to someone like Belinda at least he had to produce a valid reason for having come to Australia. Or was she just playing with him? Belinda's persistent probing into his past life unnerved him. Weren't all white Australians migrants to their own country? He recalled a sentence from a crime report he'd read in the *Age*: 'The accused would not let the victim be.' Could Belinda tell he was neither a refugee nor a displaced person, not a victim of either racial or religious persecution, and therefore in particular need to justify himself? Mark was tempted to revert to one of his own snappish student remarks, back at Old Grammar: 'Pardon me for being born!'

But he did not need to defend himself. 'Mark's going to be a doctor and a haematologist,' Sonja announced over dessert as if he were not present. There was a triumphant tone in her voice. Julia took it to be the end of the discussion, got up and put on a record. 'Good on ya!' Mignon shouted across the table, pouring herself another glass.

Mark was moved by Sonja's support. He felt like touching her hand or conveying his gratitude in some other way.

He was unsure how to express his thankfulness. Showing appreciation was another thing he would have to learn.

'I have often walked down the street before ...,' Julia howled off-key but with great emotion, drowning out the record. The others had started smoking, a ritual which seemed to signal a new turn in the conversation. It was time to be intellectual, to discuss sex, religion and politics. Never before had Mark witnessed girls talk about their flirtations and sexual exploits so openly. If he needed any reminding, he was once again made aware of being a man in a house of women where the rules of social conduct seemed well-rehearsed. What appeared chaotic, volatile and emotional to him revealed itself as a caring ritual of consensus. Catering to men was out of place. Mark couldn't help comparing them with the young women of his home town. Would they, in their own company, be as free and independent?

'Home.' That was what the dinner conversation had been about. Belinda was suspicious of Mark trying to make her city his home. Perhaps she believed only women could 'make' a home.

Mark had been in Sonja's room only once, but it looked 'homely' to him. Did she still feel at home when she visited her parents' place? For Mark, home was above all a place of the senses, to be 'sniffed out', the way he had, as a child, laid claim to the smell of the harbour, the fog and the rain. Like an animal he'd followed the scent of his native town.

Home had to be discovered, explored and taken possession of. Some people spent all their lives in places which would never be theirs. For that, a special kind of ownership was required. Otherwise they remained forever mere residents.

In the basic affinity of sense and place, houses too could smell 'right' or 'wrong'. The city of Melbourne, the suburb of Carlton, Swanston Street and this house 'smelled right'.

The streets of Carlton carried a characteristic aroma of Italian, Greek and Jewish delicatessens, espresso machines, fruiterers, pubs and wine bars. They had smelt right from the start. The most perfect odour of cooked meats, cheeses, prepared food and spices Mark had encountered at King & Godfrey's in Lygon Street, a special shop where all the flavours, smells and tastes of the world seemed to mingle. Next to an undertaker he had found a mixed business where a matronly Greek lady would slice and cut him a huge piece of delicious New York cheesecake direct from the plate. It had become something of a feast he observed on payday. As he bit into the cake its taste mingled with the smell of pickled gherkins, olives, rollmops, octopus and coffee.

Of course, it wasn't just a matter of smell. In addition to the senses, it took time to recognise oneself in, as well as to familiarise oneself with, a place. Might it not then be possible to feel at home in more than one place?

Was that what Belinda was so suspicious of?

Had he been older and the war still raging, Mark's flight from the fog-bound, rainy border town into which he was born would have constituted treason. He would have been shot by his own people. 'Home' could be a dangerous possession.

Sometimes Mark thought that to be alive meant to be on the way to somewhere else.

Perhaps it was no coincidence that most of those he loved in the past had been refugees. Both Hanna and Herr Kirsch had lost their lives in his home town. Just as there are those who stay put all their lives, there must be people who were born refugees. Mark thought of his mother who'd lost her home when his father did not return, though she lived and died a local.

Mark heard Sonja and her friends refer to people he did not know, theatres he had not been to, films he had not seen, racecourses he had never attended. Listening to their intricate gossip of love and sex, passionate discussion of fashion, money and power made him feel excluded. Mark, the newcomer, could neither share nor comprehend their excitement over names. Exclamations like 'Didn't you know, she's a

Beaurepaire?', 'Not *the* Myers?!' or 'At the Princess?' Names were a vital part of the home game. At the Clyde he'd caught a curious expression – his beloved Carlton was 'at home to Melbourne'. He remained intrigued even after finding out it'd been pub talk about a football game. Apparently the whole 'footy' season was a matter of 'home and away'.

Sonja and Mark withdrew for coffee in her room. Lying on the big bed, drowning in pillows, the veiled lamps projected their intermingling shadows across the walls and the Indian poster. From somewhere came the barely audible but strangely nagging sounds of a sitar. It blended with Sonja's regular breath. As she drew closer to him Mark watched the heaving of her voluptuous breasts. It looked as if she had turned her own body into an instrument.

When he awoke in the morning, a buoyant Sonja was already up in the kitchen humming to herself. His quiet appearance in the doorway startled her. She quickly recovered, running into his arms with a broad smile, hugging and kissing him. 'Morning, darling,' she beamed. 'Isn't it wonderful? You'll have to let me take care of you just a little bit.' Her eyes were radiant. She pointed to a pile of neatly cut sandwiches. 'I've made you a little something for the office. You can't keep eating in the pub.'

Before Mark could free himself she added, 'You don't have evening classes tonight, do you? I didn't think so. Make it seven, then, for tea. We'll be joining the others in the Bughouse later. They're showing a new Italian film. I hear it's supposed to be very good. Have you heard of it? I think it's called *L'Avventura*.'

V

Mark's first science assignment – an essay on antibodies – was due in a month. It set him in a state of panic. He'd attended all the lectures, completed all the required studies, participated in all the prescribed lab experiments. But when the time came to report on his findings he could not say what he wanted to say. It wasn't that he had difficulties with his 'second' language. He'd learnt to speak it, not merely to survive; he revelled in a new kind of freedom it gave him. Adopting the Beautiful Enemy's tongue opened up different, more precise expressions, subtler ways of thinking. Translations were old, badly built bridges, where meanings changed in the process of crossing. No two things could ever be the same. He gave up his earlier habit of relating back to his native language. It was the difference in words and meaning that mattered, not any assumed similarity or equivalence. There was really no other way of 'saying the same thing'.

Mark found the nature of speech forced its own intention, its own logic upon a knowledge unable to speak for itself. But what was it, then, he saw and read under the microscope?

He did not consider himself a religious person, but thinking about expressions of knowledge, he concluded that language was like faith. From his childhood he sensed the presence of an intelligence around him, a knowledge that just was. It was what others simply called life. Mark had learned early, for instance, that water had its own logic. There were things you could and could not do when dealing with water. It would carry or drown you, depending on your own behaviour. Down at the docks he'd loved watching paint and oil mingle with water, the circle of colours that would form, spreading a pungent smell of aniline. Whenever he got the chance, he'd taken the tiny ferry to cross the harbour, its superstructure barely above waterline. With his right hand he would measure the strength of the current and the speed of the small launch. Mark knew about water, long before he understood it. He knew it was a language that spoke to him.

As a child back home he'd communicated with rain pounding against windows, frost patterns, clouds, trees, sounds, signs and voices. Now, Melbourne's relentless summer heat, swaying palms outside the university's old sandstone buildings, roofs of workers cottages and terrace houses casting intricately patterned shadows across Elgin and Lygon Streets, red-caped nurses on Sunday afternoons leaving St Vincent's flock-like for late Mass at St Patrick's Cathedral, were becoming part of a new vocabulary.

Each place had acquired its own habit of speech.

He'd worked on the biochemistry assignment for several weeks. 'First Signs of Leukaemia', the chapter's title read in his textbook. All his life Mark had been obsessed with reading signs. To him, they were reality as the most immediate and urgent language. He'd come to think of them as the seams of the world. Learning to recognise them allowed him to witness how life spoke to itself. He'd wanted to make signs the subject of his first science essay, only to discover that to do justice to a science based not on mechanism but organism, he needed to think and write in a language external to his own mind. It was something he found he could not do. Instead of writing with 'scientific objectivity', he knew he needed to describe a process, his personal experience, of discovery. To study the sign language of life required a knowledge of his own mind's expression – and the distance separating it from other forms of natural speech. Science was the study of infinite manifestations of life declaring their presence. What he saw under the microscope were calls of intelligent life communicating with each other. How to report these living relationships in words and expressions that had no part in the process! For in human speech the word was not the thing.

Mark discovered the nature of being was a language which made everything else superimposed and 'foreign'.

Thinking about how to represent without falsification or distortion the behaviour of antibodies, he wondered whether any description – perhaps even truth itself – could ever be more than the logic and reality of one particular language. The blood pathology he remained most interested in was the human body seeking to communicate. It kept speaking to him, even as he was analysing the nature of what it was saying. He became convinced that illness, too, was an intelligent speech with its own inherent logic. To depict complex organic processes Mark needed to possess a very special power of description – a language in which appearance and innate being coincided. In his search to acquire it he realised it was beyond him. He despaired, knowing he would not be able to say what needed to be said.

Humans answered to 'given names'. Mark knew there were hundreds of thousands with whom he shared his name. The word 'Mark' did not, could not, express who he was. The language of biochemistry, on the other hand, always was what it said.

Trying to write his first scientific essay, Mark thought of the Frisian islets' 'double houses'. But they were no more than duplication. To find the proper expression for his lab experiments, more than reflex analogies were required. The language of science was like a dyke built to withstand even the highest storm tide. Did he want to walk the sea again, as he'd once done with Sannes, the beautiful boy who carried the fatal seeds of a mysterious illness?

Should he manage to submit his essay, Mark hoped that he would contribute more than his academic knowledge of the subject. The truth was he wanted to say something about himself. It was his own illness that had drawn him to the science of blood pathology. Witnessing the body communicating with itself had left an indelible impression on him.

To Mark's amazement and relief, the disease of his childhood and adolescence seemed to have disappeared. As a child, he'd been told his blood was not clotting properly, that the severe bleeding he was suffering from was a hereditary disorder. 'You can't change the blood you're born with,' one of the doctors had joked. And yet it seemed that he'd grown out of the haemophilia and anaemia. Was it pure chance that the growth of his blood's red particles coincided with his leaving home? Was it possible that illnesses of the blood were able to heal themselves? Mark knew that was a highly unscientific assertion, yet wasn't his own life proof of such possibility? (Unless, of course, his disease had been falsely diagnosed. But in that case his recovery would seem even more mysterious. For how could he measure his chances of recovering from a wrong diagnosis?)

The nature of blood, he'd discovered, its very essence, consisted of relationships. Now, studying haematology, his body spoke to him, even while he was trying to discover the logic of what it was saying. As proof of his knowledge of the pathology of blood he needed to invoke its sign language of origin. But in his attempt to discover how life spoke to itself, he was dismayed to find himself speechless.

With each new rough version it became clearer he would be unable to write the essay. He could not say what he wanted to say. Not yet. The best he could do would be to explain the reasons for his failure. But that was hardly science!

The truth was that already life in Melbourne was beginning to change him. He was no longer the same person who'd arrived in the city from the migrant camp Bonegilla.

Drawing on seven years study of what both students and

teachers had referred to as a foreign language, Mark did not entirely rely on people in the streets, in shops and trams, in pubs and cafés, imitating their accents, reproducing their colloquialisms, copying their habits of speech. Radio and newspapers helped him acquire expressions of belonging. He was surprised how all those language classes at Old Grammar were at last serving a very practical purpose. They had helped him prepare for a future far from his birthplace. Perhaps there could never be a successful adoption without at least a degree of conscious or unconscious readiness.

Yet Mark still needed to listen to all those voices around him. With almost everything he did, he became involved in a new kind of learning. Like a child he was being taught to speak, how to use words to make himself understood.

Some manners of speaking, like race callings, he knew he would never be able to follow. On the other hand, to have once studied as a foreign language what had now become his commonplace communication, to have considered the everyday familiar as something strange, lent a special dimension to everything he heard or said. There was something both intimate and alien about his daily exchanges. He was busy understanding the meaning of place.

From his studies Mark remembered a little about the evolution of the new language – that it had habitually borrowed from historical conquerors, in the process writing its own history of conquest. It was, he thought, a brilliant strategy for survival. Opening itself up to the influence of foreigners, it had stayed alive remaining itself. All Romans, Normans, Vikings and Germans could do was to enrich its beauty and add to its wealth of meaning.

If there had never been only one language, how could there ever be only one sense? On leaving school, his classics master had presented him with a Latin dictionary. It carried a simple dedication: *Semper con scientia*. With knowledge always. That was what he should aim for in life – to think, act, speak and write both consciously and conscientiously.

Mark learnt to speak the new language with the knowledge that, ironically, it had originated from his first home, the region of northern Schleswig known as *Angeln*. Many of his schoolmates, those whose parents owned farms or lived in villages south of the border town, spoke a Low German dialect known as 'Angel-ish'. Now, his new life in Melbourne confronted him with yet another local variation of 'Angelish'. When it came to language, it seemed he couldn't escape his origin. From now on he would communicate in a 'native foreign language'. Half-alarmed, half-amused, Mark discovered he'd become a child of consciousness! The realisation eased his embarrassment at having to recognise many things twice. His second childhood challenged him to speak consciously. It made him feel strangely grateful that he often recognised more than would otherwise have been apparent. Things were no longer static; without ceasing to be what they were, they revealed themselves as part of many other things. The world was in motion.

Was it possible he himself might have to learn to understand everything, including himself, in terms of relationships?

It continued to both frustrate and excite him how difficult it was to express meaning precisely in any language! More and more he discovered how the nature of speech forced its own intention, its own logic, upon a knowledge unable to speak for itself … Could there be knowledge without language?

One of Mark's favourite books had been the dictionary. As a boy he'd been attracted to certain words, developing a taste for their sounds, their spelling and the – frequently ambiguous – sense of their meaning. Some aroused, while others frightened him. Left alone, he precociously struck up conversations with new words, trying out their weight, their taste on his tongue, tentatively combining them with other words he liked. Occasionally he formed sentences made up from different languages. Later he invented a personal code almost entirely made up of strikingly unusual vowel combinations with which he managed to frighten his friends.

Unlike most of his schoolmates, Mark loved oral tests in Greek and Latin vocabulary. At home it became an intimate ritual he shared with his mother. Outside his home, walking the streets or prowling the docks, he would hum to himself foreign expressions, rehearse unfamiliar sayings or pronounce new words, over and over again. He acquired the reputation of being 'a strange boy'. Back home, alone in his room, he quietly repeated songs they'd learnt at school. *Ya se van los pastores* or *In Dublin's fair city*. He loved the sound of cockles and mussels alive, alive-o.

His own early blood illness, his chemistry set, his student microscope and his beloved globe, even his wild, improvised music were all part of his addiction to languages.

What he'd been taught in foreign language classes was the logic of speech. The knowledge that one could communicate in other tongues meant freedom, for there would always be other ways of saying things. Speaking another language, then, really meant to become a native, one's own, 'foreigner', to adopt a different way of seeing, thinking, understanding and feeling.

Part of such expression of knowledge was the increasing realisation that there could be no one language of truth. Reality spoke many tongues.

He had worked on the haematology assignment for several weeks. On the paper in front of him he read the carefully typed sentence: 'Antibodies are killers of an inherently beautiful enemy.' It shocked him when he realised what he had written. Furiously he pulled the sheet from the typewriter, chastising himself for his lack of discipline. He needed to write about the experience of discovering 'signs'. With passionate, personal precision. He read his own sentence again, fearful of going mad.

In his native language the literal meaning of madness was *being removed*. Was that what was happening to him now? Had he removed himself from the person he had been?

He was haunted by day-dreams of horror which turned

him into a mad monster, part-Dracula, part-Frankenstein, designing a grammar of blood counts, corpuscular patterns, cells of an organism defending its immunity. He was a crazy deaf-mute who in his carnal language glorified illness as The Beautiful Enemy, under constant attack from defenders of a conspiratorial health of silence, order and sterility. His nightmares took him back to the immediate postwar years, when all patients were forced to live in occupation zones to fight off infections of love, ideas and beliefs, passions they were unable to sustain. The frontier guards were under constant order to shoot to kill anyone attempting to cross into no-man's-land. But in his dream he just saluted them as he crossed into freedom.

He cleared his throat before pushing the portable away. Deeply alarmed, he decided to try again another day. There was still time.

To put into words the language of blood, to rediscover himself in 'foreign' images, was like joining those wild boys in the thick winter fog back home as they jumped blindly onto the frozen harbour.

If he was going to jump, he was determined to keep his eyes open.

VI

Curd was a law student who'd gained a high degree of prominence in student theatre, both as an actor and a director. In fact, there was never any doubt in his mind that he would become a professional actor. It was only because his parents were convinced such a precarious choice of profession required a 'reliable back-up' that Curd had, reluctantly, agreed to 'do' law.

His digs consisted of a tiny, windowless room in North Carlton that contained a stained second-hand mattress on the floor and one chair. Two rows of textbooks leaned against whitewashed walls and what Curd professionally referred to as an actor's suitcase. There was no carpet and no table. From the ceiling hung a single naked bulb. When Mark first saw the place he thought it looked like the set for a *film noir*'s grisly murder scene. The starkness of the room positively oozed violence.

They'd met one day when Mark mistakenly entered the Law School from the first floor of 'Public Exams' and found himself in the faculty library. They'd nearly collided as Curd burst through the door. He was, as always, late for a lecture.

'How do you get out of here?' Mark asked him.

'Well may you ask!' the young curly blond man replied. 'Follow me!'

They walked down the stairs until they reached a covered walk with a colonnade opening to a quadrangle. The walls of the cloister still displayed last year's examinations results. Together they entered the old courtyard.

'I've never gone this way before. I'm with 'Public Exams',' Mark explained.

'I'm just with myself.' Curd gave him an endearing, self-deprecating smile. It was a quick-witted, but seemingly well-rehearsed response. He knew the effect it would have on a stranger, making him instantly appear genuine, warm and trustworthy. He introduced himself with another characteristic gesture. Throwing his head back as if in some kind of defiance, he delivered the line 'Name's Curd – ,' before adding with careful timing, '– that's with a "c", and a "d".'

'Fine by me,' Mark imitated the light-hearted mannerisms of a fellow student.

'See you 'round!' Graciously Curd with a 'c' and a 'd' took his leave as if acknowledging the applause of an audience. Before disappearing behind one of the columns he turned around shouting boisterously, 'I'm in the caff most lunchtimes and late in the evenings.' He had managed to upstage an entire building.

Had Mark made a new friend? Who was he? The way he introduced himself made Mark wonder whether he'd met an undergraduate with a stage name.

Over the coming weeks they met regularly, mostly in the cafeteria, at Genevieve's, the Bughouse and, of course, on campus. They talked mainly about plays and films, and how society 'needed to take a good look at itself'. In the course of their passionate discussions Mark sensed that something about this acting student did not ring quite true. He watched and listened to him carefully. If he was looking for some kind of proof, he had no idea what it could be. His own curiosity made him feel disloyal, even deceitful. Why was he not simply grateful for a new friend?

Curd's language seemed somewhat literary, as though everything he said had been learnt off by heart. His pronunciation began to irritate Mark. His new friend's English was

'too good'. Of course, Mark reasoned with himself, he cultivated his speech for the stage, a theatrical affectation of the
Queen's tongue. After all, Curd wanted to be an actor.

As if to validate his use of the Queen's English, Curd told
Mark his sister was actually living at Buckingham Palace.
She was a model who'd recently married a Royal Guard, he
explained. His family's glamorous royal connection, however indirect, sounded so unlikely Mark decided it might
actually be true. But most of all, it sounded like an alibi.

He pleaded with Mark to join him on a weekend visit to
his parents. 'Got to show your face now and then – to earn
your allowance,' he explained. 'Command performance. Such
a drag. You could create a diversion by coming with me.'

Under the circumstances Mark felt he could hardly
refuse. Curd prepared him for the visit by casually revealing
that fifteen years ago his family had emigrated from a region
quite close to Mark's own birthplace. Once their families
must have almost been neighbours.

Mark was stunned. He had not been able to detect a trace
of accent in Curd's speech. How language could both hide
and reveal the speaker! Suddenly he was no longer amused
by some people mistaking his own accent for Welsh. If
speech was the most authentic passport anyone could carry,
there were people like Curd who were able to fake even this
seemingly unforgeable self-documentation. Mark tried to
hide his irritation from Curd, anxious now to find out more
about his friend's obsession to reinvent himself.

Curd's parents' house was a bungalow on the outskirts of
the city. They arrived on a Saturday afternoon to a warm
welcome. Curd complained he was missing out on Carlton
playing Melbourne 'at home'. His mother in particular
seemed delighted to learn of her son's new friend 'from the
old country'. Mark was struck by the contrast between the
random placement of the bush, its coincidental arrangement
of majestic silver gums, acacias and native pines, and the
orderly, unmistakably bourgeois European interior of the

house, complete with heavy oak furniture, tiled stove, oil paintings of forest landscapes and a cuckoo clock in the hallway.

'Isn't it *gemütlich*?' Curd imitated his mother's speech. Mark had picked up on his friend's habit of 'speaking in voices' to cover his unease. It was clear Curd didn't want to face his parents on his own. For whatever reason.

'Isn't it *wunderbar*?' Curd's mother enthused while they were consuming mountains of food 'from the homeland'. It would have been impolite for Mark to reject the stacks of dark rye bread and 'authentic' sausages Curd's father claimed to have smoked himself.

'We all lent a hand at building our great escape,' Curd's father explained. Unlike his son, he spoke with a heavy accent. 'Even Curd. That was, of course, before he started studying law and threatened to become a useless actor.' This was no more than a playful dig at his son, accompanied by a jovial pat on the back. Nonetheless, Mark watched Curd cringe at his father's remarks. He followed uneasily as his parents proudly led Mark on a guided tour of the house. Their very own design, they assured him.

The house could only be described as a foreign body, an out of place transplant from another place. It did not 'fit'. Curd alone recognised the alien nature of their home; knew it did not 'belong'.

Shortly before they were allowed to leave – Curd claimed he had to use the weekend to complete a backlog of assignments – Mark cast a polite glance at the silver-framed family photos prominently displayed on the lounge mantelpiece. He quickly recognised the royal glamour girl. As if on cue, Curd reiterated that his sister was an international cover girl working under the professional name of 'Silke'.

'As in silk. She's all class.' Mark shrugged his shoulders. He wasn't remotely interested in fashion models, even Curd's sister. But he signalled his approval with an acknowledging nod.

They were filling in time while Curd's mother busied herself in the kitchen wrapping stacks of sandwiches for 'the growing boys'. Mark, in particular, could do with them, she declared. As far as she was concerned he was decidedly on the skinny side!

Crammed between, almost hidden by two large glamour photographs of the famous sister, Mark spotted a picture of his friend's father. In the photograph he was wearing a black uniform with a peaked cap bearing a silver death's head.

It wasn't merely that Mark instantly recognised the emblems of the SS. What confused and upset him more was that the picture was clearly not taken in 'the old country'. Curd's father was photographed in a distinctly Australian landscape. Further back in the picture Mark noticed other uniformed men, soldiers, too far away to identify clearly, their formation headed by a couple of standard-bearers. The occasion must have been a formal gathering of some kind. One banner read '*Alte Kameraden*'.

Next to Silke's model poses stood the framed picture of an adolescent boy whose straight blond hair was neatly parted on the right. His eyes were gloomily staring directly into the camera. But wasn't Curd's shock of hair curly and unruly, thrown back regularly as if in constant correction?

'Time to go!' His friend grabbed him roughly by the shoulders. Mark was deeply unsettled, confused and afraid of what he appeared to have discovered.

Perhaps the boy on the mantelpiece was not Curd at all, he told himself. But there could be no doubt about the man in the black uniform. He was the same who had earlier boasted how they had all lent a hand in designing and building their 'great escape'.

Back in Curd's cell-like room they quietly gobbled their sandwiches. The atmosphere was subdued. Mark felt as if they were two prisoners being fed after their daily exercise in the yard. Whenever one of them rose from the mattress the single bulb swayed above them. In the starkness of its light their silhouettes began to cast an ensemble of wild inmates. Yet if this was, or looked to Mark like, a kind of prison, Curd clearly did not see himself in the least as being confined or shut up. On the contrary. His loft would always remain his secret hideaway, an oasis of freedom, the only place where, as he put it, 'he could truly be himself'.

Like his parents, Curd seemed obsessed with photographs. Even in this bare room Mark saw a few glossy enlargements protruding from books. After what he'd seen he dared not ask what they were. But Curd had already noticed his glances and dismissed the pictures as 'publicity shots from recent productions'.

Later that night they picked up Curd's girlfriend Samantha who lived just a block away. She too was a law student, about nineteen, a pony-tailed dark-haired beauty, cheekily dressed in a sailor suit. After a coffee at Genevieve's Mark invited them along to Sonja's and 'Les Girls next door'. Mark appreciated their standing invitation to just 'drop in' any time he felt like it, and 'to bring his friends'. Up to now he'd always come alone. Although he considered himself by now as belonging to various groups – at 'Public Exams', in tutorials, in the pub and, yes, most of all at 'Les Girls', as he'd dubbed his hospitable neighbours – Mark was unsure whether Sonja and her friends would be ready, either for a knitting ice-skater fallen on hard times or a slit-eyed 'spider woman' anxious to transliterate Chopin into sex. It wasn't altogether clear to Mark how they would respond to Curd and Sam either.

He needn't have worried about Sam. They all took to her as if they'd been friends for years. But then it was easy to like Sam. She was not only beautiful but genuinely interested in other people. An alert listener of great empathy, she knew exactly when to nod or to display other signs of agreement and when to remain thoughtful or silent. Little wonder the girls took an instant liking to her.

By contrast, their response to Curd seemed somewhat more cautious. They immediately sensed that he was 'different'. To Mark's hidden irritation Curd viewed their visit as a theatrical event, an exhibition of his 'personal wares', in a manner of speaking. Shortly after their arrival he began to imitate – not mockingly, rather with a kind of searching interest in another voice – the speech and gestures of everyone present. From the hallway, Julia, who'd gone to her room to fetch a new LP, heard what she thought was Belinda telling the others secrets of her new boyfriend. Outraged at the indiscretion she called out, 'Stop it, Linda!' Curd was disappointed there was no laughter when Julia discovered that during her absence he had been imitating Belinda's voice.

A nervous tension that no jokes or anecdotes could relax fell over the conversation. Sam did her best to mediate. Smiling apologetically, she dismissed Curd's 'habit' as an actor's *deformation professionelle*. It prompted a forced laughter, more in tribute to her good-natured temperament than in appreciation of Curd's uncanny, unsettling ability to imitate voices. Didn't he know when to stop?

'Hello, sailor!' he joked turning to Sam, this time adopting the voice of a cockatoo. When he spoke to her in Mark's distinctive, yet almost unplaceable accent, she beckoned Mark to follow her, grabbed his arm and walked out of the room.

'It's a compulsion,' Sam explained. 'I hate it. Once he starts he can't stop. It's like an illness.' Mark felt sorry for her. Having to apologise for someone you love must be very difficult.

After a final coffee Curd and Sam left. They suddenly remembered other friends they'd promised to see. 'The curse of popularity!' Curd's parting words of self-mockery appeared to be spoken in his own voice. Neither the girls nor Mark recognised it as their own.

It was still early in the evening. Mark and Sonja withdrew to her room. Lying on the bed they quietly held each other. Sensing Sonja's disquiet he thought of ways to comfort her. They tried to reassure each other by touching. For the moment his presence was all Mark could offer her. She accepted it as if it were a precious gift.

'He's not really a friend of yours, is he?' she pleaded. Silently Mark shook his head, signalling as much his own bewilderment as his desire to calm the young woman who, having made it her business to mother him, felt the urge to protect him from all evil as well.

Mark next saw Curd and Sam outside the Union Theatre where they were putting up posters for a new play. 'It's all about racial persecution in a fictional country,' Curd enthused. 'We've been rehearsing for months. You must come and see it. Sam'll get you two free tickets, if you like.'

Not a word about their visit to 'Les Girls'. Mark was surprised Curd had spoken to him in a matter-of-fact tone.

Dressed in black tights, a striped blue and white top and sporting a navy blue beret, Sam looked like a French pantomime artiste. She rushed over to Mark and with a hug handed him the tickets. 'It's for the first night,' she pleaded. 'You and Sonja, please come and join me. Otherwise I have to watch it on my own. Whenever Curd's putting on a show,' she explained, 'I have to be in the audience.'

'Why?'

She shrugged her shoulders. It was clear she had never given the matter any thought. 'That's how it is. When he's acting or directing I also attend lectures for him. Curd says it brings us closer.' She laughed dismissively, then shrugged her shoulders once more, as if demonstrating a new dance craze.

'We'll be there,' Mark promised.

One night Sonja reluctantly told Mark that her father was a famous violinist. Mark had no idea his friend came from such a distinguished family.

They had made love in the safety of Sonja's deep-cushioned bed, surrounded by projections of Indian dancers and their own moving shadows. The covered lamp in the corner of Sonja's room reminded Mark of the globe his mother had given him all those years ago, a little world that lit up at night, just like the illuminated dial of the radio that had once belonged to his father. To him, the world had always been linked to light.

Exhausted from their love-making, in a moment of serene after-pleasure when confessions and intimate truths are exchanged most naturally, Sonja told him she was an adopted child.

'My father's hardly ever home,' she told him with a soft, monotonous voice. 'Most of the time he's on concert tours, all over the world.'

Mark had heard of his name, although he could not be sure whether he had ever listened to any particular concert or recording. Chances were he had heard him on the radio. It occurred to Mark that Sonja's father must be quite old.

'Nathan's very good to me.' Her response anticipated his question. 'We never fight. And he always brings me presents from the countries he has visited.'

Mark's arms did not release her. He remained silent in their embrace.

'When he leaves my mother alone for too long she gets frustrated and starts fighting with me. That's why I don't live at home. Mum and I argue most of the time. I think we're really fighting over his absence.'

'I understand.' Mark did not elaborate. Perhaps, on another occasion, he would tell Sonja about his own absent father.

Although he was told it would be a casual meeting, Mark took the invitation to meet Sonja's parents very seriously. Not because it signalled her seriousness about their relationship. His reasons were rather more selfish – he wanted to meet her famous father.

The afternoon before their dinner date Mark went on a special expedition to the city. He knew a record shop which sold classical LPs that had 'only been played once'. The sales assistant assured Mark that his selection, a Deutsche Grammophon recording of Tchaikovsky's Symphony Nr 6, the 'Pathétique', had indeed only been played once. Their classical records, she explained, were all 'surplus' from a local radio station. It sounded a bit suspect to Mark, but when he examined the vinyl, the record did look as new, and he couldn't argue about the price.

The elegant atrium house in the seaside suburb of Brighton was furnished with scores of musical items – a grand piano next to a collection of string instruments, ivory and marble busts of composers, volumes of musical scores, histories of music.

The world-famous artist who had adopted Sonja as his daughter seemed genuinely pleased with Mark's present. 'Ah, so, ja, the Friscay recording,' he mused aloud. 'A truly memorable performance of the Berlin Philharmonic. Thank you, my dear boy.' His delight sounded a bit like muffled groaning. Despite the familiar sounds of his accent, Mark had difficulty understanding what the old man was saying.

Meanwhile Sonja's mother kept complimenting him on his 'thoughtfulness' and 'good taste'. 'You can always tell a European upbringing. You are not a musician yourself, by any chance?' she politely enquired.

'Only when I'm deluding myself,' Mark responded without a hint of irony. Turning to the father he added flirtatiously, 'I did not think it appropriate to bring you one of your own recordings.'

His vague attempt at humour misfired. The artist looked at him gravely and said, 'No, my friend. That would not have been right. It'd be like returning to a singer his own voice.' Thoughtfully he ran his fingers through his grey thinning hair, then clapped his hands, as if to call himself back to a life without music. 'But it was nice of you to come. You have known our daughter for a long while?'

Mark could not tell why, despite its underlying groan, he found the accent of the old man strangely comforting. There was something about its tone he thought he recognised, although he could not remember where he had heard it before. Then it came to him. It was a Jewish voice, so similar to the

270

accent of his own people. Only when he listened more carefully did it sound somewhat different. Mark's ears began to ring with echoes of Mr Kirsch's last words, 'Enough. No more.'

After dessert, Sonja's father placed the record on the turntable. It soon became apparent that it was scratched. Not here or there. A seemingly invisible crack cut right across the record. As soon as Mark noticed it, he pleaded with his host to turn it off. Deeply humiliated, he wanted to explain the origin of his present.

Waving his hands in a placatory gesture, the famous violinist responded with a lenient smile. Graciously he insisted, 'Nevertheless. Let us listen to the end.' Reconciled to the insistent scratch he kept his eyes closed, listening as though there were no interference at all. Sonja and her mother could barely hide their irritation. By contrast, the great artist accepted the distorting interruptions as though they were an inseparable part of the performance. He insisted on listening to the other side of the record as well, which, to Mark's great relief, turned out to be undamaged.

Only after they had heard the entire recording did Sonja's father pronounce with a quiver in his voice, 'It is a very German interpretation. One of the Berlin Philharmonics' best. How ingeniously it captures the spirit of the work and the time.' Then, looking at Mark, he said almost mournfully, 'Thank you for your thoughtful present, my dear fellow.'

Mark did not know how to fill the silence that permeated the room after that.

When they were leaving, Mark made one last attempt to explain. 'I should've bought it from a proper store,' Mark admitted. 'You see, I don't own a record player myself.' It sounded a rather pathetic excuse. He didn't want to add that he could not afford to buy one, that even the records on sale in proper music stores were too expensive for him.

The old man farewelled him with a smile. 'You look after my daughter, dear boy, and leave the music to me.' As he saw them out, his face lit up. Speaking slowly, he explained,

'Music is memory, a kind of trembling bridge rising above history. It has its own time, its own truth.' In a gesture of resignation and reconciliation he seemed to wave himself aside. 'You are still young. You must recognise music, even if you have never heard it before.' He opened the door, embracing them with sudden passion, 'You will, you will!'

From the front gate they waved back at their hosts. The famous artist had put an arm around his wife. Mark had never seen his parents that way. Slowly he turned away.

Sonja took Mark's hand. She would continue to protect him, even against her parents.

'He liked you,' she assured him in the tram back to Carlton. 'In a strange sort of way I think he even liked the record.'

That night they made love as if trying to fix all cracks of all imperfect presents in the world. Never before had Mark stayed inside a woman for so long. Sonja's body was like the cocoon of her room – a soft, deep-cushioned bed, a woman's shelter, a home of intimate generosity.

'My father wasn't away on concert tours,' Mark told Sonja, his voice carrying more bitterness than he'd intended. 'I never knew where he was.' After a moment's silence he corrected himself. 'I never knew who he was.' She lay next to him, not letting go of their touch.

'I once thought I could see him flying in the sky. Dropping bombs on his own home. The things we imagine when we are children!'

Caressing his hair, Sonja listened to the man whose home she longed to be.

Mark sighed, his eyes directed at the ceiling. 'It was a long time ago.'

Finally, in a barely audible murmur, Sonja responded. 'I understand. I mean, your own father not returning.'

'I still don't know what's happened to him.'

He was afraid Sonja might whisper once more 'I understand'. But she remained silent. Somehow she knew when not to say anything.

'Is he a father to you?' Mark asked.

'No,' Sonja replied. 'But he's a friend.'

That night, before they went to sleep, she cried. A quiet voice came out of the darkness. 'Perhaps I really wanted a father.'

By now friends seemed to enter Mark's life as if they were part of the place. University was crowded with people anxious to argue over what they thought was their most intimately personal discovery, only to learn their fellow students had been on the very same exploration. An entire generation seemed in the process of seeking to recognise itself. By its very nature knowledge was something to be shared, even if some of Mark's brightest friends denied there could ever be such a thing as meaningful knowledge. Often they were the most desperate to share their despair.

Helen was a second year honours student of English. Pale-skinned, blue-eyed, long-haired, Mark thought she bore an uncanny likeness to Lauren Bacall. They met one day near the clock tower of the Old Arts Building, where he found Helen reading an anthology entitled *The Metaphysicals*. He introduced himself with the cunning obtrusiveness of a stray cat. Her precocious response was of equal directness. As if in the middle of a prolonged discussion, she implored him to accept that 'thought was a feeling and feeling a thought'.

Anxious to please, he simply nodded. 'Sure. If you say so.'

Testing or proclaiming literary interpretations she raised and lowered her long blonde hair like a curtain.

Mark could not keep his eyes off her. He didn't know what to admire more, the bubbly cheekiness of her behaviour or the graceful movements of her body. To anything he might say Helen had ready-made literary answers, usually in the form of a quotation. She turned up her nose at his questions about the truth of poetic language before adopting a rhetorical stance and reciting in a gloriously musical voice, 'He that's mounting up/Must on his neighbour mount/And we and all the Muses/Are things of no account'. Mark had to admit she looked damned beautiful when delivering somebody else's poetic despair. He could not help staring at her watery blue eyes, sensuous lips and voluptuous breasts.

Noticing how he scrutinised her from head to toe, she challenged him with barely controlled irritation, 'What are you doing?' Mark thought she was referring to his studies.

'Haematology?!' The way she dismissively pronounced his subject it sounded more like 'alchemy'.

'Believe it or not, we biologists are also looking for patterns of meaning.' Her sceptical look challenged him to explain further: 'Or life, if you like. In fact, some patterns are quite beautiful, although scientists are not suggesting there is a connection between beauty and meaning.'

'Oh yeah?' In the same tone of defiance she asked him, 'Are you going to tell me now or later that I'm beautiful?'

Helen was not the kind of woman Mark would find easy to convince of anything. But even in her apparent impatience she didn't make him go away. In fact, it became clear she quite liked talking to the stranger who'd interrupted her reading.

She was living in a residential college on campus, Helen informed him. In case he wanted to give her a call, although she couldn't guarantee she would be 'in'. Still, she generously gave him her number. Mark couldn't believe his luck.

When he rang her the following day Helen persuaded him to indulge with her 'in the book-sniffing cult'. He instantly agreed, although he had no idea what it meant. They took a tram to the city where they ransacked a number of second-hand bookshops. Helen informed him she was looking for first editions of Matthew Arnold. The shop owners greeted her like an old acquaintance.

Mark found it incongruous to see the tall vivacious woman with spectacular film star hair stroll through rows and rows of faded books covered in dust, pull out the odd volume, knowledgably study its imprint before returning it to the shelf. Her enthusiasm and energy proved infectious. Against all intentions Mark soon found himself looking for medical titles, especially books dealing with illnesses of the blood. But there was very little in his area of interest. Medical textbooks seemed to age very quickly. Mark remembered one of his lecturers urging them not to buy an earlier edition of a standard work on blood diseases because new discoveries over the past two years had made most of its content obsolete.

In playful provocation Helen reminded him she was a student of 'timeless values'. She said it in a mocking tone, but Mark was left in no doubt that she meant it. Was there no timelessness in science?

It was in the company of Helen that Mark first went to Acland Street in the bay suburb of St Kilda. He recognised it as a kind of Jewish Carlton. The street was crowded with delicatessens, cake shops and cafés. Helen directed him to a European-looking bookshop which in its window displayed publications in various languages along with records from many countries. It also sold Jewish devotional objects and religious books.

From the moment they stepped inside Mark felt at home. He was amazed and delighted Helen had taken him to a place like this. The music, the smell, scraps of verbal exchanges momentarily took him back to the world he'd left behind. Relieved and intrigued Helen registered his smile of recognition.

'Thought you'd like it here,' she said casually as she guided him to the section holding books and records of his native tongue.

Together they went through the titles, holding book and record covers in their hands, drawing each other's attention to whatever had caught their eye. As they did so, something remarkable happened. Holding publications in the well-known language, inspecting, touching, smelling them, Mark was suddenly overcome by an alienating, even repulsive, familiarity.

Something once so intimately natural had transformed itself into a powerful confrontation. What had happened to bring about such radical change? Could nothing remain the same? If origin was permanent, why was memory busy changing it? Mark heard the calm reflective voice of Sonja's adoptive father: 'Memory is a kind of trembling bridge rising above history.' He felt ashamed without knowing why.

Surrounded by sounds and letters, signs and smells, images and voices designed to call him home, Mark was lost. Everything he saw, heard and touched made him ask the same question: 'Who am I?'

Helen's obvious disappointment over his response made him feel guilty. She'd taken him here to please him. Why didn't he want any of the books or records 'in his own language'?

He was relieved to find she herself had not discovered there an author 'of timeless values'. They left the bookshop with mixed feelings.

Over cake and coffee in Scheherazade, the café across the road, they found it difficult to argue over art, science and life as if nothing had happened.

'It's a very historical place.' Helen tried to give her voice the usual cheerful bounce, but failed. It was the only reference to the cosmopolitan bookshop she allowed herself.

VII

How long did it take to become a Melburnian? By now Mark knew most of the suburbs, the different tram and bus lines, the theatres and cinemas, a host of sports-grounds and department stores, churches, hospitals, bank branches and radio stations – even a variety of government offices. He had visited the Town Hall, been inside the Exhibition Building and, together with Sonja, bought fruit and vegetables at Queen Victoria Market. Was that enough to turn him into a 'local'?

Mark noticed how people claimed their part of the city with remarkable speed. Whole suburbs appeared to be populated by newcomers of similar background. They simply declared it their new home. In Europe your family had to have lived in one place for centuries before you could truly say 'this is our home'. Here, things happened more quickly, perhaps because there was nowhere else to go. Some homes seemed to project a kind of defiant resolution: 'This is it! We're staying put.'

Perhaps what had brought the inhabitants closer together was this one shared experience. At one stage they'd all been newcomers. They'd arrived, and now there was nowhere else to go. Living in this city (perhaps in this whole vast country that Mark had only encountered from the sky) meant remaining in a permanent state of arrival. Mark liked that idea. It made him think of the fable of the race between the hedgehog and the hare. Reading the English equivalent of the tortoise and the hare at Old Grammar, he'd discovered that in translated stories sometimes even the central characters needed to be altered. Mark wondered whether something similar happened to people who left their home country – perhaps they too needed to change their stories, if they wanted to make themselves understood. 'Ick bün all hier!' the piglike snout of the porcupine declared in perfect Low German whenever the faster rabbit arrived at the finishing line. In Europe the most unlikely creature always came first, claiming ownership of home and country, along with other privileges.

Mark found the thought of Australians being turned into refugees in their own country preposterous. He was quite certain it just couldn't happen here. Refugees were a European invention.

Hares brought to mind rabbits, a prohibited import on this continent. Yet they'd multiplied to plague proportions. Mark was amused by the thought of extending the symbolism of the race to his adopted homeland; the Aborigines would have been the hedgehogs. Not that he knew enough about the original inhabitants to be able to judge the validity of such comparison. So far, he'd only seen a couple of native Australians. They were sitting in a dry riverbed outside the camp of Bonegilla doing much the same as the inmates – smoking and drinking. It had made Mark wonder what the fence was for: to keep them out, or keep him in?

Having lived in the city for almost a year, however, he knew Melbourne was not the setting of a fable. It was nonetheless a place of constant arrivals.

Moments of panic still paralysed him. The long list of destinations on the arrival and departure board at Flinders Street Station confused him, as it had on his very first day, fresh from Bonegilla. But this time he realised that all these names – many copying well-known European cities – referred to nearby suburbs and a number of Victorian country towns.

The trains weren't going to the 'real places', he registered with alarm. Flinders Street was not at all like central stations in Europe where railway passengers departed to cross international borders, to enjoy lunch or dinner in dining cars or to travel through the night in comfortable sleepers. Mark was outraged. Melbourne's main station was fake. Its trains didn't go where they pretended to go. He felt cut off from the rest of the world. Australia was a country without borders. The only way in or out was by sea or air.

But he had known that all along. Why this sudden panic? His flight had taken him to the largest island in the world. Wasn't that where he had wanted to be?

A hot and humid Christmas came and went. Mark sent cards featuring exotic palms in Albert Park to old classmates. In a couple of sentences he let them know there was no snow in December and that he was fine. Writing to Frank Hilmer, he nearly forgot to revert to his first language. Frank had been his special friend, both in and out of school.

The campus lay deserted. Almost all students had left. Colleges were empty. In the surrounding suburbs 'Room to let' signs went up, but no one took up the offer.

To his surprise Mark had passed the first year science course. He'd failed only one assignment. His lecturer could not understand why he hadn't handed it in. He'd been so reliable in every other way. When he discovered Mark was working full-time he recommended a Pass in the subject.

During January and February Mark spent most of his evenings at 'Les Girls' or the Bughouse. He had nowhere else to go.

Like Curd, he'd come to love the poetic realism of Italian cinema, especially the films of Pasolini, Fellini and Antonioni. Sometimes Helen would join him. Afterwards they'd go to Genevieve's where many of their friends had gathered for late night drinks and discussions. It was here, after a screening of La Dolce Vita, that Sonja first met Helen.

Mignon and Sonja were sitting at a big table by themselves and waved them over. Mark was grateful for the theatricality of Curd's introductions – it created the kind of embarrassment which helped cover his own disquiet. For a few awkward moments the two young women appeared to size each other up. Then they acknowledged one another's presence with deliberately casual smiles which Mark misread as genuine attempts to be pleasant.

Samantha turned to him. 'How's Marcello?'

'He's thinking about a huge flabby fish,' Helen replied looking straight at Sonja.

Curd described the final scene as if it were a dramatic recitation. 'It was a monster – a strange, bloated monster that stared at us with dead, accusing eyes. A repulsive little crab skittered down off its back and dropped onto the sand.'

'What on earth are you talking about?' Mignon demanded to know.

Sonja's face became flustered. She was blushing, close to tears. Mark whispered something soothing in her ear. Enough to calm her down. Quietly he turned to Mignon. 'A German woman called it a schooner fish. They told her it might have come from Australia. It was horrible.'

'Well, that's how the film ends.' The triumphant finality in Helen's voice expressed profound satisfaction. It remained unclear what made her feel so deeply gratified – the entire film, its ending, Marcello, Mark or Sonja.

Samantha looked around. 'It's the most beautiful, the most haunting part. Marcello calls out to the young girl, "I don't understand … I can't hear, I cannot hear … I can't hear." And then he walks away.'

'Who with?'

'With the others.' Curd had lent his voice an Italian accent. Testing its effect he turned to Samantha, calling out *'Abbraccami forte!'* She pushed him back.

The arrival of their coffee led to talk about new lecturers, friends and the future of the country. Mark realised that in their company he truly was no longer an outsider. This was where he belonged. No doubt about it.

It was approaching midnight. The heat and humidity remained incongruously high. With one eye Mark was watching the television set located high up in the corner of the room. He recognised the newsreader Eric Pearce. (That, too, was part of being a Melburnian.) Eric Pearce was an institution in this city. Everybody watched and admired him, his gentlemanly flair, the serenity with which he would announce a tragedy, the intimacy, the irony of some of his pronouncements. To most Melburnians he was more than the news, he was the world.

Someone had turned up the sound to catch the weather forecast. Eric farewelled his viewers with characteristic charm. 'I've been reliably informed,' he assured the good citizens of this fair city, 'a cool change is just around the corner. So it's quite safe now for you to go to sleep.' His eyes twinkled as he passed on the desired prediction. Mark was again struck by the endearing intimacy of his manner. Melbourne might be a city of millions, but Eric Pearce created the illusion that reading the news could be like passing on the village gossip.

'Good night,' the great man said, leaving his viewers with the station signal.

'Perhaps we should go too,' Mark prompted Helen. 'You heard, there's going to be a storm.'

But Helen was in no hurry. 'Stay, Marcello,' she imitated Samantha. No one laughed. The subject *La Dolce Vita* had exhausted itself.

'Funny how many universities are located next to cemeteries,' Curd ventured. 'Wonder whether that's purely coincidental?' They were back to student philosophy, politics and town planning.

It was true: Carlton was surrounded by a large cemetery. Mark had walked across it once, marvelling at its Chinese and Jewish graves. From a distance the cemetery was hard to distinguish from any other suburb.

Through the open door they could hear a rumble. Flashes of lightning tore across the night sky. As yet there was no rain.

Mignon and Sonja were anxious to get home before the downpour. 'I'll walk Helen home. She's staying in college,' Mark explained as he kissed Sonja on the cheeks.

'Make sure you don't get lost!' It was Mignon who gently mocked him. Sonja left quietly without looking back.

It was easy for Curd to persuade Samantha to stay the night at his place – it was so much closer, and the first rain-drops were already pelting against the window. They left Genevieve's arm in arm, howling 'The rain in Spain'. Their voices blended perfectly, even in the send-up version of the song. Standing at the door Helen and Mark could hear them singing as they slowly disappeared into Lygon Street, inter-rupted only by well-timed growls at the rolling thunder. By the time they moved on to 'I have often walked down the street before' they were already out of sight.

'What an odd couple,' Helen chuckled approvingly.

They started running towards Swanston Street, the rain now pouring down quite heavily. They paused to catch their breath at a tramstop shelter, then raced each other down a lane past the North Building of the university. By the time they reached one of the college ovals they were completely soaked. Mark knew the field well. He'd sometimes kicked a ball around there during his lunch breaks from 'Public Exams'. Trying out the new game. The one with the oval ball. Australian Rules.

For a brief moment they were both exhausted. But it didn't take long for them to regain their vigour and high spirits.

The ground was soggy as the rain continued to bucket down. Helen responded to the thunder and lightning around them with her own exuberant shrieks. Wet to the skin she began to dance around the middle of the football field. Her usually well-groomed long hair was hanging in limp ringlets which lent her face a slightly mad, demonic look. 'Marcello!' she cried. 'Come here, Marcello!' A primal scream, demanding and unforgiving.

Mark's shoes were flooded by puddles, his clothes drenched by the rain, his skin as wet as if he'd taken a shower. With every move he made he sank deeper into the mud. Helen waved and shouted at him like a madwoman, gesticulating to the sky, pointing to her breasts and crotch.

In their embrace they wrestled each other to the muddy ground. Laughing madly, they rolled together, their faces covered with wet soft earth. Amidst muddy kisses they removed parts of their clothing to let the other inside.

For brief seconds a lightning flash illuminated her face. With wide open lips she repeated her demands: 'Come, Marcello! Come to me! Oh, how I want you!'

Mark could feel the wet soil on his tongue. He entered her with the brutality of the storm now raging all around them. Did she scream in recognition? Nearby trees were losing their branches, and the thunder drowned out any other noise. Did she cry in pain or moan with pleasure? All Mark could hear was the pounding of his own blood.

Their coming together had the precision of uncontrolled desire. Tears of relief mingled with the pouring rain and wet soil. The heavens had opened up, and so had they. The storm's water on their skin had cooled their lust, that angry want exploding inside of them.

Hysterical with pleasure and delight she would not let him go. Whispering words neither of them could hear, she waited till she felt him grow again. 'Marcello!' the trees hissed as they surrendered more of their branches. And the rain grew heavier. Like prehistoric creatures they wallowed in their own swamp. Not far from them an overhead wire had caught fire and lit up the dark. Neither Mark nor Helen noticed it. Once more they flowed into each other, the unstoppable downpour soaking every part of their bodies.

Impatient passion sated, they lay like two dead bodies in

the night. Their breath had cooled, their still thirsty lips were drinking rain. Each rubbed mud from their eyes to look at the dark. A cold wind was blowing. No lights anywhere. The whole suburb, along with the university, must have been blacked out by the storm. Silent, they continued to stare at the cloudy, starless night sky. Night enclosed them like a lovers' tomb.

Sonja and Mignon sat in the kitchen for a candle-lit cup of tea. The soothing drone of the gas stove contrasted with the violent explosions outside. It felt good being inside with the storm raging. They'd been thoroughly drenched by the time they'd reached home. Now they listened to the rain tumbling on the corrugated iron roof, feeling snug and safe.

'Cosy, isn't it?'

'Yeah. I love rain. And didn't we need it!'

VIII

A week before the start of lectures Mark found a letter addressed to him on the telephone table in the hallway. He opened the envelope on the way up to his room, curious to know who might be writing to him. It was unusual for him to receive any mail. He was exhausted and cranky, having worked with David on 'Stats' all day, only to find their figures didn't match. Lying on his bed he unfolded the formal looking letter and began to read.

Moments later an involuntary shout emanated from his room, startling his landlady downstairs. Mark could not suppress his delight at the content of the typed communication from 'The Commonwealth of Australia'. He'd been awarded a scholarship to continue his studies. How could that be? His results had not been outstanding, and he had not applied for a scholarship. Yet there it was. Again and again he read the opening sentence, 'It gives me great pleasure to inform you ...'.

All his tiredness quickly disappeared. Without hesitation he raced down the stairs, barely closing the front door properly on the way out, and ran over to 'Les Girls'. They were all home and after his announcement treated him like a hero. Even Belinda showered him with congratulatory kisses. 'I don't believe it! Well done, Mark! Good on you!

That's so … so I-don't-know!' She had difficulty finding the right words to express her delight. Passing the letter around, waving it in the air, they fell over each other with compliments. They shared in Mark's success as if it were their own.

It was time to celebrate. Genevieve's, Martini's or The Black Pearl? 'You decide,' a boisterous Mark declared. 'You're all invited.'

They ended up at Genevieve's, as always, ordering 'spags and vino'. 'One of these days we really should try something different,' Mark mocked their culinary lack of imagination.

The girls took no notice of him. They were comfortable with the place, the food, the company, their regular corner table near the window. Their favourite waiter, Luigi, delivered cutlery and glasses, while Julia and Belinda lit each other's cigarettes. Mark and 'his girls' were an exuberant lot, filling the crowded low-ceiling premises with cheers and infectious laughter. Sonja sat close to Mark, forever seeking to hold his arm or hand, congratulating him over and over again.

'I'm so happy for you,' she repeated every once in a while. Mark watched her clean his glass before pouring the wine. How he wished she wouldn't fuss so much!

Perhaps that's why he'd begun to visit her less often. He was grateful for her kindness and affection, but found he needed the company of others. Tonight they were a group of neighbourly friends, celebrating together. Had she forgotten she was part of 'Les Girls', his next-door mates?

Sonja was careful not to mention Helen to him, but it was clear she had not forgotten the night he'd introduced her to them. Soon after she'd made a point of seeing the film herself and established that 'her' Mark had nothing in common with Marcello, that reckless, immoral Italian journalist. If Helen saw a similarity, it was clear to her she didn't know the first thing about him. It disturbed her deeply that Mark had shown an interest in Helen. What was so special about her? She was just another English student, after all.

But Sonja knew why Mark had gone out with her. She despaired over the unfairness of being a woman. Helen's looks were propagated in every film and every glamour magazine. How could she fight it! The way her shoulder-long hair bounced when she was laughing or shaking her head! Sonja was deeply distrustful of what was called the glamour of female beauty. Didn't Mark realise that Helen knew exactly what she was doing, that it was all an act! Helen was acting the part of a woman, instead of being one. And her role was, of course, written by men, for the pleasure of men. Did Helen really care for Mark, or was he just part of the make-up?

Amidst the laughter and uproar surrounding her Sonja's heart missed a beat. It was a frightening thought, a terrible, horrible, unimaginable possibility. What if Helen really did love Mark? Instinctively she groped for his hand.

But Mark was busy drawing figures in the air. He was giving an impression of old Mrs Osborne, pencil in hair, carrying one of 'Public Exams" huge record books into the sacred vault. He followed it with an imitation of David knitting while skating on ice. Sonja had never seen Mark in such an extrovert mood. He was performing, entertaining the whole party. Had Helen turned him into a Curd?

'It'll be such a joy to leave all that behind!' he assured them with a laugh. 'No longer shall I be examining the public. Keeping an eye on your school record, dear Linda, exposing Julia's grade in Domestic Science.' The two women mimicked a howling outrage before another glass of wine stilled their protest in appreciative snorts of laughter.

Sonja had missed one vital fact, she realised. Mark was leaving his job. Of course! What had she been thinking! With a scholarship he would no longer have to work.

'Hadn't she listened?' Mignon mildly rebuked her. 'Where have you been?' He planned to give notice right away. Well, tomorrow. He'd be free at last. 'Imagine,' Mignon prompted. 'He'll be just like us. All day to himself.'

'Mark, just like us?' Sonja thought. But hadn't he always been special, different? How could he suddenly be like anyone else? She hadn't fallen in love with someone who was 'like anyone else'!

When Luigi banged down a bowl of steaming spaghetti in front of her, it hit her like some kind of brutal, inescapable, overwhelming evidence. Or was it already an execution? Looking around, she found the others already making pigs of themselves. She had to restrain herself not to throw the parmesan grater at them.

'To Mark!' 'To freedom!' 'To spaghetti!' 'To Luigi!' 'To Genevieve's!' 'To scholarships!'

Belinda offered her own subtle variation of the last toast, 'To scholarship!'

To the sound of hissing they all raised their glasses, before Mark requested a drink to honour a new daring ambition. 'To my own place at last!' They emptied their glasses before fully grasping the implications of what Mark had just announced.

Amidst the general joviality Julia enquired in a semi-judicial tone, 'Are you telling us you've gone flat-hunting already?' Mark did not reply, but it was clear he'd made up his mind to move away from their immediate neighbourhood.

'When are you going to leave us?' Sonja's voice was quivering, but her face retained its usual cheerfulness. Mark put his arm around her in mock comfort. 'The corpse's still warm, my dear,' he informed her.

'Marcello, don't go!' Mignon adopted the declamatory voice of an Italian actress, her hands raised dramatically in a desperate gesture as if she were about to take leave of someone foolhardy and reckless. 'The world's incredibly cruel, my darling. Molto, molto cruel! It will crush you, and it will kill you,' she predicted, relishing the operatic artificiality of her crs' lingual sound. The theatrical outburst ended abruptly in a plain voice casual request. 'Pass the parmesan.'

So he was going to leave her, as she'd feared. Sonja took a

deep breath and kept her hands to herself. She stopped eating. As she drank Mark's wine she heard her adoptive father say to him, 'You leave the music to me.' Had Nathan even then known things about Mark she'd failed to notice? She longed for his touch, to be away from here, alone with him once more, to let their bodies play the game of light and shadow.

'Well, well, well! If it isn't. What's all this, then?' It was Curd's voice imitating God-knows-who. His sidekick Samantha, dressed like a gondolier, took a fork-full of spaghetti from Sonja's plate and swallowed it in a spectacular manner. It was another one of her circus acts. '*Molto precisioso, al dente!*' the culinary trapeze artiste pronounced. '*Molto, molto, molto!*' Everyone around the table shrieked with delight and moved their chairs to make room for the newcomers.

'May one enquire whose birthday it is?' Curd asked, adopting the tone of a kind old lady as he took his seat next to Mark. When he'd learnt the cause of the celebration he spontaneously declared, 'But he doesn't deserve it! What's he done? Nothing!' They all laughed like a well-prompted audience. No one around the table felt Curd begrudged Mark his success. They all knew what he meant. Mark really hadn't done anything; he'd discovered life in Carlton, and become one of them while remaining himself. Well, good for him. But hardly worthy of a scholarship. He was lucky the people of this city had looked after him.

Assuming Mark's voice Curd announced, 'Now that I've spent over a year of my life in beautiful downtown Melbourne, I wish to advise my friends that I am returning home.' His speech was greeted with uproarious laughter. Even Mark joined in.

'But I am at home.' Mark's protest was drowned out by the noisy exuberance at the table. It came too late to take away the impact of Curd's vernacular declaration.

Samantha shouted something to Sonja about make-believe belongings.

Mignon tried to make a point about Schoenberg's twelve-tone-music, while no one was listening. 'All this chasing after atavistic harmony,' she said to no one in particular. 'It's pathetic. I simply can't listen to nineteenth century music any more!'

Julia concentrated on gulping down her food. 'These spags are much better than the ones we had at The Black Pearl last month, don't you agree?' No one took any notice of her.

'Of course nobody thought of ordering a plate for me.' As always, it was impossible to tell whether Curd actually meant what he was saying. But a few minutes later Luigi, at a wink from Mark, brought two more spaghettis for Sam and Curd. '*Al dente*. Personally, I try to avoid attending lectures,' Curd offered, 'but I'm all in favour of scholarships.' Nonchalantly he poured himself another glass and started attacking the food that was at last rightfully his.

'So, do you have any idea where you're going to move to?' Samantha wanted to know. Sonja looked at Mark. He withstood her glances as he told Samantha, somewhat mysteriously, 'Let me put it this way. I know what I'm looking for.'

Later Mark would claim the place he decided to move to found him. It was part of a strikingly unusual building in North Carlton whose design reminded him a little of the border ferries of his home town. Along the rows of diverse houses that made up Lee Street, Number 12 looked unmistakably nautical, like a vessel built of bricks. Its groundfloor windows, barred with grilles over them, had taken on the appearance of portholes. A small passageway led to the entrance of the groundfloor flat, while a low brick fence separated the living quarters from the street. Upstairs were two more apartments, the larger one on the left, right above the groundfloor residence. Mark rented the smaller one on the right which was situated on top of a garage. One of its features was a whitewashed Juliet-balcony, which barely offered room for one person to look out onto the street. If it was more decorative than practical, it was a luxury that appealed to Mark. It completed the nautical look of the house. He thought of it as a crow's nest. A small staircase led to a passageway rather like the one below.

Lee Street was an unusually wide thoroughfare leading from the neighbouring suburb of Fitzroy to the Carlton Cemetery. Most of its corners were claimed by espresso bars, Greek cafés or what Melburnians referred to as 'mixed business'. The tramline was only two blocks away, and Mark's favourite local haunts were all within walking distance. Even Curd's solitary-confinement-cell was close by. Yet from the moment he moved in, Mark sensed his new place had created some distance from his friends. It had not been his intention to withdraw, but when he realised the effect of his move he was not altogether unhappy.

The first weeks were occupied with buying furniture. Mark had no idea how much of it he needed for a one-bedroom flat. He combed the suburbs for second-hand shops and auctions. For a couple of days he slept on a mattress on the floor. Gradually he gathered what he considered to be the essentials for his new life – a large table, a couple of chairs, an oriental-looking couch with an equally exotic coffee table (its first owners had been Lebanese) and a bed. He would have to make do with his one set of cutlery and the few mugs and glasses he had in his possession. After all, he wasn't expecting many visitors. (No doubt, Sonja would have insisted on providing his 'home' with 'decent curtains', donated tablecloths, napkins and towels and offered to lend him her vacuum cleaner.)

Was he settling down in Melbourne? Mark felt ambivalent about becoming established in a permanent abode, even as he was pleased to have his own place at last. He had never got used to asking a landlady for favours, sneaking to his room after midnight, anxious not to make a noise, leaving the fortnight's rent in an envelope on the kitchen table or listening to the owner's complaints about the cost of living and rudeness of young people. Now all that at least was in the past. From now on he would not have to consider anyone other than himself.

It took a while before he met his neighbour. The man living next to him turned out to be a middle-aged, short but stockily built Italian sculptor whose name was Ernesto. His thinning black hair combed forward made him look a bit like Napoleon. One day he simply rang at Mark's door and asked him over.

The flat next door looked rather different from the way Mark had begun to decorate his own. 'Ernesto Napoleone' had turned the entire space of a two-bedroom apartment into one large artist's studio. Wherever Mark looked, he was confronted by nude statues and wooden sculptures. It gave the impression the place was, despite its size, overcrowded. There was hardly room to move.

Ernesto spoke so quickly that even without his strong Italian accent Mark would have found it difficult to understand what he was saying. Although it was barely midday when he introduced himself, Mark suspected Ernesto of being drunk. His suspicion deepened when the sculptor opened a bottle of Chianti Classico and carelessly poured them two huge glasses. Mark watched in amused disbelief as his host gulped his down like water.

'Sit down, sit down,' Ernesto urged him, even though Mark couldn't see any place where he might follow the artist's invitation. He decided to crouch, leaning his body against the wall. 'You're a student, no? A student of what? Of life? If not, everything else's a waste of time!' The sculptor waved his arms around, narrowly missing one of his creations. His enthusiasm made him impatient with Mark. He did not really want to hear anything a university person might have to say. 'Life's elsewhere!' he insisted, wine running down his chin.

'You have to be free, Marco, my friend!' he shouted. 'Free! Do you know what that means?' He ignored Mark's nodding and continued, 'All this here, Marco, all you see, is my own world, my own creation, formed and breathed life into by the freedom of my soul!'

Momentarily Ernesto seemed exhausted, or perhaps he was reflecting on the truth and impact of what he'd just proclaimed. Mark looked at the statues nearest to where he was sitting. They were mostly female nudes. As far as he could make out, there was nothing strikingly original about their shape or design. They seemed typical examples of representational sculpture. But Mark could see the careful craftsmanship of each figure. He did not doubt their pedigree as labours of love. As he looked more closely, Mark noticed many of them bore strange markings, thick white stains from a dried or frozen liquid. One nude's facial discoloration gave it the appearance of tears, as if Ernesto had aimed to create a Pietà. But the statue's arms and hands were empty.

'How long you been in Australia, amico?' the artist continued his getting-to-know-you session. Before Mark could reply, his neighbour called out, 'Australia is nothing. You hear? Nothing!'

'Where did this little man get all this energy from?' Mark wondered in amazed alarm. Surely he must be exhausted!

'We have to populate, to humanise this land. Capisce? Otherwise we'll all go back to the Never-Never!' Ernesto pronounced it 'Neva-Neva'. 'This city's got no soul. Its inhabitants don't belong here. We all don't belong here. That's why I'm creating my own people – beautiful, in perfect harmony with the land. They're the real Australians! They're a model for who we have to become, Marco, if we want to survive!'

He interrupted his exuberant speech and left for the kitchen. Shortly afterwards he reappeared with a plate of kabanas and cheese. He put it on the floor in front of Mark and started eating. To Mark's surprise Ernesto sat down next to him without saying another word. A curious silence descended. After the avalanche of words, the tirade of criticisms and accusations the studio fell ominously silent.

Quietly they looked around the room and at each other. Mark had not been prepared for such a reception and did not want to prompt another outburst. He could see Ernesto was secretly still talking to himself – he was chewing words, not food. Sweat was running down his forehead, although it was pleasantly cool in the studio. 'The guy's a maniac', Mark thought to himself, 'obsessive, neurotic, and quite mad.' Yet in his outlandishness he was also, Mark felt, strangely like-able, a kind of hyperactive child bursting with intelligence and wit, if unable to calm down. Could or should someone like that be 'helped'? Everything Ernesto said or did was a performance. But now Mark could see his neighbour was try-ing to keep his thoughts to himself. He sat on the floor next to him like a puppet with its strings tangled.

Mark thought of the 'nautical' house they shared. On their floor Ernesto's studio amounted to the bridge, his own little flat the stern. They were cast on a suburban ship in dry dock.

'Who lives underneath?' Mark finally ventured, fearing another outburst. To his surprise all Ernesto said was 'My family.' Mark had heard sounds of children playing, and in the morning he'd watched a woman collect the daily fresh home-delivered bread from the sill outside. She was dressed in black, her face almost disappearing underneath a huge scarf. Mark knew that many women from the Mediterranean were in the habit of wearing such dark clothing, but this one seemed to be trying to hide herself from the rest of the world. He'd called out to her a few times, 'Good morning!', but she'd merely nodded in his general direction. Hardly the kind of woman Mark would have thought compatible with the outrageous artist.

'I've been a monk for most of my life, you know.' Mark would not have been surprised if Ernesto had told him he'd been the pope. 'Itsa good life,' the sculptor added, 'but itsanot a free life.' Mark found it difficult to imagine his neighbour as Brother Ernesto. He asked him where his monastery had been located. 'Just outsida Roma, amico.'

His reply sounded almost nostalgic. Once more silence descended. Mark was no expert on the religious life. Better to let Ernesto do the talking. The artist scratched his head, then poured them another glass. Into the unnatural silence he announced, 'And now I live!' The feisty tone of near-belligerence had returned to his voice.

Perhaps it was just the association of words, but before he knew what he'd said Mark quoted *La Dolce Vita*. Ernesto pulled him up and embraced him. 'Si, Marcello, si! Where are you, Marcello? You remember the film? Ah, what a film! But only a film, only highly flammable moving images, Marcello.' His excitement quickly reverted from fever pitch to depression. He managed to lend even his disappointment the intensity of a true idealist. 'I've lived the life of sacred images,' he began again. 'My body was starving, my senses were crippled, my soul was sacrificed to the sign of the cross. Now I taste life, all of it, not only its spirit. And yes, my friend, it is sweet – ah, you've no idea how sweet it is!' He emptied his glass and tried to refill it. When he saw the bottle was empty Ernesto aimed it with precision. The bottle survived its passage through half a dozen statues without touching any one of them, only to smash against the wall.

From below they could hear someone banging against the ceiling. Ernesto dismissed the noise with a contemptuous gesture. *'La donna è mobile!'* he hissed in the direction of the floor before he walked over to the kitchen, emerging with another bottle.

This time he threw the cork through the room, tuned his voice and started singing, *'E non ho amato mai tanto la vita!'* He followed the sound with dramatic imitations of an invisible orchestra which he conducted with great gusto. Visibly shaken by his own dramatic performance, Ernesto stood there, a shattered man overcome by the emotion of the poignant moment. Close to tears he had trouble regaining his composure.

'Liberi, amico caro!'

Mark remained in turn intimidated and amused by Ernesto's eccentric behaviour. To convey his good-neighbourly appreciation he held out his glass and applauded. But the artist merely waved him aside, ignoring the glass, before unleashing a vitriolic attack. 'Ah, you university people! What do you know! Niente!' His outburst was followed by an avalanche of English and Italian words Mark could not understand. Finally Ernesto fell silent. He was like the sea. All Mark could do was ride out the storm. They had reached placid waters again. In the quiet he could hear his host snoring. Cautiously Mark raised himself and sneaked out of the room.

Days passed without Mark seeing Ernesto again. Occasionally he could hear hammering and other sounds of unidentified tools from the unit next door. Mark assumed the artist was at work and did not wish to be disturbed.

Returning late one night he went for the first time to the Greek corner café where he was served by a tall woman with extraordinary straight long black hair. As she turned around, Mark noticed it reached below her waist, lending every move she made the neurotic elegance of a racehorse.

Making his coffee she opened up with some friendly small talk. 'You must be new around here. At least I haven't seen you before. My name's Alexa. What's yours?' A tiny cloud of steam covered her face while she introduced herself. For a moment Mark thought she looked like a witch. He watched her as she poured the frothy milk before replying, 'Mine's Mark. I live across the road, upstairs Number 12.'

Alexa burst out cackling. 'Next to Ernesto?' Mark nodded. She did not stifle her loud laugh. 'You know he fucks his statues, don't you?' It seemed information she was proud to pass on. 'I've seen him do it. Would you believe it? He's got a wife and children downstairs, for gawd's sake!' But her disgust didn't sound very convincing. It was just too good a story. 'Those artists,' she confided, 'they're all mad!' Again she chuckled. 'You're not an artist, I hope.'

Mark put her mind at rest. As the café was empty Alexa left the coffee machine and joined him at the table.

Now Mark saw why she looked so tall. She wore black shiny stilettos with the highest heels he'd ever seen. They looked like veritable torture instruments. At the same time they unsettled him. It was strangely exciting to see a woman wear something which restricted her freedom. How anyone could walk in those shoes was a marvel. Why she didn't stumble and fall as she walked over to him?

'Seems to me you're a bit of an artist yourself,' Mark said, trying to cover his nervous excitement. He pointed at the long tapering patent leather heels. 'With balance like that you could fly a high trapeze.'

Alexa took that as a compliment. Looking down her black stockings she replied with a flirtatious smile, 'You really think so?' Mark couldn't believe a young Greek woman of her cheerful disposition would be left on her own running a street café at this late hour. 'We're about to close,' Alexa informed him as she lit herself a cigarette. She must have read his thoughts.

'Are you by yourself?' Mark asked, expressing mild concern. Alexa shook her mane. 'My brother'll be here in a moment. He'll lock up and take care of the money.' All of a sudden a thought came into her head. 'You're a student, Mark, no?' Taking a deep breath she demanded to know, 'Do you know Jimmy?'

'Jimmy who?'

'He's a lecturer in politics. In his mid-thirties. Short, with grey hair already. Walks like a drake. So arrogant. Always giving orders.'

Mark tried to explain he was a science student, that the university was a big place with hundreds of lecturers. 'Sorry, I don't know him. Why, is it important?'

'He comes round here a lot. Always at night. Bothering me. You know what I mean? He's a terrible womaniser. Won't leave me alone. He chases me. Sometimes he follows me home. Last week Dimitris, my brother, beat him up. He told Jimmy never to show his face here again.' She caught her breath. 'Still, I'm sure he will come back. If he does, you have to protect me, Mark. Promise me you will.' Mark could tell her fear was genuine, even if it was expressed in a sexually enticing manner. He hadn't realised how arousing it could be to hear a woman confess that she was scared. 'Where can I run to, Mark?'

He didn't have to come up with an answer. A bulky guy with greasy, curly black hair entered the café rattling his keys. Mark gathered it was Alexa's brother Dimitris. Together they began putting up chairs on tables. As he left, he saw Dimitris check the till while his sister wiped the tiled floor. Slowly Mark walked across the intersection to his flat. The streets were empty. Only in Ernesto's studio the lights were still burning. There was no sign of any Jimmy.

Mark spent most of the day at university attending lectures and lab sessions. He loved studying what he knew to be a mixture of medicine and science, but more recently he'd also become interested in arts subjects such as literature, painting and music. He started borrowing books from Helen which he read in the cafeteria or on the lawn. Afterwards he couldn't wait to discuss with her what he'd been reading. He no longer mocked Helen for her daring thoughts and ideas; in fact, he was slowly becoming addicted to them. Her creative outrageousness made him love her more. How much a person's interests could become an inseparable part of their being! In Helen's case one couldn't even call it an 'interest' – it was who she was. The more he shared in her excitement the closer he got to her, the more he understood her the deeper he felt his love for her. Mark came to depend on her thoughts and feelings as much as her presence. Soon a day without her seemed inconceivable.

Helen loved almost all writing, but especially the novel.

Mark, on the other hand, discovered what was to him a new language – poetry. It was the closest, he felt, to the idiom of what, in a discussion with Helen, he'd called 'carnal intelligence' – the patterns, constellations and interactive relationships of blood formations, diseases, corpuscles, the whole pathology of human life. Words in a poem always 'spoke', the way he found the body did, whether healthy or not. In fact, Mark continued to doubt the generally accepted concept of 'health'. In a poem words were signs and everything related to everything else, until the sum total was always more than the parts. Wasn't that a reasonable, truthful description of the human body, of life itself?

Helen agreed, but she remained suspicious of what she called the underlying irrational in poetry. They argued for hours about whether a poem's meaning derived from a comprehensible, logical frame of reference or a composition which contained an element of chance. Helen was willing to recognise it as a kind of magic, remnants of the sacred origin of poetry. What if life, too, still held some of that spirit?

Mark reminded his love of how they'd met while she was reading the Metaphysicals outside the conservatorium. Now, at last, he understood what she'd meant when she challenged him about the interdependence of thought and feeling. She'd excited him precisely for that reason. All he had to do was think of her to feel her presence. And while he was with her, she taught his love to think. How rich her life was! She had enough abundance to give herself away and enrich him.

He still saw Sonja, almost every day, but he didn't visit her as much as before. They met between lectures, ran into each other while shopping or at Genevieve's. Mark made a point of being especially nice to her, but the intimacy of their friendship was gone. Sonja acknowledged the change in the relationship, but still advised him to 'eat sensibly', now that he had his own kitchen, recommending Queen Victoria Market as the ideal place for 'fresh fruit and veggies'. He had invited 'Les Girls' to his place, of course, not only in exchange for their hospitality, but also to show off his 'own' place. They all praised its location, ideal size and cleanliness. Although they stayed together till the early hours of the morning, the atmosphere was not the same as at their house. Something was missing. Determined to hide the loss, everyone was on their best behaviour. There were lots of smiles and kind gestures. They virtually agreed on everything that night. Even Curd who joined them just before midnight wasn't true to form. Suddenly he spoke in only one tongue – and it wasn't amusing. Without Samantha by his side the Queen's actor failed to make a lasting impression. In the end they all found it unbearable. Mark tried to analyse what had gone wrong. Maybe the music wasn't right, or he just wasn't an entertaining host. Too late he realised the problem: his place didn't have a room like Sonja's, cast in soft light, furnished with a comfortable bed and chairs, crammed with pillows, warm, soft, feminine, intimate; nor did it have an old-fashioned kitchen or a large family lounge where they could come together over a meal, share each other's thoughts, compare lectures, discuss shopping, exchange gossip, review the day, assured in the knowledge they were friends who cared for each other.

The Lee Street evening with the girls left Mark with a stale taste. He asked himself whether he 'betrayed' Sonja. But although he felt guilty, he found it difficult to accept that he'd been disloyal to her. Love was more complicated than emotional ownership, feeling protective or caring for someone. In a way, he and Sonja had 'adopted' each other. If anything, she, in mothering him, had taken that concept more literally. Poor Sonja! After an adoptive father she had adopted a lover believing she could make him her own. Would she choose all of her men in a similar manner?

Somewhere Mark had read 'If I love you, what business is it of yours?' It sounded cruel, but in his heart he found it a startlingly daring and honest statement. 'No one has a right to love,' he decided. 'If I confess my love to someone, I cannot lay claim to that person's affections in return.' Otherwise declarations of love would amount to blackmail. But the terrible thing was that Sonja had not laid any claims on him. She just continued to express her love for him with the same care as before. It was a loyalty Mark found difficult to accept.

Sometimes he sneaked into an English lecture both she and Helen were attending. Quietly he took his seat in the last row of the hall. But no matter how careful he was not to disturb the class, Sonja would turn round and signal him a welcoming smile. It made no difference where she was sitting. She seemed to sense Mark's presence the moment he arrived. By contrast, he had trouble finding Helen, even if she was sitting close by. If he waited for her after the lecture, she was completely taken by surprise. 'Deserting science again?' she would tease him before welcoming him with a kiss.

Sometimes she spent the night with him at Lee Street. When she was there the place took on a different character. They talked as though they were the whole world, and the whole world were a mysterious, glorious work of art. Mark loved listening to her, especially when she recited her favourite texts by heart. What a memory she had! When they touched, it was the reward for a new shared discovery.

Built into one of the walls of his small living room was a gas stove. Mark and Helen would turn off the lights and sit in front of its grill. It reminded him of early school camps where they would sit around the fire sharing a simple meal. He remembered in particular how they used to prepare a cake mixture consisting mainly of flour and raisins, chop a few young tree branches into sticks, carve them clean and, having placed the thick mixture around the stem, hold it into the camp fire. When he and Helen tried it using the lounge's gas stove she told him about damper, an unleavened bread cake baked in wood ashes. It wasn't quite the same – the long sticks were missing – but Mark could see the similarity. 'I guess we both loved singing and talking with our sticks in the fire.'

Helen laughed out loud. 'What a way of putting it!' As they rotated their sticks in front of the grill, watching it turn brown and crunchy, Mark's living room became a boys' camp.

The thin hollow cakes they released from the sticks bore the shape of bottle-brushes. Mark brought butter and jam from the kitchen. As they started eating, he produced a sheet of paper and, turning in the semi-darkness to the gas fire, began to read to her.

> *the heat of burnt grass,*
> *impotent anger*
> *at an english class,*
> *men getting younger*
> *by each disciplined day,*
> *till they are schoolboys*
> *again, told to pay*
> *attention, roll-calls*
> *into another*
> *life, how to translate*
> *the humid weather,*
> *the shame and the hate –*
> *at night, the huts throb*
> *with desperate love-*
> *making, young men sob*
> *in darkness, dreams of*
> *childhood call them home,*
> *twilight rains set in,*
> *morning builds its dome,*
> *the snake sheds its skin.*

Mark's voice was sonorous, but the lines were read as if they were an objective enumeration. Any emotional pathos was kept under tight control. He had read the poem almost against its content. As Mark folded his paper, Helen moved over and embraced him. 'I can tell it's yours,' she whispered in his ear. What a different kind of embrace it was from the hugs Sonja gave him! Helen touched him just at the right moment, in just the right way and in all the right places. Recognition.

'Not bad for a would-be immunologist,' she added sardonically as she withdrew gently. 'Is that all you've written, or is there more?' In fact, there was more, but Mark felt it was too early to show her what else he'd jotted down in the hope that one day it might become a poem for her.

They returned to their 'stick cakes' and wine. Later, in bed, both felt they should have made love right there and then – in front of the gas fire, amidst the food and poetry, while they were confiding to each other their passion for words. But the way they imagined, tongued and recited each other, quoting with relish even the tiniest section of their bodies, there could be little doubt they were speaking their own language with its own vocabulary, as they were busy writing their own poem.

'If I love you, what business is it of yours?' proved a quotation 'Jimmy, the lecherous lecturer,' had either no knowledge of, or no sympathy for. Around one or two o'clock in the morning Alexa would bang against Mark's door, begging desperately to be let in. 'Mark! Please! He's after me again!'

What happened to her brother? It became something of a ritual, her nightly panic flights up the stairs, his letting her in just in time before Jimmy got to the top and started his own banging. While Alexa, top buttons of her blouse missing, collapsed hysterical inside, one of her stockings undone or her short black skirt slipped and torn, Jimmy did his best to knock the front door down. Mark was amazed none of the neighbours complained. Perhaps they thought it was Ernesto sculpting.

After about half an hour Jimmy would give up his threats of violence and start crying instead. Howling and hissing like a tomcat he pleaded his undying love and desire for his 'sweet pussy' Alexa. He even scratched the door as if he had claws. After a while Alexa calmed down – as an inducement Mark usually offered her pure gin – and began to enjoy the scene. Suddenly steadfast virgin again, she would remain unmoved by all of Jimmy's amorous advances. Once in a while she would call out, 'Go away, you dirty old bugger!' before clinking glasses with Mark. 'To you, Mark,' she'd say, 'my chivalrous knight! Thank you for saving me!' After an hour it usually turned quiet outside. The occasional sob indicated Jimmy's continued presence on the staircase. Around this time Alexa was in the habit of getting undressed and urging Mark to come to bed.

In the morning neither of them left without first checking from Juliet's 'crow's-nest' whether last night's suitor was indeed gone. When he moved in Mark had no idea how useful the tiny balustrade platform would turn out to be. Like the flat itself, it had become something of a strategic shelter.

Whenever Mark dropped in at the Greek café he was treated like a hero. Alexa had told the whole family how he continued to defend her honour against 'that wretched university swine'. Once her mother, a wrinkly old woman of dwarf-like statue dressed in obligatory black, blinked her eyes at him, crowing 'Well done, boy!' Mark felt like a dog expecting to be patted.

'Happy to help,' was his only reply.

Alexa, too, beamed satisfaction. 'No worry, mama,' she kept saying. 'No worry. I'm fine.'

It was a ritual with few variations which repeated itself over several months. Jimmy's chase finally ended when one night Ernesto emerged from his studio, hammer and chisel in his hand, trying to find out what the noise was all about. It surprised Mark that he hadn't done so earlier. Perhaps his neighbour's own creative activity, immersed in alcoholic consumption, involved such concentration that he remained oblivious to the commotion outside. As he stood there, covered in a large leather apron, he must have looked to Jimmy like an executioner from hell. Almost instantly his amorous appeals stopped. Not even his notorious whining and sobbing persisted. 'Jimmy the lecherous lecturer' had no intention of confronting the deadly apparition. With remarkable agility he took to his heels, jumping stairs three steps at a time, before racing down Lee Street like a young athlete.

'Everything all right?' Ernesto wanted to know from outside Mark's door. They opened up and let him in. His expert's eyes took one look at Alexa before he asked them to 'come over'. She was reluctant to accept his invitation, whispering in Mark's ear 'I told you about him!' But Ernesto would not take no for an answer. Putting his arms around Mark and Alexa he dragged them both over to his studio.

'I know what you're doing to your statues,' Alexa giggled nervously. 'You ought to be ashamed of yourself.'

Ernesto remained unperturbed. Priest-like he poured her a drink. 'Get that into you, holy virgin.' She gulped down the wine as if it were water. 'I will make a statue of you. To be worshipped by men for all time. You would like that, wouldn't you?' Alexa shrieked with embarrassed delight.

'What, right now?' She mimicked a model's pose. 'Like so?'

That was enough to inspire the artist. 'Get undressed, you bitch!' he yelled. 'I shall cover you in clay, my pigeon!' At his uncouth shouts Alexa turned coy and tried to withdraw, but Ernesto blocked her way to the door. Soon they were chasing each other. He caught and undressed her in one movement. She abandoned herself to the hands of a professional. Mark quietly withdrew to his flat.

After that his contacts with Alexa were restricted to the café. Yet over time they remained what Mark would have called conspiratorial friends. 'I'll dance at your wedding yet,' he would tell her, and late at night, just before closing time, she would send him home with the friendly advice, 'Don't let anyone in!'

IX

In Mark's mind the layout of Carlton consisted of a 'living tract', centring around Elgin, Lygon, Rathdowne and Grattan Streets, a 'region of the dead', the great dividing expanse of the cemetery, and a 'beyond', marked by Princess Park, home of The Mighty Blues. His home suburb was a giant hopscotch of life and death, a metaphysical terrain leading to its very own heaven and hell, where the 'beyond' revealed itself as only one spell of play, only one contest, only one sport – Australian Rules.

He shivered with joy whenever he thought of it. He'd come to a place which turned triumphs and despairs into a sublime game, and gave it the name of Australia. It elevated life to its own logic. The symbolic location of Princess Park – located as it was behind acres and acres of graves – heightened the occasion whenever the Carlton team triumphed over death, defeat and daily doldrums. The moment the Blues ran on to the ground everything was sublimated. For two and a half hours Carlton's supporters lived more consciously, fought more passionately, loved and hated more unequivocally.

The first time Mark entered the hallowed ground he instantly recognised Australian Rules was about more than football. Its spectators had all risen from the dead. He joined them watching a game consisting of the most beautiful and precise rehearsing and replaying of life's endless possibilities. With seemingly effortless grace it could demonstrate the ultimate triumph, when, miraculously, everything went right – from the centre bounce, Big Nick's inspired tap-down, the rover's speedy pass to the flanks, to the torpedo punt marked by the full-forward dead in front and the straight kick right through the middle, prompting two white flags being waved to let God know it was a goal. The opposing team didn't get a single touch. It was pure bliss.

Admittedly, it rarely happened so elegantly, but it was always possible, and it was that possibility the crowd had come to see. Mark understood immediately that 'Australian Rules' was all about concerted moves, potential triumphs or restructured failures. It played a language of variable interrelationships, an enactment of positions, actions and reactions. All those who participated or watched recognised themselves in the game.

One July night, on his way home from a college party, Mark walked along the rim of the cemetery. It was cool, with a gusty breeze blowing from across the graveside. A full moon cast silhouettes of Newman and Ormond colleges together with the last row of houses on top of Swanston Street. How he had come to love his new welcoming home with its gracious, venerable houses, quiet streets and ancient trees! By Melbourne standards Carlton was what real estate agents referred to as an 'up-and-coming' suburb, its residents a vital blend of students, migrants and artists. Mark had no idea where it had been before it gained the status of 'up-and-coming'. All he knew was that it made people come alive. It was undoubtedly Melbourne's most exciting and vivacious suburb. In its realm even the most ordinary happenings turned into celebrations.

On his way home from the college party, less than four blocks away from his apartment in Lee Street, Mark noticed mysterious flickers emanating from the cemetery. At first he thought it might be the eternal lights of some graves. But then he realised the gleams were moving straight in his direction.

Foolishly he looked up at the sky to check the angle of the moon. As he stopped walking, the lights in the cemetery also came to a halt. To make quite certain, Mark took a few steps and saw the lights begin to follow him once more. There was no doubt. He was not imagining it. Intrigued and alarmed he let his hands glide over his clothes and body. Was he wearing something glowing? Could he be responsible for projecting a light into the cemetery? It was a laughable assertion, but by now he was agitated enough to consider any explanation.

He crossed the street, away from the overgrown footpath following the cemetery boundary. The neon street lights across the wide road were moving in the breeze. Hands in his pockets he searched for 'the lights of the dead'. They had not gone away.

Whistling and humming to himself, Mark resolved to ignore them. 'How can I be followed by lights?' he reasoned with himself. 'Some sort of illusion – surely.' He took a deep breath and remembered his tongue-in-cheek invitation to tonight's party at Newman. During lab a couple of students had asked him, in the middle of an experiment, to join them in a night of 'ghosts and spirits' – a thinly disguised reference to the miracles and wonders of alcohol. When he arrived he was asked to deposit his contribution of plonk with a skeleton whose hands had been turned into a drinking tray. In the hollow eyes of the bony replica of man tiny light bulbs were flashing as its jaw moved up and down acknowledging the contribution with a sonorous voice, 'Bottoms up!' No attempt was made to hide the small tape recorder – even with the voice machine in full sight the response of 'the grateful dead' prompted mock horror and laughter. Mark was surprised college students enjoyed so much freedom! If that outrageous evening was anything to go by, he wouldn't mind living in a college himself one day. According to his self-satisfied hosts, almost everything was done for them. He wouldn't have to go shopping any more for starters. And no one would wake him at night, demanding to be let in. Mark had never considered college for himself. Taking up residence in college seemed the exclusive privilege of locals, the culmination of a traditional education. Didn't parents have to book their children in before they even entered high school?

He looked around and across the road. No one else was walking at this time of the night. Cars hissed past him, their lights on full beam. In the distance ahead he could see the corner leading into Lee Street. He was almost home.

Muffled singing could be heard from the cemetery. It sounded eerie, especially as it seemed to emanate from the area of the moving lights. Mark stopped and withdrew into the shade of an old fig tree. He wiped his eyes in disbelief as he saw first two, then three white ghost-like figures emerge from behind a row of large tombstones in what he guessed, from memory, had to be the Chinese section. With their appearance the singing stopped abruptly, and the lights quickly moved off in different directions. Was that a scream? Mark could not be sure.

He stepped out of the shade into the full beam of the street light. As he did so, the ghosts across the road seemed to slowly move away in the direction of the cemetery's exit. Hissing and other curious sounds suggested that those disappearing into the night were conferring. Some of the noises sounded almost like laughter. The other, smaller lights had completely gone.

Mark moved forward, then stopped abruptly. He needn't have worried. There was no doubt, he was no longer being followed. The whispering ghosts continued to move off in the opposite direction.

Frustrated that he could make no sense of it, Mark again checked his movements, but he was clearly alone now. Relieved and angry his mind protested, 'I wasn't seeing things!'

Back in his flat he found it difficult to fall asleep. His mother rose from her grave demanding to be left in peace. She called him a layabout and a womaniser, urging him to concentrate on his studies. 'Any news from your father yet?' she enquired, as she'd always done after Mark had listened to the missing persons tracing service on the radio.

'No, Mutti, they haven't found him yet. I thought he was with you.'

'There's no one here with me.' It was a statement of fact, her voice free of disappointment or reproach.

She must have been disturbed by Mark's witnessing the lights and the ghosts in the cemetery. He wanted to apologise to his mother, but found she was no longer with him.

How foolishly moved he still was by the silly expression of a 'home game'! Just seeing the scoreboard on college ovals spell out HOME and VISITORS was enough to shake him. He would have to learn not to be so sensitive to words. There wasn't even a game on!

To kick, to pass, to mark the ball. It was 'Heaven'. Mark followed the order of movement, the grammar of flight, the syntax of intentions. Going to Princess Park recalled his first two years in the city. He had become a blue boy, a Blues man, a player and citizen of Carlton. Sometimes, to his great surprise, Helen good-naturedly joined him in the outer, consuming vast numbers of Four'n Twenty pies. Not that she fully endorsed his extravagant description of Australian Rules as the 'poetry' of his life, but she did respond to the grace and movement of the game. 'Mock heroic,' she offered. 'Pope, rather than Wordsworth.' It was a good-natured reservation. She remained resistant to his attempts to draw her into the game plan of his life. Together he wanted them to be the HOME side.

'Time on.' The final urgency to come home. Mark had lived in this city for a number of years now. He had learnt to play Australian rules – found a room, a job, a place of his own, made friends, fallen in love, won a scholarship studying science and medicine, discovered poetry and settled in a suburb built and developed along its own strict town planning divisions of earth, heaven and hell.

Despite their seeming intimacy Helen remained curiously elusive. Mark sensed her hesitancy about the ultimate aim and purpose of their relationship, but did not speak to her about it. It was too soon. She never openly expressed any disquiet about what they were doing, but her sudden outbursts of desire were like the breaking of a storm – unpredictable, spectacular and frightening. Not so much a steadily growing affection as an impatient revelation of uncontrollable physical and emotional demands and needs. Could their relationship be no more than unresolved muddy lust and verbal passion?

Admittedly, when the downpour came, it was exciting in its awesome strength. Before Helen, Mark had little knowledge of the emotional resources and sexual strength of a woman's body. It made him feel insecure. In a disturbing way he felt 'used', not accepted for himself, as if Helen's lover could have been anyone. She had adopted him into their lovemaking, fed him with her own seemingly insatiable desire. Never had Mark felt himself so wanted – but in his gratitude he became increasingly unsure whether what Helen offered was love. In the beginning he didn't care. From the moment they met he'd been intoxicated by Helen's presence. If he thought eventually his infatuation would diminish, he was wrong. If anything, it had increased over time. It humiliated him that his love seemed to mimic the wisdom of trite and sentimental pop songs – he became convinced he 'could no longer live without her'. But he was prudent enough not to tell Helen. She would not have welcomed such mushy sentiments. She would've shot him down with a particularly acid quotation. 'If I love you …'.

Except in the throes of passion, Mark had become afraid of confessing his love to Helen. The restraint made him defensive and angry. Why was it so wrong to make another person the meaning of one's life? Wasn't that what love was supposed to be about? He remembered Helen's scathing mockery about 'settling down in the suburbs'. Scornfully she informed him she was 'no breeder', as if that was what Mark expected. But what was she? What did she want to do with her own life? Mark could not even be sure she would let him ask her, let alone tell him. Helen remained very much her own woman.

He dared not suggest what to him seemed a perfect set-up: that they might share the flat in Lee Street, live together, like so many other students they knew. Helen would've dismissed it as a kind of rehearsal of suburban marital bliss. They continued to see each other whenever they could – or whenever Helen felt like it. But there were times when Mark had no idea where she was. When he phoned her at college, someone else passed on the message that 'Helen's gone home for the weekend' or 'Helen's not feeling well' or 'Helen's in the library, working on an important assignment, and must not be disturbed'. Had he become a nuisance? Had he begun to cling to her like a limpet? Had he begun to play the part of a possessive husband? He felt rejected, and when he went to the library and found she was not there, he felt sick in the stomach. He was sure she was seeing somebody else.

But when they did meet again Helen was as cheerful as ever, and he forgot about asking her where she had been. Back at his place he made a point of inviting friends around whenever he knew she did not wish to see him. He often asked Ernesto to come over, making sure it would be a long and wild night. His flat, once the most visible manifestation of his independence, meant less and less to him now. When Curd asked him one day whether he could take someone to his place 'in private', Mark handed him the keys. The 'frozen ship' of Lee Street no longer felt like home.

The door was open, the place overflowing with people he didn't know. The stairs were crowded with couples drinking and making love. Mark found it difficult to hide his outrage at thwarted plans.

'Come in, Marcello!' Ernesto hailed him. 'How good of

you to come! Pretend you're at home – we're doing the same. My dear chap, caro amico, do join us in our celebration of life!' The way he looked at Helen, Mark found it preferable to leave the uninvited guests and book into a nearby hotel. Curd caught up with them on their way out. Sheepishly he explained that he'd ordered a number of duplicate keys and passed them around to cast members of his current theatre production. 'I didn't think you'd mind!' he pleaded. 'Bit of drama at home, you know.'

To Mark's relief Helen loved the hotel room's anonymity, their mysteriously late check-in, the luxurious pillows and sheets of the large double bed. She jumped into it like a diver from a springboard. When Mark wanted to draw the curtains she called out to him, 'Leave it! It's only the cemetery.' She was right. Lying in the dark they could see the old trees and street-lights move in the gentle night breeze. Before long they joined in their rhythm, probing their skin, seeking the depth of their passion, falling into each other like tributaries joining the mainstream's vast overflowing delta. Her short cries of delight reassured Mark that he'd pleased her.

Afterwards they stood naked at the window, looking out over the graveyard, Mark searching for moving lights or any other signs that the game was not over yet.

At the end of the academic year, after his final exams, Mark made an appointment for an interview with the Rector of Newman College. Before presenting himself to the Rector's office Mark entered the grounds, inspected the dining hall, the library, students' studies and common room, then strolled around the impressive, medieval-looking quadrangle, marvelling at the buildings' striking architecture, in particular the main section with its beautiful dome. The college, he'd read, was the vision of Walter Burley Griffin, the famous architect and designer of the nation's capital. Since most of its resident students had already left, it projected an archaic monastic atmosphere, quite out of character with the impression he'd formed from the student party earlier in the year. Then it had seemed to him a hive of happy activity, with laughter, shouts and shreds of music echoing along the cloisters.

Would he be able to live in a community like this, complete his studies in a traditional place of scholastic discipline? Mark suddenly had doubts. Admittedly his plans were still tentative, and there was no guarantee the Rector would accept him. What kind of order would be forced upon him? Would his scholarship cover the fees? And, most of all, he now realised as he caught a glimpse of the inside of the simple chapel, would a Catholic college draw him into a religious life he knew nothing about? The unadorned altar seemed stern, demanding and unforgiving. By the time he was led into the Rector's office Mark had lost all confidence.

'The Very Reverend, SJ' something or other stretched out his hands as if to bless him and welcomed the visitor with a broad boyish smile. It took him only a short while to describe the college – to Mark's relief the Rector did not bother giving him an historical overview – and what Mark could expect should he decide to become a 'Newman'. He wasn't in the business of running either a boarding or a whore house, the holy man pointed out, and 'after 10 p.m.' ladies would not be tolerated, 'except on special occasions'. The Rector did not elaborate which events might qualify for such exceptions. On the other hand, he continued, no one would be forced to observe religious rites they did not believe in. 'This is a place of light and learning,' the Very Reverend explained, 'not a seminary or a school of indoctrination. Saintliness,' he added in an attempt at theological charm, 'is purely optional.'

This Jesuit did not even ask whether he 'believed'. That in itself Mark found remarkable and reassuring.

'Had he already looked around?' the Rector enquired. If not, perhaps he would care to join Luke and him on a stroll through the grounds. Mark gave the Very Reverend a quizzical look. At the sound of the name, a door was pushed open, and a huge yellow-brown Labrador appeared. The expression on the dog's face seemed to say, 'You called, Sir?' As Mark had already seen most of the college, they would merely skirt around the grounds. During their short inspection tour Luke did not leave his master's side. The Rector referred to him as his 'Evangelist'.

Strolling through the empty cloisters and quadrangle, the Rector admitted his students were 'a bit of a wild bunch, but good boys all of them'. He seemed particularly ambivalent about Newman's continued practice of initiations. 'They went a bit far this year,' he explained. 'At the stroke of midnight groups of freshmen had to cross the cemetery singing or mumbling the Newman song. Hidden behind tombstones in the Chinese section a couple of senior students, covered in sheets, were waiting for them. You can imagine the panic among freshmen, mostly country kids, barely eighteen.' He shook his head in disapproval, but his eyes seemed to be grinning. 'Needless to say, we don't approve of this sort of thing. But it happens.' His voice faltered, as if saddened by the wickedness of the world.

'You're not a rower by any chance?' he suddenly enquired. This time it was Mark's turn to express regret.

'It's just, you see, we've never won Head of the River. One of my ambitions as Rector.'

Mark's lack of contact with Jesuits had left him unprepared for the priorities of this man of the cloth.

Nearing the chapel the Rector gave his visitor an inquiring look. When Mark nodded, he took him up the stairs to its entrance. As if by command Luke stopped dead in his tracks just outside the door. Mark couldn't help remembering the signs of butcher shops back home. Underneath the picture of a dog a text read, 'We must stay outside!' Clearly this Jesuit Labrador-Evangelist was well trained in spiritual sanitation.

Visiting Newman College offered a different perspective

on Mark's secular metaphysics of place. He could see its vital importance in the overall scheme of things that was Carlton. Unlike the Catholic church in his home town, this house of worship and learning did not appear to be a place glorifying the promiscuous, irrational or superstitious. It surprised Mark that the inside of the chapel was simple and unadorned – Newman could lay claim to being committed to enlightenment. Already it had lifted for him the meta-physical veil of death, ghosts and apparitions.

So that was what he had witnessed in the cemetery that night! A group of terrified youngsters under instructions to dare the dead! Poor freshmen! They had failed to make it to Princess Park, the true place of the world's redemption.

At the conclusion of his visit Father Pratt – Mark had at last remembered his proper name – handed him a brochure containing 'all relevant information about Newman'. In terms of relevance the 'Newman Song' appeared to rank highly. Mark chuckled as he reinvoked the unfortunate freshmen serenading midnight graves to the lyrics of 'Newman, Newman, Newman, Newman, /Show that you are tried and true men, /That you always fight for Newman, /Newman to the end.' He had a good idea of what Helen would have made of that 'poetry'. Still, it was a song of 'home'. Beyond the municipal cemetery, all they would have had to sing was 'We are the Navy Blues, We are the old, old Navy Blues …'. The world would've taken the initiates back. The worst that could've happened to them at Princess Park would've been to be kicked and pushed into the crowd. Hardly a sin. They would've fallen into, and been carried by, the human wave in front. Instead of the morbid stage-man-aged doom and gloom designed to prove they were 'Newman tried-and-true-men to the end' there would've been shrieks of joy and exhilaration.

Still, Mark was unsure whether he would be able to settle into a college lifestyle. Helen, of course, had. But Helen could do so many things. Would they continue to see each other?

They would not be able to spend nights together in college! Disappointed and undecided, he groaned his frustration. There was one relief: his life in Lee Street would be drawing to a close. Thanks to Curd's largesse in handing out duplicate keys to anyone who wanted them, it had become a place for free spirits wanting to hold or join a party, smoke pot or make love. In a rare departure from the Queen's English Curd himself had come to refer to it as a 'safe house for no-hopers and mother-fuckers'.

X

What was it about the secular and metaphysical layout of his new home? At Newman College Mark immediately recognised a reflection of the same design that characterised the suburb of Carlton. Newman's hopscotch was made up of its main hall of residence – the realm of daily living – its quadrangle which in its solemnity and dignity invoked comparison with the local cemetery (especially during the three-month absence of students) and, located behind them both, the heavenly oval where during the academic year lives were rehearsed whenever Australian Rules were played, and where once, in a magic moment of revelation, he and Helen had made love in the mud.

As it was January, and the college virtually empty, Mark was given a choice of rooms. He settled for the annexe farthest removed from the centre. His study offered a perfect view over the entire Newman campus, especially the quadrangle. It was an ideal position. From his window he could see anyone approaching the building. In addition, his room was closest to the oval and the university. Diagonally to his right was the college chapel, just rising above a couple of ancient palm trees. Straight ahead his study faced the cloisters of the older, original parts of college. Yes, with this choice he had secured a personal crow's-nest. Like the one in Lee Street, it would warn him of possible intruders.

Despite university recess, however, he was not the only resident. A final year medicine student, Father Pratt told him, had chosen to stay over the holiday period. Like Mark, he could come and go as he pleased. He lived somewhere on the upper floor of the old building. In addition, members of the English Department occupied the two suites next to the chapel reserved for staff. One was a professor working on a new Australian dictionary. Helen seemed to know all about him. There were rumours about, she confided, that he was involved in a 'messy' divorce. The other academic was an elusive Irish-Australian poet. He too was supposed to have a 'colourful private life'. Helen had shown Mark some of his poems, which he liked so much that he was anxious to meet the author. He admired how the language managed to keep just the right balance between confessing and holding back, to play out feelings against intellect, images against abstractions. It brought back memories of his first encounter with Helen, her urging him that 'thought was a feeling and feeling a thought'. That bit about 'The Metaphysicals'. Now Mark was keen to see what a 'real live poet' would be like.

One balmy night, with the window of his study open, he found it hard to fall asleep. Lying on his bed images invaded his mind, interacting, playing out possibilities, retracing events, projecting variations – following the rules of the 'Australian' game. Would it make sense to speak of a poetry of the body, an art of physiology, Mark wondered. Helen would be scathing. Well, whatever they were, these patterns and images clearly belonged to the senses. They had to be part of the very first communication, a first language of knowledge.

A gentle, recurring noise from outside, sounding like ping-pong or the serve of a tennis ball punctuated his reflections. It didn't seem to adopt a particular rhythm, but every time Mark thought it had gone away he heard it again. His curiosity was not satisfied by peering out of the window. He could see nothing, even though the gentle noise persisted. Tired and irritated he tried to put it out of his mind. For a while the sound disappeared, but he was hardly back in bed when it started again. This time Mark was determined to discover what it was.

He dressed and walked over to the quadrangle. The noise came closer, until he suddenly stood in front of a priest carrying an instrument. It gave Mark a fright because, dressed in black, the priest was indistinguishable from the night. He seemed to appear from nowhere. Perhaps he'd stepped out from behind a palm tree.

'You must be Mark,' the man of the cloth greeted him. 'I've heard about you. Welcome to Newman. I'm Father Donohue, the chaplain.'

Mark felt embarrassed and uneasy meeting a priest in the dark of night. He couldn't see his face or make out what he was carrying. 'Good evening,' he began, 'or rather good morning, Father. I live just over there' – he pointed in the direction of his study – 'and got up to investigate the strange noises.' It came close to an apology for being out at this time of the night.

'Well, investigate no further, my son,' Father Donohue replied. 'What you must've heard were my golf balls.' He offered him his club.

'You're playing golf in the middle of the night?'

The priest laughed indulgently.

'But you can't see anything! Are there actually holes in the lawn?'

'You bet there are,' he continued to laugh out loud. 'But you're quite right, my son. They're difficult to see.'

'So why do you play in almost total darkness?'

Mark didn't know what to make of the priest or this strange meeting. The droll stranger whispered conspiratorially, 'It's a kind of theological exercise, you know. For verily I say unto Thee, truth is to be found in disappearance!' His explanation was followed by a quiet or suppressed laugh.

The words of an insane priest, surely, if not the ramblings of a haunted ghost. Only now did Mark notice the spectacular white hair of the madman, an unruly mane which made it difficult to guess his age.

'I see,' Mark replied, but he didn't. 'Well, Father,' he added, 'I guess I can get back to bed, now that I know what you're doing.' He slowly walked away, before turning around to ask, 'You're quite sure you put in these holes yourself?' The priest merely chuckled to himself before he resumed practising his unorthodox drives and strokes.

'God bless!' he called after Mark as he disappeared into the dark.

Back in his room Mark pondered the priest's enigmatic statement. What could he have meant by 'Truth is to be found in disappearance'? Was he mocking his faith? Surely not. Something in Father Donohue's voice made him think he really meant it; he wasn't making a joke.

Living in college proved very different from visiting college. During the student party on Mark's first visit the place had been full of boisterous people, animated and noisy, its energy so physical the voices seemed to have taken on a life of their own. Now, by contrast, it was all very quiet. In the cloisters Mark was followed by the echoes of his own footsteps. Late at night it was easy to imagine Newman as a Cistercian monastery – weren't the Trappist monks the ones who'd taken a vow of silence? During the hot summer nights the only noise coming from outside was the welcome sound of a slight breeze – and occasionally Father Donohue's golf balls.

But early one morning – around three or four – something extraordinary happened. For once the cool change overnight so reassuringly predicted by Channel Nine's Gentleman Eric had not eventuated. Even with the window wide open Mark woke up bathed in sweat, but cleansed by the sound of hauntingly sad and beautiful music. In the distance, from across the quadrangle, someone was playing the cello. Drawn by the intensity, grace and pathos of the melody Mark stepped outside, searching for a light in a window or any other sign which might help him trace the location of the player. But what he found himself confronted with was complete darkness. The playing continued unabated.

The instrument did not seem to address itself to an audience. Rather, it appeared to be a performance for its own sake. The quality of playing was such that there could be no doubt about the artistic calling of the player. It was characterised by a quiet, dignified relentlessness, an insistence on saying what needed to be said. Mark heard in the music a barely suppressed outcry, a disciplined suffering strenuously kept under control. The playing became more and more authoritative. What kind of ghost music was he listening to? Was this another stunt from the mad priest of the night?

Mark sensed that this music – was it still just music? – derived from a source beyond trickery or virtuosity. It sounded like a quiet, dignified monologue. The supreme technical skill of the player reflected his severe control over an extremely demanding score. Variations of Bach's unaccompanied suites for cello – Mark was pretty sure of that. But, at the same time, he had little doubt that what he was listening to was someone speaking to himself. He was in awe. How could music express so much beauty with such disciplined persistence, such relentless demands? Challenge and freedom, despair and joy, tragedy and triumph seemed to coincide. It was a voice speaking to itself, but now Mark realised that more than anything it was also a call. A call to whom? He didn't know. Was he prying into someone's agony? The player seemed to conduct an intimate dialogue with himself, with different parts of himself. How could that be?

Sitting outside his room Mark became enveloped by the lament emanating from the dark. It finally ended as the first thin streaks of light appeared in the sky. The air was still warm, but Mark found his face was covered in tears. The beautiful calling had stopped.

What a strange place Newman College had turned out to be!

Sometimes it seemed like an enchanted medieval castle, one of those haunted fairy tales fortifications sheltering the ghosts of crusaders. There were things going on here, especially at night, that defied the laws of practical reason and common sense. It made Newman a sanctuary of magic and mystery, alive with unexplored secrets of the dark.

Back on his bed Mark kept thinking about the music he had heard. Surely he hadn't just imagined it? No, the memory was far too powerfully real for that. What remained with him was the expression of its playing, its recurring patterns, its persistent search for resolution. Like an echo he could hear the discipline of the exercise, the determination of the instrumentalist to see it right through to the end.

Particular phrases continued to haunt Mark. Some sounded as if the player were using all of his energy to keep the melody alive. Like a sentence which had to be finished. Or when in his childhood he and his friends had tried to keep their kites in the air. That was the most disturbing thing about the lonely musician playing in the dark. Mark could feel the almost superhuman effort that went into the performance – the exertion appeared an inseparable part of the composition. And all the while the music seemed to be calling out, demanding, begging, appealing. He'd never heard anyone play like that before.

The following day dinner was served, as always during university recess, at the high table only. Mark joined the Very Reverend Father Pratt, the chaplain Father Donohue, Michael Spencer, the English professor working on a new Australian dictionary, his colleague Sean Moloney, the Irish-Australian poet teaching in the same department, and John McCluskey, a handsome final year medical student whose sporadic attendance seemed to be taken for granted by all those present. 'Luke', the Rector's faithful Evangelist Labrador, took his seat on a chair right next to his master. Mabel, the plumpish, stern-looking matron, served them all with equal attention.

It was a curious daily gathering this, in line, Mark thought, with the peculiar nature of the college, at least at this time of the year. Conversations tended to be esoteric, full of references to people he didn't know: someone on retreat, someone else in charge of Holy Eucharist Week, another to address a Jesuit seminary. The new Dean of Studies had not yet been appointed. The only subjects Mark understood were discussions of the Head of the River, along with Newman's chances in the intercollegiate Australian Rules competition. When the Rector claimed, 'We have a strong Eighteen!', no one disagreed. Mark was fascinated by such exchanges. He listened to the table conversation as an exotic verbal orchestration, picking up early that it commanded its own unmistakable rhythm. The sequence of composition began with an opening largo of grace, followed by purely informational ritardandos, punctuated by shorter and longer pauses, sudden staccato comments and outbursts of laughter, and concluded with slow adagio reflections only occasionally interrupted by 'St Luke's' satisfied barking.

Mark would have loved to speak to the resident poet whose long wavy hair and sensuous face seemed to reflect his lyrical nature. But Sean Moloney remained almost as withdrawn as Mark. For most of the time he looked uncomfortable, even ill, his handsome hair dry and grey, his face ashen, his eyes lost somewhere in the distance. By contrast, Professor Spencer projected the very image of the good life. A gross eater and hearty drinker, his greasy black hair and shiny forehead were quickly covered in outbursts of sweat. He seemed determined not to let his 'messy divorce' interfere with the rest of his life. Every now and then he winked genially at Mark as if to signal he knew all about him.

When people spoke to the final year medical student, the tone of the conversation changed dramatically from convivial to gentle. As soon as they addressed him their voices expressed goodwill and concern. When Father Donohue enquired whether John had been able to sleep the previous night, he eliminated any doubt in Mark's mind about the identity of the cello player. As if to confirm his supposition John turned to him. 'I hope I haven't kept you awake with my playing.'

Afraid he might stop the night music Mark lied, 'You haven't. I'm a deep sleeper', then instantly regretted that his lie prevented him from acknowledging how beautiful it was.

John McCluskey, senior medical student and cello player in the dark, did not join them in the Rector's study for the customary after-dinner drink. Father Donohue took Mark aside. Assuming the professional demeanour of pastoral care, he gently told him John was suffering from terminal cancer. He spent most of his time at St Vincent's, but whenever he was well enough he returned to his room at Newman. Newman had become John's home after his parents' death in a car accident.

They often met at night, the chaplain intimated, when it seemed easier to offer him spiritual support. For John, the worst was not the pain, because its agony invariably ended in drug-induced loss of consciousness. The most horrific suffering came while he was conscious, lying in his study thinking. For the most part he'd asked not to be disturbed. The illness had made him a loner. At Newman they were looking after him discreetly, with regular checks by doctors and a nurse. His room had a special call button connected to the hospital, in case of an emergency. 'Would Mark be so kind as to put up with John's night music?' Father Donohue begged of him. 'Had he noticed,' he added as if to entice him, 'John's an exceptionally gifted player?'

'Truth is to be found in disappearance.' As a token of understanding and respect Mark quoted the chaplain's words back to him. In recognition the white-haired priest and midsummer night golfer touched his arm. 'We'll make you a member of the Church yet, my son.'

Mark spent many nights awake waiting impatiently for the lament of John's cello. For almost two weeks it did not come.

He must have been hospitalised again, Mark concluded, but decided to check John's study for signs of occupancy.

Mark entered the adjacent unlocked common room. Everything was silent now. Unlike his first visit to the college when constant shouts had come from this direction. At regular intervals voices had called students to the phone. Multiple echoes had carried their names across the quadrangle to every room in the college. The old walls were covered with pictures of former student presidents, victorious cricket and Rules teams and a list of the previous year's Newman residents. Foolishly Mark looked for his name. There were several billiard tables, with rows of cues neatly stacked away. The air was stale. Near the door were two old-fashioned telephones. The Rector had told him this was also the traditional place for initiation ceremonies. The smell of sweat and fear had remained.

From the outside he tried to look through the window into John's study. At first all he could make out was a large desk covered with books, a couple of shelves and a bed. But when he looked closer he saw it, right in the centre of the room – the large cello standing upright as if to attention, its bow neatly placed in front. The instrument looked almost human. Even through the window it projected a dignified presence. The half-drawn curtains gave the room a stage-like appearance. Mark looked for a music stand. There was none. Then he remembered. John had played in the dark. He must have known the score by heart.

In a subdued mood Mark made his way back to his own study. What would Helen have to say, if he told her about John, he wondered. John seemed to find in his art both incantation and exorcism, agony and consolation, conjuration and redemption. Perhaps ultimately all art addressed itself to death, to non-being. Would she dismiss it as one of his attempts to 'poeticise science'? 'And what do you know about music!' she would mock him. Mark remembered his own wild improvisations at the piano, his outbursts of unstructured, unchannelled, undisciplined frustrations. He was ashamed now of his precocious self-centredness. He had played then as if only he existed or mattered. By contrast, John's music was inclusive. It invoked, and kept alive, both the joy and sorrow of being alive.

Although it was raining, Mark decided to walk the leafy paths along the outskirts of the university. He had no idea where Helen was, but he felt her presence as he followed the walkways and alleys they'd taken when first they became lovers. 'If I love you, what business is it of yours?' Damn that poet! If I live, do you care? Why did he suddenly care about a cello-playing medicine student dying of cancer? Who was John McCluskey anyhow? And, for that matter, who was he?

A gentle rain cooled his face. This time he was alone and not ambushed by a storm. He was walking by himself. Passing the oval he thought of Helen, but in a different way. That night they had not been bodies in a storm – their own bodies had been the storm. Impatiently their shared desire had set itself alight and exploded. All those lights residing in his head, the lit-up radio stations and far-away places of his childhood globe still sparkling in the night! In making love with Helen the shining cities and twinkling of stars he'd encountered on his Super Constellation flight returned, as did the microscopic patterns of colour and light he'd discovered as part of his own flesh and blood. In Helen all of these lights had come to life again. Did they only shine for him? Mark still needed to be assured of his own nature, what it was that he was meant to grow into. He sensed that without Helen he was unlikely to ever find out.

Who was he?! What was he without her?

How angry he'd been as a boy that a name had already been chosen for him! Now he had to spend his whole life answering to an arbitrary word which had nothing to do with him. Mark had no doubt: John's music too had been a cry for recognition and redemption, a calling. The missing persons tracing service after the war, those roll calls of life and death, those endless names, lost, it seemed, forever. No one answered any more.

To be 'called'! All his life he'd waited for it, even as he searched for his own 'calling'. Priests may be called by God, but Mark knew he needed another person to become real. When his father had not returned from the war his mother had lost herself. The truth was she died many years before her 'accidental death'. It was horrible and tragic, but it was also so simple. She'd needed her husband to be real. In the end she was left with her son listening to the radio, waiting for his father's name.

Like John, Mark had played his young life as if it were an instrument, anxious to discover where it would lead him. Had he not followed every whim of improvisation and variation, trying to find himself? But he had not been able to make music as haunting and beautiful as John's. Was Helen helping make him real or was she offering him one more variation? She'd passed on to him the gift of poetry. But did she love him?

The university grounds lay deserted. Outside the empty cafeteria an old poster from one of Curd's productions flapped in the wind. The glue was still stronger than the gentle summer wind and rain. Swaying in the breeze it made a noise he found unnerving. It appeared to be waving at him. Would he ever escape the backyard of his childhood?

When Mark reached the cloisters of the Old Law School he sat down. A couple of years ago he'd started his new life in this very place. He recognised the window of his former office. Working for 'Public Exams' had allowed him time to examine himself. He'd just arrived in a foreign country whose authorities, after briefly imprisoning him, had released him into its midst and left him to his own devices. Freedom had first meant survival, then searching for himself. Without realising it, life in this country had forced him to discover who he really was – or wanted to be. Everything that had happened to him in this city had shaped him, most of all the friends he made.

It now seemed fairly clear that in a few more years he'd be a doctor specialising in diseases of the blood, a haematologist probably. Helen would add 'with poetic potential' to the definition. Helen! What was her part in all of this? Who had she turned him into? A 'poet'? What did that mean, 'to be a poet'? It was hardly a profession. You could never make a living being a poet, though – and here he blushed – it might be something like a 'calling'. Not like a calling into the religious life, of course; more like the kind of appeal he'd heard in John's playing, a disciplined but passionate search transforming longing into 'art'. A daring celebration recognising but defying death. Again Mark blushed. He knew he lacked John's courage, his dignity and self-reliance. Mark's 'poetry' would never rise and sing as one unaccompanied voice. He knew his words would not stand up to the night. Everything he'd done in his life became meaningless when he thought of the loneliness of the dying medical student. Mark too was alone, he too had lost his mother in an accident. He and John had that much in common. But Mark had run away from death, the flights of the Beautiful Enemy. His was a different kind of escape from the disappearance John's body and mind were suffering. He wondered where John might be, lying at St Vincent's or resting back in his room at Newman. By now Mark could will the presence of John's music. He needed it to accompany and comfort him as he retraced the hopscotch of his own life.

Would he and Helen find John's courage to face the night with more than sexual lightning? Would their bodies be strong enough to conquer their own disappearance? 'Truth is to be found in disappearance.' Would love choose them, or would they answer to it as if it were their given name?

In love's compulsion he called out Helen's name. The cloisters replied with an empty echo. Alone with the silence Mark listened to the gentle monologue of the warm summer rain.

Like the college, Genevieve's was empty of students. Mark escaped to the pub to be among people. Sonja caught up with him while he was waiting for a tram. She'd had a card from Julia. It was from Italy where she was spending the holidays with her parents and had attended one of her father's concerts. 'Would you believe it?' she enthused. The card was a glossy picture bearing the words 'The glory that was Rome'. And did he know Belinda had joined the Labor Party? 'Isn't it wonderful?', 'Isn't it weird?', 'Isn't it exciting?', she kept exclaiming. Mignon had gone to Apollo Bay with a new boyfriend. 'Hope she's found the right one this time!' She was bubbling over with news, ideas and opinions, sounding like someone who'd been by herself for too long. 'The house's virtually empty, Mark,' she pleaded. 'You will come over some time, won't you?' He agreed to see her soon, but now he really had to get going. He gestured at the tram. It wasn't his, but he quickly boarded it. He waved at her from the safety of the moving vehicle.

Going to the Bughouse was not the same. The cinema was more than half empty and no one howled at the playing of the national anthem. Of those present some actually rose from their seats to salute the Queen sitting smugly on her royal feather head-dressed horse. Several people walked out in the middle of the screening. A few times Mark had the whole Bughouse to himself. But even when a session was well attended he felt alone. He was no longer part of the same audience. There were no familiar faces. He began to resent the anonymity of spectators. For them, *Last Year at Marienbad* proved too much of an 'art movie'. A man sitting in the balcony's front row called out 'Bullshit!', another in the stalls 'This is giving me a headache!', a young bikie 'What crap!' The film's constant revisions, its form of theme and variations fascinated Mark. In patterned images of light and dark he recognised the performance of a ritualistic discipline, a cinematic rehearsal of life and death. He was certain John would have understood.

After the film, back at Newman, Mark listened to John's cello. One more night he witnessed that haunting music of celebration and lament. Sitting outside his study he cherished it as if it were played especially for him. As always, the alternately rugged and gentle, impatient and tolerant, passionate and accepting sonatas were played with heartbreak precision. Mark remained irresistibly drawn into the dialogue of player and instrument. For a while it seemed he himself became part of the music. He felt then that he understood something of what the young man was invoking. With his playing he dared the darkness to extinguish itself, to let light triumph over suffering.

A shrill tone interrupted the middle of a prolonged cadenza: the aggressively insistent, discordant sound of a telephone ringing from the students common room. Mark held his breath, hoping John would continue with his playing. Who could possibly call the college at this ungodly hour? In his disappointment Mark's inner voice was pleading with the music, 'You're stronger, you're braver; do not give in! Ignore the barking hounds!' But the sound of the cello stopped abruptly. As if the phone's impatient signal had cut the strings, the music ended on a discordant note. Suddenly only the repetitive alarm of the telephone could be heard. After a brief silence Mark could hear John's footsteps as he approached the top floor railing. A moment later the quadrangle reverberated with a gentle, quivering voice.

Mark listened in pity and fear as John called his name.

It was the Royal Melbourne. A Miss Sonja Millstein had been admitted approximately an hour ago. They found his name and address among her belongings. Would he come to the hospital as soon as possible? They'd tried to contact her family, but no one had answered the phone. The matter was extremely urgent.

When Mark arrived, a nurse with a stern face looked him over before declaring, 'About time, young man!' He had no reply to that.

'What's happened?' he asked instead. 'Is she all right?'

His questions earned him only more disapproval. With barely controlled disgust the nurse made it clear it was her prerogative to find out what had occurred.

'Is Miss Millstein pregnant? You might as well tell me. It'll all come out with the wash in the morning.' Her obvious disapproval of him made it difficult for Mark to remain calm. Her language was deeply offensive, not only to him. He wished she wouldn't refer to Sonja as if she were an object.

'I'd like to speak to the doctor, please.' Mark's request left the nurse flabbergasted. She took a deep breath.

'You've got a nerve!' she decided. 'Who do you think you are!'

'I'm the one you called, nurse. Now can I please see the doctor?'

His repeated request made her stroppy. 'You're not here to make any sorts of demands. I know your type. Before I tell you anything about the patient I've got a few questions for you, young man.'

Mark had had enough. Ignoring her, he started walking down the ward's corridor. She rushed after him waving a clipboard as if about to hit him with it. Another night nurse exited from one of the emergency wards, nearly colliding with Mark.

'Quick! A doctor, please!' he beseeched her. Just behind her a doctor emerged. Without any introduction or hesitation Mark asked him, 'Will she live?' The young doctor looked tired. There were splashes of blood on his coat.

'Who are you?' he asked Mark.

'Her brother,' he lied.

The doctor shook his head slowly before putting one hand on Mark's shoulder. 'You must understand. She was clinically dead on arrival. We couldn't revive her. Her wounds proved fatal. I'm so sorry.'

Mark froze. He was suddenly very calm. It was not the first time he'd been confronted with death, but this was different. He knew what his mother and Hanna had died from.

But what about Sonja? What wounds was the doctor talking about?

The nurse who'd demanded to know whether he'd made Sonja pregnant caught up with him. Furiously she explained to the doctor on call that Mark was not a relative of the accident fatality he'd just attended to. Mark let himself be led back down the corridor by his tormentor. He was pale and silent now, too stupefied and stunned to put up any further fight.

'Just stay there,' the nurse advised him. 'I'll see what I can do.'

She returned with a different doctor. 'Sonja's okay,' he informed him without demanding a personal identification. 'We've pumped out her stomach. You understand? She took an overdose of sleeping pills. Has she ever done that sort of thing before? I'm only asking. Please let nurse know anything at all that might help. You know what I mean.' Finally he did ask Mark, 'Are you her boyfriend?'

He had to think about that for a moment before shaking his head sadly and saying, 'No, I'm a friend.'

In the end the doctor didn't seem too worried about who he was. 'Whatever. Perhaps you can help us contact her family.' He offered his hand, then disappeared into the 'Doctors-On-Duty' room.

In the meantime the belligerent nurse seemed to have mellowed somewhat. Before disappearing she even offered Mark a papercup of coffee. To his surprise she took him to Sonja's room and left him alone with her. 'About five minutes, young man, no more, you hear! No talking. She needs rest.' She sounded almost human.

The pale face nearly drowning in a pillow belonged to a woman still alive, Mark had to remind himself. Only a couple of years earlier he had stood in front of an open coffin and said goodbye to his first love. Surrounded by the closeness of death the two women, Hanna and Sonja, looked unnervingly alike. Had he been able to pray, Mark would have thanked God for keeping Sonja alive; Father Donohue's or John's God – the one you called for in the dead of night, playing golf or cello with all your might until the body could take it no more.

'To be called.' Sonja hadn't called him. It must have been that cranky nurse who demanded his presence. Survival was an ill-tempered nurse, meaning well. 'Don't talk to her!'

Mark's anguish proved an agony of selfishness, guilt and doubt. Had Sonja really meant to kill herself? Or was she trying to punish him, her father and her mother for not loving her enough, for not staying with her? How could she do that to him? Impatiently he wished she'd give up that damn exuberance of hers, her love for him, her mothering him because of that love. 'If I love you, what business is it of yours?' Didn't she get it? If that's all she had to give, she would soon see where it'd take her. She'd nearly killed herself with love.

Sometimes those you loved were the most likely to leave you. Had he betrayed Sonja? Mark couldn't decide. He thought of Ernesto who was fond of saying 'We're always guilty'. He's a weirdo, but still. Perhaps he was right. He and Sonja had shared the intimate shelter of her bed. Now she was lying in a hospital bed as though she were dead. What part had he played in that terrible transformation? All he could do was to make sure her mother would come and see her later. Surely she wasn't … Mark was back in Bonegilla. As he wiped the cold sweat off his forehead he could hear the scathing voice of Wolfgang: 'Sooner or later all chicks turn into mother hens.'

He was anxious to leave. Regardless of whether he'd betrayed Sonja or not, she'd been good to him. She'd given him her love, and he'd given little in return. Perhaps that's how men were. He'd told her about the death of his mother. He didn't want Sonja to take her place. Mothers couldn't help themselves, but he wanted her to help herself. He was grateful for her love, but he wanted her to help herself. Mark knew he couldn't do it for her. He simply couldn't. She'd have to grow up and be herself. Taking an overdose of tablets when she didn't know what to do with herself was unworthy of her.

He knew Sonja was a generous woman, but he wanted her to be stingy with her generosity.

Mark gently kissed her forehead, then left the room, ready to assure the almost human nurse that he hadn't spoken to the patient.

Curd and Samantha passed on the latest gossip. Had he heard that Sonja had attempted suicide? They were discussing *Accatone*, the latest Pasolini film of robbery, prostitution, misunderstanding and chance. It was so hot inside Genevieve's, Samantha was into her third granita.

'Justice,' Curd reflected, 'when all is said and done. What is it? What does it mean? It merely supports whoever happens to be in power. The rest is revenge, politics and morality. You're always quoting that bloody Irish poet of yours, Mark. How does it go? He that's mounting up/Must on his neighbour mount/And we and all the muses/Are things of no account. Couldn't have put it better myself.'

Samantha nudged him in the ribs. 'But they say she's going to be all right,' she changed the subject. 'Poor Sonja. Such a loyal friend. Always so ready to understand.'

Mark took one of her cigarettes and nodded his agreement. 'She's a good kid.'

'I say,' Curd said.

Mark played along. 'What does Curd say?'

'I say, would you like to be in my new play? I'm looking for a lead with an indecipherable accent, if you know what I mean. The quintessential outsider who is at the same time the voice of society. It's a play by a Swiss, would you believe. What do you say?'

'I say, I say, I say.'

There was a sideshow going on somewhere, and Samantha didn't like it. 'Some other time, Curd,' she begged him. 'Not now.'

'Well, think about it, Mark. You'd be perfect. A three-week season at the Union. Your character's name is Andri. What do you say?'

They left after midnight. No one mentioned Sonja again. Her mother had taken her home. She'd be all right.

Monday the students would return. Or arrive. Another year, another class, another language, another poetry. Last year was as *passé* as a past affair. *Last Year at Marienbad*. Mark walked the quadrangle of Newman, knowing that college would not be the same. When Father Donohue visited him in his study late one night Mark knew John McCluskey had died. 'Don't tell me!' Mark yelled at the chaplain before he could say anything.

How quiet the nights would be!

Still, friends would return, not only in college. Mark visited the dictionary professor. Together they danced to his favourite record, Louis Armstrong's *Hello Dolly*. 'It's so nice to have you back where you belong.' One alcoholic night Mark listened to the professor telling him about the ambiguity and difficulty of defining words. He responded using the terminology of haemophiliacs. The professor kept playing his LP over and over again. 'This is Louis, Dolly.'

Mad Father Donohue approached him in broad daylight. Would he like to say goodbye to John at the requiem at college chapel?

Mark spent the last days before the beginning of the new academic year waiting. The new student president informed him that 'seniority' would save him from the official college initiation. How could he have explained that he would in fact have liked to cross the cemetery at midnight, before walking on to the ground of Princess Park in the morning and aiming a ball at the big sticks!

Mark knew what he was waiting for, but he couldn't have explained it to anyone. He stayed up most nights. Over the weekend parents accompanied their sons to their new 'home', successful Catholic parents expecting to reap the benefit of their son's education. The first telephone calls were relayed across the quadrangle. Still, Mark was waiting.

Saturday night came and went. Young students unpacked their suitcases and claimed their rooms.

The bewildered Irish poet rushed across the college campus as if he had something to hide. One night Mark managed to spend at least a couple of hours drinking with him. The diminutive Sean Moloney kept playing his favourite ballads. Odetta's *Foggy Dew*. Or I know where I'm going, and I know who's going with me. 'My handsome, winsome Johnny.' After that, it was time to vomit. Into a bucket or whatever could be found. *The Irish Revolution* was a poem. 'O rocky voice,/Shall we in that great night rejoice …'.

Sean Moloney's voice haunted Mark. Where had he come from, that Irish Australian singer, that foreign native who came and went as he pleased? Was that what Mark, too, was turning into – a foreign native? Ah, but he wasn't Irish. There was something about the Irish in this country. They were tributaries rather than mainstream, loved and hated, a people with their own tongue even when they spoke English. Sean Moloney did not speak, he sang. Like John, he raised his rocky voice against the dark, for all who were longing to be at home.

The nights were still warm. Eric Pearce's TV weather forecast proved more reliable as February arrived when the 'cool change' did in fact eventuate like an ancient prophecy fulfilled. In the darkness the music may have gone, but the voices were back. Mark could hear them until two o'clock in the morning. Then the last lights were turned off. The quadrangle sank back into silence, darkness and dissolution. In the absence of music and voices Mark began to write lines he could not have otherwise explained or justified. He collected poems under the title *a kind of dying*, requiems for John, his own feeble attempts to write against the dark. A good poet, he discovered, would have to be a doctor, a priest and a musician. And still he was waiting.

Lectures started again. Now in his third year of 'science and medicine', Mark had found himself, or he had been found. He was determined to learn the language of the body, to gain what his friends mockingly referred to as 'carnal knowledge'. He would have preferred to call it the immunology of life. His mother no longer called on him except in nights of despair. Darkness would remain, but needed to be fought with life's own 'antibodies' – the joys of love, the knowledge of oneself and the discovery of home. The women who had given him love stayed alive, remained a part of his life, remembered and cherished for the gift they gave. He resided in a college of strange gatherings, a place where life and death met in the echoes of a quadrangle, where Mark himself was inescapably drawn into the local presence of heaven, hell, life and death. And still he was waiting.

If there was a spirit of place, Mark had answered its summons. Living at Newman was different from anything he had imagined. He was neither born into, nor did he convert to its faith. But the college's monastic architecture conveyed energies of a very worldly presence. Its cloistered reflections and quadrangled echoes relayed the search for a knowledge it called God. He had been there only a short time, yet already the place had challenged him to discover the divinity of all expression. 'God' was language, music, the body growing, the body dying, the hundred metre hurdles, golf, 'Australian Rules' and all the other unimportant things of daily living. The ritual behaviour of men at the local. The words we mean and do not mean. The love without which there can be no God. Even without its Irish resident, Newman was a poetic meeting place. Not the school poetry recited or learnt off by heart, not the materialised vision of the printed page. It was a presence rising from the dark. Mark had known it when the college was almost empty, when in nights of disappearance faith played a game against itself while music followed life into eternity. Its truth was unfamiliar, daring and witty. Those who found it bore witness in their search. Mark had tried to invoke it with his own words. And still he was waiting.

When Sean Moloney was filled with the spirit he started to dance and sang of an Ireland he'd never seen. When Mark tried to compose unaccompanied words he celebrated the poetry of the senses. His rhymes mourned losses, his metres cast lines, his images paid homage to the clean dark. And still he was waiting.

He attended lectures and lab sessions, took notes and wrote assignments. He went to the Bughouse and afterwards to Genevieve's. He took part in one of Curd's productions, read novels, plays and poetry, but above all learnt the language of inherited blood, the range and limits of its immune response. He became obsessed with antigens, antibodies and what the lecturer had described as the extraordinary promises of immunotherapy. Immunology would be the science of the future.

He spent time with his old friends and made some new ones. In St Kilda's Scheherazade he sat with old survivors of the concentration camps studying the numerology of survival. And still he was waiting.

When it came, it was one of many, and he very nearly missed it. After lunch and dinner the quadrangle was crowded with names. Like kites they flew uneasily above waves of gowns moving in different directions. Walking alone from the dining hall Mark had already reached his study when he heard the call. A freshman's croaky voice kept repeating his name. He had been called. This time he moved slowly, looked up to the railings, then ran in the direction of the students common room. He ran as fast as he could, afraid he might be late.

Acknowledgments

All characters are fictitious. References to 'Storm's Ghost Rider' allude to Theodor Storm's novella *Der Schimmelreiter* (1886/88). The lines 'If I love you, what business is it of yours?' are a quotation from Johann Wolfgang Goethe's novel *Wilhelm Meister* (IV,9); '… das meiste nämlich/Vermag die Geburt' ('… for birth determines most in life') from Friedrich Hölderlin's poem 'Der Rhein'; 'He that's mounting up must on his neighbour mount/And we and all the muses are things of no account.' from W. B. Yeats' poem 'The Curse of Cromwell'; 'O rocky voice,/Shall we in that great night rejoice?' from W. B. Yeats' poem 'Man and the Echo'. The poem 'Bonegilla' is taken from the author's collection *waiting for cancer*, Brisbane 1985.

Work on the novel was supported by an Arts Queensland Grant and a writer-in-residence appointment at the University of Florida.

An earlier version of Chapter 1, Book One appeared under the title "The Annunciation" in *Imago*, and an abbreviated version of Chapter II, Book Two under the title "The Beautiful Enemy" in *Kalimat*.

Special thanks to Bruce Dawe, Michael Wilding, Jack Hibberd, Alex Skovron, Judith Lukin-Amundsen, Manfred Durzak, Oliver Garate, Tom Shapcott and my empathetic editor, Susan Addison. I am particularly grateful for the continued support of Marguerite S. Jurgensen.

Finally, I would like to thank my wife for her patience, encouragement, inspiration and love.

If you enjoyed this book, join **Indra Members** at

www.indra.com.au

and tell us whether you would like to receive:

- invitations to book launches
- special offers on Indra titles
- information about new releases